Just Breathe

Just Breathe

BONNIE J. JAMES

BALBOA
PRESS
A DIVISION OF HAY HOUSE

Balboa Press books may be ordered through booksellers or by contacting:

Balboa Press
A Division of Hay House
1663 Liberty Drive
Bloomington, IN 47403
www.balboapress.com
1-(877) 407-4847

Because of the dynamic nature of the Internet, any web addresses or links contained in this book may have changed since publication and may no longer be valid. The views expressed in this work are solely those of the author and do not necessarily reflect the views of the publisher, and the publisher hereby disclaims any responsibility for them.

The author of this book does not dispense medical advice or prescribe the use of any technique as a form of treatment for physical, emotional, or medical problems without the advice of a physician, either directly or indirectly. The intent of the author is only to offer information of a general nature to help you in your quest for emotional and spiritual well-being. In the event you use any of the information in this book for yourself, which is your constitutional right, the author and the publisher assume no responsibility for your actions.

Any people depicted in stock imagery provided by Thinkstock are models, and such images are being used for illustrative purposes only. Certain stock imagery © Thinkstock.

ISBN: 978-1-4525-5573-7 (sc)
ISBN: 978-1-4525-5571-3 (e)
ISBN: 978-1-4525-5572-0 (hc)

Library of Congress Control Number: 2012913394

Printed in the United States of America

Balboa Press rev. date: 8/06/2012

To my husband.
ILY

Acknowledgements

Thank you x 1,000,000 to Kristen Fairgrieve, a.k.a. KrissyPants. Every single day I am so grateful for the friendship, the giggles, and the stories that we share. You'll never know how much your help (and education on dashes) has meant to me. I couldn't have finished this book without you!

To Heidi Baker, I cannot express how thankful I am for your friendship and support all these years. When I told you years ago that I wanted to write a book you were as excited as I was, and you've been cheering me on ever since. Your honesty and encouragment means the world to me. Thank you, so very much.

To Simone Simon, thank you for reading my manuscript with such a sharp eye, for making me smile with your color-coded editing, and for enjoying my characters as much as I do.

Thank you to my mom, dad, and sister. Since I was little, you've supported and appreciated my endless desire to write stories. Amy, you were my very first writing teacher, and my favorite.

Thank you to my family, my friends, and my local MOMS club. All of your love and support has completely overwhelmed me!

A huge thank you to Kari Sletten. You've not only managed to create a beautiful website for me, but continuously kept me on track when I needed it. You are amazing!

To my sweet, adorable, crazy little boys, thank you for giving Mommy "quiet time." I love you!

And most of all, to my husband, Kerry. Your support, honesty, and patience have been endless as I follow my writing dreams, and I am the luckiest girl alive. Because of you, I will never wonder "what if...". I love you.

Chapter One

"A fire truck!" Sam cried. The young boy leaned out his window and pointed toward a brick fire station as they slowly drove by. One of the firemen beside an old pumper truck lifted his head and waved.

"He waved, Mom!" Sam shouted, bouncing in his seat. "That fireman waved to me!" Below his feet, a fat Boxer pup named Goliath wiggled in his bed of blankets. He whined and lifted his ears in momentary interest.

Lola Sommers smiled as she smoothed her son's hair. The soft breeze caressed her cheeks through the open car window and she turned to see the fireman's gaze follow them down the street. The taxi crossed over a wide iron bridge that straddled the river and they rounded the corner, losing sight of the station. Sam turned fully in his seat to watch it disappear out the back window.

"How much longer?" he whined as he faced the front again.

Lola patted his knobby knee and smiled at the way his little legs were not yet long enough to bend over the seat.

"Only one more minute," she answered quietly. She tilted her head to get a better view out the front window. Searching the road, she nudged Sam with her elbow and pointed past a row of houses as they

1

neared the other end of town. "It's tucked in there," she said, gesturing past a grassy field and into a small patch of forest.

Childhood memories flooded Lola's heart. She could see them, feel them as if they'd happened yesterday. There were summers of freedom and sunshine and dandelions, swimming with new friends and the feel of silky cold water licking her sunburned skin. There were endless days of riding bikes, running wild at the tiny county fair, and celebrating the fourth of July under a shower of fireworks.

Lola nibbled her lip as the taxi slowed and turned onto a gravel driveway. They rumbled down the lane, over an old wooden bridge that shuddered beneath the car's weight. A lazy creek moved through the forest and sparkled from the sunlight. Moving around one last bend, the taxi stopped in front of a haunting white house.

"This is it," Lola whispered. She peered out the taxi window at a leaning red shed and a rusted classic truck that melded with the earth it stood on. Laughter bubbled from her throat. "It hasn't changed one bit."

Sam burst from his side of the taxi, nearly falling in a heap on the dirt below him. Goliath bound from his bed and wiggled out the open door, falling in the same fashion.

Moments later the taxi barreled back down the driveway, leaving a heap of luggage, a wide-eyed boy, and a very exhausted Lola in its wake.

"Don't go near the water," Lola warned as she watched her son zip past her, heading to the back yard to explore. "The rocks in the creek are slippery and if you fall you'll get a concussion." Sam offered an indulgent nod before running off.

Lola glanced anxiously at the spacious yard and patch of forest surrounding her. With a sigh she dragged two heavy suitcases, nearly the same weight as she was, onto the enclosed wooden porch of her aunt's home. She dropped them on the creaky floorboards and bent to pull a key from beneath a potted plant. A small pumpkin-colored tile leaning against the plant blazed the word *Namaste.*

"Hello, Aunt Louise," Lola whispered, touching the glossy tile for a moment. She wondered where her aunt's wanderlust had taken her today. Perhaps she was meditating in an ashram or wandering an ancient city. Lola sighed. She could really use a hug from Aunt Louise. She'd always been so good at listening, truly listening, to Lola's troubles.

The door creaked open and Lola gave it an extra push with her foot. It was dark and cool inside. Every shade and curtain was closed, but tiny rays of sun leaked in through uncovered spaces on windows. Dust floated through the air, carelessly riding the waves of movement in the room.

Lola dropped the bags and wrapped her arms around herself as more memories flooded in. It was here on the cool tile floors that she learned to dance the Polka with her aunt, around and around the room until they were both dizzy and breathless with laughter. She smiled at the small wooden table where she used to sit with her Uncle Gilbert and play cards in the evening, sometimes by the light of the lantern as a summer thunderstorm raged outside. She could still smell the spicy scent of soup made from fresh vegetables and the comforting aroma of warm bread straight from the oven, sliced and slathered with salty butter.

Lola turned a circle in the kitchen and caught sight of her reflection in a small mirror on the wall. Disappointment swept over her. Who was the woman staring back at her? Deep shadows hung beneath her dull brown eyes and lines were etched permanently into her forehead. She touched a finger to her cheeks that sunk from losing too much weight and trailed the tight line of her lips. Stepping across the room, she pulled the mirror from the wall and shoved it in a cupboard.

Moving through the kitchen, Lola opened curtains and windows and felt a fresh breeze rustle the stale air. She slipped into the darkness of the next room that was filled with plush couches and chairs. Rows of shelves were stuffed with colorful books and albums. An old record player was the only sign of technology in the space. She kneeled over the couch and pulled back the heavy curtains, wrenching the windows open to let the dust escape.

The view gave Lola goose bumps. Stands of pine and maple trees stood tall beside the trickling creek. Purple wild iris bloomed beside the water. A striking crimson cardinal landed nearby and hopped on the ground, glancing up with a sideways stare as if to greet the newest guest of the forest.

"Mom, there's a tree house in the back!" Sam cried as he ran past the window. Lola winced at his words. Images of Sam falling from the tree, a broken arm, sprained ankles… it was disaster waiting to happen. But her worries quickly evaporated as she watched Goliath bounce behind Sam, tripping over his own huge paws and wriggling with so much excitement that he couldn't follow in a straight line. It made Lola laugh, the sight of her son and his puppy, exploring a new place with so much excitement and pleasure.

It was going to be a good summer, Lola reassured herself. Even with all of her worries, she could feel it in her bones that this was what she and Sam needed. They could take a break, reenergize and get focused again. Just take some time to breathe.

Breathe, Lola repeated as she gulped the fresh air that whispered in through the open windows. It was ripe with pine and moisture and sunshine. Surrendering herself to the peace, she flopped onto the chair she'd been kneeling in. Dust exploded from the cushions, and Lola sneezed.

"ALL SET!" MATT CALLED as he wrapped the last of the fire hose into the pumper. He banged on the side of the town's oldest fire truck to get the driver's attention. Stepping back, Matt watched Gabe's reflection in the huge side mirrors as he maneuvered into reverse and backed the old beast into the station garage.

Brushing his hands together to get the last of the soap and dirt from them, Matt glanced toward Main Street and grinned. The whole town seemed happy today, content with the simple pleasures of life. People strolled down the sidewalk, wandering in and out of local shops, more to gossip and catch up than to shop. Children rode by the station on their bikes, lollipops in their bulging cheeks and colorful flags whipping behind them as they enjoyed the freedom of summer vacation.

"I better head home," Gabe announced as he reached Matt's side. The tone of his voice made a huff of laughter burst from Matt's chest. He surveyed Gabe with a grin. The man may have had a beefy, powerful frame and an intimidating air, but he turned to mush at the mere mention of his family.

Matt watched his best friend cross bulging arms over his chest and eye the town carefully. As the county's juvenile detention officer, Gabe always seemed to be searching for signs of trouble.

"Rena wants to go shopping before the game tonight, so I have the rug rats to myself," Gabe said, still scowling out at the town.

"Think you can handle them for that long?" Matt teased. He squinted into the sun and waved to old Mrs. Matthews as she crept by in her rusty blue Oldsmobile.

Gabe glanced at Matt with uncertainty. "I don't know. They're a handful when the boss isn't around."

If Matt hadn't known better, he'd swear his burly best friend was scared of the two small children that awaited him at home. He was about to poke more fun when a yellow taxi rushed by, heading out of town.

"Jesus, can that asshole go any faster? Where's the Sheriff when you need him?" Gabe growled as he watched the bright car disappear down Main Street. "What the hell's a Pine City cab doing here, anyway?"

"It was headed east a few minutes ago," Matt said, nodding toward the bridge. "A little boy in the back seat waved to us." He didn't mention the woman sitting beside the boy, whose intense dark eyes were still etched into his mind.

Gabe scowled after the taxi and grumbled. He took a deep breath and nodded toward his truck.

"Good luck," Matt said, thumping Gabe's back. "I'll finish up inside." He watched as Gabe strode away, his shoulders bent in surrender.

"First thing I learned in teacher education classes," Matt called through his laughter, "don't let them see your fear or they'll eat you alive."

Gabe turned toward Matt before climbing into his truck. His eyes twinkled and a smirk played over the often serious look on his face. "Don't get too cocky, pal, or I'll pawn them off on you tonight."

Matt watched Gabe's rusty maroon truck rattle onto the street and disappear in the same direction as the little boy had gone earlier. He stood for a moment, staring out at nothing in particular, his mind chewing on the sight of the city cab and its passengers. Matt turned and walked slowly to the fire station.

It didn't bother him that they were strangers. New people often traveled into town, especially in the summer. Hope River was near some popular parks and trails, which often brought outdoor enthusiasts to the area. The town relied on these visitors in the summer months.

No, it wasn't that they were strangers.

Perhaps it was the fact that they came from the city. City people in general made Matt uneasy. They didn't seem to appreciate the relaxed pace of small towns. They were always in a rush, always trying to get to the next thing, never slowing down enough to realize that now was all they had, all they needed.

Ali had been that way, Matt reminded himself. He slammed the station door behind him at the thought.

It took quite a burst of energy to heft her suitcase onto the bed. Lola wiped her forehead and sighed. It had been a long day, traveling all the way from their little townhome in San Francisco to this big dusty house in Hope River, Minnesota.

Lola pulled back the bedroom curtains and opened the creaky window, leaning out to peer down at Sam. He sprawled on his belly in the front yard, unusually covered in dirt and dust as he collected bugs in an old plastic cup.

"Sam, don't get stung by one of those bugs," Lola warned. She looked across the yard to the creek that trickled over rocks and burbled past fallen branches. "And don't go near the creek," she repeated. There were only a few inches of water moving at a lazy pace, but she'd heard all the horror stories of children drowning in just one inch of water.

Lola's heart thundered at the thought. She'd already had enough worry with Sam to last her a lifetime.

Turning to face the room, Lola took in the warm cream color of the walls and the plush bed. It looked so inviting after such a long day. She sunk her fingers into the handmade quilt, then lay down and stared at the ceiling.

What am I going to do? How can I fix us? She ran a hand through her long, dark hair and sighed.

It had been a couple of years since Travis' death. Slowly she had picked herself up, tried to piece their lives back together and be strong for Sam. She was doing okay now. The days were no longer as painful and lonely as they once had been. She had gotten back on her feet with a little job at the magazine and Sam, though often quiet and despondent, had been busy enough in kindergarten to keep distracted. But now the job was gone and an empty summer lay ahead for Sam. They needed to figure out what was next.

A light breeze blew over Lola and she sat up and stared out the window. She could still see Sam, sitting beside Goliath in the gravel driveway, now collecting small rocks and lining them up in rows. The cup of bugs lay beside him, tipped over as if the insects had orchestrated a courageous escape while their captor was distracted.

The breeze blew a little harder, making goose bumps spring from Lola's flesh. She lifted her knees to her chest and nestled her hands into the pockets of her jacket. Her fingers touched a crinkled note and she pulled it out and studied it.

It was a letter from Aunt Louise, dated two weeks ago. Lola flattened it against her knee, smoothing the wrinkles. She smiled at the graceful handwriting that filled the paper, the words that she had been so grateful to read.

> *I have a proposition for you, Lola-girl. It seems to me that you and Sam need a little peace and quiet to recuperate. The timing may be perfect, as your mother tells me that you have recently been released from your job.*

Lola rubbed her eyes and sighed. That was one way of putting it. The job had been working out so well. Perfect hours as an assistant in the advertising department of a photography magazine. Perfect wage to help pay the bills so she didn't have to dip into Travis' insurance money. Perfect in every way except for the fact that the magazine went bankrupt last month, leaving her an unemployed single parent.

I can't believe that I've been traveling for nearly two months now. I'm having such a wonderful time that I've decided to extend my stay through the end of the summer. But my poor home has been neglected for too long already, and I'm in need of a house-sitter. Could our timing be any more perfect? Please go to Hope River and enjoy a vacation with Sam. It used to be your favorite place when you were a little girl, remember? Take a break from your worries in the city. I promise you won't regret it.

No, she knew she wouldn't regret it. Lola never had, even when she was a young girl and leaving behind a summer full of friends and adventures in the city.

Just as Lola had done so many years ago, she and Sam would make the most of their time in Hope River. They would recuperate, relax, and get back on their feet. They'd decide which direction to face and return to their family and friends in San Francisco with a new plan.

But first thing's first, Lola decided as she got to her feet and headed across the hall. It was time to settle into this place for a month or two. She would start by unpacking Sam's suitcase.

SAM HAD ALWAYS BEEN a little packrat, but this? No wonder his suitcase had felt ten times heavier than hers. While Lola's bag was stuffed with camera equipment, summer dresses, and more shoes than she'd care to admit she owned, Sam's was packed with Legos and toy cars in every available space. Even the inside of his baseball mitt was crammed with toys. She tipped the suitcase upside down and watched colorful bouncy balls roll onto his bed.

After Sam's clothes were all tucked away in closets and drawers, the question of storage for his endless toys sprang to mind. Lola looked around the room for an answer. It came in the form of a worn wooden desk in the corner, one her uncle had built for her the first summer she'd visited. She grinned at the memory.

The pine desk may have been twenty-two years old, but it had held up well. And if Lola remembered correctly, it also held her initials. With a little smile, she pulled the top drawer open to search for the tiny letters she'd etched years ago. They were covered by something that stole the breath from her chest.

It was an old journal, bound in brown leather, the texture soft and worn as a favorite old blanket. Her mother had given it to her before her last visit to Hope River.

The journal's spine crackled as Lola opened it. Her bubbly childhood handwriting filled the pages with dates, short notes, and doodles. Stuffed between the pages were old yellowed Polaroids of the creek, the house, trees and flowers, rocks and wildlife. There were blurry, awkward captures of birds and insects and random pieces of nature, a few photos of her aunt and uncle, and even a self-portrait of Lola. Each picture flooded Lola with sweet memories she had tucked away. She laughed quietly while she sifted through them, then stopped on the last one, her smile fading.

It was of Lola and three young girlfriends, at a dance on one of her last nights in Hope River. Her heart fluttered at the long lost memory of that evening. There had been a boy that night - not in this picture, but somewhere in the background of her memory - his eyes inviting, his smile handsome and confident. His hands had been warm on her waist as they'd danced. Three sets of eyes bore into her back as her girlfriends watched in jealous awe. Lola remembered how beautiful the boy had made her feel, the way he looked at her, his voice so comforting…

The memories faded as soft voices floated through her open bedroom window across the hall. She shook from her thoughts and tossed the journal back in the desk drawer. She slipped down the stairs to check on Sam.

9

Lola hopped from the bottom kitchen step and peered through the wall of windows that overlooked the porch. Sam stood awkwardly, talking to another little boy slightly taller than him.

"My mom said we're staying here for the whole summer," Sam told the boy in a small voice. He dug his toe in the dirt as his new friend's eyes widened in excitement.

"So maybe you can come over sometime," the boy suggested. He bent to the ground and inspected the perfect lines of rocks. "Cool, did you make this?"

Sam's face slowly brightened as he nodded, his timid eyes softening and his lips spreading to form a tiny smile. A smile that Lola hadn't seen for so long that it took her breath away. She leaned against the window and watched in shock as Sam's grin slowly grew.

The boy continued with excitement. "Do you have any brothers or sisters? My sister is eight months old. Her name is Grace." The words tumbled from him and Sam shook his head quickly.

"No, but I have a dog called Goliath." He pointed toward a blanket of grass where Goliath slept in the sun.

Recovering from her shock, Lola slipped through the porch and opened the screen door. "Hey, guys," she said as she skipped down the stairs. The wooden door clapped behind her. "Sam, who's your new friend?"

Sam stood quickly, his face bright with pride. "His name is Caleb. He's our neighbor," he added brightly.

"Does your mom know you're here?" Lola asked Caleb. She shielded her eyes from the bright afternoon sun and took in Caleb's handsome features.

"I do now!"

Caleb flinched and grinned sheepishly. "That's my mom," he said, nodding toward a short, pretty woman as she marched over a wooded path toward them. A pudgy baby girl on her hip squealed at the sight of her brother. They stopped on the lawn beside Lola and the woman held out a hand.

"Hi, I'm Rena. We live next door. And I guess you've already met Caleb," she added with an accusing glance toward her son.

Lola laughed. "It's nice to see Sam making friends already. I'm Lola. And who's this?" she asked, placing a finger in the little girl's outstretched hand.

Rena wiped the curls from her daughter's forehead and pinched her dimpled cheek. "This is Caleb's sister, Grace."

"She's a pain in the butt," Caleb offered.

"Caleb," Rena hissed. "That's not nice to say." She gently smacked the back of his head, then smirked at Lola and rolled her eyes. "She's starting to get into his toys now that she's crawling."

Lola wiggled her finger in Grace's grasp. "You're too cute to be trouble," she teased. The little girl grinned wide and a dollop of drool slid down her chin.

"We saw a taxi drive in here a little while ago," Rena began. "Caleb's curiosity must have gotten the better of him." She glared at her son again. "Though he should have *asked* before he came barging over."

Caleb lifted guilty eyes to his mother and shrugged. "Can I go pet Sam's dog?" he asked.

Lola laughed. "Go ahead. He loves tummy rubs."

The women watched their sons race to the puppy and settle in the sun beside him. Goliath wiggled for a moment before giving in to the pleasure. He flopped over, exposing his belly.

"So you must be Louise's niece?" Rena asked, adjusting her daughter on her hip. "She said you might be coming. We've been keeping an eye on the house for her, but it's not the same as having someone live here. Caleb will enjoy having a buddy next door." She glanced at the boys, now roaring with delight at the body parts they found on Goliath's pink underside.

Lola turned toward the noise of Sam's laughter. She quickly blinked away the surprise and cleared her throat. Returning her attention to Rena, she smiled weakly. "Have you lived in the area long?" she asked.

Rena nodded, her hazel eyes watching Lola curiously. Her smile was friendly, but she seemed to sense something. "I've lived in Hope River for about fifteen years," she answered. "But my husband has lived here all his life. We met in high school."

"I used to visit my aunt in the summers until I was thirteen," Lola added thoughtfully, wondering if she'd ever met Rena's husband. She didn't remember much about the kids in the area.

"Mom!" Instantly Sam was beside Lola, jumping up and down in a frenzy. "Mom, Caleb has baseball practice tonight. He said we can go watch him! Can we go? Please?" Sam pulled on Lola's shirt and pleaded with bright gray eyes. Eyes that reminded Lola so much of Travis.

"I suppose, if it's all right…" Lola glanced at Rena.

"Of course! It's Little League, so the whole town shows up." She laughed and rolled her eyes. "Big event for a small town, you know." She shifted Grace's pudgy body on her hip once more and pried her little fingers from the gold chain around her neck. "It's at the park, on the other side of the Main Street bridge. Have you been there before?"

"I used to jump off the rocket slide there," Lola said, laughing a little. She glanced at Sam who listened with wide eyes and wished she hadn't planted the idea.

"The kids still do," Rena laughed. "Practice starts at six. Everyone will be excited to meet you. I bet the whole town already knows you're here."

Lola nodded and tried to keep a bright face, but her heart sank. In a small town, a newcomer would attract a lot of attention. She had hoped to get away for some peace and quiet this summer, not cause a spectacle. But Sam's unusual excitement made Lola swallow her dread and smile.

"We'll see you this evening," Rena said, winking at Sam. She lifted a scolding eyebrow at Lola. "Don't be a stranger. We're just through that little clump of forest if you need anything."

Lola nodded, holding back a smile. She was going to enjoy having this bossy woman next door.

"C'mon Caleb! Daddy's going to be home any minute so I can go shopping." Rena turned once more to Lola. "Can I get you anything while I'm out? Groceries or anything?"

"Oh, no, we're fine. Thanks. We'll walk to the grocery store tomorrow."

"Walk?" Rena asked, skepticism wrinkling her forehead. "It's at the other end of town."

"Oh, we'll be fine," Lola said, waving off Rena's concern. "We walk everywhere in San Francisco, we're used to it."

Rena's eyes widened and her mouth popped open. "Okay. Well, let me know if you change your mind." She held out a hand for Caleb to join her.

"See you tonight, Sam!" Caleb called over his shoulder. "Bring your baseball glove!"

Lola watched in stunned amazement as Sam bounced on his toes and giggled.

Chapter Two

The evening was warm and breezy, the kind that Lola had relished as a child. She held Sam's little hand in her own, swinging them together as they strolled down the uneven sidewalk. Old memories flooded Lola's mind - a warm breeze on her skin, a colorful summer dress that made her feel like skipping, her pink painted toenails peeking out of white flip flops. She felt ten years old again.

"There's the school." Lola pointed to a red brick building that sprawled along the opposite side of the street. She watched Sam's eyes light up as he hopped over a crack in the sidewalk. "There's a gigantic playground in the back. We'll go there soon."

They skipped over the pedestrian crossing just before the bridge, moving in the opposite direction of the fire station. It was only another block before they reached the park where cars filled the parking lot and people herded to the baseball field. Lola's stomach curled anxiously as she watched them. She glanced down at Sam and squeezed his hand. "Rena wasn't kidding," she mumbled.

Lola was surprised by how many people greeted them as if she and Sam had been a part of the town for years. Men tipped their hats with a genteel "good evening," and old women patted Sam's head as if they'd known him since he was a baby. As Sam and Lola reached the ball field, a familiar smile beamed at them from behind the field's backstop. Rena waved them over.

"There they are!" she called as they neared, bouncing Grace in her arms. Rena leaned over to tap Sam beneath the chin. "Are you ready to watch the kids play?"

He leaned into Lola's bright sundress with shyness, but grinned at Rena and nodded.

"You love baseball, don't you." Lola stroked his hair behind his ear, thinking of the few times she'd watched him play catch with Travis. "Is Caleb out there already?" She looked at the outfield where children tossed baseballs to each other in haphazard form. Some were focused on practicing while others leaned over to build sculptures in the sand.

"He's tossing balls in the outfield." Rena turned slightly to call behind her. "Gabe, come meet Lola and Sam."

A handsome, stocky man turned from the batting cage and lifted his head in greeting as he walked over. He extended a muscular hand and smiled gently at Lola. "Nice to meet you," he said with a deep, stern voice.

As Lola shook Gabe's hand, she narrowed her eyes in thought. She had seen his blue shirt before, and as she examined the emblems of fire and axe she realized where. She glanced up into Gabe's dark eyes and smiled. "You're one of the firemen we drove by this afternoon."

A gasp of recognition escaped from Sam's mouth.

Sudden realization passed over Gabe's face too. He lifted his chin in understanding. "That was your taxi," he said, eyes narrowed. "That's a long drive from Pine City."

"Not as long as the flight from San Francisco," Lola answered with a weary smile.

Gabe whistled and settled his hands on his hips. "Just the two of you visiting?"

"And my dog Goliath, but he's home sleeping right now," Sam blurted. Still in awe over the fireman, he'd momentarily forgotten his shyness.

Gabe bent so he was eye-level with the boy. "You must be Sam," he said, holding out a beefy hand. Sam shook it cautiously, then wrapped his arm around his mother's leg.

"Caleb told me you like baseball," Gabe said.

Sam nodded. He pulled his hand from behind his back to reveal a small glove, the leather still stiff with newness.

"I used to practice with my dad," he said.

A tiny frown flashed over Gabe's forehead. "Oh yeah?" he asked. "Are you any good?"

Sam glanced up at Lola, then back at Gabe. He lifted his chin and nodded. "I can catch fly balls. And I hit really hard too."

Laugh lines spread over Gabe's cheeks. He straightened and called toward the field, "Hey, Coach!"

Lola's heart quickened as another man glanced in their direction. He wore the same shirt as Gabe but was taller and leaner. His intense blue eyes narrowed at Lola as if trying to place her.

Gabe elbowed the coach when he neared. "I think we found ourselves an outfielder. Sam here says he can catch the pop flies."

Sam's eyes widened and he nodded solemnly. "And I can hit 'em real hard too," he added.

The realization of where this conversation was heading made Lola's stomach lurch. She planted a sturdy hand on the top of Sam's head and pulled him close.

The coach frowned at Lola's movement but quickly brought his gaze back to Sam. "I knew there was something special about you when you waved to me this morning," he said. Sam gasped again and his face bloomed with a gigantic smile.

The coach revealed a disarming smile of his own. "Would you like to play with us?" he asked. He lifted his gaze from Sam's face to Lola's and his eyes lingered.

"Awesome!" Sam jumped and Lola lost her grip on his head. She held a hand out in front of her, suddenly panicked, desperate to stop the disaster she knew was coming.

"I don't think..." Lola began, shaking her head and frowning deeply. But Sam had already accepted a team hat from Gabe and was fixing it on his head.

Lola tried to keep her voice level as she continued to protest. "Oh, he's not... Sam! I don't know about this..." She reached for him again until a soft hand squeezed her arm.

"He'll be fine, Lola," Rena assured from beside her. She watched Lola curiously.

The air felt heavy in Lola's chest and her head ached with a worry she knew all too well. But Sam beamed at her, his glove ready in his hand and Little League cap crooked on his head.

"Can I, Mom?" Sam pleaded. "Please?"

Lola glanced at the coach, his eyes like cold mountain water as he waited for her answer. She half nodded, then closed her eyes and took a deep breath. When she opened them, Sam was cheering and bounding toward the field, arms raised high as he charged to the other children. Gabe followed, but the coach stopped when Lola grabbed his arm.

"Sam isn't like the other kids," she warned, digging her fingers into the muscles of his forearm. She glanced at the field, wincing at how the other children towered over her little boy.

The coach scowled and lowered his head toward Lola, meeting her eyes. "Why? What's wrong with him?"

"There's nothing wrong with him," Lola snapped. "But he's... he's fragile. He was born with a heart defect."

"Oh," the coach whispered. His eyes softened. "He can't play sports?"

"No. I mean, it's not that... he can play. He had three surgeries when he was a baby and he's strong now, but he doesn't play rough games with other kids, and I don't want him to get hurt." Lola lay a hand over her heart and tried to breathe.

The coach nodded curiously. "So the doctors say he *can* play sports?" he asked.

"Well, yes, but..."

Slapping her shoulder, he let out a breath of laughter. "Then he'll be fine. Don't worry, this isn't a contact sport. They just hit the ball and run around the bases."

Before Lola could argue again the coach turned and casually jogged to the center of the field. He joined Gabe and the children and began a series of stretching exercises. Sam stood beside Caleb, a huge grin on his face, reaching to the sky and then to his toes with the others.

Lola watched, willing the worry and tears to disappear. Her bewilderment over Sam's smiles mixed with fear that twisted in her throat. She turned to the bleachers that were half full of parents and townspeople. They quickly looked away to the field, to each other, their whispers floating in the air, pretending they hadn't been eavesdropping. Lola climbed up the first stair and slumped beside Rena.

"Are you okay?" Rena asked. She pulled a bag of Cheerios from her pocket and popped it open for Grace.

"I guess." Lola nodded and feigned a smile, then watched her son's every move. Still slightly annoyed, she pulled her camera from her bag - silently thankful that she always had it available for surprises like this - and snapped a few shots of Sam while he practiced. It helped to smother her worry.

"I love watching them out there," Rena said, shading her eyes against the evening sun. "They're so cute together."

Lola felt her shoulders loosen as the kids began their jumping jacks. Maybe this really was a low-impact sport. Nothing to worry about. "They are pretty adorable, all those little bodies trying to keep up with each other." She took a few more pictures of the kids running around the outfield, gloves in hand and excitement bright on their cheeks.

Rena laughed. "Oh, the kids are cute too. But I meant the guys - Gabe and Matt. They've known each other since they were four. They can practically read each other's minds."

Lola shifted her gaze to Gabe, and then to the brawny man beside him. "So that's his name? Matt? I never got a chance to ask him, he was too busy brushing me off." She folded her arms over her chest and glared at him.

Rena gave an indulgent laugh. "Oh, Matt's a good guy. He's great with the kids." Rena watched him for a minute, then turned back to Lola.

"Sam was born with a heart defect?" she asked. A flash of apology passed over her face. "I was eavesdropping. You get really good at it when you live in a small town." She ran her fingers through Grace's blond curls while the little girl sucked on her Cheerios.

Lola nodded. "The doctors discovered it before he was born, so the minute he came into the world they whisked him away to surgery. He's my little miracle."

"And look at him now." Rena's eyes shone when she glanced back at the field. Together they watched for a moment as the kids ran the bases, chasing the coaches and trying to tag them.

"He had two more surgeries as a toddler, but the doctors say he's fine now. He should be able to do everything a little boy is supposed to do."

"But you're still protective."

Lola nodded, then narrowed her eyes at Matt once more. Rena kissed Grace's pudgy cheeks and touched a reassuring hand to Lola's arm. "I would be too," she decided.

AN HOUR OF LITTLE League practice felt like ten hours to Lola. She was exhausted by the end of it, having watched every move that Sam made, feeling herself tense and jump whenever he ran too fast or tripped over someone in the outfield. Despite her worry, she'd kept up a friendly conversation with Rena and even bounced Grace on her knee for a few minutes.

"Do you need a ride home tonight? I drove the minivan, we can squeeze everyone in," Rena said, scooping Grace back into her arms.

"No thanks. It's a beautiful night. We'll be fine walking." Lola lifted her face to the sky, now a stunning mixture of blue and pink from the setting sun. She could have studied it for hours, taken endless pictures of the swallows diving after evening bugs, but the crowd began a roar of excitement that brought her attention back to the field.

"Go, Sam!" Rena shouted beside her. "Run all the way, honey!" The rest of the spectators cheered and clapped, some standing to show support.

Lola saw a streak of yellow dart from second base to third and recognized her son. She stood quickly, unsure if the shouting that came from her chest was from excitement or fear. "Sam!" she screamed.

The noise lifted one level higher as Sam continued from third base to home. Little bodies in the outfield tumbled over one another until a tall girl with pigtails finally grasped the ball and lobbed it to Gabe at the pitcher's mound. Gabe let it roll to his feet, then turned and tossed it in slow motion to Matt near home base. Sam's rosy face contorted with the effort of moving his little legs so fast and he dove over the plate like a leopard on his prey.

"Sam!" Lola screeched again, but it was drowned out by cheers from the crowd. Sam's body slammed to the ground. His helmet, two sizes too big for his head, rapped the dirt and bounced with his body. He slid across home plate before Matt could tag him, dust and dirt clouding the scene. There was a sudden pause of silence, and then a wild roar from everyone as they cried, "Home run!" and "Great job, kid!"

The only words that tumbled from Lola's mouth as she jumped from the stands and ran through the gate to her son were, "Oh my God! He's not moving!"

His body was still sprawled over home base when she reached him.

"Sam!" Lola fell to her knees, about to roll him over to check if he was still breathing. Sam lifted his head and peered up with a wild grin. Dirt covered his nose and chin and sweat melded with dust across his cheeks.

"That was awesome!" he gushed. He pulled himself to his knees. "Mom, did you see that? I got a home run!"

Lola grabbed her chest, holding back the sobs that threatened to escape. "Samuel Parker Sommers! You scared me to death!" She ran a hand over her forehead and stood, trying to catch her breath. Leaping up, Sam brushed his legs off and grinned at the crowd. His eyes danced with excitement as he pulled off his helmet and received high-fives from his teammates.

Matt rubbed the top of Sam's head, grinning wide. "Good job, Champ! You have one heck of a swing." Sam beamed up at Matt, then ran to the field with the other children.

The fear and anger in Lola's chest continued to bubble. She turned on Matt and glared. "I thought you said this wasn't a contact sport," she insisted. Her tone took Matt by surprise. He froze, mouth slightly open for a moment before responding.

"It's not a contact sport," he acknowledged, resting his mitt on his hip.

"The kids were tripping all over each other in the outfield," Lola growled. "And Sam nearly broke his neck when he made *contact* with the ground just a minute ago!"

Matt frowned. "That's what they're supposed to do in baseball. Run and catch the ball, fall on the ground, dive to home base when they get a home run." His voice had turned equally clipped, frustration clouding his features. The crowd emptied the bleachers, unaware of Lola and Matt arguing under their breath.

"Besides, Sam's fine. Look at him," Matt added, pointing toward the infield. Sam was chasing a ball and laughing, trying to grab it with his mitt. "Don't you think you're overreacting a little?"

"Overreacting?" Lola asked through clenched teeth. But before she could begin another round of verbal assault, Matt jerked with surprise and reached above her head.

"Head's up!" he called, and Lola quickly turned to glance over her shoulder. An amazing flash of pain spread through her temple, making bright spots pulse behind her eyelids. Slowly, darkness loomed around her.

"*Roll* the balls in, Ethan!" Lola heard Matt shout, and then there were strong hands on her shoulders as she knelt to the ground. She held the side of her throbbing head, keeping her eyes closed for a moment as she tried to let the pain wash over her.

"Are you okay?"

The ringing in Lola's ears was almost as painful as her head. "Wow, that hurt," she mumbled.

"Sit down," Matt's deep voice instructed. "Let me see."

She felt a firm hand peel her own from the side of her head and then tilt her by the chin. The scent of fresh soap mixed with a pleasant cologne. She breathed it in deep before opening her eyes, and found Matt kneeling incredibly close. His shoulders, wide and muscular beneath his blue t-shirt, were close enough for her to lean her chin on. She was tempted - and slightly nauseous. She felt Matt's thumb brush over her temple and winced.

"Didn't break skin," he said quietly. "But you need some ice. You'll have one helluva lump there in the morning."

Lola braced her hands on the ground and tried to lift to her feet, but Matt took her by the elbow.

"No, I'm fine," Lola insisted as she tried to push him away. Her hand fell on his chest, and when she pushed her palm into him all she could feel was hard, curving muscle. She wobbled, and when Matt took her elbow again she didn't fight his touch.

"Let's get you some ice," Matt said, guiding Lola toward a bench with a cooler perched at one end.

Suddenly getting her bearings again, Lola pulled back from Matt and turned toward the field. "Where's Sam?" she asked, panic rising in her throat.

"He's with the other kids." Matt lifted his chin in the direction of the playground, where Lola saw Caleb and Sam zipping down the slides. Rena and Gabe, along with a handful of other adults, sat in the nearby grass and watched the children.

"I'm fine now," Lola said, trying to wave Matt off. She touched the side of her head and felt the hot, wide lump.

Matt laughed quietly, watching Lola with his striking blue eyes. "You're stubborn aren't you?" he asked. "You need some ice for that or it's going to swell to twice the size."

She felt her shoulders drop and scowled through the pain that radiated in her head. "Fine. But only for a minute." Lola followed him to the bench and plunked down beside the cooler as Matt dug out a handful of ice. He wrapped it in a towel and handed it to Lola. She frowned for a moment, then gently rested it against her temple.

"Do you have a headache?" Matt asked. He planted his hands firmly on his hips, interrogating her with an edge of experience.

Lola scowled up at him. "I just got hit in the head with a baseball. What do you think?"

Matt nodded, undeterred by her snide attitude, and twisted one side of his mouth in thought. She watched him glance quickly over her bare legs and then toward the field.

"I need to examine you."

"Excuse me?" Lola pulled the ice from her head and gave Matt an accusing stare.

He met her gaze with his own, this time serious and determined. "I'm a trained paramedic. I need to make sure you don't have a concussion."

Lola's mouth, still open in protest, formed an embarrassed "oh". "I'm fine," she assured.

The corners of Matt's mouth lifted and he glanced over his shoulder toward the playground. "Either let me examine you or I'll tell Rena to take you to the clinic in town. You choose. Either way we need to make sure you don't have a concussion so you can take care of your son tonight and wake up for him in the morning."

Matt's voice was stern and he stared hard at Lola like a determined teacher would at a student. It made Lola shrink a little.

"Fine. Now who's the stubborn one?" She watched as a small smile returned to Matt's lips, a cute one that caused handsome lines to pile up on one cheek.

"I just need to check your eyes and ask you a few questions." He pulled a first aid kit from beneath the bench, then rustled through it before pulling out a tiny flashlight. He knelt in front of Lola, close enough that their knees bumped.

"Look at my eyes," he instructed, his voice soft and low. She obeyed, studying the intensity of his blue irises. Tiny flecks of gold hid deep within them. Lola swallowed loudly.

Matt turned the light off, but his eyes remained on Lola's face for an extra moment. He brought his fingers to her chin, warm and strong and electric, and turned her head so he could examine the lump. Lola lowered the ice to her lap and closed her eyes.

"What's the date today?" Matt asked.

She opened one eye and peeked at Matt, frowning.

"Just humor me," he said, that little smirk lifting from his lips to his eyes.

Lola sighed and cleared her throat. "June fifth," she said quietly.

Matt took her chin in his hand and turned her face back to his. His touch was gentle.

"How many fingers am I holding up?" he asked, using his left hand.

"Four." His ring finger was bare. Lola felt the wedding band on her left hand and wiggled it between her fingers.

"What's your name?"

"I'm seriously okay." Lola huffed and lifted her eyes to Matt's. His eyes sparkled with humor. He set his hands on both sides of the bench, surrounding her with strong arms, bending so close that she could see a tiny scar on his lip. Goose bumps prickled her skin.

"I know you're okay," Matt answered softly. "You don't have a concussion. But I still would like to know your name."

She cleared her throat and scooted back an inch. "I'm Lola. Sommers. Lola Sommers."

Matt leaned back onto his heels and studied her for a moment. He offered his hand, and when Lola shook it she couldn't help but notice the rough calluses, the strength of his fingers.

"Matt Dawson. Nice to meet you."

Lola gave a small smile and watched him slide beside her on the bench. She put the ice back on her throbbing temple and turned enough so she could see his face past her hand.

"Thanks for the ice," she said. "And for checking my head. I suppose I can't be mad at you anymore."

The corner of his mouth lifted. "I'm still not sure why you were mad at me in the first place."

Lola tried to control the anger that built in her chest once again. She glanced at the playground and watched Rena gently push Sam on the swings.

"See that little boy over there?"

Matt nodded, his eyes following hers to Sam and Rena.

"He's my world." She turned back to Matt, looking fiercely into his eyes. "It makes me very protective."

Matt remained silent, a small frown of confusion his only response.

Lola took the ice from her head and rolled it back and forth between her hands.

"It took three surgeries before he was two to fix his heart, to make sure it would never fail him. I can't tell you how many times I feared losing my little boy. I never want to see him hurting again."

Matt nodded in understanding. He glanced at her left hand and lifted his eyes to the playground. "It must have been awful for you and your husband."

Nodding slowly, Lola leaned back, looked up to the sky and gulped in a deep breath. "My husband died two years ago. It's a scary responsibility keeping your child safe all on your own."

Matt's gaze moved to the ground and he folded his hands together. "I'm sorry. I didn't realize..."

"I know I'm overprotective of Sam," Lola interrupted. She faced Matt and shook her head in shame. "This is the first time I've ever let him play ball with other kids. It was only with his dad before, or my father." Lola gave a tight smile and nodded, then dumped the ice and towel into Matt's hands. She met his crystal blue eyes with her own and studied him for a moment. "He had a lot of fun today. Thank you."

"He's a good little ball player. Hits harder than some of the kids twice his size." Matt dumped the ice into the cooler and leaned back on the bench. "We hold T-ball practice every Thursday night, and have a couple of competitive games at the end of the summer. If you're sticking around a while, you're welcome to join us."

"We'll be here for the summer," she said quietly, glancing again toward Sam on the playground. She shifted to the edge of the bench, feeling ready to flee from the comfort she found in this strange man's presence. "We're going back to San Francisco at the beginning of August when my aunt returns."

"Who's your aunt?"

"Louise Hamilton. She lives at the end of town near the fairgrounds."

Matt's posture changed then, such a slight movement that Lola wouldn't have noticed it except her senses were on high alert. If she hadn't seen Sam racing toward her, the others following behind him at a slower pace, she would have taken more time to consider Matt's reaction. But Sam reached her quickly, covered in sweat and dirt and looking thoroughly happy.

"That was so much fun!" he gushed, panting as he leaned against his mother. Lola pulled him into her lap and peeled the ball cap from his head. His hair stuck to his forehead and curled over his ears.

"I'm glad you had a fun day, baby." Sam's warm dirty scent reminded Lola of a wet puppy. She rested her forehead on him, then peeked at Matt. He watched them quietly, a tiny lift to his lips.

Lola considered not bringing it up, but Sam was so happy that she couldn't deny him the pleasure. "Coach said you can play on the team all summer, if you want," she told him. Sam jumped from her lap, fists pumping into the sky, and gave a whoop of excitement. Caleb joined in and the two boys hopped on the dirt making a bath of dust rise into the air. It floated over Rena and Gabe as they arrived.

"Are you sure you don't want a ride home, Lola?" Rena asked as she gathered her sleeping daughter from her husband's huge arms. "There's plenty of room."

The evening had darkened quickly and Lola could feel the exhaustion from their day settling into her bones. Had it really only been this morning that they'd left San Francisco? It already felt like weeks.

"Actually, I think I will take you up on it." Lola ran a hand through Sam's hair and thought of the bath and snack and bed-making they still had to tend to. She turned to Matt, suddenly shy and uncertain. "Thanks, Coach," she said with a little nod. He smiled in return, his stunning eyes causing somersaults in Lola's gut.

"BE GOOD FOR MOMMY," Gabe lectured, lifting his son to eye level and planting a kiss on his nose. "I'll be home in a few minutes."

Caleb jumped from his dad's arms and then crushed himself against Matt's legs. "G'night, Uncle Matt," he said, squeezing his legs tight. Matt grabbed Caleb by the waist and flipped him upside down, tossing him over his shoulder.

"I think I'll keep you with me tonight," Matt teased. "I'm a little hungry after all that exercise." He took soft bites from Caleb's side and pretended to chew on his arm. Caleb flailed and screamed in delight, grabbing Matt's head for balance.

"You really will be keeping him tonight if you don't stop winding him up," Rena scolded. Her eyes twinkled and a smile threatened her lips, but Matt knew when he'd better listen to the boss. With one swift move, he set Caleb upright on the ground. He leaned over to kiss the top of Rena's short curly hair and peeked into her arms at the sleeping Grace.

"They sure are cute when they sleep," Matt whispered. He softly tapped her button nose.

Rena looked up at Matt and winked. "Come to dinner tomorrow night, okay?" Turning to Gabe, she leaned in for a quick kiss. "Don't be too long, handsome," she added, and wiggled her eyebrows at her husband.

If Matt hadn't spent the last fifteen years with these two lovebirds, he wouldn't have believed they'd been married for nearly as long. He envied their relationship, still full of fun and electricity. He also couldn't be happier for his best friend. It was what every good man deserved - a playful and loving wife; healthy, happy children; a good home and secure job.

As Matt turned toward the baseball diamond to collect the evening's bags, he heard Sam's little voice fill with concern as he and his mother left the field. Matt glanced over his shoulder and listened, watching Lola's curving figure and long slender legs.

"What happened to your head, Mom?" Sam asked, gaping up at the small red knot on Lola's temple. She brushed a hand over her hair and laughed. Her smile was infectious and Matt caught himself grinning with her. "Oh, I just got hit with a ball, no big deal."

"Did it bleed?" Sam asked as he pulled her along by her hand.

Lola shook her head. "No, your coach looked it over and said it's fine. He put some ice on it for me and I'm all better now." Matt smiled feeling a strange twist in his stomach.

Sam swung his mother's hand in his. "I'm glad you're okay,

Mommy." He glanced over his shoulder and locked eyes with Matt, then smiled and gently waved. His small round face held the same curious expression that Matt had seen at the fire station and surprisingly, his heart swelled.

"So what's their story?" Gabe asked, walking up beside Matt and lifting his chin in Lola's direction. He bent to toss the baseballs into a black sports bag while Matt continued to eye the beautiful stranger in the bright sundress.

"I don't know much," Matt answered, watching Lola and Rena herd the children into a light blue minivan. He sighed and looked down at Gabe, watching him silently for a moment. His gaze blurred as his thoughts sifted through the evening.

Gabe zipped the sports bag closed and stood. He elbowed Matt in the stomach. "You gonna talk or just daydream about those long legs you've been eyeing all night?"

A burst of air escaped Matt and he let out an uncomfortable laugh. He walked to home plate and grabbed it, shaking the dust from it a little longer than needed.

"Buddy, I haven't seen you give that much attention to a woman since Ali."

Matt laughed lightly again, but frowned when his heart clenched at Ali's name. He avoided Gabe's eyes and collected the baseball bats instead. A small glove lay abandoned beside the fence, probably forgotten in the hustle at the end of the game. Matt smacked it against his thigh and watched the dust float to the ground. "All I know is that she got hit in the head with a ball. I just gave her some ice and checked her out for a few minutes." He turned to find a stupid grin consuming Gabe's face.

"Hell, you checked her out, all right. While I wiped baby drool off my shirt at the playground, I saw you two over here. And if you'd've stared at her any harder just now you'd have burned a hole in her back."

Matt rolled his eyes and headed for first base. Halfway there, he rubbed his forehead and sighed, giving up. Her smile wouldn't release him, and neither would those dark eyes. Eyes that he remembered from childhood.

"She's only here for the summer," he called to Gabe, who stopped what he was doing to listen. Gabe watched as Matt rounded the bases, picking them up and shaking them hard as he spoke. "She and Sam are house-sitting next door to you, in fact."

Gabe nodded and shifted, hands on hips. "That's what Rena said. They met this morning. She said Lola and Sam are real nice, but that's all I heard." Gabe watched Matt stride toward third base and studied him with narrowed eyes. "What's going on in that thick head of yours?" he asked.

Matt stopped in front of Gabe and let out a long sigh. "She's a widow," he answered quietly. "Her husband died two years ago." He tossed the bases into a pile beside the small glove and walked toward the bench.

Gabe nodded, silent as he watched Matt. He shoved the small glove in the bag, then picked it up with the bases and followed Matt. "Then you two have something in common, don't you."

"Guess so." Matt grabbed the cooler and first aid kit and walked silently with Gabe to the parking lot. When they arrived at Matt's black truck, Gabe watched him toss the bags and bats into the truck bed. He tossed his own armload in and faced his best friend again.

"It's been seven years, buddy."

"I realize that." Without looking at Gabe, Matt slammed the truck's tailgate closed and walked around to the driver's side. Gabe followed his lead and climbed into the passenger seat.

"You haven't dated anyone since Ali died."

Matt gunned the truck to a start and threw it into reverse. "I realize that too."

"So maybe it's time you get out there again."

Matt shifted into gear and eyed Gabe uncomfortably. "I don't know anything about this woman." He lifted a finger to correct himself. "Other than the fact that she's only here for a couple of months."

"It doesn't have to be her. Just get out there and find someone, anyone. Don't you think it's time to give it another try? *Seven years.*" They looked out their windows in momentary silence. Houses passed slowly by, front porch lights bright in the dark night. Then Gabe let out a little ripple of laughter that made Matt jump. "Hell, according to Rena there's a line of women waiting for you to wake up."

Matt turned away, hiding his embarrassment. He'd had his share of attractive women ask him to dinner or out for drinks. But he always had something else he had to do. Like working with the kids. Or helping someone with house projects. Volunteering for the fire department or first responders. There were always plenty of excuses.

"I know Hope River has pretty slim pickings, but Rena knows plenty of women over in the Pine City area. There's bound to be someone you'll be interested in."

Matt turned to Gabe and frowned. "You trying to get rid of me? This is my home. It always will be. I'm perfectly happy in Hope River, with or without someone to share it with."

"You don't have to move to date someone. Besides, maybe the lucky girl will like Hope River."

Matt shook his head. As he pulled into Gabe's driveway he saw lights from Lola's new summer home twinkling through the small forest that divided the lots.

"I already tried that. Didn't work out so well, did it?" He glanced at Gabe, then back to the woods.

Gabe pulled off his seatbelt and slouched back on his seat. Shaking his head, he looked at Matt for a moment, his eyes dark and serious. "Shit, Matt... fine, suit yourself." He opened the heavy door and slid out, then turned back. "See you tomorrow night. Boss is making your favorite." Gabe frowned a little, but a smirk spread over his lips. "She feeds you better than she does me."

Matt smiled gently, nodded. "That's because she loves me more."

Gabe's cheeks lit up with a boyish grin and he slammed the door in response.

WHEN LOLA ENTERED THE kitchen late that evening, her hair piled into a wet mass on her head and her skin still damp from a long, steaming shower, she felt an unfamiliar lightness in her body. She glanced around the dim room, at the tiny light above the kitchen sink and the colorful coffee mugs arranged on the countertop. She ran her fingertips over the round wooden table that was so charming and inviting, and realized what it was.

Contentment.

For the first time in a very long time, she felt a wave of peace at being exactly where she was. Everything was okay. She was okay. At this very moment, life felt okay. Her little boy had smiled today, numerous times. He'd played baseball and made friends, and she'd even heard him laugh out loud. The sound had been sweet music to her ears, and five hundred pounds had lifted from her shoulders. For the moment, no worries about tomorrow troubled her, no ghosts from the past were breathing down her neck. It was just her and the quiet evening, the peace of the house, knowing that the trees and the creek nearby were all protecting her from pain tonight.

Lola pulled her camera from her bag and looked through the evening's pictures. There were a few of Sam with his cute baseball cap, of his smile and laughter as he practiced with his new friends. She felt her own smile grow as it dawned on her... perhaps this was the first time in a long time that she'd smiled for Sam too.

When Travis was still alive, Lola had always had her camera ready to capture the joy that their little family shared. She loved photography and the act of recording sweet memories. But these last years, there hadn't really been much to photograph that made her or Sam smile. They had been living in a sort of haze, going through the motions, just trying to make it through the day, and then the next. Perhaps all Sam had needed was a little fun, and to see Lola happy again too.

Lola sifted through the pictures some more, stopping on one of Sam in the background, catching a ground ball. His coach was in the foreground, walking toward the camera, a wide smile on his face as he spoke to Gabe.

Lola gently touched the lump on her temple. Her head throbbed a little, though probably not from the accident as much as from the photo in front of her. She pressed the zoom button and studied it for a moment.

Matt was incredibly handsome. He had beautiful straight teeth.

Slight crow's feet were etched beside his stunning blue eyes and a few flecks of gray spread at his temples.

Was he married? She hadn't seen a ring on his finger. And she had deliberately looked.

Lola rolled her eyes. Why was she thinking about this? She rubbed a hand over her aching temple, then pulled some aspirin from her purse. Her earlier contentment was quickly slipping away. She gulped down the pills with a glass of water and stared out the kitchen window, into the sweet darkness of the night. It was so quiet here. Almost too quiet. She could hear every warning bounce around in her head, every word trying to bring back the worry and fear. Grabbing her laptop case from the floor, she heaved it onto the table in frustration.

This was exactly *not* what Lola had come to Hope River for. Romance was supposed to be the last thing on her mind. It had only been two years! She pulled her laptop open, started it up and found the file named résumé. Pulling out a notepad, she studied the notes and lists she had written inside. Then she unfolded the old résumé that was tucked between the last pages.

Sitting back at the table, she gazed at it all and took in a deep breath. *This*, she reminded herself, this was why she was here. To get back on track, to focus on finding a job, to make a plan, plot a path, get busy.

When Travis died, Lola had decided it was time to step up. No more relying on others to take care of her and Sam. A job, their home projects, caring for her son, she took care of it all. She had learned to keep busy, to keep her mind off of that empty, aching feeling in her chest. And she had figured out how to keep Sam busy too, how to show him that she was strong and that she would take care of them. But when Lola lost her job, she had suddenly felt suffocated, panicked, and completely without a focus or a plan.

And now it was time to get back on track. For her sake, and for Sam's.

Chapter Three

When Lola stumbled down the stairs at 5:30 the following morning, it wasn't the brightness of the early sun that surprised her. Nor was it the loud and boisterous trill of bird song beside the creek. What surprised Lola was that four old women were sitting on the floor of her wooden porch with legs crossed and eyes closed. They quietly hummed as if it were a natural part of the morning.

Lola peeked at them through the closed glass door of the kitchen. Should she interrupt them? Ask who they were, and why, in God's name, were they chanting on her porch so early in the morning? Lola rubbed a hand over her forehead and tried to tuck an unruly tuft of hair behind her ear. She noticed her reflection in the glass window, saw dark circles beneath her eyes, disheveled hair, a tattered old t-shirt and sweats for pajama wear.

"Coffee first," Lola whispered as she backed away from the door. She slipped to the far corner of the kitchen to inspect the coffee maker. It looked fully functional - a bit dusty, but the clock flashed when she plugged it in. She pulled the carafe out and sniffed it, then checked the filter. It was all clean and ready. Now if she could only find some coffee. Any brand would do. Indian, Columbian, heck, even Folgers.

Her search unearthed only a handful of tea bags. She flicked off the coffee machine, quietly filled the teapot and set the stove burner on high. She pulled a chair from the small kitchen table and collapsed into it. *Way too early*, Lola told herself, and laid her head in her arms on the table. Minutes passed, and the quiet voices on the porch lulled her back to sleep.

"Well, Lola Mason, I didn't know you were here!" a woman called from the doorway. "I thought Louise's house was about to burst, and here you are sleeping on the table!"

Lola jerked upright, her heart in her throat. She tried to see past the blur in her eyes. She hadn't been called by her maiden name in years. And the surprise of this woman's voice, along with the wild hissing sound of the teapot, sent Lola's heart rate skipping. She jumped up and moved the whistling teapot off the stove and was caught in a huge hug. The white-haired woman squeezed the breath from Lola and then held her at arm's length to get a good look.

"It's been so long!" the woman cried. A joyful smile spread over her face. She shook her head, then pinched Lola's cheek. "You're all skin and bones, dear. We need to get some meat on you. Girls, come meet Louise's niece!" she called over her shoulder. Lola turned and smiled as she wracked her brain for a clue as to who this woman was.

One by one, the other ladies peeked into the kitchen and smiled. "This is Rae," the woman continued, walking back to the door to pull a tall, gray-haired friend into the kitchen. Rae waved and smiled wide. "And Betty, our youngest member of the yoga group." Betty put her hands together in front of her and bowed slightly toward Lola. "And this here's Anne."

Anne, a pudgy woman with a kind face, drew close to Lola and held out a hand. "Louise has told us so much about you, and Sam too. He sounds adorable - is he visiting too?"

Lola nodded, still unable to find words as she shook Anne's hand and scanned the others' faces. Was every day in Hope River going to start out this strange?

"Yes," Lola finally stammered, her voice like sandpaper. "He's upstairs sleeping. I'm sorry I interrupted your…" Lola frowned, letting her words drop. She gestured toward the porch.

"Oh, heavens, it's fine. We just heard the teapot going off," the first woman said. She eased around the table and turned off the red burner that Lola had abandoned. "I think we're the ones who interrupted you," she laughed. She set her hands on her hips and eyed Lola.

"You don't remember me, do you dear?" she asked. Her friendly eyes squeezed closed while she let out a boisterous laugh.

Lola studied the woman and shook her head. "No, I'm sorry. You're a friend of Aunt Louise?"

"I'm Dolly Martinson. Last time we saw each other, you were up to here," she said, putting a hand out level with her heavy bosom.

"Dolly?" Lola jumped at the sudden recognition and then leapt forward to embrace her at once. "It's been twenty years!"

The four women clucked and cooed over Lola while she explained her arrival to Hope River and her surprise at finding them on the porch.

"Louise didn't mention that you all meet here every…" Her voice faded into a question. She hoped the sentence didn't end with *day*.

"Once a week," Dolly said with a nod. "Louise, Anne, and I started this yoga group about four years ago. Rae joined two years ago, and Betty's been with us for just a few months."

Betty smiled wide and pretty, showing pearly white teeth and a dimple. "Louise is going to bring back so many new poses after her little trip overseas," she said, her voice ripe with excitement.

"Do you practice yoga?" Anne asked, gesturing toward the porch.

"Oh, no. No." Lola shook her head and took a step back. What she wanted more than anything at the moment was a cup of something hot and caffeinated. "You all go ahead. You won't hear a peep out of me."

"Nonsense," Dolly insisted. She took Lola's hand and pulled her to the kitchen door with the others. "It's a gorgeous morning, and I have a feeling that what you need right now is a chance to get centered. It'll make your day go so much smoother."

Lola scrunched her face in protest as she was pulled into the cool morning air of the porch. She tugged at her ratty t-shirt and oversized sweatpants and watched Anne open a small bench at the end of the porch. She pulled out a thick blue yoga mat and unrolled it beside the others. "You can use your aunt's spare mat," she said with a grin.

"Let's get back to it ladies," Dolly called, and she effortlessly folded herself into position. The other women were silent as they moved into their poses as well.

Lola crouched and crossed her legs awkwardly one over the other, trying to straighten her posture as the others did. Her knees popped like gun shots and her ankles cracked, damaged from her younger days of ballet.

Dolly's voice soothed them with instructions. "We'll move into Child's Pose next," she lulled. Lola followed Dolly's lead and mimicked the others' moves. She laid her chest on her knees, her forehead on the mat, and stretched her arms above her head. Her back cracked in three places. She peeked out from behind her arms, watching the silent women who looked as though they had fallen asleep in strange positions. *Sam used to sleep this way*, she thought, *with his tiny butt in the air and his legs tucked beneath him.* A giggle threatened to escape Lola's lips, but she gulped it back and pressed her forehead harder into the mat. How in the world had her first morning come to this?

"Now slowly lift to your feet," Dolly continued, her voice mesmerizing as she practically floated over her mat. "This next one's called 'Thread the Needle'."

Lola followed Dolly's hypnotic voice, each move making her feel as if she were tying her body in a knot. As instructed, she pressed her cheek and ear against the floor, twisted her left arm through a loop in her right, and ended up with her rear end aimed at the sky.

"Is all the blood supposed to be pooling into my head?" Rae squeaked from her mat, breaking the silence. Lola would have laughed out loud if she'd had the air to do so. Black spots flashed in her eyes and the small lump on her temple throbbed.

Dolly's voice remained calm and reassuring. "It will take a while to get used to these poses, and you'll eventually find what feels right for you. Just remember, ladies," she said, untwisting her body so she could face everyone. The others unfolded themselves as well, and Lola let out a huge breath of air that she hadn't realized she'd been holding.

"Everything I teach you here is optional. The only requirement in yoga," Dolly pulled in a deep breath of air and blew it out softly, using her arms to accentuate, "is to *breathe*."

Lola smiled. *Just breathe*, she heard her mind whisper. *What an appropriate mantra for the summer.*

By SIX A.M. THE sun was high enough to cast streams of light through the canopy of trees and onto the porch. The cardinals and robins understood this earthly gesture and sang with delight, while the hum of bees stirred the air. Lola lay on her back, arms to her sides, hips, shoulders and head pressed deeply into the mat. She felt as if she were in a gentle coma, sleeping but still fully aware of the sounds and movement around her.

All five of the women lay in this position, resting at the end of their yoga session, breathing and meditating. But the peace quickly ended as a little voice called out from the kitchen door and a fat puppy erupted onto the porch. Goliath snuffled each woman's face and hair before they could rise, causing screeches and yelps of surprise.

"Hi baby!" Lola cried, laughing as she sat up. She held her arms out to her little boy, who rubbed his eyes and scowled at the bright morning. He walked timidly between the cooing, laughing women and folded himself onto his mother's lap. Wrapping Lola's arms around his head, he peeked out with curious gray eyes.

Anne, whose red hair was messed from the puppy's excited nipping, gathered Goliath into her arms and nuzzled him. "Who is this?" she playfully scolded while Goliath wriggled and licked at her fingers and chin. Dolly, Rae, and Betty exploded with laughter.

"Meet Goliath," Lola said, squeezing Sam a little tighter. It had been an unexpected morning, but she was more delighted with this day than she had felt with any other in a long while. "He's ten weeks old."

Anne picked up one of his paws and held it in her palm. "Look at the size of him! He's going to be huge." Goliath wriggled so hard that he flopped from her arms and tumbled to the floor. He righted himself, bound over to Betty, and barked. Betty jumped, causing more rounds of laughter.

"Goliath wants to play," Sam said, reaching a hand to his puppy.

"And you must be Sam." Dolly leaned toward him and smiled. "Your Great Aunt Louise has told me all about you. I'm so glad you're visiting Hope River." She brushed a hand gently over Sam's arm in welcome.

Goliath put his nose to the wooden floor and sniffed his way to the screen door. He found the soft, green welcome mat and squatted.

"Goliath! NO!" Lola shouted. She threw Sam into standing position and reached for the puppy. "Don't go on the...!"

Everyone watched as Goliath relieved himself on the rug, then wiggled with delight in response.

THE RICH SMELL OF coffee welcomed Matt as he strolled into his tiny first floor apartment kitchen. He rubbed a hand through his spiky wet hair and tightened the lip of the towel over his bare waist. He hadn't slept well last night. A cold shower this morning and a jolt of caffeine were essential to get him focused on the day.

He filled a red mug to the brim and lifted the steaming liquid to eye level. *Mr. Dawson ROCKS*, the mug read, and Matt smiled. "So does summer vacation," he murmured, toasting the memory of his 7th hour Advanced Biology class. Now if only he could train himself to sleep past six a.m., he would enjoy his break from teaching high school even more.

It had taken him hours to fall asleep the previous night, and Matt struggled with the reasons. Too much Mountain Dew before bed? Perhaps he shouldn't have watched that stupid horror flick so late, either. He had never been spooked by those movies, but always had stupid dreams afterward. Matt brought his coffee around the kitchen island and sat on one of the leather stools. The skin of his bare chest and arms prickled from the cool morning breeze as it blew in through the open windows.

When Matt glanced at the two black sports bags beside the kitchen door, he knew. It wasn't the caffeine high or the movie that had disturbed his sleep last night. It was a pair of alarming brown eyes and thoughts of a beautiful woman in a sexy summer dress that had kept him awake. An endless replay of her hair whispering over flushed cheeks and dimples peeking around pink lips as she smiled at her son.

"Shit," Matt mumbled, rubbing the palm of his hand into his eyes. It was such an irritating, unexpected reaction to have to someone he had only known for thirty minutes. *Thirty-five,* his mind chided, *if you count a blurry memory from twenty years ago.* Blurry memory or not, his reaction to her yesterday had been just as jarring as it was back then.

Matt huffed a long sigh. He'd only been a kid then. A kid without a care in the world, just as he should be feeling this morning. He sipped his coffee and stared out the window at the quiet neighborhood street, trying his best to clear his mind.

Plenty to do today, he reminded himself. He was on call for the fire department. Needed to wash his truck - the thing was filthy. Dinner tonight at Gabe and Rena's house. And he'd promised Mrs. Elmer that he'd stop over to fix her leaking toilet. He'd need to pop into Charlie's hardware store for the part.

So what's their story? Gabe's voice echoed in the back of Matt's mind. He hadn't told Gabe everything he knew - what was the sense in it? It had been twenty years. He barely remembered her, and she obviously had forgotten completely. Why wouldn't she? They'd been so young.

Lola's dark eyes flashed before Matt and he set his coffee down with a clap. He glared at the bags of Little League equipment. It wasn't a surprise that he'd forgotten to dump them in the closet the previous night. There had been a lot on his mind.

A small leather baseball glove poked from the end of one bag, catching Matt's attention. He picked it up and stuffed the tips of three fingers and his thumb inside of it. The glove was tiny on his large hand, and stiff. It looked like it hadn't been used more than a handful of times. Matt turned the glove over and read the name written in black block letters. *Samuel P. Sommers.*

Kneeling beside the sports bag, Matt studied the name. Sam was a pretty cute kid. Great ball player, despite his tiny size. Apparently the little guy had fought a tough battle early in life, though you wouldn't guess it watching him on the field. He remembered Lola's concern about her son's heart, about his safety, and Matt's own heart trembled with understanding. He knew what it was like to worry over the health of loved ones. In his own life, it had caused the biggest heartaches Matt had ever known.

The alarm from the first responder radio startled Matt from his thoughts, and he stood, baseball mitt still in hand, and listened intently. The dispatcher relayed a double car accident on County Road B, issuing a response from the Hope River fire department and a few surrounding units. Matt abandoned his coffee and the sports bags and headed for his room to throw on some clothes. He tossed Sam's mitt beside his wallet and keys, making a mental note to drop it off at their place later in the day. *I'm just the coach, returning the kid's glove,* Matt told himself. *Just part of the job, right?* He bolted through his apartment, eager for a distraction.

"COME, GOLIATH!" LOLA GENTLY tugged on the leash and tried again to convince her stubborn puppy that being pulled by a leather rope was a good thing.

"Can we go to the playground today, Mom?" Sam asked, jumping over cracks in the sidewalk. He squinted up at his mother and shaded his eyes from the bright afternoon sun.

"It depends on if we ever make it to the grocery store and back." Lola yanked on the leash this time and Goliath reluctantly trotted a few feet toward her.

It was a long walk down Main Street, past the school, over the bridge, and into the center of town with a hesitant puppy and an energetic child. Lola wiped a bead of sweat from her forehead and contemplated a rental car for the summer. Her cool cotton skirt and tank top could only provide so much ventilation. An open car window as she breezed down the road sounded like a brilliant idea. And since when did Minnesota summers get so humid? She didn't remember feeling this much warmth and exhaustion when she was a kid.

"Where are the fire trucks?" Sam asked as they passed the deserted station.

"There must be a fire or an accident somewhere." Lola lifted Goliath into her arms and caught up to her son, who stared at the station with a curious expression.

"How can my coaches be firemen too?" he asked.

"Well, in a small town like this the firefighters are volunteers. They have other jobs, and they just come to the station when they're needed." Lola noticed the handful of vehicles parked on the side of the building and wondered if any of them belonged to Gabe or Matt.

Matt. Lola's heart tripped over itself for a moment and guilt washed over her. Was she supposed to be attracted to another man, so soon? She rolled the wedding band around on her left hand. She couldn't remember Travis' smell anymore, but Matt's cologne and fresh soap scent from the previous evening still lingered in her mind. His powerful blue eyes, solid muscles on his arms and chest… it quickened her pulse and squeezed her chest, and she hated herself for it.

Goliath licked Lola's chin and yipped.

"You're looking quite pleased with yourself," she scolded. She wrapped his leash around her aching arm - twenty pounds felt a lot heavier when she was trying to get somewhere - and picked up the pace.

"When will we be there?" Sam moaned.

Lola eyed the grocery store four blocks down the street and took a deep breath. "Not soon enough," she grumbled.

THE GROCERY BAGS MADE a loud thump as Lola dumped them on the floor beside the refrigerator. She grabbed a large glass from the cupboard and moved to the sink. "Sam, drink a cold glass of water before you go out to play," she called. He came bounding beside her, still full of energy. Lola watched him gulp from the sweating glass and gave a weary smile.

"How you still have so much energy is beyond me, kid." She pulled her hair from her damp neck and wrapped it in a knot, then took a few gulps of cool water herself.

Her first trip to Hope River's grocery store had been an awful experience. Though, now that they were all home safe and sound and no one had heat exhaustion, it was a *little* bit funny.

And it was typical, Lola thought. She had a knack for creating disasters every time she tried a new adventure, and this had been no exception. She'd carried Goliath practically all the way to the store, wondering with every step why she'd brought him in the first place. Once there she'd tied him to the bike rack while she and Sam ran inside. When they'd returned, five grocery bags between them, Lola found a sleeping Goliath who was not even the least bit interested in walking home. So while she carried Goliath under one arm and lugged three heavy bags with the other, Sam skipped ahead with two light bags full of bread, chips, and eggs. Eggs that hadn't made it home without at least one crack in each shell and chips that were surely in a thousand tiny pieces by now. It was the longest, most painful walk she had ever experienced, and Lola planned to look up car rentals the moment she unpacked the groceries. Though, perhaps a nap was in order first. After all, she'd been up since the five a.m. surprise yoga session.

Exasperation pulsed through Lola as she shoved the eggs in the fridge. Behind her, on the old wooden table, she could feel her laptop beckoning her to begin the job search, could feel her résumé scolding her for taking so long to get to it. Lola slammed the refrigerator door closed and leaned over the sink, blowing out a tense wisp of air. If this was supposed to be a relaxing vacation away from the city, a time to regroup and refuel, it certainly wasn't starting out that way.

As if in answer, a cool breeze blew in through the open windows, calm and refreshing on Lola's moist skin. She glanced outside where Sam played beneath the tree house with his favorite Tonka trucks. Goliath lay in the shade on the cool green grass, his nose shining from the gallon of water he'd lapped up upon their return.

Lola envied the puppy's freedom, his ability to lie beneath the quiet blue sky and nap whenever his body pleased. She studied him for a moment, sprawled on his side and twitching himself to sleep. With a heady sense of abandonment she decided to join him.

On the way out the door she grabbed her résumé. Revising it in the sunshine wouldn't do any harm.

Chapter Four

"Want a beer?" Gabe asked, lifting his bottle to Matt in greeting. Rocking back in a lawn chair beside the grill, he watched Matt stride toward him. "You deserve one after the day we had."

A light burst of air escaped Matt's lips and he nodded in agreement. "Helluva morning, wasn't it? I just talked to a nurse at Fairview, she said the woman's in stable condition. The kids will be able to go home with their dad this evening."

Gabe dug an icy bottle from the cooler and held it out for Matt. "A good reason to celebrate."

"I'll take you up on it in a minute." Lifting a child's baseball glove, Matt gestured toward the trees that separated Gabe's and Lola's yards. "I'll just run this over quick."

Gabe stared, his beer tipped at his lips. He didn't take a sip, just watched with blatant curiosity.

"What? Sam left it at the game last night."

A wicked smirk lifted the corners of Gabe's mouth. "I'm sure he'll be happy to see it." He watched Matt move toward the woods. "Tell Lola I said hi," he called in a juvenile sing-song voice.

Matt glanced over his shoulder and rolled his eyes at Gabe, but couldn't help the tiny smile that pressed on his lips. They may be decades older now, but Matt still enjoyed the glimpses of the child he knew in his old friend.

All thoughts of childhood quickly disappeared as Matt emerged through the thick trees. Instead, they were replaced by heart palpitations at the sight of Lola lying in the grass beside the creek. Her feet were bare, toenails painted a subtle, feminine pink, her legs stretched on the soft ground. It was those legs, Matt decided, that kept making his knees weak. Tanned, long legs, perfectly shaped like a dancer's. A short flowing skirt the color of buttercup edged up her thigh and teased the curve of her hip.

The sun partially lit her slender body, dancing over her skin as it peeked between the foliage of the trees. Her back faced Matt, shoulder blades exposed by the cut of her summer top. A fuzzy puppy curled against her body. Neither seemed to notice that a single piece of paper, caressed by the warm breeze, was floating toward the creek.

The puppy lurched from his slumber as Matt caught the paper in his fingers. There was an awesome howl from the little bundle of fuzz, and it charged Matt like a pit bull. It stopped four feet from Matt's towering shadow, unsure if it should wiggle with delight or growl a warning. So it did both.

At the same time, Lola jerked awake, tucking her legs beneath her and touching a hand to her forehead. She ran her fingers through her straight, dark hair and steadied herself into sitting position. The whole scene made Matt laugh out loud.

"Sorry," he said, lifting the paper and smiling. "Your work was about to go for a swim." He let his gaze dance over her pink toes and yellow skirt, up over the curves of her chest, past the delicate skin around her collarbones, until his eyes met hers. No longer the intense dark ones from yesterday, Lola's eyes were now soft and sleepy, as liquid and inviting as a melting Hershey's Kiss.

Lola clambered to her feet and called to the puppy, smothering a smile beneath soft pink lips. The tiny dimples erupting at the corners of her mouth twisted at Matt's gut.

Lola smoothed her skirt with anxious hands. "This is Goliath," she said, pointing at the puppy as it inched toward Matt. She brushed fingers over her pink cheeks and cleared her throat.

Kneeling to Goliath, Matt held out his hand, palm down. The pup wiggled toward him, sniffed his fingers a moment, then ran anxiously back to Lola. She picked him up and buried her face in his fur.

"You surprised us," Lola said, her words muffled into Goliath's fawn-colored coat. Her dark eyes, narrowed in amusement, lifted to meet Matt's. "I don't normally sleep on my lawn."

The paper in Matt's fingers rustled as he held it out for Lola. Droplets of dew and a smudge of dirt had stained it. "You're in a small town now, you can do whatever you want on the lawn."

Laughter bubbled from Lola's throat as she watched a smirk build slowly on Matt's lips. She covered her mouth with her fingertips and pressed her giggles inside.

"I'm sorry I startled you. I'm having dinner at Gabe's and wanted to bring this by." He lifted the baseball glove and offered a small smile. "I thought Sam might want it back before next week. He must have forgotten about it after the celebration of his home run."

Lola's face turned instantly white. She dropped Goliath to the ground and whirled to face the house. "Sam!" she cried.

A little voice answered from the backyard, and Matt watched Lola's shoulders ease. She lifted a hand to her temple and rubbed, then turned back to Matt. "Sorry. Thank you, he'll be happy to see it." She accepted the glove and bent the stiff leather in her hands.

Stuffing his fingers into his jean pockets, Matt tilted his head to get a look at Lola's temple. "How's your head feeling today?"

Her face clouded with a moment's confusion, and then understanding filled her eyes. "Oh. It's fine. I'm fine. I woke up this morning and everything," she said with a grin.

It was instinct for Matt to reach out to Lola, to lift her face gently by her chin. He let his fingers brush below her jawbone as he studied the small lump, then pulled away, catching himself before he lingered too long. "Barely any bruising," he mumbled. He crossed his arms over his chest and willed himself to stop touching her.

From the side of the house, Sam charged to them, his short legs pumping so quickly that Matt thought he might tumble from the exertion. "Hi Coach!" Sam called. His cheeks were flushed and eyes sparkled. His hair was damp with sweat.

"Where were you?" Lola asked, an edge to her voice. She glanced at Matt in apology. "I'm not used to all this space," she explained. "Our townhome in San Francisco is tiny and has an even tinier fenced-in yard." She pulled Sam into her arms and squeezed him against her chest. "You're not supposed to wander off, remember?" she whispered into her son's hair.

Sam grinned up at Matt but seemed to turn a little blue. "Mom, you're squeezing too hard," he whispered. Lola released him but still wrapped a hand over his shoulder.

"Coach brought your glove by. You left it at the game last night."

Sliding the glove on his fingers, Sam grinned up at Matt. "Thanks, Coach!"

"No problem," Matt answered, ruffling Sam's mop of golden curls. His eyes met Lola's and for a moment they stared awkwardly at one another. He watched her throat move, heard the audible click of her swallowing.

"It's warm today, isn't it?" Lola fanned herself with the paper that had tried to find relief in the creek. "Is it normally this warm? I don't remember it being so warm… in the summer…" She dropped her eyes to the ground and shook her head.

Matt sighed. He was making her uncomfortable. And why wouldn't she be? He was creeping up on her while she slept, staring at her, touching her every chance he had. He shifted, taking a step back from Lola, giving her some room. "It's not normally this humid in June," he agreed. He lifted a hand to say goodbye.

"We walked to the grocery store this morning and nearly melted," Lola added, winking at Sam. He grinned up at her, then looked expectantly at Matt.

Matt frowned. He glanced between Lola's pretty face and the old rusted Chevy truck parked in the lawn behind her. "Why didn't you drive?" he asked.

Sam and Lola both followed Matt's gaze and studied the tarnished, bulbous truck beside the shed. Grass had grown so tall around it that the wheels were half hidden.

"Oh, that old thing," Lola said, waving it off. "It doesn't work." She turned back to Matt and frowned at his expression. "Does it?"

"Your aunt was driving it this spring..." He shrugged and tried not to laugh at the way Lola's eyes suddenly popped.

"The back tire is flat," Sam announced. He ran through the tall grass, disappearing behind the Chevy. "But you can fix that, right Mom?" he called.

When they reached Sam they found him on his belly, chin propped in his hands as he studied the folding rubber of the flat tire. Goliath sat on his haunches beside him, head cocked as he seemed to study the tire as well.

Lola frowned as she surveyed first the tire and then the entire truck. "I'm sure I could manage..."

"Have you changed a tire before?" Matt asked. Judging from the look on her face, he already knew the answer. Sam and Goliath peered up at Lola, waiting patiently for her response. She frowned and slowly shook her head.

"I could help you out tomorrow."

Sam jumped to his feet and bounced on his toes with fists in the sky. "Awesome, we have a truck!" He ran away with Goliath, singing and pulling dandelion heads as he skipped.

Lola watched Sam and nibbled her bottom lip. She met Matt's eyes with her own deep brown ones and lifted a shoulder. "I'm sure I can figure it out by myself."

There was a stubborn look in her eyes. Matt had seen this attitude in so many of his high school students. He knew the drill.

"I'm sure you could. But I'd like to help."

Lola wrapped her arms over her chest and eyed the tire. With a sigh, she finally gave a single nod. "I'm sure I'll catch on fast. It won't take long." She patted a hand over the round fender and then glanced quickly at Matt. "Thanks," she said.

"No problem. I'd help tonight," he added, glancing at his watch, "but I'm actually supposed to be at Gabe's for dinner right now."

Lola flinched with the realization that she was keeping Matt from his evening. "Go! Tell Rena I'm sorry I kept you." She waved her hands to shoo him away, then touched her mouth with her fingertips when she saw the amusement on Matt's face. A smile was building on her lips, one Matt wished she'd let surface. Her face probably lit up like a flower when she smiled.

Matt glanced down at her pink toes and smirked, then lifted his eyes to Lola's lips. Instinctively, he brought his hand to her face. Before he could stop himself, he felt his fingers curve gently below her jaw. *Hands off!* His mind scolded, but her body moved toward him like a magnet before he could pull back.

"You have some dirt..." Matt whispered, and he rubbed his thumb gently over her lower lip.

Lola's cheeks burned. She quickly rubbed her fingers over her lips and began to turn away.

"You're making it worse," Matt laughed, then caught her hand in his. "This truck will need a good wash after you fix the tire." He gently turned her hand over to expose dirt on each of Lola's fingertips and at the base of her palm.

"God, I'm filthy," she murmured. She tried to step back from Matt, away from her embarrassment, but he caught her softly by the arm and brought her back to him.

"Here," he said quietly, and lifted her face toward his once more. He rubbed Lola's chin with his thumb, pressing a little harder this time.

"You're not going to spit on your thumb now, are you?" she asked, a smile finally blooming on her cheeks. Matt's heart pounded. Damn if that smile wasn't even prettier than he'd expected.

He examined his thumb as if considering. Then he pulled something from his back pocket, shook it once beside them, and lifted it to Lola's chin. He rubbed it gently over the dirt smudge. It was a white cloth, soft from age, and when Matt released her, it was Lola's turn to laugh.

"Is that a handkerchief?" she asked. She took it from Matt's hand and felt the smooth thin cloth between her fingers.

"I haven't seen one of these since I was ten. I thought only eighty-year old grandfathers carried hankies."

Matt lifted an eyebrow. "It used to belong to my eighty-year old grandfather, actually," he said. "My Nan gave me a bunch of these when he passed away."

Lola's forehead crumpled. "Oh, that's so sweet." She gently set the handkerchief back in his hand, her fingertips brushing softly over his skin. God, she was torturing him. Her touch was warm and soft, her lilac scent sending shivers down his belly.

"You're just lucky I don't blow my nose with it like Gramps used to do," Matt teased. Lola's smile turned into a slight grimace.

"What exactly do you do with them?" she asked, wrinkling her nose.

Matt shrugged. "Use them to wipe dirt from pretty women's faces, I guess." He shuddered internally. Had he really just given her that horrible line? What was he, nineteen again? "But you might need a little stain remover for this one…" he added, reaching again for Lola's chin.

She playfully pushed on his chest, but not before Matt gently caught her hand in his. He let his fingers whisper quickly over hers, feeling the warmth of her skin, the cool smooth band on her finger.

Lola brought her hands to her chest and absently twisted the ring on her finger, glancing to the ground and avoiding Matt's eyes. Her smile faded, the light in her eyes dimmed.

Shit, just leave her alone. Matt looked away and cursed himself. "I better get back to Gabe's." He watched Lola's eyes for a moment as they scanned the ground, his shoes, then lifted to meet his gaze. There was such a sudden emptiness in those dark eyes, such loneliness.

"Why don't you two come over for dinner?" Matt asked. "Gabe and Rena would love to have you." It seemed like a nice gesture until he saw the alarm rise in Lola's eyes. And suddenly Matt felt a rush of unease spread over him as well.

What was he doing? Life was easy and simple right now. He didn't need to add any complications.

Lola glanced toward Sam at the side of the house. She shook her head, then smiled politely. "We can't. It's a nice offer, but we've had an exhausting day and Sam should go to bed early." She nodded fervently, then sighed.

"Maybe next time," Matt said, feeling an odd mixture of relief and disappointment. He lifted his hand in a gentle wave as he backed toward the path.

"Tomorrow morning, about nine?" Matt called over his shoulder before disappearing into the forest. Lola stared after him in confusion.

"The truck," he added with a smirk.

"Oh! Yes, sure. Nine! Just fine… with me." She nodded quickly again and gave an awkward wave.

As Lola moved in Sam's direction, Matt slid into the shadows and cursed himself once more. What was he thinking? Of course she wouldn't want to join them tonight. She just wanted to be left alone. He of all people should understand.

After all, it wasn't that long ago that he'd felt the same way.

GABE EXAMINED HIS WATCH and gave an evil smirk as Matt emerged from the woods. "I thought I was going to get your share of the ribs," he teased. He studied Matt as he settled into a lawn chair beside him.

"I could use that beer now."

Gabe leaned over a tiny cooler and rustled through the ice. He pulled out a cold bottle of beer, twisting the cap off before handing it to Matt.

The two men sat in silence for a minute, watching the heat rise from the charcoal grill in front of them.

Finally, Gabe sighed. "Are you gonna tell me what's going on, or do I have to set Rena on you?"

Matt shook his head. "There's nothing to tell."

"Hell there isn't. I haven't seen you this stirred up since…" He stopped and scowled at the grill, then turned back to Matt. "…high school, probably. Senior year. It's like being eighteen all over again."

Gabe took a sip of his beer and let Matt sit in silence for a moment before he continued.

"I heard Lola calling for Sam. Everything all right?"

Matt nodded, eyes still on the busy air that lifted from the grill. He watched as it made the trees wiggle and wave like a dream. He turned to Gabe with a slight frown. "She sure is sensitive with that kid. If she smothers him any more she'll drive him crazy."

"Hell, I can't imagine taking care of the kids by myself. I'd probably be overprotective too." He lifted his eyebrows in thought, then added, "That's what the boss is for. She's good at keeping the urchins in line."

At that moment Rena's voice, loud and bossy, called to Gabe from the kitchen. Gabe flinched as he glanced at the house.

Rena appeared at the screen door and pushed it open with her side, holding Grace in one arm and a plate heaped with saucy ribs in the other. "Grace needs to be changed, honey."

Gabe scowled at his beer and then eyed Matt for a moment, who returned his gaze with a grin. "I'm busy manning the grill. Besides, Matt needs my support right now."

Rena lifted her eyebrows and stared at Gabe for a full ten seconds. Knowing it was no use, Gabe sighed, put his beer down and pointed at Matt. "It's your turn next time, buddy."

Lifting his daughter into his arms, Gabe smooched her soft dimpled cheek. She wiggled and squealed, happy to be washed in her daddy's love.

"Hey Matty," Rena said, joining Matt at the grill. She smiled wide as he rose to kiss her cheek.

"Relax, I'll do this," he said, taking the plate of ribs from her. "You get the rest of the night off." He motioned for Rena to sit and began placing the ribs on the grill.

Rena patted Matt's back before settling into a chair. "I knew I liked you for a reason," she teased. She glanced at the sandbox where Caleb concentrated on filling buckets of sand, then looked up at Matt once again.

"How's Lola today?"

Matt casually lifted his shoulders. "She's fine. I just ran over to give Sam his glove."

Rena nodded, watching Matt curiously. "You were over there for half an hour."

"You timed me?"

"Of course I did. Tell me everything."

Matt laughed and set the empty plate beside the grill. He carefully covered the grill and adjusted the smoke vent before settling beside Rena. "We just talked for a few minutes and looked over her aunt's truck." Matt met Rena's eyes, trying to gauge her response.

She frowned. "That's it?" she asked.

"That's it."

Rena shook her head, knowing. "That is not *it*. You're blushing."

Matt rubbed a hand over his cheekbone and smiled. "I don't blush."

"Yes you do! Look, right there." She poked a finger into Matt's cheek. Laughing, she sat back and watched Matt look down at his hands, smiling at his own secret.

"You *like* her, don't you?" Rena teased, with a voice she surely would have used in middle school. She sat back in her chair, lifted her face to the sky and closed her eyes. "I haven't had a chance to get to know her very well yet, but she seems really nice," she added.

Matt glanced at Rena whose eyes remained closed. Maybe it would be easier to admit this while she wasn't looking at him.

"She is nice. And funny too."

Rena peeked at Matt and grinned, then closed her eyes again. He heaved a big sigh and folded his hands over his chest. He might as well just tell her, she'd drag it out of him eventually.

"There's something about her, Ree. Scares the hell out of me."

Matt's smile faded and he looked at Rena, who was now watching him intently. He shook his head and opened his mouth to speak, but no words came.

Reaching over to pat his arm, Rena's smile faded too. "It's not going to be easy, Matt. But Ali's in the past now. It's okay to move on. Take a chance."

Pain washed over Matt. "I don't know anything about her."

"Then get to know her. Have a little fun."

"She's only here for the summer."

"Then have a summer romance!"

Matt shot Rena a strange look that made her laugh.

"Just get back out there Matty. You need to enjoy yourself again."

The screen door clapped behind them and Gabe stomped down the steps with Grace wiggling in his arms. She pulled on his nose and cooed her secret garbled language.

"What are you feeding this kid?" Gabe asked his wife, who smiled up at them proudly. "We'll have to fumigate the house. I don't know if I should burn the diaper or bury it."

"She just discovered how much she loves peas." Rena pulled on her daughter's toes and grinned.

Glancing between Matt and Rena, Gabe's expression fell. "You told her, didn't you?" he asked Matt, disappointment and jealousy heavy in his voice.

"Told her what?"

Gabe scowled at his wife as she laughed. "I've been his best friend for twenty-eight years and you can't even let me talk to him first," he scolded.

Matt shook his head, then stood and pulled Grace into his arms. "I think it's time we go play in the sandbox with Caleb," he decided. He lifted Grace high into the air and watched her close her eyes in delight. "Your mommy and daddy are crazy," he whispered.

As Matt walked away, he heard Rena's voice trying to soothe her pouting husband. "Sit down honey," she said. "I'll fill you in."

Chapter Five

✦

The following morning, as he walked toward her front porch and enjoyed the quiet whispers of the forest, Matt heard Lola scream.

"Noooo!" she shouted. It echoed out of the old white home into the silence of the morning.

Matt picked up his pace, bounding up the porch stairs in one giant leap. As he opened the screen door, Lola rushed from the kitchen with Goliath in her arms, a soiled rug dangling in her fingertips and a frustrated scowl on her face.

"Everything okay?" Matt asked, his breath catching in his chest. He felt suddenly winded, but knew he was in better shape than to blame it on his rush up the stairs. He watched Lola step onto the porch and tighten her hold on Goliath. The puppy wiggled at Matt's sudden presence, but it could have bit him and he wouldn't have noticed.

It was Lola, he realized with a jolt of panic, that had so quickly taken his breath away. He felt an unreasonable need to protect her, and that scream had kick-started his heart. In addition, she was wearing another summer dress, this one sleeveless and exposing silky shoulders. The dress was white with soft printed flowers, flowing to her shins but cut so that her long legs peeked out. The buttons strained the tiniest bit over her breasts and the top one had popped open to expose a hint of cleavage.

Matt quickly pulled his eyes from her chest and swallowed.

"Good morning!" Lola chirped. Her eyes were still dark and frustrated but she smiled politely at Matt. She brushed past him and pushed the puppy out the porch door, tossing the rug in the grass. "Bad dog!" she scolded. "*That's* where you go potty." She pointed to the tall grass beside the stairs and then wagged a finger at Goliath as he sniffed around.

Matt smirked. "House training's not going so well?" he asked.

Lola let the door clap behind her and leaned on the frame. She closed her eyes for a moment, rubbing weary fingers over them. "Not good at all," she mumbled.

Matt moved beside Lola and watched Goliath out the porch window. "We had a dog when I was a kid," he said. "His name was Barnie." He laughed at the thought. From the corner of his eye he noticed Lola's posture soften. "My dad took all the rugs out of the house for the first month because Barnie thought they were patches of grass."

Outside Goliath sniffed the ground and tiptoed through the tall green grass. Lola watched him carefully.

"I've heard that dogs don't like to go to the bathroom on long grass," Matt added, glancing at Lola with teasing eyes. "Probably tickles."

Lola scowled at the lawn. The grass was nearly six inches tall. She sighed and shook her head. "I keep having to remind myself why I got a puppy," she said, her voice low and quiet.

Matt looked down at Lola as she gazed out the window. He elbowed her softly, playfully. "And?" he asked.

She looked up at Matt, her eyes showing the sad emptiness that he'd noticed the day before. "Sam really wanted one. And I wanted to see him smile again."

Matt glanced down at Lola's hands, folded gently over her arms. Her wedding ring glistened in the morning sunlight.

"What about you? Are you smiling again?" he asked.

Lola looked quickly at Matt, studied his face for a moment, and then forced her gaze back outside. She fixed a strained smile on her lips. "Sure. Sam makes me smile every day." She watched Goliath bounce around the yard for a moment longer, then moved away from the window.

"Can I offer you some coffee?" she asked.

Matt pursed his lips and nodded. "Sure, thanks."

TEN MINUTES LATER, GOLIATH, Sam, and Lola followed Matt as he rolled a new tire from his truck toward the old Chevy. "Where'd you get the tire?" Sam asked, skipping beside Matt.

"My friend Mike owns the auto shop downtown. He has a few extras."

Lola squinted from the bright morning sun and surveyed Matt's face. "I'm paying you for that tire," she scolded, knowing full well that he didn't get it for nothing.

The look Matt gave her reminded Lola of the day she'd been thumped on the head at baseball practice. It was the teacher glare, one that made her feel as though she'd be staying in at recess.

"Don't worry about it," Matt said. He and Sam tipped the tire over beside the flat.

Lola crossed her arms in frustration. She wasn't about to take handouts, especially from a man she had only met two days ago. She would take care of herself now, and was about to tell Matt when he interrupted her.

"Do you have a jack?" he asked, glancing Lola's way. His sky blue eyes danced over her dress before they lifted to meet Lola's gaze. The way he studied her, and the way his blue cotton shirt stretched over his broad shoulders made Lola forget what she'd just been debating in her head.

"Probably somewhere in there," she said, pointing toward the weathered red shed. "What does it look like?"

Sam stood between the adults, watching the conversation unfold, and gave Matt a sideways glance. The two of them burst with laughter.

"You wanted to change the tire by yourself and you don't know what a jack looks like?" Matt asked. Sam shook his head in disappointment.

Lola frowned at Sam, then met Matt's eyes with her own narrowed ones. "I'm sure I could figure it out." She leaned over to grab Sam and tickle him, and he wiggled and screamed until she let go.

"Do you know what a jack is for?" Matt asked when he'd calmed his laughter.

Lola set her hands on her hips and lifted her chin. Of course she knew what a jack was for! She wasn't an idiot. It had just been a very long time since she'd had to take care of herself. Travis had made sure of that. Which was exactly why she needed to learn how to manage life on her own now.

"Of course I know. It's used to... fix a flat tire." At the look on Matt's face, Sam fell to the ground in a heap of giggles.

Without a word, Matt shook his head and grinned at Lola. He turned toward the shed, dusting his hands together as he moved.

"I'll help you, Coach!" Sam cried, leaping up from the ground.

Matt held out a hand so Sam could slap it. "Deal," he laughed.

"You two have no faith in me. I really could figure it out," Lola called.

Before he disappeared into the shed, Matt turned back to Lola and nodded. "I'm sure you could. But for today, just let us boys show a little chivalry, okay?" He patted Sam's back and smirked at Lola, his face nearly as adorable as her son's.

"Fine," she said, "but I get to help too."

"You can start by locating the jack." Matt's voice echoed as he slipped inside the small building. Lola followed, letting her eyes adjust for a moment before Matt turned on the single light bulb above them. It was a musty, creepy space, surely full of black hairy spiders and diseased mice. She was about to warn Sam, who peeked eagerly behind old boxes, but bit her tongue when she noticed Matt watching her. She moved to one wall and pretended to know what she was looking for.

"Mom, there's a lawn mower!" Sam cried, pointing to a dirty, greasy, and ancient contraption. Lola grumbled and turned away.

She pretended to search for the jack, but as the minutes passed she could only focus on Matt. She watched him bend on strong legs as he searched, marveled over the way tendons and muscles danced in his solid arms as he reached. His hands were wide and worn with physical work, and memories of his fingers on her skin the previous day made her heart jitter.

What was wrong with her?

"There it is," she announced, pointing toward the shadows at the front of the shed. She moved toward it, then tilted her head sideways to take the whole thing in. It seemed… different than the one her father used when he changed tires on their old Cadillac.

Matt was suddenly at her side, looking back and forth on the wall. His forehead crumpled in confusion. "Where is it?" he asked.

Lola pointed once more. "Right there," she said with a frown. It was a large, awkward piece of metal in the corner, covered in dust and cobwebs. How could he not see it?

"That thing?" Matt asked. He looked at Lola to clarify, and when she scowled and nodded her head, a lopsided grin slid over his lips.

"You mean this?" he asked again, moving forward and touching it, just to make sure. The top of the metal contraption bounced slightly. Were jacks supposed to bounce? Lola felt the doubt creep in, and nodded sheepishly.

Laughter interrupted Matt's words. He glanced at the metal heap, brushed a hand over his jaw, and tried to contain his humor. "That's actually a food scale," he said, trying to hold himself together as he turned it toward them. The wide, round face of the scale was cracked and dirty, the rusting plate holding inches of dust.

Lola sighed. Another one of Uncle Gilbert's treasures. The man had collected more junk than an antique store.

Sam giggled behind Lola, and although she wanted to hold her head high and remain proud, her composure fell apart. She started to laugh too. And laugh. And along with Sam and Matt, she laughed until her sides hurt.

AN OLD RUSTY JACK was finally located behind even older tool boxes. Lola stood beside Sam and Matt, arms crossed, a stubborn set to her chin. She watched as Matt lifted and fastened the new tire in place, then turned a bolt with strong fingers. Sam handed Matt each of the remaining bolts as he needed them.

"I bet I could have figured this out," Lola insisted with a frown. Matt peeked over his shoulder, his eyes meeting Lola's legs and the soft cotton dress that half covered them. While he continued to twist the bolts, he let his eyes travel from her legs over the full length of her body until they reached Lola's eyes. He raised his eyebrows and smirked.

"I bet you would have tried to change the tire with that dress on too," he teased.

"What's wrong with my dress?"

Sam grinned at his mom, clearly amused by the adult conversation.

"Nothing's wrong with your dress. It's very pretty. And very *white*." Matt snuck another glance at Lola's legs and then focused his attention back to the tire.

Pulling on the fabric of her skirt, Lola inspected it. "Well, I'm a California girl," she clarified. "I have a lot of summer dresses. I thought I'd get good use out of them here."

"I like your dresses Mommy," Sam said, beaming at his mother. "You look pretty in them." Lola rubbed a soft hand over his cheek.

Matt smiled, but didn't look at Lola. He kept his eyes strictly on the tire, nodding in agreement. "I like them too," he said softly.

Before the blush on her cheeks could fully bloom, Sam was on his knees digging through the tools. He picked up a long heavy one, swinging it up to his face for a better look.

"Sam, please be careful," Lola cried, grabbing the tool from his hand. She could see it clearly - a chipped tooth, a bloody nose, a broken foot when he dropped it from his little hands. The child was going to give her an ulcer.

"What is that thing?" Sam asked, unphased by his mother's panic. Lola turned it over in her hands. She would have given a clueless lift of her shoulders and brushed the question off, but Matt was watching her carefully. He thought she *was* clueless.

"It's a... a tool," Lola answered as she ran her fingers over the smooth silver metal.

"What's it used for?" Sam asked.

Lola tried not to glare at her son. Did he have to be so inquisitive? "It's used to... help change tires." She spotted the curved end of the tool, the shape at the top - exactly the size and shape of the bolts that Matt fastened to the tire. "It's a bolt changer," she decided, giving a little nod of confidence.

Not at all impressed, Matt cocked his head and stared. "It's called a tire wrench," he corrected. "It tightens these bolts so they're secure."

"You were a know-it-all in school, weren't you?" Lola grumbled. She tossed the wrench to the soft grass beside her and the heavy end clipped her toe. An instant stream of curses filled her head, but outwardly Lola only grabbed her foot and bit her lip. She blinked back the tears that stung her eyes, then simply squeezed them closed as the pain zipped over her nerves.

"Are you okay?" Matt was standing in front of her when she opened her eyes, a concerned lift to his forehead but a small grin on his lips. *Damn those lips.* Lola nodded quickly and sucked in a breath. Her toe, her entire foot - hell, her entire leg - had gone numb while a dull ache radiated through her chest.

She had promised herself the previous day that she wouldn't do this again. She wouldn't get so close to Matt that she could see the tiny flecks of gold in his blue eyes, the small curved scar on his lip, the extra lift on the left corner of his mouth when he smiled. Yesterday she would have let those lips touch hers. For a moment she had actually thought they would. And worse still, she wished they had.

But not today. Not in front of Sam, who stood inches away and watched them with the careful eyes of a curious little hawk. And really, not ever, because... just because.

Lola pursed her lips, still fighting the urge to swear, to scream, to run. She shook her foot a little, then turned and limped toward the house.

"I'm going to go find something useful to do," she called over her shoulder, and didn't turn back at the sound of Sam and Matt snickering.

When Lola returned, Goliath scurrying at her heels, she held her camera to her cheek and adjusted the lens. The morning light was perfect, soft and sweeping beyond the canopy of trees surrounding them. Beneath the tall oaks and swaying aspens, a gentle light cast shadows onto the ground and glittered over the moisture still hanging in the air. Lola stood beyond the old Chevy and studied it with an artistic eye. She captured a few pictures of its imposing stature and rusty red hue, of the way the separation between ground and tires had all but disappeared.

The shadows hid Lola as she turned her focus on Matt and Sam, just finishing the bolts on the wheel. Lola watched them working together through the lens, Sam's tiny frame next to Matt's large one, still very much strangers but looking so much more like father and son as they exchanged mechanical secrets. They stood close, heads bent together in quiet conversation as Matt instructed Sam on releasing the jack, helping him with large hands over Sam's small ones.

With a shaky sigh, Lola snapped a few more pictures, helpless as her heart tugged with a feeling of comfort and hope that she was too scared to acknowledge.

"Mind if I use your sink?" Matt asked, inspecting his dusty, greasy hands. He checked his shirt - only a little dirt smear at the bottom - and looked down at Sam as he studied his own grungy hands. Sam had seemed to enjoy being Matt's helper, soaking up every ounce of manly conversation like a sponge. It had been fun to hang out with the little guy for a while. Also a bonus was spending more time with Lola, soaking up her gentle beauty, her quick sense of humor, her stubborn personality. She intrigued him.

"Sure, go on in," Lola answered. She led Sam up the stairs behind Matt, herding them both into the kitchen.

"Are you a photographer?" Matt asked as he pumped pearly green soap into his palm. It smelled nice, like sweet cucumbers in late summer. He turned to watch Lola over his shoulder.

"Oh, no, this is just a hobby." She slipped the camera strap off her shoulder and settled the Nikon on the kitchen table. It was the same smoky black color as her laptop, which, along with a tall stack of files, took up one side of the table.

"I work for a magazine." She shook her head, quick to correct. "I mean I *used* to work for a magazine. I was an assistant in the advertising department." Lola scowled as she watched Matt dry his hands on a towel decorated with lemons. "The magazine went belly-up two months ago, along with my cushy job."

Sam squeezed between Matt and the sink, reaching on tip-toes for the soap. He was about nine inches too short.

"Here, Champ, I'll give you a hand." Matt lifted Sam by the waist and watched him squirt a palm full of gooey soap. He rubbed his hands together until they were oozing green, then watched the sink fill with water and bubbles. By the time they were finished, Sam's shirt was splattered and Matt was holding back laughter.

"Thank you!" Sam grinned. Matt set him back on his feet and Sam zipped into the other room in a blur.

Returning his attention to Lola, Matt found her watching him carefully. She nibbled her lip and then looked away.

"That's actually why Sam and I are here for a few months," she continued absently. "No job plus summer vacation, we thought we might as well take advantage of it. I'll take the time to fix up my résumé and look for another position." She gestured toward the table and shrugged. "That's the great thing about technology, I guess. I can apply for jobs and do interviews even if I'm halfway across the country. Hopefully I'll find something back in the Bay Area by the end of August."

City people, Matt reminded himself as he leaned against the countertop. They really did make him uneasy. "What kind of jobs are you applying for?" he asked. He watched Lola move across the kitchen to the fridge.

"Entry level, mostly. Assistant in marketing or advertising offices. That's the only experience I have." The refrigerator light flickered and then died as Lola reached in for a jug of lemonade. Without seeming to notice, she turned to Matt and raised her eyebrows. "Would you like a glass?" she asked. Matt shook his head, lifting a hand in a thankful gesture.

Lola's voice lowered as she continued. "I got pregnant with Sam in my last year of college. Travis and I married right away, and he finished his law degree while I stayed home with Sam. I never went back." As she opened the cupboard door, the handle turned loosely in her fingers and the door shifted an inch lower. Matt found himself itching to grab a screwdriver and tighten the thing up, but a bigger part of him wanted to hear the rest of Lola's story.

"What were you studying in college?" he asked, returning his eyes to her soft face. She tilted her head away from his gaze and sighed.

"Fine Arts. Never really worked out though."

For a moment the only sounds in the kitchen came from Lola's bare feet padding over the tile, the whispers of the refrigerator door opening and closing, the crackle of the ice in Lola's glass of lemonade. And then a rhythmic drip from the kitchen sink that was starting to set Matt's nerves on edge. He turned toward the sound and watched as drops of water escaped the faucet in ten second increments.

"This house could use a lot of fixing up," Matt murmured. He tightened the hot and cold handles. Although the dripping ceased, water began to slowly ooze from one handle, making a rivulet down the basin. He turned to study Lola again, watching her sip the cold lemonade, looking so innocent and pretty and... *unhandy*. The unreasonable, protective ache he'd felt earlier returned with a vengeance.

Moving to the table, Matt ripped a small piece of paper from her notebook and grabbed a pencil from beside the files. "Lola, if you need any work done on your aunt's house this summer, I want you to call me." He wrote his phone number in a quick scribble over the scrap of paper, then handed it to Lola. She took it in her fingers, looking the number over with surprise.

"That's really nice of you, but… don't you have a lot of other things to keep you busy? Like the fire department? And a job?" *And a family?* Matt could see the last question in her eyes and it made him flinch. Once upon a time, he thought he'd have all of that. But not anymore.

"Being a handyman actually is my job in the summer. I do carpentry work, a little plumbing, sometimes electrical work."

Lola glanced at the scrap paper again, then back into Matt's eyes. "And when it's not summer?"

"I'm a science teacher at the high school."

Lola's face brightened with a smile that made his chest tighten.

"So it's *Mr.* Dawson," she said with a little laugh. She pointed an accusing finger at him. "Now it makes sense. The other day at practice, that felt like a good old fashioned teacher scolding." Lola smiled wide, her dimples peeking from the corners of her lips. Involuntarily, Matt took a step toward her.

"You needed a scolding," he said, glancing at her temple. The bruise was only a tiny bit yellow now. He lifted his hand and lightly brushed his thumb over it, then pulled away just as quickly.

Lola's cheeks flushed. "Is there anything you don't do?" she asked. She folded the corners of the scrap paper between finger and thumb while she studied him. "Volunteer fireman and paramedic, handyman, coach, and now teacher…"

Matt shifted, uncomfortable with the attention. "Keeps me out of trouble, I guess. It's nice to give back to the town when I can."

"I need an array of skills like yours," Lola said, glancing at her computer. "My résumé is looking pretty sparse right now." She slipped past Matt and set his number on the top of her files.

"But once I get things in order around here, I'll dive in. Fix up my résumé, send out some letters, make some calls and see if I can get any phone interviews. Before I know it I'll be settling into a new job and Sam and I will be back on track."

Matt watched her eyes fall, her face clouding for a moment. And then she lifted her face to Matt's and gave a confident smile. It made Matt's stomach drop like a bowling ball.

A true city girl, he reminded himself. The playful freedom that she exuded with those beautiful bare toes and flowing dresses was very deceiving. The true Lola had plans, had a deadline, had a lot to get to and little time to do it. She wanted to be busy, just like the city that she came from.

Just like the one she'd return to in a few short months.

Chapter Six

*W*here had the day gone? Before Lola knew it, she was washing dinner dishes in the small porcelain sink, up to her elbows in white bubbles. Sam brought his plate and cup to her, his eyes heavy with exhaustion.

"You look so tired, baby," Lola said, leaning over to kiss the top of his head. "Why don't you go to bed early tonight? You're not used to all this fresh air."

Sam straightened, shaking his head in denial. He yawned and then covered his mouth. "I'm not tired," he said with a grin.

Lola smiled at her son while she drained the sink. It would be a good night to tuck him in early and get some things done. But the sudden tapping of puppy nails on the tile floor interrupted her mental to-do list. Goliath wandered toward the front door, his head low as he made a beeline for the rug.

"Sam, take him outside, quick!" Lola cried, swinging her sopping hands toward the porch.

Sam sped around the table and grabbed Goliath by the collar. The puppy tried to put on his brakes, but Sam was strong enough to drag him outside. Lola watched them for a minute, her hands dripping blobs of soap suds onto the floor.

The sudden silence that filled the room was surprising. Though, even in this quiet old house, in this quiet little town, silence didn't last long. Slowly, new sounds arose. Bubbles popped beside Lola's feet. A monotonous tick-tock floated from the antique owl-shaped wall clock next to the stairs. Sam's soft voice floated through the screen door, encouraging Goliath to pee. It all flowed together to form a strange kind of lullaby.

At times these new sounds comforted Lola, but at others it put her on edge. Shouldn't she be doing something more than listening to the sounds of the world around her? Didn't she have work to do, a job to find? A plan of action to write and implement?

She turned back to the sink and watched the last of the suds swirl clockwise down the drain. Her skin glistened from the soap left behind. Pulling a towel from a nearby drawer, Lola wiped her hands and peeked at Sam out the porch windows. She watched him crawl into the hammock that swung between two leaning oak trees, trying to convince Goliath to join him. Lola felt like joining him too.

She probably would have, but there was a nagging in her gut that wouldn't leave Lola alone. It grew stronger as she looked at the kitchen table, one side taken over by her laptop and files, books about job searching and a stack of folders stuffed with résumé information. It all scolded her to begin her work. She frowned at the laptop and then, like a rebelling child, pulled her Nikon from the table.

Now this, she thought as she fiddled with her camera, *this* was what felt good. Feeling the weight in her hands, knowing that what she captured with the lens would never disappear. The beauty, the light, the texture, the feelings, stored forever the moment she pressed the button. When she held this camera, focused on something in front of her right then and there, everything else faded away. All the worries of the future, all the heartache of the past - it all disappeared.

Lola cradled the camera against her chest and turned toward the porch. Tonight she needed to follow her little boy's lead. She needed to relax and enjoy the evening. Her résumé and job search could wait a little longer. She had the whole summer, right?

Lola tiptoed barefoot down the wooden porch stairs. She didn't want to disturb Sam, who rocked silently in the hammock beside the creek with Goliath tucked beneath his arm. Sam's chest rose and fell with such rhythm that Lola knew he'd fallen asleep.

It felt as though the night had whispered to the forest that bedtime was near. Birds sang lullabies in the bows of trees while they settled their nesting babies. Branches swayed with the soft breeze, and even the creek seemed to quiet its gurgling. A thin stream of sunlight spread over the yard and then disappeared behind the horizon. The world glowed a strange golden color.

Lola held her camera to her eye and focused on a birch tree leaning beside the creek. It bent, as if stooping to kiss the water goodnight, and the creek sparkled like a contented child's smile.

Her focus changed then, zooming in on her little boy swaying in the hammock. Lola knelt on one knee and studied him through the lens, felt her heart swell with unspeakable love. How could one little soul consume so much of her heart?

The light faded quickly around her, making Lola desperate for a few last photos. She lay on the ground, adjusting her focus again, and snapped a picture of a buttery dandelion. A tiny black cricket hopped in the shadows, and Lola followed closely behind. The evening light held while Lola wandered the creek and woods, taking photos of everything that beckoned her attention.

When Lola reached the side of the house she was face to face with the old Chevy, glistening from the good cleaning that she and Sam had given her that afternoon. A few puddles still remained beneath the tires, the tall grass flattened by the water, but the body of the old beauty shined. With the setting sun glowing perfectly against the truck, Lola took one last picture.

She stood for a moment, feeling small beneath the towering trees and darkened sky, and felt a peace that she wished could be bottled and saved forever.

SAM HAD DEFINITELY GAINED a few pounds since they'd arrived in Hope River. Lola's legs and back had screamed with proof as she'd carried him up the stairs. She watched Goliath turn circles on Sam's bed until he finally settled into a ball, nestling into the crook of Sam's knees. Sam rubbed his face into his pillow, his eyes closed and a tiny lift on his soft lips.

The evening had cooled quickly once the sun went down. Lola moved to the window and pulled it closed, letting only a tiny breeze seep into the room. She wrapped her hands over her chilled arms and stared into the thick forest.

The only requirement here is to breathe, Dolly had said. The words whispered through her mind, over and over, chanting in rhythm with her heartbeat.

It occurred to Lola that perhaps there was another, more important goal for this summer other than searching for a new job and a new plan. Maybe she was here for a bigger lesson. One where she learned to accept life as it was and move forward.

She smiled at the thought. If only it were that easy.

THE NEXT MORNING IT was business as usual. Specifically, Goliath's business.

"No, Goliath! Bad dog!" Lola cried as she swooped down at the porch door to grab the puppy. She patted his bottom in frustration. "You're supposed to potty *outside!*"

She didn't catch him in time, though, and he continued his business in a haphazard line all the way out the kitchen door and through the porch, like an air tanker sprinkling to the flaming forest below. Lola dropped him gently into the grass, which was tall enough to tickle her shins, and sighed in exasperation. When was this dog going to learn?

She watched him sniff the long grass and then trot in a zigzag toward the driveway, his nose still hovering over the ground. A hundred new scents had probably arrived overnight with the scampering little critters of the forest. They might even be watching her from two feet away. She couldn't see the ground through the thick, long carpet of grass anymore. Lola sighed again. It was probably time to mow.

But first there was a doggy mess to clean up inside.

It didn't take long before Lola was swept up in the hum of the morning. The coffee maker groaned with percolation, the stove hissed with pans of frying eggs and simmering pancakes. Outside the open kitchen window the birds recited their cheery morning songs, clear and crisp as the fresh morning air.

"Sam, breakfast!" Lola called toward the family room where he'd planted himself for cartoons. Sam appeared seconds later, his eyes bright and his cheeks lifted in a mischievous grin.

"You sure look chipper this morning," Lola said, eyeing Sam with suspicion. Either he had found a little trouble already, or he had a new outlook on life before eight a.m.

"What are we doing today?" Sam asked. He climbed into a chair beside Lola's laptop and pile of books and papers. Lola turned her back on it all as she filled Sam's plate with scrambled eggs and fluffy pancakes.

"Well, we should take the Chevy into the shop. What else do you feel like doing?" Lola glanced at her laptop and tried to shrug away the guilt. One more day off wouldn't hurt, right?

"Can we go to the playground?"

Lola smiled. Her sweet boy had been waiting patiently for three days to visit the school's playground. She nodded, and Sam celebrated with fist pumps. Lola pushed the long curls from his eyes and made a mental note to find a hairdresser as well.

Lola slid a stack of pancakes and a pile of eggs onto her own plate and marveled at how her appetite had grown in the last few days. Maybe it was all the fresh air and walking they'd done, but it had been a long time since Lola felt... *hungry*. And from the way Sam was devouring his breakfast, it seemed he felt the same.

As Lola set the dirty pans in the sink, she discovered a small stream of water oozing from the hot water handle. She had noticed it before, but it seemed the leak had grown overnight.

Tightening the faucet handle didn't work. Neither did wiggling the handle around. That actually made a bubbling sound and more water oozed from the base. The stream was becoming a river.

"Looks like we need to visit the hardware store while we're at it,"

Lola murmured. She turned to Sam and watched him stuff a piece of pancake drenched with syrup into his mouth.

"This time we'll drive," she added with a wink.

"WELL!" A STURDY OLD man declared as Lola and Sam walked through the jingling hardware store door. His word carried more of an accusation than a greeting. "You must be the relatives staying in Louise's old place!"

Sam stuck close to Lola's side but his eyes wandered the store, filled top to bottom with gadgets and thingamajigs that were a feast to a little boy's eyes.

"Yes, I'm Louise's niece, Lola," she said, surprised by the recognition. "And this is my son Sam."

Sam's eyes bulged with surprise as the old man walked toward them.

"Doesn't take long for news to spread in this small town," the man said, his voice low and gravelly. "Welcome to Hope River." He held out his left hand in greeting and Lola tried not to let her eyes bulge like Sam's did as she shook it. Because while the man's left arm and hand were as beefy as the rest of his body, his right arm was... missing. He leaned over, eye level with Sam, and held out a lollipop that he'd pulled from his overalls pocket.

"Think this will be all right with your mom?" he whispered to Sam. Sam's eyes lit up and he glanced at his mother for approval. She grinned and nodded. Sam gently took the lollipop and whispered a thanks.

"You're welcome young man. My name's Charles Dupont, but you can call me Charlie. Around here I'm even known as One-Armed Charlie." He winked at Lola, his eyes crinkling with humor, then looked back at Sam in all seriousness. Sam nodded uncertainly.

Charlie flicked the empty right sleeve of his checkered flannel shirt with his left hand. "Lost it in a farm accident a few years back. I can still do most everything like I used to, except paddle a boat."

Lola and Sam frowned together, and Charlie's lips twitched. He lifted a finger in the air, moving it around and around in gesture. "Just go in circles, see." His face was still as he watched the pair in front of him, then it cracked into a warped grin.

It was Sam who giggled first, a little eruption of noise from his chest that turned into uncontrollable laughter. He looked up at Lola, who was still not sure if it was a laughing matter, and giggled so hard that tears touched his eyes. The sound was contagious, and Lola couldn't help but join him.

When they'd all caught their breath, Charlie rested his hand on his hip and lifted his graying bushy eyebrows. "So what can I do for you folks today?"

It took some strange hand gestures and a few sound effects, but eventually Lola explained the problem with her aunt's kitchen sink.

"Sounds like you need a new rubber washer," Charlie decided. He led them down a short aisle of faucet displays and boxes, stopping in front of a row of open bins. He pulled a selection of rubber washers from the bins and tightened his lips in thought.

"Problem is, we don't know what size you need," he murmured. Lola frowned at the donut-shaped washers in his hand.

"Hey Mom, our faucet looks like this one!" Sam stood halfway down the aisle and pointed at a box in front of him. Lola joined him and gave his shoulders a little squeeze.

"Sure does, baby. I think it's the exact same one."

Charlie shuffled beside them, dumped his handful of washers into Lola's palm, and pulled the box from the shelf. "Smart kid, this one," he said with a wink toward Sam. Sam's cheek, bulging and taut from the lollipop, grew even wider with his proud smile. He and Lola watched as Charlie maneuvered the box open with one hand, then knelt to the ground. He fiddled with pieces and parts in the box until his sausage-sized fingers pulled out a flat washer the size of a dime. He lifted it to Lola, his breath raspy.

"Find a match in there?" he asked, gesturing toward Lola's hand.

"Oh! Well, this one matches," Lola answered. She plucked the tiny washer from her hand and held it between finger and thumb. *And what does a washer do?* she wanted to ask. Maybe Google would have some answers for her.

"Do you have a Phillips screwdriver at your place?"

Lola slowly lifted her shoulders in answer. "Louise may have a tool kit in the house, but I'm not sure where." She followed Charlie down another aisle, his shoulders so wide they nearly touched both sides. *And why will I need a screwdriver, exactly?* she wanted to call to him. Lola glanced at Sam as he skipped behind her, wishing he would have the answer.

Charlie stopped next to a display of screwdrivers, pulled one off the wall and handed it to Lola. "This should do the trick," he said. He watched as Lola studied it carefully.

"Replacing the washer is probably the easiest thing to fix on a sink."

Lola raised her eyebrows with uncertainty. "I guess I'll figure it out. I just use this to..." She let her voice trail off and made a face.

Charlie seemed to float with her question before he realized she needed an answer. "...unscrew the handle so you can get to the washer," he finally answered. "You'll need to pry the cover up to get to the screw. It's pretty simple."

Lola nodded, still uneasy. "And I can do that with this thing?" she asked.

"Sometimes you can just pull it off with your fingernails. But if that doesn't work, a flathead will do it. You have one of those at home?"

Lola glanced at Sam who returned her unsure expression. Charlie surveyed them both before frowning.

"You sure you're up for it? I've a handful of handy friends who'd be more than willing to help you out."

Lifting a hand in the air, Lola quickly waved Charlie's concern off. "No, we'll be fine. Sam's a good helper," she reassured, smiling down at the eager grin on Sam's face. It was a simple project, Charlie had said so himself. What better time than now to practice taking care of themselves?

"We should buy a flat... one too, just in case," Lola said, glancing at the wall of screwdrivers. Charlie nodded and pulled one down for her, laid it in her palm beside the other.

There we go, Lola told herself. *Flat one, Phyllis, and a washer.* She'd have that sink fixed in no time.

They followed Charlie to the counter where he rang up the bill on an old fashioned cash register. Lola watched it spit a thin sheet of paper from the top like her old toy used to do when she was little.

"Fifty two dollars and twelve cents," Charlie said, squinting at the register. Before Lola could protest, Charlie frowned and shook his head. "Well, that's not right is it?" He looked over the counter at Sam and made a face, then pulled his glasses from the pocket of his shirt and fixed them on his large nose.

"Must have fat-fingered something," he mumbled. Sam erupted in giggles again and leaned into Lola, pulling playfully on the light fabric of her jersey dress. She watched him for a moment, snuggling into her with a smile on his lips and a lollipop dangling from his mouth, and felt her heart expand.

It was a marvel how easily his smiles now appeared.

SAM WAS SWEATY FROM a romp on the playground and ready to relax when they returned to the house. But not Lola. She was ready to get to work. Anything to avoid that résumé. Sitting on a swing at the playground, watching Sam climb and crawl and slide for an hour had given Lola too much time to think. Which meant too much time to worry over all that she should be doing in order to return to California with a plan.

With a cleansing sigh, she dumped the plastic bag of hardware store items beside the sink. The screwdrivers fell with heavy thuds, and the washer nearly rolled into the basin.

Sam stood beside Lola and examined the pieces.

"What's this one do?" he asked, pointing to the washer.

Lola frowned and plucked it off the counter. "Apparently this little thing will stop the leaking." She watched the water slide from beneath the handle and make a steady path into the sink. "Now we just need to figure out exactly where it goes."

Lola lifted Sam onto the counter so he could get a closer look. She turned the soft rubber washer over in her hand, inspecting it. Did it screw on? She lifted a screwdriver into the other hand. Did this unscrew the old part somehow? Where exactly *was* that old part?

The faucet continued to ooze, and Lola rubbed her fingers over its cold smooth base. How did this thing come off? The washer must be inside of it, at the bottom probably. She ran a thumbnail along the base, huffing with uncertainty. Pull this up with her fingernails? Was Charlie joking? She'd need more force than that to pop it off.

After a minute of staring and contemplating, Lola finally turned to Sam and frowned. "Well, it's not going to fix itself, is it?" she asked him. Sam giggled.

Taking both screwdrivers in her hands, she inspected the tips. One was flat and smooth, the other pointed. "Pry the cover up to get to the screw," Lola repeated to herself. Charlie had said so. "You must pull the faucet up with this one," she continued, keeping the flat-ended screwdriver and handing Sam the other. She nudged the tip of the flat end between the faucet and the cracked rubbery film that used to seal it all together. She gave it a gentle push. Nothing moved.

Lola shoved the screwdriver in harder, angling her grasp as far down as she could before putting weight behind it. She leaned on the screwdriver, even lifted to her toes and gave a little hop for extra effort. The base of the faucet creaked and moaned as the space between the sink and the faucet grew.

Another hop, this one more like a giant leap, and then Lola shoved the screwdriver in with as much power as she could muster. God, was it supposed to be this difficult? She was panting with the effort. She glanced at Sam who eyed the loosening faucet and scooted a few inches back.

Finally there came a tiny crackling, as if an old warped seal was slowly peeled off, and Lola fell forward. Metal scraped against metal as the faucet lifted halfway off the sink. An eerie *crack* echoed through the kitchen and for a fraction of a second Lola felt relief that she'd finally loosened it up. Surely she could just pop it off now. But before she could congratulate herself, a spurt of water thrust from the base and jutted into the air like a fountain.

Screaming, Sam jumped down from the counter, water splattering over him in heavy drops. He ran behind the kitchen table and ducked, still screeching at the top of his lungs.

Lola nearly joined him. But the awful thought that this vicious spray would not stop on its own kept her beside the sink. She wrestled with the twisted faucet, trying to push it back into place while dodging the cascade of water. In the noise of the background, someone's panicked voice yelped, "Oh shit! Oh shit!"

Was that hers?

Lola let out a high pitched moan. Each time she moved the faucet, water sprayed in different directions and with different velocities.

"Mom, make it stop!" Sam cried, his eyes and mop of hair the only thing Lola could see beyond the table.

"I can't!" Lola shouted back, and then shot herself in the eye. She flinched with surprise, making her change the direction of the spray so that her arms and chest were soaked.

A little blur of brown fur rushed into the room, and Goliath was at Lola's feet, barking and wiggling and jumping on her bare legs. He licked her skin, drinking up the fresh droplets of cool water that sprayed down to him.

Lola began to giggle as she watched Sam hide behind the table and felt Goliath's soft tongue slip over her ankles and toes. Her giggling turned to deep laughter, and she buckled over while still holding the faucet, spraying the kitchen curtains and windows. Her laughter shifted to wheezing until she was gasping for air, pushing into her side with an elbow. She looked at Sam, who watched his mother in curious wonder, and the thought finally hit her with full force: *What am I going to do?*

With Sam's brave help, Lola managed to get a large metal mixing bowl angled over the top of the spraying fountain so that the water dove back into the sink. It wasn't the tidiest idea, since water seemed to ricochet off the bowl and spatter onto Lola, but there was now a tiny semblance of control. They also managed to prop a small pail beneath the sink to catch water that flooded down the pipes and dripped to the tile floor.

"Should I call 911?" Sam bellowed as he watched the scene unfold. Water dripped from his eyelashes and trickled down his cheeks. If he hadn't been smiling Lola would have thought the water was tears.

"No! God no," Lola cried, shaking her head. She could just imagine it.

"911, what's your emergency?"

And Sam's despairing little voice, *"My mom broke the sink, send an ambulance!"*

Lola dropped her head to her shoulder, trying to smother her shame. This was, without a doubt, the biggest screw-up she'd managed yet. Why couldn't she just do something right for once?

She knew it was time to call for help, a different sort of 911. She gave Sam the instructions.

"Hi Coach!" Sam cried when he heard Matt's voice on the other end of the cell phone. He smiled and nodded, and then pointed at his mother.

"My mom needs your help. She kinda flooded the kitchen."

Lola dropped her head back to stare in agony at the ceiling. God, there was even water up there!

"He wants to know if you're okay," Sam called. Lola nodded feverishly and adjusted the bowl to stop it from spraying the cupboard.

"Tell him I'm fine. *I'm fine!*" she shouted again, so that Matt might hear her. "I just need help fixing the faucet! It's spraying water everywhere!" She laughed a little and then hung her head again. Matt was going to find such a disaster when he arrived - if he even could. What if he wasn't in town?

Abruptly, Sam hung up the phone. Lola froze. "Is he coming?" she asked.

Sam nodded. "He said he'll be here in a minute."

Lola's shoulders fell with relief, causing water to spray the window. She repositioned the bowl once more, this time fighting back tears. If only she could crawl beneath the sink and hide. Goliath licked the floor vigorously, trying his hardest to lap up every spare drop of water.

"Sam, will you let Goliath out?" Lola called over the noise that sounded much like a waterfall. "He'll need to potty soon." Sam obliged, pulling Goliath into his arms, now a feat since the puppy was getting heavier by the day. They lumbered outside to the warmth and sunshine, the screen door slamming behind them. Lola held her position in the kitchen, alone.

THE LUMP IN HIS throat nearly choked Matt as he barreled over the small bridge and parked beside the Chevy. Sam and Goliath watched him from the porch stairs, waiting patiently.

"Is your mom inside?" Matt called, slamming his truck door.

Sam bounced down the stairs and greeted him. "She's holding the sink together!" Droplets of water stuck to his ears and hair and his shirt was drenched. But his eyes sparkled with excitement, surely a good sign. Lola couldn't be in *too* much trouble.

When Matt walked into the kitchen, trailed by Sam and Goliath, he couldn't hold back the laughter.

"What...?" he started, shaking his head, but the words were lost. It was like a circus act: Lola balanced on tip toes, leaning into the sink as far as she could reach, one hand holding the faucet in place, the other holding a bowl over a geyser of water. The cabinet door was splayed open, showing a bucket of overflowing water at Lola's shins.

"Oh, thank God!" Lola cried. Her expression, desperate and guilty and incredibly thankful, told Matt everything he needed to know.

Beginning with the fact that the water was still on. Quickly kneeling beside Lola, Matt shoved his head and shoulders into the cabinet. He maneuvered around pipes and supplies, bumping Lola's legs with his side as he wedged himself in. She shrieked, and Matt heard water spray against glass before Lola's voice broke out, sharp and frustrated. "What are you *doing?*" she cried.

Matt's fingers moved quickly as he twisted the water valve. The pipes hissed and moaned as the water flow ceased. A sponge and set of matches floated on the bottom of the cabinet. Gingerly moving around the full bucket, Matt backed out of the cabinet and faced a pair of wet, shimmering, shapely legs. He glanced up at Lola's glistening face, still covered with a mixture of remorse and relief.

"Finally!" Sam cheered and gave a delighted little wiggle. He smiled at Matt, then looked at his own shirt and shorts, soaked completely through. "Now I gotta go change my clothes," he muttered. He bolted up to his bedroom with Goliath behind him.

Matt leaned back against his heels. The sudden silence of the kitchen was nearly deafening. "What happened?" he scolded Lola. He tried his best to hold back a smile, but it was difficult. She was just so damn cute, standing there shivering and drenched to the bone, her eyes huge and pitiful. He stood and moved beside Lola as she leaned over the counter. She dropped her head to the cool countertop, released her grip on the faucet and dropped the bowl in the sink with a terrible clatter.

"I was supposed to turn off the water first, wasn't I?" she whimpered into her arms. "There was a little leak..." She hid her face, making her voice weak and her words garbled.

Matt let out a sigh of relief. She was fine. He let his hand rest on the dip of her back for a moment, his fingers sliding over the soft fabric of her dress. God, how he wanted to protect her, to comfort her. He touched the curves of her side as he pulled her near him, wrapped his fingers around her waist, and for a moment he forgot why he was there.

Lola pulled herself off the counter and met Matt's gaze. Her eyes were bright and apologetic, her face only inches from his. "Thank you," she whispered. Then laughter took over and she covered her cheeks with the palms of her hands. "The sink had a little leak - remember, you saw it? - and Charlie told me to use this thing to fix it." She picked up the screwdriver and swung it under Matt's nose.

Matt grasped the screwdriver before it impaled him. He frowned at Lola.

"How...?" He glanced at the faucet, lifted and mangled on one side from being pried from the sink. "You used the screwdriver to pull off the faucet?"

Lola plucked the tiny washer from the counter and let it roll in her hand. "And apparently this was supposed to stop the leaking?"

Matt watched Lola's face and smiled gently. For a moment he let his eyes skim her frame, hugged nicely by a smoky blue dress, long at the sleeves and short at the legs. It was wet in sporadic places, clinging to her arms and chest and revealing curves that were making Matt's stomach knot. He pulled his eyes from the dress and took the piece from Lola's hand, inspecting it between his finger and thumb. Then he lifted his eyes to Lola's and nodded.

"This would fix the leak," he said as he leaned across Lola and popped the cover from the top of the handle with his fingers. "As long as you use it to replace the part... in here."

Lola leaned beside Matt and peered into the handle. Her mouth dropped open in horror. "Oh my God, Matt, look what I've done."

Matt's laughter filled the kitchen. He set the washer down behind her and left his hand braced against the countertop, then lifted the other to her dark hair. A large drop of water clung to one of her small low pigtails, and Matt brushed it off with a fingertip. He could smell the sweet scent of her shampoo mixed with the crispness of water and metal.

"You'll need a new faucet, obviously," he said softly. He couldn't help the teasing tone that he knew was building in his voice. "And a couple of new hoses, probably."

He lifted her chin so he could see those chocolate brown eyes. "I really think you should let me fix it this time. And we'll make sure the water is turned off first."

Shivers danced down his spine as she laughed.

Chapter Seven

"I've got a bone to pick with you, Charlie," Matt called as he entered the hardware store. Charlie shuffled out of the paint aisle holding a handful of small brushes.

"What'd I do now?" He asked with a curious grin. His eyes followed Matt as he walked toward the faucet and sink repair aisle.

"I hear you told Lola how to fix a kitchen faucet."

Charlie scowled. He joined Matt, watching as he inspected a box full of jangling faucet pieces. "I didn't tell her *how* to fix it, just gave her the parts. She said she knew what she was doing." His voice hitched a little, anticipating a good story.

Matt glanced at Charlie and smirked. "Well, you should have told her to turn off the water first."

A huge rumble of laughter spilled from Charlie.

"She pulled the whole damn faucet off looking for the washer. There's more water on her ceiling than in Hope River."

Charlie's body shook as he wiped tears of amusement from his eyes. "Not very handy, is she?" he said with a snort. He slowly moved toward the counter, his laughter trailing after him. "I should have told her I'd come over and fix it. She's quite a pretty one, ain't she?" he added.

Matt glanced at Charlie and nodded. A flash of Lola's wide brown eyes and wet, pink cheeks flashed through his mind. He could still feel the curve of her back on his fingertips. "Sure is," he said quietly. He pulled the box from the shelf, grabbed two faucet hoses from a bin, and joined Charlie at the counter.

"That Sam's a cute kid too," Charlie added, leaning against the counter as he watched Matt dig in his jeans pocket for his wallet. "If I was thirty years younger I'd be howlin' after those two. Pretty young widow with a cute kid…" his voice trailed off for a moment while he studied Matt. "Haven't seen a dress like that or a pair of legs like those in years." Charlie's voice huffed out of him as he accepted the cash that Matt handed over.

"Yeah, well, that dress and those legs will be hightailing it out of town in another month, so don't get too attached."

Charlie handed Matt his change and used his arm to support himself against the counter. "She could always change her plans. Just needs a good reason to." He raised his bushy eyebrows at the idea.

Matt frowned in return, then shoved his wallet back in his pocket. He slid his purchase off the counter and lifted it in the air as a gesture to Charlie. "Thanks," he said, and turned toward the door.

A few steps later, as Matt pushed the door open and listened to the bells jingle, he turned back to Charlie and pointed a finger in his direction. "No more home maintenance advice to pretty women who wander into your store," he scolded his old friend. Charlie laughed and waved him off. "In fact," Matt added as he moved out the door and into the sunshine, "don't let Lola buy anything anymore. Tell her to come find me first. It's probably safer that way."

LOLA WAS TOWELING GOLIATH off in the warm sun as Matt parked beside the old Chevy. She looked up from her perch on the bottom porch step and offered him a guilty smile.

"Charlie apologizes for setting you up like that," Matt said, smirking at Lola as he stepped from his truck.

"Oh, no! I hope you didn't give him a hard time. I'm the idiot who made the mess." Lola stood, her eyes wide with apology.

"Well, either way, I don't think he'll be eager to sell you anything from his store for a while." The creases beside Matt's eyes made Lola's stomach swirl. She turned away and watched Goliath roll in the grass.

"I guess that's only fair," she laughed, shaking her head. "I really thought I'd be able to figure it out." She covered her cheek with a hand. Surely Matt thought she was the world's biggest dope.

"This should fix the mess you made," Matt teased, lifting a plastic bag of supplies in front of him. All Lola could do was shake her head and try to ignore the deep blush that was creeping from her cheeks to her neck. *Idiot,* she repeated over and over in her mind. She hung her head and gestured for Matt to go inside.

Lola followed Matt up the stairs, trying her best to calm her churning stomach. She told herself she was just embarrassed. But who was she trying to kid? The jittery nerves were coming from something else too. Her gut was twisting and turning because of Matt's presence, because she couldn't keep her eyes off of the snug fit of his jeans or the wide, strong shoulders that she wanted to run her fingertips over.

She nearly bumped into his back as he stopped at the porch door and held it open for her. Lola slipped inside, avoiding his gaze.

Moments later, and much to Lola's chagrin, she continued to find herself studying Matt's body. This time it was his strong legs, one bent, the other straight out, jutting into the middle of the kitchen while he worked beneath the sink.

Lola nibbled on a fingernail as she watched him. She eyed the toolbox beside his knee, full of old, worn tools. Strange how it gave her a sense of safety that she hadn't felt in a while - a sturdy, reliable man fixing broken parts of her life, willing and able and generous. Strange... and frustrating. His voice startled her back to the present.

"Can you hand me the wrench?" he asked, holding a hand out. Lola bent over the toolbox, trying to remember which one was the wrench. None of them looked like the one he'd used on the Chevy.

Matt sighed. "It's the one that looks like Pac Man."

"That's the one I was going to pick," Lola grumbled. She glared at the shiny metal Pac Man tool. There was more than one kind of wrench? Good God, how was a normal person supposed to know this? She pulled it from the box and set it in his outstretched hand. His fingers touched hers, and for a moment Lola was paralyzed.

"Lola, I think we should set some ground rules," Matt said.

Lola gulped. Ground rules for how much she could ogle him? For how many times he could touch her in one day and light her skin on fire?

"Like what?" she asked, her voice small.

He shifted under the sink and Lola watched a muscle bulge in his forearm. "From now on, I think it's best if you don't buy any tools unless you actually know their names and exactly what they're used for."

Relief zipped through her body. She laughed out loud and kicked Matt's sneaker with her bare toes. "That's not fair!" she cried. "I was only trying to fix my aunt's leaking sink! I shouldn't be banned for that."

"That's exactly my point," Matt continued, his voice steady. "If you have the desire to fix something, great, but first you need to make sure you understand exactly what it is you're fixing. And you need to know, for example, what this tool-" he grappled with the few tools beside him before he held out a screwdriver, "-is called."

"That's a Phyllis screwdriver!" Lola shouted through her laughter.

"*Phillips*, Lola. A *Phillips* screwdriver." His voice was choked with laughter. "And what's it used for?"

"To screw things!"

Matt lifted his head and stared at Lola, then rolled his eyes. Giving up, he adjusted his body so he could reach around the pipes. His strong legs slid as he shifted and his shoes braced against the white tile floor. His shirt lifted over his torso a few inches to reveal a tanned washboard stomach.

Lola sucked in a breath of air and bit her bottom lip. She looked at the ceiling and fought for control. "So if a screwdriver isn't used for fixing a faucet, then why did Charlie tell me to buy one?"

"It is used for fixing faucets. It's just that Charlie was too distracted by your pretty dress and long legs to tell you which part it's supposed to fix."

Lola froze for a moment, her heart pulsing from the compliment. Were these Matt's words, or was he just relaying the thoughts from a lonely old man at the hardware store?

"How about from now on you just ask for help before you start fixing anything. Deal?" he asked.

Lola sighed. "Deal."

Matt crawled from beneath the sink and collected his tools. The kitchen was quiet except for the ticking of the owl clock and Goliath's snores beside the stairs. Whispers of child's play floated from Sam's bedroom upstairs. While Matt seemed to be completely comfortable working in the kitchen, Lola was beginning to feel herself unravel. She moved to her purse on the kitchen chair and pulled out her checkbook.

"I'll write you a check for the materials and your time," she said, trying to steady her fingers. She rummaged blindly through the bottom of her purse for a pen.

When Matt finally answered, his voice was so close that she jumped. She turned to find him inches behind her, reaching for the box of new faucet parts on the table. His fingers hugged her side, steadying himself as he reached around her. Lola closed her eyes and hoped he wouldn't notice the goose bumps that sprang on her arms.

"Don't worry about it, we'll figure it out later." Matt's words were soft next to her ear. "Let's just get your kitchen back in order first." Lola glanced over her shoulder and watched his lips widen into a teasing smile.

There she was again, so close that she could see the tiny white scar on his lips, the flecks of gold in his stunning blue eyes. She nodded, but was otherwise frozen by his closeness. His hand was still on her waist, his eyes locked with hers, and she swore that if his lips came any closer she wouldn't be able to stop herself.

Matt's warm touch fell from her side and he cleared his throat. He glanced at the box in his hand, then turned quickly toward the sink. Together they looked at the mangled chrome faucet that half-dangled into the basin.

"Maybe I should have Googled 'how to fix a kitchen sink'," Lola offered. She elbowed Matt when he snorted.

"There's a perfectly good excuse for this," she continued, desperate to explain. "For the last six years I've been so focused on Sam that I haven't even considered taking care of anything else." *Including yourself,* her mind scolded. "My husband was a lawyer, so he was never home to work on projects. He insisted we pay for a repairman whenever we needed to have anything done." She looked at her hands, her mind filling with memory. "Our place is pretty new so we don't have many problems anyway." Lola leaned into the counter, twisting her wedding ring as she spoke. She knew she sounded like a spoiled brat.

"I'm not used to being in a place that needs so much... attention." She gave a weak smile as her eyes met Matt's. He nodded in understanding, then turned to the sink, slowly pulling the old faucet parts from the basin and dumping them in a plastic bag. As he opened the box of new parts, his fingers moved more and more slowly until they stopped.

"I'm here if you need help, Lola," he said, his voice quiet. "With anything." When he turned to look at her, she saw something in his eyes. They were bright and serious... and so comforting. So reassuring. He wanted to protect her, to help her save herself from this whole mess she had fallen into.

"That's why I gave you my number," he continued. "Next time call me first and I'll save you a lot of trouble." Matt's lips curved into a gentle smile, turning Lola's knees into rubber.

"Thank you," she whispered.

Lola watched Matt in silence as he arranged the new faucet parts on the countertop. His hands were so big, so tanned and tough and sure. Every ounce of him exuded confidence and security. He was protective of everything around him - his work, his friends, the community...

"So, what about you, Mr. Dawson?" Lola asked, suddenly curious. She studied his strong jaw line and straight nose and the shadow of stubble that covered his chin. "Do you have someone at home to fix things for?" Her heart clenched as she waited for his answer.

Matt gave a small laugh and shook his head as he kept his gaze on the faucet parts in front of him.

"Not anymore."

Lola opened her mouth to ask more, but Sam thumped down the stairs, his arms full of construction toys.

"Mom," he called, breathless and rosy-cheeked, "can I go play outside?"

Lola nodded. "But stay where I can see you," she said, pointing a stern finger at her son. Goliath jumped from his slumber and wiggled to the door, waiting for Sam to let him outside.

Matt turned to watch them. "They seem to like it here," he said.

Lola watched Sam bound down the porch stairs into the long grass. "They do," she breathed, feeling her own lips spread into a pleased smile. "I'm glad we came here this summer." She looked up to find Matt watching her as intensely as she'd been studying him earlier.

"I thought after a spell we'd feel a little better in San Francisco, but..." Lola looked at her hands as she gripped the countertop. She shook her head. "These last years weren't easy for Sam, and I'm sure I was no picnic either. We've had a lot of support from Travis' parents, and Sam's pretty close to them. But it's still been hard." She shrugged her shoulders. "I guess what we really needed was to just get away for a while. Maybe we'll have a fresh perspective when we go back."

Matt watched her, a pity in his eyes that she didn't want to see. She gave him her bravest smile. "Thanks for helping me out today."

Matt reached for Lola's hand, taking it gently in his own. He held it for a moment, then squeezed it softly in the only appropriate gesture he seemed to be able to find. "Anytime," he whispered.

Matt studied Lola's face, his eyes gentle and caressing. Both he and Lola seemed to feel overwhelmed with an emotion for which they weren't ready. He let go of her hand and returned to the faucet, while Lola turned around to lean against the counter and face the porch door. The breeze had picked up outside, and Lola watched it gently dance through the oak trees and whisper over the long grass. She hugged her arms over her chest and inhaled a steadying breath.

It was time, she knew. Time to move forward, to let go of the past. Time to stop feeling sorry for herself and start taking care of herself. Time to believe that she actually could. And now, for the first time, she realized that half of knowing how to take care of herself and Sam was knowing how and when to ask for help. Knowing that it was okay to ask for help, that needing it was not the same as being weak.

"With respect to your earlier rule-setting," Lola said, her voice quiet, "I have one more favor to ask you." She looked at Matt, letting a small smile peek from her lips.

Matt glanced up from the newly installed faucet. His eyes brightened as he waited. "Anything," he answered.

"ARE WE GOING IN the spooky shed again?" Sam asked, his voice high with excitement. He followed Lola and Matt to the rustic red shed that leaned in the late afternoon sunshine.

"The spooky shed?" Matt repeated. He lifted an eyebrow at Lola. This explained a few things. He dropped his gaze to her legs, which were now covered from knee to toe in her aunt's oversized neon green rain boots.

Lola frowned in response.

"Yeah, Mom said it freaks her out. And that it probably has diseased mice and big hairy spiders." Sam's face was bright with the thought.

A visible shudder rippled through Lola's body and Matt laughed out loud. He rubbed a hand over her arm and felt her skin prickle with goose bumps. "You want me to go in first?" he teased. She stuck out her tongue.

"I'm fine," she said, lifting her chin. And there it was, that cute, stubborn part of Lola that he'd so quickly come to adore. They slipped inside the shed and clicked on the lone light bulb.

"There it is!" Sam cried, pointing to an old push lawnmower in the far corner. Cobwebs draped over the handle and dust clung to the grease on the engine cover. "I wonder if it still works."

Matt watched Lola glance anxiously at the floor, probably looking for mice, and couldn't help the grin that spread across his face. Even with crazy boots and a jittery expression on her face, she was still so beautiful. Her mocha hair, pulled into two small tails over each shoulder, made her look as innocent as a child. The soft skin of her neck and collarbones was sprinkled with freckles. Her lips, soft and pink and supple, her dark eyes that showed every emotion she felt - it all mesmerized Matt. So much so that he barely felt Sam pull on his fingers.

Matt shifted his gaze from Lola and focused again on the old lawnmower.

"Think it'll work, Coach?" Sam repeated.

Matt brushed his hand over Sam's head. "Let's give it a try." He wiped the cobwebs off the handle, to the groans and squirms of Lola and Sam, and pulled the mower out into the sunshine. Looking it over, he shook his head and glanced at Lola. "This doesn't look promising," he muttered.

After checking the gas tank and pushing the choke a few times, Matt wrapped three fingers around the cord and pulled hard. Nothing. He pressed the choke once more, then pulled again, this time starting the engine. It chugged and choked and shook for a moment before rumbling to life. Lola smiled and Sam jumped up and down with cheers. Goliath darted over to investigate the sudden commotion.

"Do you know how to use this?" Matt asked Lola over the noise of the mower. She wrinkled her nose and shook her head.

Why was he not surprised? But he'd give her credit for admitting it. At least she hadn't said she'd just Google it.

"Sam, take Goliath and go watch from the stairs," Matt instructed, pointing to the porch. "You shouldn't be close in case it spits out a rock or stick."

Sam obeyed immediately, happily running with Goliath to the house. Matt took Lola's wrist and pulled her beside him. He pointed to different parts of the mower as he spoke.

"Gas goes in there," he said, then lifted a small dipper and added, "oil in there." He straightened and looked carefully at Lola, studying her as she seemed to process this new contraption.

"This keeps the motor running," Matt said, nodding to the wire handle that he held down with his right hand. "You have to hold it down while you mow, and just let go when you want to turn off the engine." He released the handle and the mower went silent, suddenly intensifying the sounds around them. An ovenbird's throaty call broke through the forest, followed by the breeze rustling branches and leaves.

Matt watched Lola carefully. She looked so pretty and dainty and... unsure. "I don't know about this," Matt said. He shook his head. "You, pushing a lawn mower around this huge yard. It just doesn't give me a good feeling."

Lola crossed her arms and shifted on her feet. "I'm capable," she said with a frown.

He studied her for another moment, his eyes wandering over her oval face and slight body, down her shapely legs to the tips of her neon boots. "You'll have to cover your legs when you mow."

"I have jeans."

"And wear goggles."

Lola rolled her eyes. "My sunglasses are in the house, they'll do the same thing."

Matt frowned. "And absolutely no flip flops."

"Yes, sir, no flip-flops." Lola gave a mocking salute, then dropped her arm to her side. A tiny smile slipped over her lips. "Matt, just teach me how to mow the damn lawn. I'll be careful."

MOWING THE LAWN HAD never been a sensual experience for Matt before. But with Lola, everything seemed to turn him on. Especially when he was close enough to feel her body against his, to touch her soft skin, to smell her flower scent that made him shiver with longing.

It had only taken a few minutes to show her how to start the mower, and soon Lola could do it on her own. He'd stood behind her, his arms hovering around her shoulders while she practiced using the machine. It had been frustrating because more than anything, he wanted to wrap his arms around her body, pull her to his chest and sink his face into her hair, her neck, her skin. It was nearly painful to hold himself back.

But he did. And ten minutes later, after Lola showed him that she could run the mower completely by herself, Matt felt the need to go home and take a cold shower.

Matt threw his tool box in the back of his truck and turned to find Lola right behind him. She gave him a firm look. "Tell me what I owe you for everything, labor included."

Matt frowned as he closed the tailgate. "Don't worry about it," he said. He didn't want her money. He just wanted to help her. To protect her. He needed to do that much.

She let out a frustrated sigh. "Fine, I'll start with this and figure out the rest later." She lifted a knee and used it as a platform to scribble numbers on a check, then slapped it against Matt's chest.

He stood still, letting her hand rest on his heart and enjoying every moment of the feeling.

"Take it," Lola warned. Her eyes narrowed and Matt had to smile at the stern glare she'd perfected.

"Lola, the only payment I want is a promise that you won't do any more 'fixing' in that house," Matt answered quietly. His thoughts wandered to the old gas stove, the ancient water heater, every faucet and pipe and outlet in every room. "Next time you or Sam could get hurt." He gently laid a hand over hers. "I don't want you to pay me. Please." They stood like this for a moment, staring at one another.

Lola finally slipped her hand from Matt's chest and crumpled the check. "Then let me make you a nice home-cooked meal some night," she said, her voice soft. "Please," she added when Matt began to protest.

Matt's shoulders loosened and his stomach actually growled. A nice meal, in Lola's company, with little Sam and Goliath running around... it sounded perfect. Too perfect. Nearly dangerous. He smiled and pulled gently on one of Lola's pigtails. "Okay. I'd like that."

A beautiful grin spread over Lola's lips and Matt was tempted to kiss her on the spot. But he knew better. Lola didn't want anything to do with a relationship, and he wasn't about to risk the easy friendship they'd built.

Matt was tugged from his thoughts when Sam came next Lola and snuggled into her side.

"Bye, Coach!" he said, bouncing a little on his toes.

Matt grinned and pinched the boy's chin. "See you at practice, Champ."

Chapter Eight

❧

Baseball practice could not come soon enough for both Sam and Lola. All week, Sam had begged Lola to practice with him. Each day they'd pitched and thrown and pretended to hit home runs. Sam loved diving for bases now, but each time her little boy collapsed to the ground, throwing his body and his fragile heart into it, Lola still cringed. She preferred they just play catch.

For Lola, baseball practice meant she'd have a chance to see Matt again. She missed him. She missed his crooked grin, the way lines tickled his cheek when he half-smiled at her. Those bright eyes, his large warm hands, those wide shoulders and rippling muscular arms... her list went on and on. Lola hadn't felt a lusty ache like this for quite a while, and since she couldn't ignore it - God knows she had tried for the last three days - she might as well nourish it. A little ogling at baseball practice wouldn't hurt.

The Chevy, now set for the summer thanks to Mike's Auto Shop, rumbled over the gravel driveway toward Main Street. Lola glanced in her rear view mirror and laughed quietly. The lawn had been quite a chore, but surprisingly relaxing. Once she got the hang of using the mower, and got over how uncomfortable it was to cover up from head to toe in the heat, the job had been kind of fun. It was mindless work where she could let her thoughts wander and just soak in the scent of the freshly cut grass and the hum of the mower. There were a lot of trees and house and shed to go around, and she'd missed some long patches here and there. But she'd get better, she told herself with a smile. She had all summer.

At the park, Lola slid from the truck's cab and lifted Goliath out, then helped Sam jump to the pavement. He wore his baseball cap a little crooked, a sleeveless shirt and matching shorts, and a smile that took over his whole face. Lola wiped a smudge of dirt from his cheek and noticed the extra freckles he'd accumulated that week. Playing outside was doing him so much good.

"Can I go now?" Sam whined, trying to pull away from Lola's cleaning. She laughed and nodded, and Sam raced to the baseball field as fast as his little legs would take him. Goliath tried to follow, but Lola held tight to his leash and let him pull her along.

The evening was beautiful. After a warm day, the soft breeze was welcoming. The sky blushed a brilliant pink as the sun set over the park. Lola walked slowly, letting the gentle wind tickle her bare shoulders and finger through her hair. Her legs were warm with a touch of sunburn, and her toes wiggled in her white flip flops. She watched as Sam joined Caleb and Gabe on the baseball field.

Lola tried to act casual while she looked for Matt. But he was nowhere in sight, and her heart fell with disappointment. She glanced back at the parking lot, scanning the vehicles for Matt's black truck, but it was missing. Where could he be?

Lola heard someone calling her name and turned back toward the baseball field. It was Rena, waving to her from the bottom row of bleachers. Lola led Goliath over and settled beside her, smiling and waving to others who greeted her in the stands.

"Don't you look cute," Rena said, pulling Lola into a half hug, which was all she could manage as her other arm struggled with a squirming little girl. Grace squealed and pointed to Goliath. "Da!" she shouted.

"You have the prettiest clothes," Rena continued, taking in Lola's meadow green strapless dress. "I could never pull that off with these saggy nursing boobs and baby fat," she added with a laugh.

Lola elbowed her friend, feeling her cheeks warm with the comment. "I actually don't get to wear these dresses a lot in San Francisco's cool weather. Some of them haven't been out of my closet for years." She wiped a hand over the stretchy ribbed bodice and pulled at the top to hide any cleavage. She suspected Hope River already had enough to gossip about.

"I haven't seen you guys around this week," Rena said, adjusting Grace on her lap. "Caleb's been asking every day if he can play with Sam. We even walked over on Tuesday morning, but you were out."

Lola leaned in to tickle Grace's pudgy bare toes. "Now that we have the Chevy to drive we've been wandering a lot. Playground, groceries, hairdressers…" Lola glanced out at Sam and smiled, happy to see that his hair no longer curled around his ears or covered his big gray eyes. "I think we've been in all the shops on Main Street and met nearly every person in town. They already know who we are, so I'm trying to remember names and faces. Everyone's been so friendly," she added.

"I love Hope River," Rena said, her face lighting up with a smile. "There are just enough people to make it a small town but not so many that you lose track of everyone. It's like a great big family. You don't have to like them all, but you put up with them because you're all in it together." She laughed and turned to Lola, eyebrows raised. "You know, for some people that's a turnoff, everyone knowing everyone else's business. And being a counselor, I get to know more than enough of everyone's business… but I really enjoy how close-knit this town feels."

Before Lola could respond, she felt the pull of Goliath's leash and turned. Her voice stuck in her throat as she noticed Matt kneeling beside him, nuzzling nose to nose and rubbing his ears with vigor. Goliath fell in a happy lump to the ground, exposing his belly.

"Hey, Matty," Rena called. Grace squealed and thrust her arms in the air in delight.

"Looks like I made it just in time," Matt breathed, glancing at the field. Still crouching beside the bleachers, he pulled a t-shirt from his sports bag. He quickly grabbed the bottom of the black long-sleeved shirt he wore and flipped it up over his head. The tanned skin of his stomach rolled with muscles, his arms bulging as he pulled the shirt in one swift movement from his body. Lola's breathing stalled and her ears began to hum. She couldn't tear her eyes from the beautiful feast in front of her. When she finally yanked them away, hoping he hadn't seen, she noticed women in the stands frozen for a momentary gape as well. Even old Fran Jones, owner of Main Street Café, tripped as she ogled Matt on the way to her seat.

Matt quickly thrust his arms in his t-shirt and pulled it over his head, letting it slide down his chest and settle at his waist. A collective sigh of disappointment floated from the women in the stands.

"Hey, pumpkin," Matt said, reaching over Lola's lap to pull on Grace's outstretched hand. Lola begged the butterflies to stay in her stomach. She froze, willing herself not to react to Matt's musky scent or the closeness of his body. But she nearly jumped out of her skin when his arm brushed over the top of her legs as he stepped away.

"Everything go okay?" Rena asked, and Matt nodded, adjusting the black bag over his brawny shoulder.

"Yeah, Unit Five had it covered. A small accident on the highway, no serious injuries." He reached down to pet Goliath one last time, then glanced at Lola before moving to the baseball field, sending a tiny smile her way. His eyes were bright and cautious, and she swore she saw unease in them before he turned away. Lola watched him, her heart dancing and flopping. Against her better judgment, she let her gaze linger over his snug-fitting black shorts and his tight muscular legs. The man looked like he had run a thousand marathons.

"Was he at a first responder call?" Lola asked Rena, trying to shake herself from her stupor. She continued watching Matt at he lowered his baseball cap against the setting sun and pulled his glove on. He jogged to the field where the kids swarmed him with hugs and excited cheers.

Rena nodded, watching the field too. "It came over the radio about an hour ago, so Matt told Gabe to come here and he'd go to the scene. I'm glad it wasn't serious. It always makes me nervous when my guys go out on a call."

Lola turned to Rena and studied her for a moment. She liked the woman. She had a comforting way about her, a friendly and open personality that made Lola feel at ease. She seemed protective and trusting and made people feel safe.

Lola squinted, remembering their earlier conversation. "You said you're a counselor?" she asked.

Rena's hazel eyes brightened and she bounced Grace on one knee. The little girl gurgled and drooled over a set of plastic keys. "Yep. I've been at the high school for eight years now. Matt got me the job when I graduated from the U of M." She nodded toward the field where Matt and Gabe were rounding the kids up for some pre-practice stretching.

"He sure is cute, isn't he?" Rena offered, smiling wide at the bodies on the field. Lola frowned, unsure if Rena was talking about Matt or Gabe or one of the kids. She'd been confused by this conversation before.

"Matt came over yesterday to help Gabe fix the brakes on my minivan. He said he'd been to your place to fix a broken faucet over the weekend." Rena slid a playful look toward Lola and grinned.

If Lola's cheeks had burned any hotter, they would have set on fire. She swallowed hard and glanced down at Goliath, sleeping in a fat ball beside her feet. She wrapped the leash around her wrist and took a deep breath. Why did she feel like *she* was in high school again?

"Did he tell you what I did?" Lola asked, hoping to cover why her cheeks were burning. Rena fell for the bait, and Lola filled her in on the mess she'd made. They laughed together through the story.

When Lola finished, she shook her head. "Hopefully I won't be breaking anything else in Louise's house and disrupting Matt's days anymore."

Rena let out a sigh as her laughter passed. "Well, it doesn't sound like Matt minds helping you out," she replied. A knowing smirk touched her lips.

Lola couldn't help herself. Her curiosity had finally built too high. She watched Matt roll the ball with Sam while she formed the question she'd been wondering for days.

"How long has Matt been divorced?" she asked, trying desperately to sound only half interested.

Rena turned in surprise, pausing for a moment. She shook her head. "He's not divorced. His wife died seven years ago, from ovarian cancer."

A wave of shock rippled through Lola and she felt her heart swell. No wonder he had shown Lola so much understanding. "How awful," she whispered.

Rena turned to watch Matt on the field, her face falling with sadness. "It was awful. Watching Matt go through it all, trying to be so strong. And it was even worse with all they'd been through right before..." She stopped herself and glanced at Lola, then shook her head. "I have a real soft spot for that man. He's like a brother to me, and to Gabe."

Lola faced the field again. As if he knew she was watching him and unraveling his secrets, Matt's eyes met hers for a brief moment. His face grew solemn, his eyes guarded, and more unease flickered over his expression before he turned away.

"All I want is to see him happy," Rena continued. "He deserves someone special. He has such a big heart and so much to give to the right woman - if he'll just let someone in again."

"AREN'T THEY A PRETTY sight?" Gabe asked as they stood near the pitcher's mound. The shouting and laughter that had been flooding their ears faded as the gaggle of children ran to the bench for a water break.

Matt followed Gabe's eyes, not toward the children, but to the front row of bleachers where Gabe's wife and pudgy-cheeked daughter sat beside Lola. The two women talked and laughed as if they were old friends.

Matt grinned at Gabe. "You sure are a softie underneath that grumpy-ass front you like to show this town," he teased. He lifted a bottle of water to his lips and guzzled half of it.

Gabe rolled his eyes. He folded his arms over his chest, surveying the children and the stands like a watchdog. "Maybe I am," he agreed. "But they are a sight for sore eyes, aren't they? All three of them." He nudged Matt with his elbow and snickered. "I saw you do a double take at Lola when you got here."

Matt glanced at Gabe and huffed, letting a guilty grin lift his cheek. He thought about playing dumb, but this was Gabe he was talking to. The man sniffed out lies and truths from others for a living. And hell, they'd known each other for twenty-eight years. There was no sense in trying to hide anything.

"Those dresses are making my head spin," Matt admitted quietly.

Gabe laughed. "More like what's *under* those dresses. She sure stands out in the crowd, doesn't she."

"I've been trying to avoid her since Sunday. I almost skipped out tonight so I wouldn't see her."

"What the hell are you avoiding *that* for?" Gabe asked with an astonished frown.

The look that Matt slid Gabe would have made most people shrink. But Gabe just stared at him, dumbfounded.

Matt shook his head. "Because *that* is going to be leaving just as quickly as it came, and I'm not about to get wrapped up in it."

Before Gabe could respond, the kids surrounded them, eager for a practice game. Matt lifted his glove in the air and grinned down at the children. "Who's ready to play ball?" he shouted. Screams of delight and bouncing little bodies raced in every direction.

AFTER PRACTICE, EVERYONE WANDERED home by foot or piled into rusty old vehicles. The breeze had picked up as the evening wore on and the air had grown heavy. Lola could feel a storm brewing above her, the same feeling that was in her chest.

She lifted Goliath into the Chevy and unhooked his leash, then gave Sam a boost into the cab of the truck as well. She felt as exhausted as they looked. All this fresh air and activity was overwhelming. As she turned to walk around the back of the Chevy, she spotted Matt crossing the field. He moved toward his truck, frowning absently at the ground.

Lola glanced around. The parking lot had emptied quickly. Other than Lola's Chevy and Matt's truck across from her, only one other car was left at the far end of the lot. She watched Matt for a moment, studying his lean body and long gait as he moved.

God, she found him attractive. It wasn't just his toned body and rugged good looks that charmed her, though they certainly helped. His appeal went so much deeper. He was intelligent and witty. He made her feel safe. He had a way with children that made her heart melt. And he held a respect with the people of Hope River that she knew had been hard-earned.

Lola rallied her courage. "I finished the entire lawn without mowing my foot off," she called carefully. She stepped out from behind the Chevy and leaned against the tailgate, smiling as Matt faced her. His grin grew slowly, and he finally nodded in acknowledgement.

"How long did it take you?" he asked.

Lola looked at the ground and kicked a rock with the tip of her flip flop. She peeked up at Matt and grinned. "Two days. It isn't the prettiest, but I figured it out."

Matt laughed. He walked slowly to Lola, staring at the ground as he neared. He flexed one hand open and closed over his keys.

"With this heat you'll have to start mowing again tomorrow to keep up. The grass grows like crazy in this weather." He lifted his face to the sky and studied the dark clouds as they rolled overhead. "Looks like we'll get some rain tonight."

It was all Lola could do to keep herself from moving into Matt and laying her hands on his chest. She wanted to touch him, to invite him to wrap his arms around her. She ached with loneliness. Was he lonely too? Lola looked into his eyes, clear and bright as a blue summer sky, and felt desperate to keep him near her.

"Come over this weekend," Lola breathed out quickly. Her smile faded, along with her confidence. "For dinner, for helping me out this week," she added.

"You don't have to make me dinner," Matt began, his expression conflicted. But before he could continue, Lola interrupted him.

"I want to. Come Saturday night. I'm much better at cooking than I am at repairing things." She smiled hopefully but still felt herself shiver with the threat of rejection. Why was she doing this to herself?

Matt laughed quietly. He reached a hand to her cheek and thumbed a strand of hair from her skin. "Okay. I'd like that," he added with a quick nod.

Matt peeked over Lola's shoulder, lifting his chin toward the passenger door window. "Looks like you have a pretty tired boy tonight," he said.

Lola turned to see Sam's arm leaning out the open window, his head resting peacefully on top of it. His eyes were closed and he breathed in a slow, deep rhythm. Lola smiled. "I guess so." She anxiously smoothed her hands over her hips and turned back to Matt. "It's been a big first week here. I better get him home." Walking past Matt around to her side of the truck, she looked at him one last time before she pulled the driver door open.

"Saturday evening, about six?" she asked. Matt gave a little nod. She waited to climb into the Chevy until his lips curved into the small smile that had become a therapy for her heart. Her chest simultaneously fluttered and ached, and she didn't know whether to smile or cry.

"SLEEP TIGHT, SWEETHEART," LOLA whispered. She kissed Sam's forehead and smoothed his hair, watching him yawn so big that his eyes watered. She leaned over to turn off his bedroom lamp, but Sam's little voice made her pause.

"Mom," he asked, his voice sleepy.

"Yes?" Lola shifted back onto Sam's bed and bent her face down to listen.

"Will I ever have a dad again?" he asked, his eyes fluttering open and closed as he fought the sleep that so desperately wanted to come.

Lola felt her body flush and she swallowed the pain of the question. She nodded, trying to get her mind ready with a good answer. But how could she answer it? She often wondered herself if there would ever be a man who could take Travis' place. She ran her finger's through Sam's hair and caressed the soft skin of his earlobe.

"You'll always have a dad, honey. He'll always be your father, whether anyone else comes into our lives or not."

Sam's eyes were closed now, but he frowned and licked his lips before he spoke. "But I'd like someone to play baseball with, like the other boys at practice. Someone to play catch with."

Lola leaned over and nuzzled into his soft cheek. "You have me," she whispered.

A little smile lifted Sam's cheek, and just before he drifted off, he opened one eye to peek at his mother. "But you throw like a girl," he said with a soft giggle. Lola watched him fall asleep, a smile on her face and tears welling in her eyes.

LOLA REACHED THE BOTTOM stair to the kitchen and found it still staring at her - the laptop, a pile of notebooks and papers, a stained and rumpled résumé. It was all in the exact place she had left it a week ago, untouched and accusing. Lola scowled and moved to the windows.

Outside, the night was dark and rumbling. The distant groan of thunder warned of a coming storm and lightning blinked above the trees. Lola called to Goliath in his small plush bed in the corner of the kitchen. "Potty time, Goliath," she urged, but he only rolled to his side and continued to snore.

"Aren't Boxers supposed to be energetic?" she laughed. She scooped one hand under his plump, soft belly and propped him upright on all fours, then patted him on the fuzzy bottom until he moved off the bed. Goliath stretched and yawned, then wiggled a greeting to Lola before he made it to the doorway. At the rug he sniffed and considered squatting, but Lola shoved him onto the enclosed porch with a gentle foot. He lumbered outside to the fresh-cut grass and squatted, keeping a wary eye on the sky. The clouds overhead churned and rolled and the trees seemed to whisper in anticipation. With a shiver, Lola called Goliath back inside. They settled on the lone cushioned chair in a corner of the porch, rocking and waiting as the storm brewed.

At first only a few drops of rain thrummed on the roof, but soon the sound doubled and tripled until it became an exponential downpour.

The sky belched a constant grumble, gorged and miserable. Lola closed her eyes and listened, lost in the drumbeats of rain. When she opened them, one burst of lightning lit the night into day, and then a single clap of thunder split the dark in two. Rain pelted the roof for a minute, then ceased. Just as quickly as the storm had come, it was through.

Lola listened to the forest grow quiet. The only sound that remained was of rain dripping from the trees to the saturated ground. The house was silent. Sam always did sleep like a rock, once he was out.

She could relate to the storm tonight, could nearly feel it in her bones. She had a similar storm surging inside of her, roiling and struggling, groaning in misery. But her storm wasn't passing through as quickly. That was the frustrating part, she decided. She didn't know what she should do next. She didn't know what she wanted.

Continuing to rock on the quiet porch, Lola sorted through her thoughts. There was one thing she did know: she didn't want to be alone forever. She wanted Sam to have a father figure in his life once more. Someday, she wanted to fall in love again. To move on with life and let go of the past.

How she'd do this was the million dollar question.

Lola sighed, considering. It seemed that her heart had broken in two during the last years. Half of it held Travis, his memory, the joy he brought to her life and Sam's. It also held a small amount of anger, that he'd left her alone with Sam to fend for herself. Before and after his death. He had always been so busy, often absent. And now he was gone forever.

It wasn't his fault, she knew. But it didn't calm the frustration or ease the loneliness.

The other half of Lola's heart was yearning to be noticed again. To be held, to laugh and smile and dance, to be touched. She was ready for life to move on. Lola shook her head. How was she supposed to hold her heart together when both sides were so conflicted?

Her thoughts moved easily to Matt. Deep inside, she knew it wasn't wrong or unfaithful to be attracted to another man. It had been two years without Travis. They had never talked about it, but Lola knew that he would have wanted her to find love again, for her and for Sam.

Just as she would have wanted the same for them if she'd been the one to leave.

So what was holding her back now? Why was she having such a hard time letting herself befriend Matt, letting him into her life?

Part of her knew the answer. It was because of Sam. She didn't have the luxury of thinking only of herself now. She had Sam's heart to consider. It was fragile, so incredibly fragile. Losing his father was trauma enough for one lifetime. He wouldn't survive another heartbreak, losing another man so important in his life. Lola couldn't take any chances.

The phone's loud jangle startled Lola from her thoughts. She set Goliath on the floor and ran inside. "Hello?"

The line crackled, and for a moment there was only silence. "Lola-girl!" came a woman's voice. "Did I wake you? What time is it there?"

Lola smiled and gripped the phone to her ear, sinking gratefully into a chair at the kitchen table. "It's nine-fifteen. How are you Aunt Louise?" Lola wrapped her free arm around herself in the hug she felt from her favorite aunt.

"Oh, darling! I'm having the *best* time! You should see the ashram I'm staying at, I feel like I'm reenacting *Eat Pray Love!*" Her voice carried musically through the phone, and Lola leaned back to listen to the stories. She let herself get lost in Louise's soothing voice and tales, joining in her aunt's contagious laughter.

"And tell me how it's going there," Louise insisted.

"Oh, everything's fine. We're both doing fine. Sam's having a blast! And our new puppy Goliath has settled in like this is home." Lola smiled as she watched him turn three circles before curling into a sleepy ball on his bed.

"And how are *you* doing, Lola-girl?" Louise's voice lifted in the knowing tone that Lola remembered well.

"I'm fine! I'm doing fine." She wrinkled her nose, wondering how many "fines" she could squeeze into one conversation. "I've met a lot of people from town. They're all very nice."

"Really! That's wonderful. Who have you met so far?"

Lola listed them off. "All the ladies in your yoga group - I met them the first morning I was here. They asked me to join them, you can imagine how well I fit in there." Louise laughed joyfully on the other end.

"And Sam's joined the baseball team, so we've met lots of kids, and your neighbors, the Westons."

"Oh, they're a lovely family aren't they? That Grace is precious," Louise added.

"And Sarah at the salon, she cut Sam's hair. She's real friendly. Fran at the Main Street Café - we had a piece of cherry pie with her. And we met Charlie, at the hardware store…" Lola's voice cracked and she laughed at herself and her awkward tone.

"Charlie, oh he's a hoot, isn't he?" Louise giggled, delighted to hear of her old friends.

"Oh, and Louise, I broke your sink! Matthew Dawson helped me fix it." Lola felt the heat flood her cheeks.

"Oh, splendid! That old sink's been dripping for years, I'm sure it wasn't your fault," Louise laughed. Lola squeezed her eyes closed, but before she could confess, Louise continued. "That Matt Dawson's such a nice young man, don't you think? Handsome, too. He's always doing so much for the town."

Lola rubbed a thumb and finger over her eyelids and sighed. If only she could tell Louise how much Matt Dawson did for her.

"So tell me what's bothering you, Lola-girl. I can recognize the flatness in your voice even when I'm half a world away."

Lola shook her head. "Nothing's wrong, Louise. I promise. We're doing fine." She cringed - there was that word again.

"I've known you a long time, sweetheart. I know when there's something on your mind." Louise sighed. "And I also know that you'll tell me in due time. Just remember something for me, okay?" Her voice had turned soft, matching the quiet of the night and the gently dripping raindrops beyond the kitchen window.

"You've been through one of the most painful losses you'll ever feel - I know. I still miss my Gilbert every single day. But your *heart* knows what's best for you now, not your head. Your mind is probably full of all the things you should be doing now, telling you what's right and what's wrong. But you listen to that big heart of yours, sweetheart, and let it lead you where it wants. Even when it scares you to death, just listen to it." She paused a moment, her voice nearly a whisper. "Lola-girl, it's time to trust that your heart has plans that you never could have imagined - good plans, I promise. And that happiness that you thought was lost forever *will* return."

The night grew quiet then, not even a snore from Goliath could be heard. Even the raindrops seemed to be silenced, the hum of the house frozen. Lola let out a deep breath that hitched as she swallowed her tears. She nodded into the phone, smiling and crying at once, remembering what happiness had felt like. She gulped down a sob and swallowed the knot in her throat, knowing, trusting, that happiness would return. Knowing that, already, in this tiny town of Hope River, it was beginning to.

Chapter Nine

The following morning, just as the kitchen began to fill with the glowing light of sunrise, Lola set the kettle on the stove and pulled five mugs from the cupboard. She rolled her shoulders as she found the tea bags and sugar, relieved to feel yesterday's tension dissipating after a little early morning yoga.

"This is a lovely camera, Lola," Anne said, picking up the Nikon D90 from the clutter on the table. She lifted it to her nose and inspected the buttons through her bifocals. Lola moved beside her, pushing her laptop and piles of papers out of the way while the other ladies settled around the table.

"Do you do much photography?" Dolly asked.

"I've been getting into it more lately, since Sam and I arrived. There's so much to photograph around here. It's just beautiful this time of year."

The women all nodded and clucked in agreement.

"Can I see some of your favorites?" Anne asked with eager eyes. "The pictures that come through the shop are rarely very good."

"Oh, I bet you've seen it all at your little store," Betty giggled. Anne rolled her eyes.

Something clicked in Lola's brain. "You own the photo store beside

Sarah's salon? Ritz Pix?" she asked. She turned fully toward Anne in surprise. Of course. *Anne Ritz*, she said with a mental slap of the forehead. "Sam and I peeked in there earlier this week but it was closed."

Anne nodded, looking slightly worried. "I'm only open a few days a week now. There's not enough business to keep the place open full time. So many people are doing their own photo processing these days."

"I'm telling you, Anne," Rae scolded, "you need to expand or something, change the place up a bit!" Anne waved her off as if they'd had this conversation one too many times already.

Lola gestured toward her camera as she tended to the whistling teapot. "You can just flick through the pictures right on that screen," she said over her shoulder. She filled the mugs with steaming water and dropped the tea bags in. She turned with tray in hand and was surprised to see the women gathered behind Anne, eyes and smiles wide.

"Oh, that's stunning," Anne breathed as she thumbed through the pictures. The others added their own noises of approval and appreciation.

"Lola, these are professional quality," Anne seemed to scold. "I didn't know-"

Rae interrupted Anne, pointing a finger at Lola. "You have to submit a few to the fair's photography contest this summer!" The others nodded and hummed in agreement.

"Oh, I don't..." Lola shook her head and frowned as she set the tray of mugs on the table. "... I'm not..." A tiny tug in her stomach made her pause and clamp her mouth shut. She watched the women, lost in the photos once again, oohing and ahhing in unison. It had been years since she'd been complimented on her photography skills. Six years, to be exact.

"What kind of fair?" she finally asked.

"The Hope River Fair!" Betty chimed in, lifting her eyes to Lola's. A ringlet of dyed blonde hair fell over her forehead and she wiped it gracefully back in place. "Why, it's the biggest event of the summer, next to the Fireman's Ball."

"The fair starts next Friday, one week from today," Anne warned. "Participants need to submit their photos this week."

"Anne oversees the contest, you know," Dolly told everyone, still watching as Anne continued to sift through pictures.

"Ohhh!" The four women gasped together, clutching their chests and shaking their heads.

"This one is precious!" Rae said, pointing to the camera. With her heart thumping, Lola rounded the table to stand beside them. On the small camera screen was the photo of Sam and Goliath asleep in the hammock, taken their second evening in Hope River. Their silhouettes snuggled together, a warm glow of sunset their backdrop. Lola smiled at the memory of how adorable, and exhausted, they were that night.

The look Anne gave Lola when she turned to her sent shivers down her spine. "Promise me you'll enter some of these photos, Lola. Come by my shop today and we'll get a few ready before the deadline."

THE AIR-CONDITIONING WELCOMED LOLA and Sam into Anne's shop that afternoon. Outside, Main Street hummed with Friday afternoon busyness. Townspeople meandered from window to window, sometimes popping in and out of shops. Children followed in little red wagons and bikes, ice cream cones dripping in their hands.

"Mom, look!" Sam called, running to a photo collage of hot air balloons on the wall. He stood on tiptoe trying to get a better look.

"Hey, you two," Anne cried as she appeared from a back room. She met Lola at the door and wrapped her in a warm hug, then bent beside Sam and peered at the pictures with him.

"Do you like those balloons?" Anne asked. Sam nodded eagerly, his eyes wide with awe. "We don't see hot air balloons around here much, but I have some little ones over there," she added, pointing to a corner of the store. A bundle of colorful balloons floated beside a desk. Sam skipped to them, pointing to a bright yellow one.

"This is a cute place, Anne," Lola said, taking in the shop while Sam collected his prize. Small and cozy, one wall was filled with photo machines, the other with shelves of cards, magazines, and picture frames. A long desk stood in the corner, a computer on top and rows of cubbies behind that held sealed envelopes of photographs. A second room behind the desk, the one Anne had come from when they'd arrived, was dark and seemingly empty.

"Well," Anne sighed, lifting her arms out while she studied the place. "I've had it now for fifteen years. Used to be that all I did was process film, but nowadays with the digital cameras most people print it themselves at home or use these machines." She pointed an accusing finger at the self-processing machines and shook her head. "Doesn't give me much to do anymore."

She ran her fingers anxiously through her hair. "I've been thinking about fixing the place up a little, but I'm not sure what I want to do with it. I don't want to go spending too much money on perking up a place that doesn't really get much attention." Anne shook her head, then focused on Lola. She suddenly seemed to notice the camera dangling over Lola's shoulder and snapped to attention. "Let's print some of those pictures of yours!" she said, jumping slightly.

Startled by the change in thought, Lola jumped a little too. She fumbled with the camera, pulling the disk out and handing it to Anne. She followed her to one of the self-processing machines and watched Anne navigate the screen with expertise. A handful of photographs appeared, and Anne stood back and smiled.

"Look at these beauties," she marveled. Lola eyed the pictures on the screen and let a smile escape. She hadn't realized how colorful the photographs were. Flowers and birds, butterflies and trees all popped from the screen in stunning hues. There were eerie morning landscapes and softly shaded scenes of farms and forests that she'd captured during the week's adventures. Crisp close-ups of Sam and Goliath made her smile, and even a few photos of the faded crimson shed and the rusted Chevy... they weren't half bad. She stepped closer to Anne, trying to steady her pumping heart.

"What do you think we should print?" she asked in a small voice.

Anne shook her head and sighed. "Oh, Lola. How will we choose? They're all so beautiful." She turned to Lola and squeezed her arm, meeting her eyes with her own sincere gaze. "Louise didn't tell me you're a photographer. Honey, these are amazing."

Turning back to the screen, Anne placed her fingertips over her lips in thought. "You're allowed to submit one picture in each of three categories: people, nature, and man-made. You'll have to choose your favorite from each. I just can't decide."

Lola felt as though she were under water listening to Anne's voice. It all seemed surreal. She had always loved photography, had studied it in college. She had even let herself dream, once upon a time, that she might create a career out of the art. But never had she truly let herself believe that it was possible, that she was good enough to impress anyone. She felt her heart clutch with doubt.

But Anne urged her on. It took little pats of assurance and Anne's unbridled excitement, but five minutes later Lola had chosen her favorites. And from Anne's murmurs of delight, Lola figured she'd chosen well. With one last gulp of hope, she pressed a fingertip to the screen. The machine churned and whined as it came to life.

Anne turned to Lola and smiled, giving her a playful wink. "The judges aren't going to know what hit them this year," she laughed.

BY SATURDAY AFTERNOON, ALL thoughts of photography and contests had disappeared. Now, for a completely different reason, Lola was a nervous wreck.

She'd readied the ingredients for their dinner with Matt, given Sam a good bath, even laid out a dress - a favorite of hers, sleeveless lavender and pink with a high waist and soft material that flowed to her toes. And then scolded herself a million times over for getting so worked up about nothing.

Lola vigorously shook a rug at the bottom of the porch stairs to keep her mind off the fact that Matt would arrive in less than two hours. Sam and Goliath lay on a blanket in the shade, lazing and reading books, completely unaware of her jittery nerves.

Suddenly, Caleb burst through the trees, branches snapping and shaking, and Lola nearly jumped out of her skin. He greeted her as he passed, then joined Sam and Goliath. Rena wove over the path behind him, Grace nearly asleep on her shoulder.

"Hi, neighbor," Lola called. She joined Rena on the grass and ran a hand over Grace's soft blond curls.

"I have a message for you," Rena said, offering a tight smile. She hefted Grace's chunky body in her arms and then turned her attention toward the boys. "Caleb, don't get comfortable, we have to go to Grandma's in five minutes." Returning her gaze to Lola, she smiled again, but her eyes gave her away. "It's from Matt. He didn't have time to call you."

Lola felt her stomach lurch. She tried to paste a pleasant smile on her face and act like she wasn't suddenly sick to her stomach.

"The guys were just called to a fire at Hanson's place," Rena said. She took a deep breath, seeming to steady herself. Although her expression was brave, worry filled her eyes.

"Is everyone okay?" Lola asked.

Rena nodded uncertainly. "I'm sure it's fine. But Matt said he'll be late for dinner." The worry lifted from her features and a mischievous smile spread over her lips.

"Oh, that's fine," Lola said, desperate to act calm. "I was just making a little something to repay him for fixing my kitchen."

She knew that Rena was no idiot. It would be easier if she just confessed now, got it over with. But Rena played along. "He'll probably be a few hours late," she said, touching a hand to Lola's and squeezing. Then the worry slipped to her forehead, wrinkles building on her pale skin. "Last I heard the fire was on both floors of the home, so the men have a lot of work ahead of them."

Lola's heart clenched at the thought of Gabe and Matt, along with the other brave men and women she'd met in this little town, fighting against such a dangerous beast. She wrapped Rena in a hug and held tight. "Gabe will be fine," she whispered. "They'll both be fine."

Rena swallowed hard, then peeked at the boys to make sure they weren't listening. They had their heads together over a book of robots, deep in conversation. She lowered her voice to a near whisper.

"I hate it when they have to go out like this. I'm a ball of nerves until I hear from them again." She wiped a fingertip beneath her eye to catch a tear. "We're going to visit my mother. I need a distraction to stay sane."

Rena wrangled Caleb from the blanket and books, said a quick goodbye and returned through the woods.

Matt would be fine, Lola heard herself repeat over and over. He was trained for this. He'd be arriving for dinner before she knew it.

She headed inside to get ready, to slowly begin cooking dinner. She was determined to have it warm and welcoming when he arrived.

BY NINE P.M., LOLA was filled with more emotions than she knew she had. Fear, anger, sadness, and relief all roiled together in the pit of her stomach. Her nerves were like a live wire, jumping at every sound.

Ninety minutes earlier, Rena had called with news that the fire was extinguished and no one was hurt. So Lola had paced and waited, tidied the table countless times, folded and refolded the soft dinner napkins until she thought she would scream.

She'd tried to reassure herself. Surely it took hours to secure things after a fire. There would be damage and cleanup to deal with before any of the men and women could leave the scene. The grieving owners to take care of, arrangements to be made.

Now it was late and Lola knew she needed to face the possibility that Matt may not come over at all. Perhaps it was a good thing, she considered. It was silly for her to explore these romantic feelings for Matt, ridiculous when she would only be returning to California in a short time. She and Sam had family there, a life to ease back into. Travis' parents were waiting patiently for their only grandson to return.

Lola sighed. She'd had too much time in the silence of the evening, trapped with her own wandering thoughts and fears. It made another awful thought crawl through her body.

Perhaps Matt was relieved that he wouldn't be coming over.

Perhaps he'd never really wanted to come over in the first place. What if he found this the perfect excuse to avoid seeing her tonight?

Stupid, she decided. That's what she was. She should have paid attention when they spoke after baseball practice. Hindsight was clear now - he had wanted to say no. But she hadn't given him much choice, had practically begged. And he was too nice to turn her down.

The sting from these thoughts was difficult to swallow, but even more so, Lola was disappointed for Sam. She had set him up for more heartache. He had been so excited to see Matt. He had taken a bath without fuss, put on the tidy clothes he only wore for school, hauled his toys away to his bedroom, leaving only a baseball glove and ball out in case "Coach" felt like throwing a few. And when Sam's bedtime had passed and Lola said it was finally time to crawl in, she'd put her son to bed with quite a pout on his face. To say he was disappointed was an understatement. He'd tried so hard to hold the tears in and keep a brave face when Lola had kissed him goodnight.

With a sigh, Lola pulled the plug from the kitchen sink as she finished washing up the dinner pots and pans. She looked out the window above the shiny new faucet and stared at her reflection. *All that worry for nothing,* she scolded. The dress, the makeup, doing her hair, a special dinner and a bundle of nerves, all down the drain. She shook her head, more than annoyed with herself. "Probably for the best," she whispered.

And then, as if in rebuttal to her words, two small lights caught her eye. They reflected off the window, and when Lola turned she saw headlights across the wooden bridge. Moments later, a black truck pulled up beside the house.

He'd made it after all.

Lola's eyes welled with a rush of relief. She wiped her hands quickly on a towel and rushed through the kitchen, her bare feet whispering over the smooth tile. Stepping into the cool air of the porch, she leaned out the screen door to welcome him.

The exhaustion on Matt's face and in his slightly slumped shoulders nearly broke Lola's heart. He walked slowly toward her, lost in his thoughts as he made his way. Closer to the house, he glanced up, his steps faltering when he noticed her. A slow, handsome smile spread over his lips, and an appreciative sigh lifted from his chest.

"You're a sight for sore eyes," he murmured, making Lola blush.

He stood at the foot of the stairs and stared up at her, an expression on his face that she couldn't read. His hair was still damp from a quick shower, his cheeks as rosy as if they'd been sunburned. A navy polo shirt stretched graciously over his broad chest and around the tight muscles of his shoulders. For a moment Lola couldn't speak, could barely breathe. He was just so damn sexy.

"Hi," she finally returned, her voice husky. God, how she wanted to slide into his arms and kiss away the aches of his day. It was such a wonderful, delicious idea.

Matt lifted a child's fireman hat. "I brought this for Sam. I suppose he's sleeping by now."

Feeling the blood return to her limbs and brain, she gestured for Matt to come inside. "He's out cold, but you can put it in his room. I'm sure he'd love waking up to it tomorrow. He was really looking forward to seeing you."

Matt's lips tightened in a disappointed smile. He walked up the stairs and stopped in front of Lola. His eyes, now the color of cobalt, were dull and tired, the usual sparkle faint. He glanced at her lips, then lifted his weary eyes to Lola's and gave an apologetic smile. "I'm sorry I'm so late," he whispered.

Lola shook her head and laid a gentle hand on his chest. She couldn't help herself, she had to reach out, needed to touch him. The man who took the weight of an entire town on his shoulders deserved some comfort. "I'm just glad to see you," she said. She slid her hand from the hard warmth of his chest and gently clasped his fingers in her own. Slowly turning, she guided him inside.

It was tempting to keep walking through the kitchen and up the stairs. She would have liked to drag him all the way to her bedroom… if it wasn't such a ridiculous, but tempting… and bad, bad idea.

In the bright light of the kitchen, Lola felt herself begin to tremble. She dropped Matt's hand and turned to face him. "Is everyone okay?" she asked. She stepped back, suddenly aware that they were only inches apart. Another step back, and she bumped into the kitchen table. She watched Matt slowly study her dress, from hem to waist to collarbone. His blue eyes, simmering with heat, met hers and held.

"The Hansons are okay, but their house is lost. The first floor was burned completely, the second damaged from smoke and water. They'll have to rebuild, start all over."

Lola didn't know the Hanson family, but she knew their farm. She and Sam had driven past it during the week, taken pictures of it from the top of a countryside hill. The old white farmhouse and charming barn had been picturesque in the afternoon sunlight with fields of golden grass the perfect backdrop. There had been fat dairy cows chewing on long green weeds, oblivious to Lola's lens, and a weathered sign blazing *Hanson Family Farm* at the end of the gravel driveway, swaying peacefully in the breeze. She was sure there was nothing peaceful about the place now.

"What will they do?" Lola asked.

"They had good insurance, so Earl said they can easily rebuild. And they have a daughter in town, Sarah, and her husband Clint. They'll stay with them for a while until they can get back on their feet."

"Sarah from the hair salon?" Lola covered her mouth in shock. She hadn't realized.

"She was there when it started in the kitchen. She was quick to call 911 and get her parents out. I think Earl would have gone down with the place, trying to put it out by himself."

Lola brought a hand to her stomach at the thought. It shocked her how, after such a short time, she felt so much attachment and protectiveness over this little town and its members.

The room was silent until Matt shifted and dug a hand in his pocket. With the other, he lifted the fireman hat to Lola. "Think Sam will like this?" he asked softly.

He stepped closer to Lola, his scent of a simple, fresh soap and crisp cologne making her heart jump. She studied his face, the way his warm cheeks made him look nearly feverish and how his eyes were slightly swollen from exhaustion.

Suddenly she was certain. If she didn't move away from him she'd surely pull him into her arms and make a fool of herself.

"He'll love it," she said with a quick nod. She pointed to the stairs that led to the bedrooms. "You can take it up to his room if you like.

First one on the left." She watched him turn and quietly creep up the narrow stairs. He slouched to clear the ceiling of the stairway and his wide shoulders nearly touched the walls.

When Matt returned, Lola was at the microwave warming up their dinner.

"Sam's a hard sleeper. I knocked over some toys and he didn't even budge."

Lola smiled. "He's always been a good sleeper. He gave me a scare with everything else, but he's never struggled with that." She pulled some utensils from the drawer and glanced at Matt. "Are you hungry?" she asked, hopeful.

A grin crossed his face. "Starving. I haven't eaten since noon." He rubbed a hand over his stomach as he walked around the table. When he stopped beside Lola, she could feel the heat from his body beside hers. She closed her eyes and breathed deep to steady her heart.

Matt rubbed warm fingers on the back of her arm. "I really appreciate the meal, especially after such a long day. It smells delicious."

You smell delicious, Lola thought. She gave Matt a quick smile and stepped to the table to set out silverware. She could feel his eyes follow her, wandering over her body. His gaze made her skin prickle with goose bumps.

Really, truly, she begged her conscience, *such a terribly bad idea.* She turned to find him leaning against the kitchen counter, completely oblivious to the war raging in her heart. He looked so perfect, standing there as if he were a normal part of her world.

"You must be so exhausted," Lola said, desperate to interrupt her thoughts. "I don't know how you guys manage it."

Matt rubbed a hand over his jaw, his stubble making the sound of sandpaper. "Yeah, a day like this really knocks it out of you. Not just the physical labor of hauling the hoses around and the work, but the psychological part of it. Worrying if the guys are safe, if everyone's out of harm's way, if the family will be all right, if we can save anything for them…" His gaze settled to the floor and for a moment he seemed lost in the events of his day. "It is exhausting," he confirmed, snapping his gaze back to Lola. "But I feel worse for the Hansons. We did what we could and now get to walk away, back to our normal lives. They're left with the disaster, with so much more to worry about."

Lola sat down at the table. All the emotion raging through her, from Matt's presence to the memories of her own loss, made her knees too weak to hold her up.

"I remember that feeling," she said. "Everyone goes on with their normal lives while you're trapped in a world that's fallen apart." They stared at each other for a minute, Matt nodding in understanding.

Silence threatened to swallow the evening whole, but Matt quietly cleared his throat. "Lola, I hope you don't mind my asking. What happened to your husband?"

Lola lifted her chin and met Matt's gaze. "He was in a car accident." The pain that flashed in Matt's eyes made her look away. She twisted her hands in her lap. "It was only a few miles from our home, on his way to work. The driver of an eighteen wheeler broadsided him, and Travis' internal injuries were too severe. He didn't even make it to the hospital." In the silence that followed, Lola could hear herself swallow, hear the clock ticking in slow motion.

"I'm sorry," Matt whispered.

Lola nodded, then looked up at Matt through blurry eyes. "Rena said your wife died of cancer."

He gave a little nod before pulling a chair out from the table. He settled into it, his knee brushing against hers, his fingers tapping lightly on his leg.

"About seven years ago." He looked curiously into Lola's eyes, uncertainty passing over his forehead. "Did Rena tell you the rest?"

Lola frowned. "There's more?"

"I had a daughter, too. Anabella. She was born three months premature. She lived for two days."

Lola touched her fingers to her lips. "I'm so sorry."

Matt shrugged. "After we lost Anabella, Ali was never the same. We were never the same. She didn't want to be in Hope River to begin with - she didn't really like small towns. She only came here because I had a teaching offer. But when Anabella died, things just fell apart."

Lola reached across the table and covered his hand with her own. Slowly, he turned his palm and wrapped his fingers over hers.

"We struggled through another year before Ali announced that she wanted to separate. She wanted to move back to the city, closer to her family, out of this small town and away from her pain and the memories of Anabella. She felt awful. She'd lost so much weight and was always sick. I said I'd look for a job there, but she didn't want me to come with her." Frustration clouded his eyes. He squeezed Lola's fingers, then slid his hand from hers.

"A few days before she was going to leave, we found out she had ovarian cancer. Stage four. She didn't even want to fight it. She stayed in Hope River and just gave up on everything. She died a month later."

For a moment Matt seemed lost in the memories. Then he blinked and focused on Lola, a light slowly returning to his eyes.

The beep from the microwave made Lola jump. She moved on wobbly legs to the counter, pulled the hot plate out with a towel and nearly dumped it on Matt's shirt when she turned. She hadn't heard him rise and move behind her.

"Let me help," Matt said, taking the towel-wrapped platter in his hands. The steam rose up in curls toward the ceiling. "It looks delicious," he added with a thankful grin.

After they'd settled at the table, creamy chicken and mashed potatoes dished onto their plates, Matt paused before taking his first bite. His eyes flickered with apology.

"I'm really sorry I couldn't make it earlier. I was looking forward to hanging out with you and Sam all evening."

Relief washed through Lola's chest, along with a million tingles of pleasure up her spine. "I'm just glad you made it at all. I was worried about you." She watched his eyes glimmer at her words. And then a slow, teasing smile spread across his lips.

"The Queen of Disaster was worried about me?"

Lifting a heaping fork of mashed potatoes, Lola readied it for a launch across the table. She lifted an eyebrow in warning.

"Hey, don't waste that," Matt laughed. With a quickness that surprised Lola, he plucked the fork from her fingers and shoved the mound of potatoes in his mouth. His eyebrows raised in appreciation. "You may not be able to fix a broken sink," he mumbled through swollen cheeks and a mischievous smile, "but you can sure fix a good meal."

"HOW'S THE JOB SEARCH going?" Matt asked when they'd finished their meals. He'd noticed the computer and pile of papers had moved to the countertop. Lola wrinkled her nose.

"It's not." She piled their dishes together and set them in the sink, the clatter reflecting her frustration. "I'm finding too many other things are distracting me." Her lashes fluttered as their eyes met.

"Like destroying kitchens?" Matt teased.

Lola lifted her chin a fraction. "I haven't caused any trouble this week."

"That's true." He laughed at the sparkle in Lola's eye, the stubborn set of her jaw as she smiled.

Moving to the sink, Matt bent and reached for the dish soap in the cupboard.

"Oh, no you don't," Lola scolded. She pulled him back using a warm, strong grip on his forearm. "You've done enough work for today. You get the rest of the night off."

When she turned and walked toward the other room, Matt couldn't find the words to argue. His mouth had gone dry and breathing turned shallow. The way her pink and purple summer dress hugged every curve of her body, the way she'd lifted a teasing brow over those sexy chocolate eyes - it was making the blood rush from his limbs. He didn't even have the ability to walk.

Ever since he'd arrived and saw Lola, he'd felt it. She wasn't giving him the strongest of signals, but there was something. The look in her eyes, the caress of her fingers on his skin, the sway of those hips as she invited him to join her. He didn't know what was more dangerous, acknowledging these acts or falling for them.

Matt finally felt the blood pumping through his legs again and joined Lola at a shelf of old records against the family room wall. He had to make a conscious effort to keep from touching her.

"This is quite a collection. Any good ones in there?" he asked. His eyes couldn't yet focus on the album names. He was too busy trying to clear his head. But the moment he caught the soft scent of lilacs floating from Lola's hair and noticed the small dip in the skin of her silky shoulder, he knew it was a lost cause.

"I have a few favorites in here, actually. This was my uncle's collection. I used to listen to a lot of this old music when I came to visit." Matt watched Lola pull a dusty record from the shelf and examine the cover. His eyes wandered over her small fingers and the creamy skin of her arms, down her long silky neck and over freckles that sprayed her chest down to warm, swollen...

Clenching his fists, Matt forced himself to breath slow and deep. He was like that horny teenager from all those years ago, losing his head over the beautiful girl with the seductive brown eyes. Without a quick distraction, it was a good bet he'd do something stupid real soon.

He knelt beside Lola and forced his attention to the shelf. He could do this. *Just concentrate.* Fingering through the records, he let the artists and songs sink into his brain. He pulled a sleeve from the selection and held it out in front of him.

"I haven't heard this one in years," he said with a little laugh. He forced himself to ignore the whisper of her dress against his arm. He turned the sleeve over and stared at the list of songs.

Had any of these songs played on that warm summer night so long ago? He couldn't remember the music. He only remembered the warmth of her hands on his shoulders, soft and timid, the scent of bubble gum floating from her pink lips, the knot that formed in his stomach as she revealed tiny dimples at the corners of those lips.

"Bon Jovi," Lola read over his shoulder, shaking him from his walk down memory lane. He watched her trace a finger over the cover and then take it in her hand. "Their music reminds me of middle school. God, those were awkward times," she giggled. "Do you like them?"

Matt nodded. "Sure. 'Livin' On A Prayer', 'Bad Medicine' - they bring back some interesting memories. I'm surprised your uncle liked them though."

Lola gave a little laugh. "Uncle Gilbert loved all music. One minute you'd find him dancing with Louise to Frank Sinatra in the kitchen, the next he'd be singing rock and roll with Guns N' Roses. He was hilarious."

Matt didn't remember much of Gilbert in his younger years, only that he seemed eccentric. Now, he decided he would have liked the guy.

Opening the ancient record player, Matt lifted an eyebrow at Lola. A slow smile spread over her lips, and without a word, she nodded. Matt lifted the flimsy vinyl from her fingers and flipped a switch for the turntable. It slowly came to life, spinning in lazy circles. The speakers crackled and hummed as Matt set the record in place.

"Do you remember dances at that age?" Matt asked, referring to their middle school days. He studied Lola's face, wondering if she'd reveal anything, uncover any long lost memories.

"You mean all the girls sitting on one side, staring at all the boys on the other? Whispering in one another's ears, hoping the cute one would be gutsy enough to walk across the dance floor and ask her?"

Matt laughed. "You know the boys all hated dancing. It was the most miserable few hours of our lives."

Waving a hand, Lola dismissed his teasing. She turned toward the record player and slid the volume higher until they could hear the beat of the first song. A tinny chorus of "I'll Be There For You" wailed through the speakers, and she laughed before leveling the sound.

It occurred to Matt that he could change the subject now, he could forget any connection they once shared. He could leave it in the past where it belonged in all of its awkward adolescent glory.

Aw, what the hell.

"When I was young," Matt began, stepping closer to Lola, "dancing at the Fireman's Ball was the worst." With the music still softly beating around them, Lola lifted her eyes in interest. "All the adults were at the bar and tables, but still watching, which made it ten times worse. I never liked to dance at those things." He turned to Lola and narrowed his eyes, concentrating on the memory. "But when I was about twelve, there was this one particular girl I couldn't stop watching. I remember thinking that she was stunning. She had long dark hair and deep brown eyes. She wasn't from around here."

Lola's eyes widened and her mouth dropped open in surprise. "That was...?" She shook her head, closed her mouth. "Did you ask her to dance?" The smile that spread across her lips, and the twinkle in her eyes, told Matt she knew the answer.

"I did." Somehow his hand had moved to her waist and his fingers slid gently along her back.

Lola studied Matt for a moment, her eyes locked with his. "I only went to the Fireman's Ball with my aunt and uncle once." She nodded, as if she could suddenly see it clearly. Her hand reached and rested on Matt's arm, her fingers brushing lightly on his skin. "I sat by my girlfriends near the dance floor and listened to them whisper about the cute boys across the room."

Quiet laughter rumbled in Matt's chest. He could see it, see her, as clear as if they'd transported twenty years back in time.

"There was a handsome boy, a few years older than me," she said, squinting at the memory. "He walked toward us and I was sure he'd ask one of the other girls to dance." Her smile grew and Matt could see that she knew. She remembered. "But he didn't ask one of them. He asked me."

"And what did you think of him?"

While her one hand remained on his arm, the other moved to his chest. She brushed soft fingers over his shirt, slightly tugging on it. "He was tall, really good-looking. His eyes were bright blue like the sky. He was lean and confident and walked across the dance floor full of kids and adults, straight to me." Returning her gaze to him, she smiled so wide that her eyes crinkled.

Matt took her free hand in his and brought it to his heart. With his other already on her waist, her fingers already wrapped over his shoulder, they swayed gently together, their bodies vibrating with warmth. "Would you like to dance?" Matt asked.

"I think we already are."

He pulled Lola closer so that her hips bumped against him. Her scent was no longer the sweetness of bubblegum, but the flowery aroma of a beautiful woman. Matt rested his lips in her hair, breathing her in.

"I can't believe that was you," she laughed, shaking her head in disbelief. "You never told me your name."

Matt pulled back enough to see her sparkling eyes. "I went to your aunt's house the next day but you were gone. You'd already left for California." He rubbed his thumb against her chin and smiled. "You were the first girl to ever break my heart."

"Oh, that's awful," Lola murmured, burying her face into his neck. Her lips brushed against his throat, causing a flash of lust to threaten the strength of his legs. He gripped her hand and hip just a little tighter, then leaned to whisper in her ear.

"When you drove by the fire station in that yellow taxi two weeks ago, I knew I'd seen you before. But I didn't realize who you were until that first ball game." He loosened his tight hold so he could see her face, see that her eyes had darkened with a hunger he felt in his own body.

"I remembered these eyes," he continued. He lifted his hand and brushed a thumb over her cheekbone, tracing to the corner of her almond-shaped eye. "And these lips," he added, touching a tiny dimple.

A little sigh escaped Lola's mouth before Matt moved to cover it with his own. He watched her eyes flutter, then close, until he lost himself in the warmth and moisture of her lips. She pulled him closer, until her breasts crushed against his chest, until their clasped hands were trapped between them. Her free hand slid from his shoulder to his neck, her fingers caressing his skin and tangling in his hair.

It was hard to control himself. But somehow, he managed. If he hadn't been trying so hard, he might have picked her up and carried her to the couch, laid her down to enjoy even more of her. He certainly wanted more. But her mouth was soft and gentle, exploring, and her breath came in quick, anxious sounds. When her lips parted his tongue tickled hers, lingering in the sweet warmth. Her breath hitched and caught in her throat and she crushed her mouth against his with such need that Matt nearly pulled her to the floor.

And then she froze. When Lola pulled away, her eyes grew wide with shock and her lips opened, ready, Matt was sure, to give him an earful.

"This..." Lola shook her head, dropped her hand from his neck. "This is a bad idea." She nodded wildly. "*Really...* bad idea." A little giggle erupted from her mouth and she covered it with her fingers. She pulled her other hand from his, using it to push gently off of Matt's chest.

"That... I..." She brushed her fingers over her mouth and laughed. "I'm sorry. I think I got caught up in the moment."

Matt nodded, thrust his hands in his pockets and smiled even though he wanted to grab her and taste her soft honey lips again. "It must be the music," he added, and laughed when Lola burst with more giggles. Frustration and hilarity swirled together in his brain, making Matt dizzy.

But really, Matt scolded himself as he tried to calm his head and his heart, it *was* a bad idea. She may be incredibly attractive and smell like a flower garden, and she may taste sweeter than watermelon on a hot summer day... but she was leaving in two months.

"I'm leaving in two months," Lola confirmed, as if she'd read his mind. Her smile quickly faded and worry lines rose on her forehead. The swirls in Matt's stomach turned into a sharp ache.

"And I have Sam to think about," she added quietly. With the sudden jolt of reality, she turned away, wringing her hands at her waist.

He couldn't stand it. He couldn't bear to see Lola beat herself up over this, couldn't stand that he'd caused it by not controlling himself. "Hey," he soothed, stepping toward her. He reached out, touching her arm gently. "I'm sorry. This is my fault. I just..." He shook his head. Just what? Fell in love the moment I saw you? "I got caught up in it too. I'm exhausted, not really thinking clearly. I should go home."

Warning bells rang through every muscle of his body as Matt lifted his hand and brushed a finger gently over her neck. He touched a strand of soft hair and sent it whispering over her shoulder. The creamy skin of her neck was exposed, and Matt let himself feel her warmth, feel the rapid beat of her pulse.

It was simple, really. He could turn and walk out the door and ignore this evening, ignore the racing in his chest. Ignore that this woman was making him feel something he had never felt before. But when Lola leaned her cheek gently against his hand and closed her eyes, he knew the truth.

Eventually, he would give in to loving her. And she would break his heart.

He clenched his jaw and closed his eyes too. Nothing about this, about what they both seemed to want, was rational. It had been seven years since he'd lost Ali, and still he struggled with opening up to someone new. How could he expect anything from Lola while she still suffered from her own loss? How could he expect anything good to come of them when she was only here for the summer?

They stood like this for a moment before Matt heard his own voice, strange and distant. "I should go." He gave a small, uncertain smile, and waited for Lola to look at him. It seemed that hours passed before she lifted her gaze, her eyes dark and confused. Her chest rose in a visible gulp of air and she lifted her chin and nodded.

"Thank you for dinner," Matt said quietly. He let his hand brush over her arm as he turned. With every muscle screaming in protest, he strode toward the kitchen. Before disappearing around the corner he turned and stole one last glance.

Lola stood in the same place, her eyes focused on her hands as they twisted the small diamond band on her finger. Regret and anger flashed through Matt as he watched, her pain palpable and raw. He escaped through the kitchen and out the door before he could change his mind, before he could turn back and make everything worse than he already had.

Chapter Ten

❧

Sunday morning, as the two small churches of Hope River filled with townspeople, Lola did her praying in the kitchen. Dirty bowls and pans filled the sink and countertop. The oven had been pumping heat since 6a.m. Lola fanned herself with an oven mitt while she looked over the mess.

All this chaos and still she couldn't take her mind off of last night.

"Are we gonna eat all this food?" Sam asked. He held a bowl of soggy Corn Flakes that he'd been slurping in front of the TV. Lola smiled at the way her son's Spiderman pajama bottoms crept up his shins, proof that her little boy was indeed growing. He looked comical with his too-small pajamas and a red fireman hat on.

"No, it's for our new friend Sarah. Remember the nice woman who cut your hair last week?"

Sam nodded but frowned, still confused.

"There was a fire at her parents' house last night and we're bringing them a few meals to help."

Sam adjusted his fireman hat with pride. "Is that the fire that Coach fought last night?"

Lola nodded, a bubbling sensation rising in her stomach. She didn't want to think about Matt right now, but it seemed he was the only thing on her mind. His warm hands wrapped around her waist, fingers caressing her neck, lips soft and warm against her own... she could still feel him. Still taste him.

"Run upstairs and change so we can take these to Sarah," Lola told Sam, desperate for distraction. Sam spun on the slippery tile and raced to the stairs, holding his fireman hat in place.

"Be careful in the bathroom," she called after him. "No climbing on the sink." Sam glanced over his shoulder and gave Lola a playful grin, then rolled his eyes before disappearing upstairs.

Turning back to the kitchen, Lola pulled a pan of lasagna from the oven and laid it on a cooling rack. She moved the ham and cheesy potato casserole from another rack, testing that the dish had chilled. Wrapping it in foil she set it next to the stack of sandwiches she'd made earlier. With a huge sigh of satisfaction, she turned to the kitchen sink, no longer visible under the mass of dirty dishes.

"Nothing like a little cleaning to take your mind off things," she whispered.

THE SUN WAS HIGH as the Chevy zigzagged along the narrow country roads outside of town. Armed with the meals she'd made and eager to show support, Lola headed for the Hanson Farm, where Dolly had told her most of Hope River's residents would be found.

Sam dangled an arm out the open window, lost in the blissful thoughts of summer. His hand opened to catch the wind, to feel its silky caress against his skin, and contentment settled in his eyes. Lola tugged on his ear and gave him a smile.

The wind whipped Lola's hair in circles as she picked up speed. She watched the countryside open up to waving fields of glossy green corn stalks and bright red farms with tractors plodding along the dirt driveways. The air was warm and soft against her palm as she held it out the window. She made an airplane with her hand, lifting it up and down in the current of air as she drove. She giggled with Sam, feeling ten years old again. All the worries of life in San Francisco seemed far from her mind: the job search would wait, Sam's school would wait, her feelings for Matt would...

Lola brought both hands back to the wheel and focused on the road. *Best not to think about that right now*, she scolded.

It was when they rounded the bend that their expressions changed to ones of awe. Half a mile down the bumpy road they could see the Hansons' two-story farmhouse blackened and weary. But it wasn't the devastation of the house that made Lola's mouth drop in surprise. It was the line of cars parked along the road and filling the long driveway, the number of people that slowly walked a path to the farm like worker ants marching to their queen. The burned house was streaked in black and gray, crispy and dusty as charcoal, but the vibrant colors of the people as they swarmed the farm took Lola's breath away.

She pulled in behind the line of cars and lifted Sam and the meals out of the cab.

"Good afternoon, young man." The familiar voice boomed from beside them and Charlie winked at Sam. Lola watched him shuffle toward them with a cardboard box of food and supplies in his arm. "Lola," Charlie said in greeting, grinning wide.

"Hi, Charlie." She stifled a laugh as she watched his eyes dart to her legs and then just as quickly away. He certainly didn't have anything exciting to look at today, considering the bland denim overall dress Lola sported. She probably looked like she belonged on the farm, just needed a straw hat to accessorize.

"Shame about this place, isn't it?" Charlie said as they slowly made their way to the farm. He looked toward the house and all of its damage. "Lucky the fire didn't spread to the barn."

"Do you know them well?" Lola asked. They turned onto the dirt driveway that split the farmhouse from the barn and sheds.

Charlie nodded. "Known Earl since I was a kid. I used to do a lot more with him when I had the farm, but now I just see them on occasion."

The crowd of people around the farm filled Lola with pride. There were groups milling around the house, some deep in conversation, some sharing laughter and smiles. Burly men, wearing shirts with fire department emblems on them trudged in and out of the house, inspecting the walls and windows and bringing salvageable items out to the yard. Children ran and played in the dirt driveway, crossing over to pet horses and play with kittens outside the barns. And far behind everyone was a busy group that Lola recognized as the Ladies Auxiliary, sorting food on tables and supplies into boxes, smiling and laughing as they worked. Lola waved to Anne and Dolly, then moved beside the woman she'd been seeking.

Sarah stood tall against an older woman, her arm wrapped protectively around her shoulders. The gray-haired, weary-eyed woman sniffled into a tissue and thanked the couple she spoke with.

"I'm so sorry," Lola whispered as Sarah turned to her and gasped. She wrapped Lola in a fierce hug and gave Sam's shoulder a tight squeeze. "It's so nice of you to come. I know, it's devastating… but I'm still so thankful my parents are all right." She wiped a tear from the corner of her eye and tried to smile.

"Everyone has been so generous," she continued, turning toward the crowds of people. "We've had offers of places to stay, people who want to help rebuild, and the donations…" Sarah placed her hands over her chest and tried to control the tears that threatened to return.

Lola held out her armful of meals, two dishes wrapped in foil and stacked gingerly on top of one another. Sam thrust his bag of sandwiches in the air as well.

"You made this for us?" Sarah cried, clasping her hands together. She took Sam's cheeks in both hands and planted a kiss on the top of his head, then wiped another tear from her eye. "I just can't believe the kindness," she whispered, and again she wrapped Lola in a hug.

It took Lola and Sam a few minutes to make their way to the donations table. Familiar faces greeted them as they moved, patting Sam's head and pinching his cheeks. When they finally reached the table, Lola handed the meals to one of the many auxiliary ladies and watched her place them in coolers beside the house. Meals and kitchen supplies overflowed from boxes, and Lola marveled at the incredible generosity of the community.

"Coach!" Sam bellowed from behind Lola. She turned to watch

Sam run across the lawn toward Matt, arms open wide. He collided with Matt's legs, crashing and then bouncing back as if he'd hit a brick wall. With a handsome grin, Matt scooped him up in his arms, lifting him to eye level.

The sound dimmed around Lola as she watched Sam and Matt. The way they looked at one another, the comfort they seemed to share - it made her heart flutter and sink all at once. She took in the way the skin crinkled beside Matt's blue eyes as he grinned, the way Sam laid his hands comfortably on his shoulders and whispered secrets in his ear. Matt held her precious son in his arms like Sam was his own. She couldn't deny that they looked like father and son.

The thought terrified her.

Sam slid back to the ground and returned to Lola. "Coach is here!" he called, panting as he reached her. She nodded and smiled, trying hard to keep her expression light.

Matt's face was unreadable as he approached, but his eyes studied Lola's with intensity. She shivered, even as the warm sun beat down on them.

Before he could speak, Matt was intercepted by a round man in sooty overalls, his face gray with exhaustion. He clapped Matt on the back and shook his hand with both of his own.

"I can't thank you enough, Matthew," the man said, tears springing to his eyes. Matt pulled the stout man to his chest and hugged him tight, slapping his back as they embraced. After a moment, the man pulled away and sniffed hard, wiping his eyes with the back of his beefy hand. "Your guys did one hell of a job last night." He glanced at Lola and tried to smile through his tears.

"Earl, this is Lola Sommers and her son, Sam," Matt said. "They're staying at Louise Earnhart's place for the summer."

Earl turned to Lola and took her hand, wrapping the other over hers in warmth. "Thank you for coming, Lola," he said with a smile. "I can't tell you how blessed Maddy and I feel, all of you coming out."

"Sam and I made a few meals for your family," Lola said, nodding toward the coolers of food. "I'm so sorry this happened."

Shaking his head and lifting his chin, Earl took in a chest full of air. "I'm just thankful nothing else was caught in the fire." He glanced down at Sam and winked. "The cows and horses are just fine, and so are we. That's what matters most, right?" he asked. Sam nodded and gave an uncertain smile as he snuggled up to Lola's side.

After thanking her profusely for the meals, Earl moved to greet other groups of visitors. Lola and Matt stood beside one another in silence, watching the crowd. Sam was the first to spot Caleb walking with Gabe toward the house.

"Can I go say hi?" Sam whispered urgently. Lola nodded and watched him tear across the lawn in greeting.

"If those meals are anything like last night's dinner, Earl and Maddy are in for a treat," Matt said.

Lola laughed softly and wrung her fingers. "It's just lasagna and a casserole. I thought they'd need some help with meals for a few days, but I didn't expect..." she gestured in the general direction of the huge crowd, her eyes misting as she did. "This is amazing."

"Doesn't take long after word gets out for everyone to pitch in." Matt stuffed his hands in his jean pockets and studied the ground.

"Lola, last night..." he began. Lola lifted a hand to stop his words, but he continued. "I'm sorry about what happened. I didn't mean to upset you."

Lola shook her head in desperation. "It's okay, really." To stop herself from reaching to him, touching him, she wrapped her arms tight over her chest. She lifted her eyes to his uncertain ones, blue and clear as the sky above, and gave a gentle smile. "*I'm* sorry. I had a nice time last night, I really did. I'm just..." She smiled and shook her head when she couldn't finish the sentence.

"I know." His face showed that he really did understand what she couldn't say.

Two little bodies surrounded them then, and Sam and Caleb clung to Matt with hugs and giggles. Gabe joined their small group and clapped Matt on the back.

"You didn't get enough of this place last night either, huh?" Gabe teased.

"Hi, Lola," he added, leaning over to kiss her on the cheek. "I hear this jerk nearly stood you up last night." Matt's eyes narrowed at the comment.

"I can't believe he came over at all, with the night you guys had," Lola answered, hoping that the flush on her cheeks would be attributed to the warm sun. "I'm glad everyone's okay."

The men nodded, then looked at the house.

"It was quite a sight," Gabe said. He pointed to the first floor of the house and scowled at the memory. "I haven't seen flames like that in years. How many of us were here, anyway?" he asked, turning toward Matt.

"Twenty-five in all. A couple of trucks came from Summersville to help out too."

"Hey, Chief." A man of intimidating height and curly dark hair stood beside Matt and slapped his back. He offered a hand, shaking both Matt's and Gabe's.

"Clint," Matt answered in greeting. He shook the man's hand tightly and gave his arm a friendly smack.

"We cleaned out the first floor this morning," Clint said with a nod toward the farmhouse. "Brody and Will are getting some equipment so we can move up to the second." A handful of men slowly joined them, greeting one another and discussing the plans to clean up. Their voices mixed together as they listened to Matt's instructions and bounced around ideas.

Lola watched the men, some with familiar faces, some she'd never met, and felt her heart expand. This wasn't just a community, she mused, it was a brotherhood. She glanced toward the Ladies' Auxiliary, at the cheerful faces of the women who worked together. A sisterhood. Never had she experienced such protection and caring, such a huge sense of family. Rena's words echoed in her mind - *just one big family, all in it together.*

Could her heart expand so much that it might burst, Lola wondered? She rested her hand over her chest, over the ache that was making her eyes sting. Her gaze fell on Matt once more, on his easy smile and reassuring eyes, on the way the men listened to him with such respect and reverence. Her breathing came in deep raspy gulps

133

and her throat burned from trying to keep the emotion of her sudden realization inside.

It wasn't just the man she was falling for, but the whole town along with him.

Lola grasped Sam's hand in hers and whispered to Gabe that she and Sam were leaving. With her head down, she hurried through the crowd.

She heard her name called in Matt's deep voice, could feel his questioning blue eyes burn at her back. Lola pulled Sam behind her and fled.

IT WAS AMAZING HOW much Lola could get done when her heart and mind needed a distraction.

By Monday afternoon, every surface of the house was dusted, every floor vacuumed or scrubbed. Windows were sparkling clean, the kitchen was spotless, and even the lawn was mowed again. Twice.

On Tuesday Sam and Lola drove through all of the surrounding towns within a twenty mile radius, visiting the shops of the main streets and enjoying lunch at a small Norwegian diner. They sampled new flavors of ice cream at a drive-in and even tried out a quaint little candy shop, bringing home more bags of chocolates and sweets than they could consume in the entire summer.

Wednesday, after yoga with the ladies, Lola and Sam ventured to the Green Hills State Forest, only five miles outside of Hope River. They packed a lunch and made a day of hiking through the woods and along the stony shores of the river. When they returned home, covered with sunburns and scrapes and bug bites galore, their exhaustion was nearly blissful.

Still nothing could keep the anxious feelings from creeping back into Lola's chest.

It wasn't until Thursday morning, as Lola nursed her hot cup of coffee in the kitchen and scratched the tiny bumps on her ankles, that she admitted why she'd been keeping so busy.

She'd do just about anything to avoid a job search that would take her away from this peaceful little town.

Today would be different, she decided. Today she was determined. She'd had time to clear her head, to put things into perspective. Yes, this was a lovely little town, and certainly, Matthew Dawson was a delicious specimen of a man. But her visit to Hope River was meant to be a short reprieve, and soon she and Sam would return to San Francisco. The Bay was their home, where family and friends awaited their return and the life they knew would move forward.

Outside, the sky was gray and gloomy and the temperature had cooled drastically. A light drizzle hung in the air. The weather was familiar to Lola, much like the foggy mornings of San Francisco. It felt like the kind of weather that was planning to stick around for most of the day. So while Sam played with Legos in the family room and watched cartoons, and Goliath snored on his bed in the kitchen, Lola decided it was time to dust off the laptop and try again.

She wrapped a thick sweater around herself and with a sigh, opened her laptop. Topping off her coffee, Lola settled into a chair with her legs folded beneath her to preserve warmth, and stared at the blank computer screen.

The morning was deliciously quiet. Sam's soft voice floated over her as he spoke to his Legos and Goliath's sweet gusty snores whispered through the kitchen. Lola closed her eyes and listened to the hum of the refrigerator, the patter of raindrops off the eaves. If she listened closely enough, she could even hear a quiet, argumentative little voice in her head.

It spoke softly, urgently, with an intensity that made her heart jitter. It told her a truth she'd been avoiding, one that she'd known long before she'd ever arrived in Hope River. It wasn't just the new job search that Lola was dreading.

Her heart was weary. It felt lost and empty. For the past eighteen months she'd been working in a career that didn't satisfy her. Before that she'd been home, feeling stifled and frustrated, as if a creative force was being smothered inside. And now she was looking for another job that would continue the pattern.

Lola opened her eyes and sighed with the realization. She stared at the blank screen, felt the smooth squares of the keyboard beneath her fingertips and decided that five minutes of surfing the internet wouldn't hurt a thing.

She typed in a few keywords. The pictures that popped up on the computer screen boasted of a small and colorful town snuggled against a lazy river, of friendly people, good fishing, and gorgeous countryside. Lola scrolled down the page and read over a list of facts. The last one made her smile.

Hope River, population 1,208. It had nearly doubled since she was a little girl. The web page banner flashed photos of well-kept houses, a cute main street full of shops, and old iron benches flanked by colorful pots of petunias that lined the street.

Lola moved the cursor over tabs on the top of the screen - recreation, mayor's office, schools, fire department. She clicked on the last link and grinned when a picture of the volunteers popped up. Her smile grew wider as she recognized the handsome face in the middle of the back row. *Matthew Dawson, Volunteer Fire Department Chief,* it read. Matt stood tall beside the serious Gabe, an amused smile on his face.

The school district website was next. Lola could hear a voice nagging in the back of her mind to just focus on her résumé or search for a job, but she couldn't reel in her curiosity. She clicked through the school links until she found a list of high school faculty. Rena, known as Mrs. Irene Wesson, was listed as a specialist - High School Counselor and Director of Career Services. Her smile was soft and inviting, her eyes twinkled with a certain knowing. Further down the list, Lola found what she'd been searching for.

Matthew R. Dawson, Science Teacher and Athletics Director. Lola laughed; an Athletics Director as well? Clicking on his name, she watched with a grin as a picture of Matt and five of his students appeared. Even in a photograph of him on a school website, he took her breath away. He had that same smirk and those intense blue eyes that she'd found herself falling for, those wide shoulders and strong hands wrapped around the arms of students who adored him.

It took Lola five more minutes to convince herself to stop snooping. When she finally closed down the website, she pressed fingers over her eyelids and sighed.

Enough was enough.

"QUITE A CHANGE FROM the last few weeks, huh?" Rena asked as Lola joined her and Grace on the single stand of wooden bleachers. Lola settled beside them on a dry wool blanket and shivered in her raincoat. It was the first day since her arrival that she'd worn jeans, and her toes felt unusually cramped in her white sneakers.

"At least the rain stopped," Lola answered, glancing at the sky. She leaned over to take Grace's chubby hand in her own.

"The kids are going to be filthy by the end of practice." Rena nodded toward the field where the children were already covered in layers of mud.

As Lola glanced up, it wasn't the sight of the children stomping in mud puddles or throwing clods of wet dirt at each other that made her breath catch. It was Matt, kneeling in front of her son, laughing and gently holding his shoulder. He tapped a finger on the bill of Sam's cap and patted him on the back, sending him off to join the others. As Sam's face brightened with a wide smile, Lola's smile faltered and her heart began to stutter.

"Matt sure is good with Sam," Rena said quietly, noting the expression on Lola's face.

The lump in Lola's throat was hard to swallow. "Sam adores him, too," she answered quietly.

"You sound worried." Rena pulled a blanket over her daughter while she waited patiently for Lola's response.

"Sam's getting so attached," she finally answered, trying to keep her voice steady. "He already lost his dad. Now it seems I'm setting him up to lose another father figure."

The counselor in Rena seemed to kick in. She laid a gentle hand on Lola's and squeezed. "Honey, it's healthy for Sam to look up to other men, especially now. He needs good male role models in his life again." Rena looked at Matt and smiled. "I don't think there's a better one out there."

A familiar ache threatened Lola's chest. She rubbed a hand over her heart and took a deep breath. Matt was an incredible role model for her son. But he was also turning Lola's world upside down with feelings she didn't know were possible. How would she deal with it all? How would Sam?

As she watched Matt, frowning at her own complex thoughts, he turned and tossed a few balls toward home plate. He called over his shoulder for the children to gather for warm-up, and then lifted his gaze to the stands. His eyes met Lola's and locked, and Lola felt her brain go fuzzy.

Just breathe, she coached herself, inhaling the damp earthy scents of the field. She tried to recall Dolly's quiet voice and the calming yoga advice that she offered. But Lola's lungs threatened to burst as she held the breath inside.

With a curious lift of his eyebrows, Matt's expression softened and a whisper of a smile swept over his lips. He winked once, so quick she wondered if she'd even seen it at all. And when he turned back to the hoard of children bouncing at his feet, Lola let the air gush from her lungs until she thought her eyes would cross.

"Mom, did you see me catch that fly ball?" Sam cried, running to Lola at the end of practice. His eyes were wild with excitement and he nearly bowled her over in the wet grass beside the field. Lola laughed, pulling him into an awkward hug as she tried to keep his wiggling body from smearing mud on her jeans.

"That was a great catch, baby. And you threw it right to first base just like you're supposed to." Lola bent at the waist and pulled his cap from his damp forehead so she could see his eyes. "I'm proud of you," she whispered, marveling at the tiny dimples that pierced his cheeks.

Before Lola could smother her little boy with kisses, Caleb had him by the waist, lifting him high enough that Sam's feet dangled.

They giggled together, even as they threatened to topple over. Then Caleb set Sam back on his feet and faced him with huge eyes. "Are you going to the fair tomorrow?" Too excited to listen to Sam's answer, he continued. "My dad said I can go on the Tilt-A-Whirl this year, and the Fun House too!"

Sam whirled to his mother, his face bright with hope. "Can we go, Mom?" Sam begged. He jumped up and down, grabbing Lola's coat, pulling her toward him with his excitement.

"Um, okay." Lola grimaced, peeling his hands from her jacket before she tipped over. A flash of panic raced through her mind - unsavory carnies, stomach aches from the greasy food, even the *idea* of losing Sam in the crowd...

"Awesome!" Sam shouted, pulling her arm and her thoughts back to the moment. Lola swallowed, slowly nodding, thinking that maybe she could use Goliath's leash to keep from losing her son. But before that thought was fully formed, Lola had another idea. Perhaps she could sneak a peek at the photography contest while they were there.

Sam's grip left Lola's arm as he ran to greet Matt.

"Coach, we're going to the fair tomorrow!" Sam cried, and Caleb saddled up beside him and bounced with joy as well. "Are you going?"

Matt bent and scooped both boys up, one in each muscular arm, squeezing them to his sides. He was covered in as much mud as they were, as if they'd all used it as war paint. "I suppose I will, sometime this weekend."

Sam's eyes grew wide with a sudden realization. "You can go with us!" he shouted, turning to Lola. "Mom, he can come with us, right?"

Lola froze, her mouth unable to form an answer as she watched Matt's eyebrows lift in surprise.

"That's a great idea," Rena decided as she and Gabe joined them. She wrapped a firm hand around Lola's arm and squeezed. "We can meet you three there and the boys can go on the rides together."

"And the men can drink beer together," Gabe added under his breath. Rena nudged an elbow in his stomach, making Gabe wheeze.

"Sure," Lola finally answered, nodding a little spastically. "I mean, if you want to…" she gestured toward Matt and then let her hand fall to her side. He looked just as stunned as she felt.

Clearing her throat, Rena looked between Matt and Lola and lifted an eyebrow. It seemed to snap Matt from his silence. He knelt to the ground to set Caleb and Sam on their feet, then ruffled a hand over Sam's golden hair.

"Sounds like fun," he answered. His blue eyes studied Sam and Caleb and finally landed on Lola. And slowly, much more slowly than Lola's blood was rushing through her veins and pumping to her heart, one corner of Matt's mouth lifted into a curious smirk.

Chapter Eleven

❧

"You know, Sam, you can call me Matt when we're not at baseball practice." The softly spoken words floated to Lola from the porch stairs. She watched from behind the thin lace curtain in her bedroom, saw Matt hold her son in a gentle hug against his chest after Sam had jumped into his arms in greeting.

"Okay, Coach." Sam covered his mouth and giggled, scrunching his shoulders to his ears in embarrassment. "I mean, Matt."

"That's more like it." Matt let Sam slide from his arms back to the stairs. He ruffled Sam's hair, which Lola now noticed was getting blonder by the day. They were cute standing there together, Sam mirroring Matt as he leaned against the railing and waited patiently for Lola. She was scared to go out there, scared to look into Matt's face and see the truth, the uncertainty, in his eyes. She pulled the curtain back and mustered her courage.

"Hey, guys!" she called down as she leaned out her window. She slipped a gold earring in her right ear and felt her hair brush over her jaw. "I'll be down in one minute."

Sam's shoulders dropped in frustration. "C'mon, Mom," he whined, "we're gonna be late! Caleb will go on all the rides without me."

Matt looked up at Lola and grinned. It made her heart jump so fast that her knees began to wobble. She smiled in return and then quickly backed away from the window until her legs hit the bed. She knew she should rush down the stairs, knew she'd been keeping Matt and Sam waiting long enough. But the extra minute she took to sit on the bed and steady her heart, to catch her breath and fan her warming cheeks was not only helpful - it was absolutely necessary.

"THIS SMELL IS MAKING my eyes water," Lola complained, covering her nose with one hand. She had a vice grip on Sam with the other hand.

"You're such a city girl," Matt teased. He led Sam and Lola into the barn at the north end of the Hope River Fair, grinning when he saw Sam's reaction to the animals.

"Baby pigs!" Sam shouted. He climbed up the wooden railing and leaned as far into the pig pen as he could. Lola and Matt stood behind him, their bodies close enough that their arms touched. It was a warm day, but it still made goose bumps rise on Lola's skin.

She looked up at Matt with a grimace. "You're not even bothered by the smell?" she asked.

Matt's eyes narrowed with laughter. "My uncle owns a farm in Wisconsin. I used to help him out in the summer. You get used to it after a while." He elbowed her playfully and then moved close to Sam, lifting him off the railing and farther into the pen so he could pet the piglets. Lola fished around in her purse for sanitizer and suddenly realized that someone was lifting her son into a stinky pig pen and she was hardly phased by it. Either she was too busy being bowled over by the smell, or she was actually beginning to lower her defenses about her son's safety.

They moved past the pens of cows and horses, Lola nearly gagging as the stench fried her nostrils, Sam becoming ever more excited about each animal. When they reached the end of the long barn, Lola burst from the building and gasped for air.

"Maybe we should visit the craft shed next," she said, rubbing a layer of sanitizer into her hands and then Sam's for the fifth time. Sam rolled his eyes at Matt.

"What?" Lola scolded. "These animals are full of germs, and I bet you'll be wanting to get your grimy fingers all over a corn dog in a little while." She eyed Matt, who studied her for a moment before holding his hands out as well. She squirted an extra-large blob of sanitizer on them and laughed as Matt rolled his eyes at Sam.

After the craft barn, which had Sam moaning over how boring handmade quilts, clothing, and jewelry were, they did indeed buy some corn dogs and sat together under the shade of a huge tree. Caleb found them there first, Rena and Gabe trailing behind, holding hands and flirting.

"Well, aren't you two cute?" Lola teased around a mouthful of food. "Where's Grace?"

Rena grinned. "My mother took her for the afternoon." She pointed a finger at Lola and raised an eyebrow. "Anne caught me a minute ago and said you're supposed to go to the Arts & Crafts barn at four o'clock." She frowned a little, waiting for an explanation.

Lola blushed and tried to concentrate on the corn dog in her hand. She licked ketchup from her finger, dabbed the corners of her lips with a napkin, and sighed. "I entered a few pictures in the photography contest. It was Anne's idea."

Matt's eyebrows shot up in surprise and Rena's lips popped into a perfect O. But before the questions could pour out, Caleb interrupted everyone.

"Mom, can me and Sam go on the bumper cars?" he pleaded, pulling on Rena's arm. Sam shoved the rest of his corn dog in his mouth and jumped up, his eyes begging Lola the same question.

"We'll take them," Gabe cut in. He motioned for Lola and Matt to stay put. "You two finish your lunch. We'll be back in a few minutes."

There were few people Lola trusted enough to take her son out of sight at a fair, and it surprised her that she found it so easy with a couple she had only met two weeks before. But without the slightest worry, she watched them walk toward the bumper cars, all four bodies linked together by their intertwined hands.

"They sure are a nice couple." Lola nibbled on a potato chip as she continued to watch them.

Matt nodded and finished his corn dog off in one bite. "Yeah, they're good together," he said, then washed his lunch down with a bottle of water.

"So, the photography contest, huh?" Matt asked, lifting a brow. His eyes seemed proud, somehow, and it made Lola's chest warm. She shrugged, turning quickly to hide her blush.

Lola reached absentmindedly to her ankle and scratched the raw skin there. She was so wrapped up in the painful satisfaction of scratching that it took her by surprise when Matt grabbed her hand.

"How long has that been there?" he asked, frowning as he studied the menacing red bumps on her skin. He released her hand and reached for her ankle, taking it gently in his fingers.

"I don't know, maybe a day?" A rush of panic spread through her at the look on Matt's face.

He ran a thumb over her ankle bone, up the length of her calf and stopped at her knee. Warning sirens slowly blazed to life in her brain as her skin hummed from his touch.

"Have you been walking in the woods the last few days?" Matt asked.

Lola cleared her throat anxiously. What had she managed to do now, catch jungle fever? "We went hiking in the Greenhills on Wednesday. What's wrong?" Her voice sounded squeaky, so she closed her eyes and took a steadying breath.

"I don't suppose you've heard of poison ivy."

When Lola opened her eyes, she found a questioning smirk on Matt's lips and a twinkle in his eyes. He glanced again at her leg, pushing the hem of her skirt just above the knee. "Small plant, three leaves, glossy green. Causes a rash of small bumps on the skin about a day after contact." He glanced at Lola and lifted an eyebrow. "Sound familiar?"

Matt's fingers glided from her knee up the side of her thigh, making her head spin. "Jesus, Lola, it goes all the way up-" He'd nearly reached her hip before Lola's hand covered his. She glanced around, suddenly thankful that the shade of the oak tree was protecting them from curious eyes.

He suddenly seemed to realize he wasn't at an accident scene or administering first aid, and Matt chuckled and leaned back in surprise. "Sorry... just... making sure you're all right." His eyes crinkled as he watched Lola, still pressing his hand against her hot skin, still staring at him in surprise. The sudden lust she felt from his warm touch made Lola clasp her hand tight over his. A feverish hunger flashed in his eyes and he smirked. "I could do a full body exam later, if you like."

Lola let out a surprised rip of laughter and pushed Matt over on the grass. She brought a hand to her chest to hold her fluttering heart in place and watched Matt pull himself upright. He grinned and rubbed a hand through his hair, watching as her fingers moved back to the red bumps on her leg.

"Scratching makes it spread," Matt warned, scooting beside her again. Taking her wrist in his hand, he pulled her toward him. Lola watched as his forehead scrunched and eyes narrowed.

"What were you doing, rolling in the stuff?" Now he had her arm in his hands, turning it over to inspect the irritating little bumps that traveled from her forearm to her elbow. His fingers traveled to her shoulder and lifted the hair from her neck, making her shiver.

"It's on your shoulder and neck too," he scolded, shaking his head. Although his voice had taken on the teacher tone, his blue eyes danced with humor. "You really are the Queen of Disaster, aren't you?"

Lola gave a helpless shrug and let out a breath of laughter. "So, what do I do for poison ivy?" The reality of it hit her quickly and she felt dread spread through her chest. Just what she needed - doctor visits, infection, medication...

Matt sighed. "Start by putting some calamine lotion on it for a few days. If it doesn't go away or gets worse, you'll need to see the doctor for a shot." He glanced at her leg again, at the bright sunflower dress that had slipped halfway up her thigh and her fingers as they rubbed over the raw skin. He elbowed her and shook his head. "Stop scratching."

Lola moaned and rested her chin on Matt's shoulder. The bumps were uncomfortable, but it seemed she could face just about any predicament with Matt by her side. She didn't want him to let go, didn't want him to stop looking at her with those protective, sexy blue eyes. "Is there anything you don't know how to fix, Mr. Dawson?" she asked quietly.

For a moment, Matt frowned. And then his eyes softened, his lips lifted in a gentle smile. "Just one thing," he answered, running a finger over her cheek. "But I'm working on it."

IT WAS LATE AFTERNOON before the bumper cars and fun house had lost their appeal, before stomachs ached from too many funnel cakes and tubs of fried cheese curds. The boys hitched rides on the men's backs and everyone looked ready to call it a day.

"I just have to stop and see Anne for a minute, baby," Lola said, brushing a finger over Sam's cheek. He laid his head on Matt's back, his arms draped comfortably around him, and let his eyes close.

"I think we'll head home," Rena said, checking her watch. She tucked a hand around Gabe's brawny arm and smiled. "Grace has probably worn my mother out by now."

Lola and Rena hugged goodbye and the boys gave exhausted waves. Lola faced the Arts & Crafts barn with jitters in her stomach. She frowned and rubbed her fingers absently over her elbow.

"Stop scratching," Matt murmured for the hundredth time, then took her hand in his. He pulled her gently toward the barn until she stopped and dug in like a mule.

"You don't have to come with me," she nearly whispered. Guilt and fear mixed in her chest. She looked at the man who'd been stuck with her all day, had bought endless tickets for games and rides and food even when she'd protested, and was now carting her son around on his back. Surely he just wanted to go home and relax.

Waves of insecurity and vulnerability passed over Lola and she realized, too, that she didn't want Matt to see her photography. She didn't want him to see her face when she spoke with Anne, when she saw that her pictures were nothing special and she'd failed.

"I can take Sam," Lola said, holding out her hands.

Matt glanced over his shoulder at the little boy who had faded into a light sleep. "It's all right. I like lugging the little guy around.

Besides," he added with a mischievous grin, "I want to see your photography."

Lola considered arguing. She was desperate to send him somewhere, anywhere else, but Matt grabbed Lola's hand and pulled her into the barn.

"Lola!" Anne cried, waving frantically from the far corner. Her smile was a mile wide and her eyes bright with excitement. "Get over here!"

A crowd was gathered around a wall of photographs in a collage of vivid colors and black and whites from floor to ceiling. Anne nearly jumped on Lola, taking her hand in her own and pulling her into the crowd.

"You won!" she squealed, shaking their hands with excitement. Others turned and smiled, patting her back and shoulders and arms in congratulations.

"Which one?" Lola finally murmured as she scanned the wall. Her eyes focused to take it all in - colors and textures that made her speechless, scenes that took her breath away. She saw not one, but three of her pictures had awards hanging from them. Two first-place blue ribbons, one second-place red. And while Anne continued to squeeze Lola's arm and go on in her ear about the judges and comments, Lola couldn't help but turn toward the back of the crowd, seeking the bright eyes and sweet smiles of the men who held her heart. They stood tall behind the others, Matt carrying Sam on his shoulders. A huge proud smile lit up Matt's face and Sam offered a sleepy grin and a thumbs-up.

At that moment, Lola couldn't think of a more perfect award in the world.

"Is this Lola Sommers?" a woman with a curious, high-pitched voice asked over the phone later that night. Lola frowned and sat up a little taller at the kitchen table. Her laptop was open in front of her and she had been slouching over her résumé, staring blankly at it for the last twenty minutes.

"Yes, this is she…" She rubbed her eyes and sighed. "Can I ask who's calling?"

"My name is Myra Jenson. Anne Ritz passed your phone number on."

Lola's frown transformed into a surprised scowl. She had seen Anne a few hours ago at the fair. She hadn't mentioned a thing about a Myra or a phone call.

"Hi Myra. What can I do for you?" Lola folded her legs beneath her on the kitchen chair and caught herself before she indulged in a good ankle scratch. The left side of her body was covered in a dried pink coating of calamine lotion. And still, it itched like crazy.

"I saw your photographs at the fair this afternoon, and I'm just floored, Lola. Your pictures are stunning, especially of the boy and his puppy in the hammock."

Lola felt a proud smile spread over her cheeks. "Thank you. That's actually a picture of my son and our boxer pup."

"Oh, honey, it about made me cry, it's so sweet! I'm calling to ask - what is your pricing like?"

Lola froze, her left hand hovering over the keypad of her computer. "My pricing?"

"I've never had professional pictures taken before, but now that my young grandchildren are visiting I think it's time I try it. They're all so fun at this age; I just have to capture their sweet little faces before they grow up."

Lola fumbled for words. "Um, Myra, I don't… I'm not…"

"You just name your price, honey, and I'll pay it. As far as I know there aren't any professional photographers within a forty mile radius, and I suspect you'd be the best anyway."

Lola cleared her throat, hoping she'd find her voice. She stood quickly, shoving her chair so fast that it nearly tipped backwards to the floor. Goliath jumped up from his slumber and skittered across the tile floor in fright.

"Myra, I have to be honest. I'm not a professional photographer. It's really just a hobby."

Myra's shrill voice fell into a long, happy laugh and she breathed out a whistle of surprise. "You could have fooled me! All of your pictures are so gorgeous, I figured it was your profession. Well," her voice lifted and Lola was sure she could hear a smile in her tone. "Would you like your first client?"

As she returned the phone to its cradle twenty minutes later, Lola was certain she had misunderstood. A stranger had just offered to pay a handsome amount of money for Lola's photography services. All it would take was one afternoon next week, her dependable Nikon camera, and the patience to photograph three small children at a park.

Could it really be this easy?

No, Lola decided. It couldn't be. She shook her head as she returned to her chair at the kitchen table. Her legs were tense from pacing the room and her hands trembled from the excitement.

It wasn't just taking the photos, Lola reminded herself. It was making sure they were good - no, excellent - and ensuring that the pictures would capture all three children in their most honest and gleeful moments. It was sorting through and choosing the best photos, developing them to perfection and presenting them so that Myra, *her first client* - Lola squeezed her eyes closed at the thought - would be completely and utterly satisfied.

Was this really happening?

Lola banged her laptop closed and jumped from her seat to grab the phone. Once again, her chair teetered and nearly fell, scaring Goliath once more. She dialed a familiar number with shaky fingers and raised the phone to her ear.

"Hi Anne, it's Lola," she began, trying to calm herself. She couldn't help the thrilled squeak in her voice. "I think I'll be in your shop a bit next week." She stretched her arms above her head, and in the soft moonlight that seeped through the kitchen window, indulged in a silent little dance.

HE WANTED TO BLAME it on the spring peepers, those tiny sand-colored frogs in the marsh behind his apartment that had the lungs of a piercing siren. About fifty of the little buggers, peeping in endless unison, were keeping Matt awake until the wee hours of the morning. He glanced at his clock for the hundredth time - 2:30 a.m. - then turned it around so the neon glow wouldn't blind him. Even the moon, perfectly round and bright outside his window, was incredibly annoying. He rolled over and beat his pillow with a fist.

Matt knew what was really keeping him awake. He closed his eyes and tried to invite sleep, but images of Lola continued to creep onto the screen of his mind. Her pretty sunflower skirt, bright and flowing just above her knees, its happy color accenting her golden legs. The whole long, curving, toned length of them.

Matt adjusted his pillow again, then rubbed one eye. Took a deep breath.

Next, Lola's smile popped onto the screen. Matt's gut warmed. He wanted to kiss those tiny dimples at the corners of her mouth. He knew when she was really happy, when she found something really worth a smile or a laugh because those dimples would appear, like little gifts to the person who'd incited them. And Sam. Sam was special. Damn if he didn't like that kid more than any he'd ever known. He could make Matt smile with just a little grin or by simply running into his arms and crushing him with hugs. Sam may be tiny, Matt mused, but his personality was huge, once he trusted someone enough to show it.

It was a strange feeling, the way Sam made Matt feel so special. He imagined it was the kind of feeling he would have had as a father.

But what frustrated Matt most, and was really causing this sleepless night, was that he didn't know what to do with Lola. Only a week ago, after holding her in his arms, dancing to soft music and losing himself in their surprising make-out session, she had told him that it was a mistake.

No, what had she called it? *A bad idea.* Even worse.

But Matt sensed something in her - a need, an ache to be together. He felt it when they were close, he could see it in her eyes and feel it when they touched. They'd been together the entire day, had touched and teased and flirted, held hands as if it was the most natural thing in the world. What the hell was he supposed to do with that?

Matt was sure the only real thing he would get out of this deal was heartache. Lola and Sam's time in this small town had an expiration date, and every day, every tick of the clock, was a reminder of that. Matt could spend all the time with them that he wanted, enjoy their days and laughter and fun together, but in August there would only be one outcome. Lola and Sam would return to California, and Matt would once again be nursing a lonely heart.

He rolled onto his stomach and yanked the pillow over his head. Perhaps suffocation would help with this sleep problem, he thought. With weary exasperation, he pulled the edges of the pillow in tighter.

Chapter Twelve

❦

It turned out that Goliath was the one that made Tuesday's photography session such a success. As Lola quickly discovered, it was hard work keeping three little girls, ages four months to five years, smiling and cheerful for two hours straight. Especially all at the same time. But give them a puppy to play with and not only were there endless smiles, but also the glowing, twinkle-eyed, mouth-wide-open laughter that was so fun to capture on camera. And Goliath hadn't seemed to mind the attention at all.

Which was lucky, because at first Lola hadn't been sure if it was smart to let Sam bring the puppy. But she'd wanted Sam to behave and to keep busy while she was working with her very first client, and it seemed a decent idea.

Now, Lola sat on a blanket in the afternoon sun, Goliath snoring beside her while Sam and Caleb ran through sprinklers on the lawn. She balanced the laptop on her knees as she clicked through the pictures of the girls, admiring their matching pink dresses and the little silk bows in their hair. Even the baby had worn a pretty pink bow velcroed to a wisp of curls, and in most pictures she was squealing with delight. The perfectly timed extra-large bottle of milk had helped, and so had Goliath's soft nuzzles and gentle kisses.

The three year old had been hesitant at first, Lola mused, but in the end she was rolling around in the grass with Goliath as well, letting him nibble on the frills of her sleeve. Myra had been so excited about the session that she'd pulled Lola into a hug at the end, her face beaming and her voice high-pitched with excitement. "I haven't laughed this hard in years!" she'd exclaimed.

Smiling at the thought, Lola wrapped her arms around herself and squeezed. She hadn't enjoyed herself that much in years, either.

Lola stretched her bare feet in front of her and lifted her face to the warm sun. At that very moment, life was nearly perfect. Her son was happy, healthy, and safe. They were basking in a relaxing and carefree summer in a town that offered an unexpected coziness, almost a feeling of being home. And for the first time ever, Lola was excited about a job.

"Photographer," she whispered, trying out the title. She could see herself pursuing it, feel the potential for a real career in it. If only she was brave enough.

Lola squinted one eye at the boys, drenched and laughing uncontrollably, and felt her heart flutter. Sam was *happy*. So happy that it made her chest swell. She hadn't expected Hope River to heal her little boy or to give her a new direction in life.

Fiddling absently with her wedding ring, Lola considered. Perhaps there was something to this photography thing, a new profession she had never considered. Would she let herself dream of it, believe in it?

She glanced down at her hand, her ring hanging sideways on her finger, and touched the small diamond setting. Was she brave enough to move on with life, she wondered? To give in to new adventures? And to a new love?

THE FOLLOWING AFTERNOON LOLA found herself behind the counter at Anne's photo shop, the two of them admiring the pictures of the three girls. They clicked through the photos on Anne's computer, taking their time with each one, laughing over the sweet expressions Lola had captured. Sam was spending the afternoon at Caleb's, so the shop was silent except for the crooning women.

"Myra is going to flip when she sees these," Anne reassured. She squeezed Lola's arm and grinned so wide that it made Lola's throat tight. "You really do have an eye for photography, Lola."

Goose bumps lifted on Lola's arms. She had to share her exhilaration before she burst. "God, it was fantastic," she gushed. "I could have taken pictures all afternoon. I'm still pumped. I wish I could do it again."

Anne turned to Lola and folded her arms over her chest. "Then why don't you?"

The flush was quick to flood Lola's cheeks. She shrugged, wishing she hadn't let the yearning in her voice get away from her. "Oh, I couldn't...it's just not..." She shook her head, keeping her eyes on the computer screen and away from Anne's curious ones. "It's just too risky. I'm not professionally trained - I never even finished my college degree. It wouldn't be a stable job and I need to find something that works with Sam's schedule." She frowned and shook her head harder, trying to push away the hope.

Anne clucked her tongue. "You're not giving yourself enough credit, Lola." She pinched Lola's chin and made her turn and look her in the eye. "You're *talented*, young lady. You could make a good living from it."

Lola flushed harder and fumbled for more excuses. "I don't think I'd get many clients in San Francisco. The competition would be stifling."

"Who's talking about San Francisco?" Anne cried, waving a hand carelessly in the air. "Hope River could use a good photographer. Heck, you could set up that back room as a studio. It hasn't been used in years." She threw an annoyed glance to the darkened room behind them, then grew still. For a moment, she frowned, until slowly her face bloomed like a flower discovering sunlight.

"That's actually not a bad idea," Anne nearly whispered, her eyes wide at the thought.

"Oh, Anne, I couldn't..." Lola frantically shook her head, trying to deny what an enticing idea it was. "We have a home back in California, and... Travis' family is there. Sam is comfortable at his school and, and our friends..." her voice hitched as she eyed Anne with desperation, begging her not to consider it.

They stared at one another in silence until Anne wrapped a reassuring hand over Lola's shoulder. "Seems to me that you have just as many friends and family in Hope River. And you're happy here - there's a light in your eyes now that I didn't see when you first arrived." Returning her gaze to the pictures on the computer, Anne tapped one of Sam laughing and playing with Goliath at the park. "That handsome little boy sure seems happy too."

Lola shifted her feet and nibbled her lip, staring intently at the screen. A million reasons to say yes to such a crazy idea ran wild through her mind. But fear was a stronger persuader.

And at the moment, it was winning.

"DO YOU HAVE PLANS Saturday evening?" Rena asked Lola as she handed Grace to her willing arms. They stood together in the baseball field parking lot as Rena pulled a cooler of snacks and drinks from her minivan.

Lola's bottom lip jutted out. "No plans. Why?" She made a goofy face at Grace and watched her lean backward in giggles. Her fingers reached and grasped a lock of Lola's hair.

"Grace, no no, honey. That hurts Lola." Rena squeezed her daughter's hand until it popped open and freed Lola's hair.

"My sister is getting married," Rena continued. "It's a last minute thing. I'm not so sure about the guy she's saying 'I do' to, but I want to be supportive." She glanced at Lola, whose eyebrows rose in surprise. "I know. She just announced it last week. I don't know why she can't do things the normal way." Yanking on the handle of the cooler, she maneuvered it to roll behind her, then shoved the van door closed. "Anyway, my gift is to pay for the photographer."

Lola stopped smooching on Grace's cheek and frowned. "Who's the photographer?" she asked.

"I was hoping it would be you."

If she hadn't been holding Grace so tight in her arms, she might have dropped her. She let the surge of surprise wash over her before locating her voice. "I... I would *love* to. Are you sure?"

"Of course I'm sure. I wouldn't ask you if I wasn't. After I saw your photos at the fair I knew you'd be perfect."

"Rena, I'd be honored. Thank you," Lola breathed, and squished a kiss into Grace's chubby cheek in celebration.

"There is one condition, though," Rena added, making Lola turn quickly. "You can't laugh at the bridesmaid dress she's making me wear. In fact, you have to promise to take as few pictures of me as possible. The dress is *mustard* color, Lola. It looks like something from Grace's diaper." Rena shuddered at the thought and Lola let out a whoop of laughter.

The women threw themselves into planning as they reached the bleachers. They settled into their seats, Lola handing Grace over as she tried to settle her excitement and sort her thoughts. Portrait ideas, camera equipment, details of where and when and how all filtered through her brain. She'd need a sitter for Sam, she realized. But before her mind could chew on that thought, movement in the baseball diamond caught her attention. The tall, lean man who walked to the bleachers seemed to catch everyone's eye.

"Good evening, folks," Matt said with a smile. His voice was strong and steady and he stood before everyone with hands on his hips. Lola could easily imagine him commanding an unruly classroom of teenagers.

"We're going to play a full game with the kids tonight, practice all of the skills they've been learning these last weeks. It gets a little chaotic though, so we'll need some volunteers."

Two young fathers clomped down the bleachers toward Matt. An older, eager woman joined them, a baseball glove under her arm. Matt greeted them with a handshake and thumps on the back.

In the outfield the children wiggled with excitement, cheering and waving. Near third base, a little body jumped, arms flailing with effort.

"Mom!" Sam hollered, gesturing both hands wildly. "Mom! C'mon! Come and play!" His voice was full of pride, and like a terrier puppy greeting a favorite visitor, he jumped up and down, nearly panting with the effort.

Lola frowned and gave a quick shake of her head. She waved her hand in a silent no. But Sam persisted. "C'mon Mom! Please!?" he begged.

It was the pitiful puppy eyes that finally made Lola stand and follow the others to the field. She glanced back at Rena, who laughed and gave an encouraging thumbs-up, then joined the adults near home plate.

Matt's frown as she stood beside him told Lola all she needed to know. He sent the others to various positions on the field, then turned and stared.

"You're kidding, right?" he asked.

"What? I can handle it."

Matt looked down at her feet, at her bright pink toes, his eyes dancing. "You're wearing flip flops and a skirt," he said, as if Lola hadn't noticed.

She planted her hands on her hips. "So? I don't have to run the bases, do I?"

Matt scowled, but Lola could see a small twitch of laughter building. "I don't think it's a good idea. You can't even walk in bare feet without tripping. Remember last time you were out here?"

Lola returned the scowl and absently lifted a hand to her temple. "I'll watch for flying balls this time." She planted her flip flops solidly in the dirt and lifted her chin. She was determined to do this simply because he thought she couldn't.

With a sigh, Matt grabbed a glove from the dusty ground and set it on top of her head, palm open like a leather hat. "You're sticking close to me, then. You can be catcher." He started to back away, and finally, his cheeks spread into a wide grin that made Lola's knees wobble. "Keep your eyes up," he warned.

"Go, Lola!" Rena called from the stands, cheering and pumping her fist, an amused grin on her face. She lifted Grace's arms and pumped them as well.

Shaking her head and willing the blush to stay away, Lola refused to scan the stands. She was already certain that every pair of eyes was watching her with an abundance of curiosity.

THE GAME MOVED ALONG smoothly, with Matt pitching and Lola scrambling after the ball. The children swung until they made contact, each of them getting a chance to run the bases. Gabe and the other adults in the outfield made sure to take their time returning the ball to home plate.

Matt orchestrated the game with ease, and, to Lola's annoyance, kept a close eye on her. More than once he'd sent her a scolding glance or shake of his head when she dared to trip over her flip flops or drop the ball on her foot. With his eyes constantly on her, and with all of the bending and chasing, she was thankful she had chosen her comfy denim skirt for the evening. Its thick, strong fabric was straight over her hips and didn't flutter in the evening breeze.

Once in a while a kid would crack the baseball just right and send it to the outfield, causing the crowd to cheer like it was the World Series. Little legs hustled around the diamond, sometimes missing a base or heading in the wrong direction, but they would always make it home to a cheering crowd before the ball was tossed back to Lola.

At the end of the game, when Lola's arm was actually tired from lobbing the balls to the pitcher's mound, Matt announced that he would hit the last ball. He sent the kids to the outfield, promising that he'd hit it far. Some children hugged the bases, hoping to catch a grounder, while others placed themselves against the outfield fence in hopes of witnessing a home run. No matter where they stood, their little bodies wriggled in anticipation of how strong their coach was.

Lola was certain that Coach was strong. She'd been studying his biceps for the last hour, nearly drooling over his forearms as he caught and threw the ball. His quick and powerful legs, his tight waist and broad chest that Lola decided she'd like to get her hands on… had all mesmerized her enough to nearly cause another head injury. With a frustrated sigh, she backed as far from home plate as possible and nearly passed out when Matt bent in front of her with baseball bat at the ready. He pointed to left field, making the children in that area squeal with excitement.

Panic rose in Lola's throat as she watched Gabe wind up his pitch. She took another step back and clutched at her glove. "God, he's going to kill me," she whimpered, shrinking against the chain-linked backstop.

Matt turned at home plate and offered a smug grin. "The ball won't make it to you, don't worry." He swung the bat a few times in practice.

The crowd rippled with laughter behind Lola. Rena shouted and whistled to Gabe and he gave her a heart-stopping smile. And then he leaned forward and focused.

A true fear of Gabe's strength made every muscle in Lola's body tighten. She might have made a run for it, hidden in the stands behind the safety of the backstop, but his quick smile and wink in her direction kept her flip flops planted in place. He lined his body up and lifted his arm for a fast pitch.

For Lola, it wasn't hard to imagine these men in their youth; Gabe the cocky pitcher and Matt the all-star hitter, both twitching with strength and eagerness. The crowd howled in excitement now, as they likely had years ago, all eyes on Matt as he bent and squared his shoulders.

Raising his hand behind his shoulder, Gabe's body moved with the momentum and skill of a seasoned pitcher. With one prayerful gulp of air, Lola closed her eyes and held her glove in front of her face. The air hissed with movement and she heard a loud crack followed by cheering from the stands. She peeked over the tip of her glove, watching the ball arc through the evening sky to left field. It landed with a thud on the soft grass beside the fence, and every single child let out a war cry as they charged in one direction, their little legs and outstretched arms focused on the same goal.

It was mayhem from there. Gabe shouted at the kids to throw him the ball while jumping wildly at the pitcher's mound. Matt jogged to first base, laughing and trying to stay upright as he watched the hilarious scene unfold. The kids dove for the ball, bodies over bodies, scrambling and pushing and grabbing until one little girl crawled from beneath the pile with her fingers clenched in victory. She ran a few feet, threw the ball to a friend who in turn twirled and threw it forward. When Matt passed second base the kids screamed and swarmed toward him. Lola planted herself on home plate and held her glove in the air, laughing and shouting with the others. The crowd behind her was wild on its feet.

Sam caught the ball next. He threw it hard enough to reach Gabe's glove, but by then Matt had passed third base. A few children had caught up to him, grabbing his arms and legs and pulling on his shirt. Their little feet lifted off the ground, but Matt continued to charge forward as they dangled from his body. They laughed and screamed and clung to him and it seemed it was all Matt could do to keep himself from tipping over in a fit of hilarity.

"Catch, Lola!" Gabe shouted, and Lola lifted her eyes just in time to see the ball racing toward her head. She opened her glove, squeezed her eyes shut, and felt the sting of the ball smack into her palm. Her glove closed securely around it, and at the same time as she opened her eyes, she thrust her arm toward Matt and the dangling, cheering children.

The look in Matt's eyes should have warned her. She knew too late that tagging him was the least of her worries. Soon she would be fresh road kill. With the momentum he'd built she knew the impact was coming. She braced herself, and with laughter that she couldn't hold inside, watched it unfold in slow motion.

Later, when she'd replay the scene in her mind, she knew her favorite part would be Matt's expression. The children clinging to him like ticks and dropping off behind him in a cloud of dust had been pretty hilarious too. But it was the look of pure joy in Matt's eyes that she loved the most. He was so sincere, so real. And so darn strong, which she noticed when he plowed into her, arms open wide so he could pick her up and whisk her across home plate along with the other ten screaming children. And just as quickly as he'd swept her up, he set Lola down before tumbling to the dusty ground with every single child piled on top of him. For a moment he was nearly covered from head to toe by wriggling, giggling, hysterical little bodies.

It took a few minutes for Lola to peel the children from him. When she found Matt beneath the layers, he was covered in dust and grinning like a child himself. She set kids upright, dusting them off and sending them to their parents with triumphant smiles.

"You even have dirt in your ears," Lola laughed as she watched Matt pull himself to his feet. She rubbed dust from his earlobe and couldn't resist giving it a little tug.

"You enjoyed that, didn't you?" he said with a dry smile. "Watching them mob me like that." He rubbed a dirty hand over his ribs, checking to see if they were all intact.

"I'm just glad you didn't run me over."

Stepping in front of him, Lola shook her head and surveyed his dusty face. "You're filthy. It looks like the kids mugged you." She licked her thumb and lifted it to the smudges on his cheek. Matt froze, staring at her with wide, panicked eyes. Only when she paused an inch from his cheek and grinned with devilish charm did he realize she was teasing.

"That's disgusting," Matt moaned.

"But you were going to let me, weren't you?" she laughed.

"I was paralyzed with fear." Matt grabbed Sam's shoulders as he ran up beside him. He pulled him in close, giving the boy a friendly shake.

"Does she do this to you?" he asked, and Sam only laughed and skipped toward the long grass, kicking white fuzz from the tips of dandelions.

Dusk quickly settled as the crowd walked to parked cars and trickled onto sidewalks. The echoes of excited voices replaying the evening's events floated back to Lola. Her heart felt light as she listened, as she watched her son skip through the field to chase grasshoppers.

"I think I swallowed dirt," Matt announced, clearing his throat. He rubbed his eye with a dirty finger and then, showing pure exhaustion from the evening, dropped his hand to his side. Impulsively, Lola slipped her hand over his and squeezed.

"Thank you," she said softly. She smiled up at Matt's surprised eyes and continued to hold his hand.

His forehead wrinkled curiously. "For what?"

Lola laughed. "For letting me play tonight." She swallowed the lump in her throat and rubbed her thumb over the back of Matt's hand. "I can't remember the last time I laughed so hard." She squeezed his hand once more before releasing it. She would have liked to hold it longer, to lean her body against him and feel his lips on hers. The memory of wrapping herself in his arms, falling into his kiss, made her shiver. But she knew Sam was nearby, and others watched them as well. Instead she stopped beside the truck and lifted her eyes to Matt's.

He surprised her as he leaned in close and reached for her face. "I like to see you laugh," he said, gently pinching her chin.

Before Lola could respond, before she could lean inches forward and taste his dusty lips, Sam was beside them. He was a wiggling, sweaty ball of energy.

"You're just as filthy as your coach," Lola teased, stepping away from Matt. She ran a hand over Sam's damp hair and made a face at the wreckage of his clothes. But the grimy child didn't seem to bother Matt. He plucked him from the ground, lifted him over his shoulder and pretended to throw him in the back of the Chevy. "You'll have to ride back there tonight," he teased, making Sam squeal with delight.

Lola studied their giggles and rough-housing, their identical dirt and sweat-covered skin, their rumbling laughter. She rubbed the side of her neck as the thought hit her.

"Hey, Coach," she said, watching as Matt set Sam on the ground and wrapped a strong arm around his shoulders. He turned toward Lola, only half listening as he assaulted the boy with tickles.

"I'm looking for someone to watch Sam on Saturday night while I'm working at Rena's sister's wedding. You wouldn't happen to know anyone I could trust, would you?" She tried her best to put on a thoughtful expression.

Matt lifted Sam from the ground, holding him at eye-level. "I do happen to know *one* very good sitter," he said. He raised an eyebrow at Sam. "I hear he has a lot of experience with kids and he's never lost one. Yet."

Sam giggled as he wrapped an arm around Matt's shoulder, his other hand resting on his dirt-streaked chest. He glanced hopefully at Lola and then back to Matt. "You?" he asked with a grin.

"Only if your mom doesn't mind us eating pizza and watching cool guy movies all night."

Lola crossed her arms over her chest and scowled. She pretended to consider as Sam held his breath and crossed his fingers. Finally, she grinned and nodded.

"Yes!" Sam cheered. He jumped so hard in Matt's arms that he nearly tumbled out before Matt planted his feet firmly back on the ground.

"Pizza and movies!" Sam yelled, skipping around the truck. He stopped with a sudden thought and big round eyes when he reached the tailgate. "Can we stay up 'til nine o'clock?"

Matt glanced at Lola in questioning surprise. *The kid's never stayed up til nine o'clock?* his eyes implored. Lola flushed and laughed, covering her eyes with a hand, and Matt turned back to Sam and grinned wide. "Buddy, we might even stay up until nine-*thirty.*"

If he'd announced that ice cream was free for the rest of their lives, Sam could not have shown more excitement.

Chapter Thirteen

✧

"**W**as that an awesome guys' night, or what?" Matt whispered. He took the stairs to Sam's room slowly, savoring the warmth of the little boy's body against his chest, his head snuggled into his shoulder. Matt could feel Sam's cheeks lift in a smile against his neck.

"It was *totally* awesome," Sam sighed.

As Matt laid the boy in his bed, Sam's eyes closed and his breathing grew deep. Matt tucked the blanket under his chin and stood over him, watching for a moment. He studied the way Sam smiled while he slept and the soft pink shade of his cheeks.

Turning off the bedside lamp, Matt sighed at the conflict in his heart. He was head over heels for this boy. And head over heels for his mother. And even knowing the consequences of falling so hard for them, he couldn't change the way he felt.

By the time the old Chevy's headlights filled the darkness of the kitchen, Matt was half asleep on the family room couch, Goliath snoring beneath his arm. He didn't hear the porch door creak open. When Lola finally leaned in the doorway of the family room, Matt stretched his arms and yawned. He rubbed the haze from his eyes and smiled at Lola.

"Hey." Lola smiled wide at Matt, her eyes sparkling like champagne.

"How'd it go?" he asked, his voice husky with sleep.

The way her smile lit up her entire face, Matt already knew the answer. She was beaming. And so damn beautiful.

"It was amazing," Lola began as she settled beside Matt. He watched her fall into the cushions of the couch, felt her shoulder brush against his. With an oath of self-control, he crossed his arms over his chest.

"I had so much fun. It felt like I was only there for twenty minutes. Before I knew it the bride was throwing the bouquet and the couple was off in their limousine. I can't believe I just got paid to be a part of it." Lola squeezed her hands together in her lap and sighed wistfully.

"You should have seen the cake, Matt," she continued, her eyes wide. She turned and brushed her fingertips over his arm, unaware of the shivers she caused. "It was like someone painted the design on. I've never seen anything like it. I took some fantastic pictures of it. And the flowers!" She lifted her hands in the air at the thought. "Pink tulips and white calla lilies - they were absolutely stunning."

Lola sucked in a breath, her smile still wide, then seemed to realize she'd been talking nonstop since she'd nestled beside him. She turned to Matt, blushing at the way he watched her. "How was Sam?"

Matt grinned as he brushed the back of his fingers over her cheek. Why would his hands never do what they were told? He quickly tucked his fingers tight beneath his arm. "He was great. Out cold by 8:30. I did everything I could to keep him up past nine, but it was a losing battle."

Lola nodded, smiling fondly at the thought. "He's an early bird, always has been. Did he eat well for you?"

"Every last bite. We had a contest, who could shove the most chicken nuggets in their mouth at once."

Lola's eyes widened in alarm. Her silence told Matt that he should have kept that little tidbit to himself.

"I won," he added promptly, hoping to soothe her panic. "Sam had two - one in each cheek - and I topped out at twelve."

Lola's eyes grew even wider. "Twelve? You can shove twelve chicken nuggets in your mouth?"

"I could have done more, but he made me laugh. It wasn't pretty."

He was glad to see her eyes soften, her lips widen into an appalled smile.

"Speaking of not pretty," he added quickly, "how awful did Rena look in that bridesmaid dress?" He was looking forward to teasing her. Great ammunition for the next time she decided to get cheeky.

Lola slapped her hands on her legs and let out a low groan. "It was *horrendous*," she muttered, squeezing her eyes closed.

"Gabe showed me the dress yesterday. He thinks Rena should save it for Halloween next year, make a wicked witch costume out of it." He laughed at the thought.

"I tried not to take too many full-body pictures of Rena, but I had to get a few group shots of the wedding party. The rest I aimed for shoulders up. She made me swear five times that I wouldn't show anyone when I develop them."

They laughed for a moment before a huge yawn consumed Lola. She stretched, kicking off her black heeled sandals with the movement. "God, my feet are aching. I should have known better than to wear these today. I haven't been on my feet for that long in ages."

Matt studied her slender feet and painted toenails. "You probably haven't worn shoes for that long in ages," he teased.

She waved him off with a grin and rested her head on the back of the couch. The faint glow of the moon filtered through the window behind them, accenting her profile. Her nose turned up slightly at the tip, Matt noticed, and there was an elegant shadow below her cheekbone. Her upper lip curved and dipped like an hour glass. She left him nearly breathless.

"Let me see those toes," Matt said. Although she looked tired, he wasn't yet ready to leave. He needed to touch her again, and her feet seemed safe enough. He lifted Goliath from under his arm, laying him gently on Lola's lap. Moving to the end of the couch, he held his hands out in expectation. Lola glanced at him from the corner of her eye and frowned.

"You don't want to touch my feet. I've been on them all evening."

Matt rolled his eyes. "I'm a sports coach and a paramedic. You really think your tired feet will bother me?"

Lola considered, then slid sideways on the couch. She leaned against the arm, gently laying a foot in Matt's hand. As he squeezed the stress from her feet, he could hear everything around him relax. Goliath breathed heavily, falling back to sleep. Outside a whippoorwill sang its endless song. The house settled and creaked, and Lola moaned as she buried her body further into the couch. Her eyes fluttered with relief, her chest rose and fell in slow, even rhythm.

"You have magic hands," Lola whispered. She sighed as he ran his fingers along the soft skin of her foot.

Matt sighed. "I wish they really could perform magic," he answered quietly. He concentrated on her warm toes, brushing a thumb over the pretty nails. "I used to rub Ali's feet a lot. I didn't know how else to help when she was so sick at the end."

Lola opened her eyes and studied Matt. Absently, she twisted the ring on her finger. "Ali was lucky to have you."

Matt let out a quick breath of air. Lucky wasn't exactly the word he would have used. It wouldn't have been Ali's choice either, he knew. She had been miserable in Hope River, miserable with him after the baby died. Her life could have been so different if she'd never met him. Her ending so much less tragic.

His hands skimmed over Lola's ankle and he moved his fingers to rub the curve of her calf.

"Tell me more about your night," he said, desperately needing to change the subject. "What was your favorite part of the evening to photograph?"

Lola smiled and settled back into the couch, her body relaxing. She slowly closed her eyes, bringing the evening back to her.

"The exchanging of the vows," she answered softly. Her smile widened until dimples peeked from the corners of her mouth. "They were so honest, so real. They wrote their own, and when they read them," Lola laid a hand over her heart, "it was incredibly romantic. Their smiles were shining, and their eyes twinkled with tears... I just love that I captured it for them." She opened her eyes to find Matt grinning at her.

"Have you always loved photography?" he asked.

Nibbling on her bottom lip, Lola considered. "I've always had an interest in it. It was my major in college before I dropped out." She tried to give a careless shrug, but Matt knew better.

"Do you ever think about pursuing it?" he asked. He switched to her other foot, starting at the toes and working his way down.

Lola chewed on Matt's question. He watched different expressions pass over her face, her eyes flicker with hope and then quick disappointment. Finally, she rubbed her cheeks with her hands and sighed.

"If I had the luxury of letting myself dream, then yes, a career in photography would be wonderful. But I don't. I have Sam and the life we've built. I am solely responsible for him and his future."

Lola shrugged helplessly, watching Matt's hands pause as he listened. "I can't go back to school right now. And I can't start up a new business in San Francisco just like that. I owe Sam as much stability and normalcy as possible."

Matt's heart sank fast. He remained silent, resuming a massage on her calf, concentrating on his hands. He felt it building, a frustration and resentment that he couldn't quite find the source of. The words tumbled out before he could check them. "Seems like you already have something started here." *With a business, with this town...with me,* he wanted to add.

Lola wiggled her toes and shook her head, her eyes dimming hopelessly. "I couldn't do that," she said quietly. She ran fingers absently through her hair, over and over, lost in thought.

"Sam and I..." she lifted her knees to her chest, wrapped her arms around them in a protective gesture, "...we have a home in San Francisco. He was comfortable in his old school, with his old friends. He's already been through so much change." Her eyes were pleading, begging Matt to smother the flicker of hope he offered. "This is just supposed to be a summer vacation. We're going back to normal - our new normal - in a month. I can't just..."

It pained Matt to see Lola's eyes fill with such frustration, such misery. He didn't want to hurt her, to make her life, or Sam's, any more painful than it already had been. He touched her chin with a gentle finger and lifted it until her eyes met his.

"Hey," Matt said calmly, trying to smile kindly, to hide the burst of emotion and disappointment he felt in his gut. "Don't worry about it. You'll figure everything out. Nothing has to be solved this minute." He tried hard to keep his voice soft and soothing, and Lola seemed to feed off it. She pursed her lips, and nodding in agreement, closed her eyes as Matt's fingers left her skin.

Perhaps it was time to head home, Matt thought. And to finally let go of any hope that they could be something, anything, together.

"How long did you keep Ali's things after she died?" Lola asked quietly. Her eyes were still closed and her voice soft. Matt turned and studied her for a moment, surprised at the question. He shook his head, trying to rearrange his thoughts.

Clasping his hands together in his lap, he took a deep breath and cleared his throat. "I gave a lot of it to her family after she died. It took me a few months to give her clothes to a shelter. A few years to pack up her pictures and some little things around our house."

Lola gave a slow nod. "Most of Travis' things are still in our house," she whispered, searching his eyes for some sort of understanding. Matt watched her face scrunch in fresh pain. "His clothes take up half of my closet. I looked at them every morning when I dressed. His toothbrush is still in the cabinet next to mine. Even his keys are still hanging beside the door." Lola shook her head sadly. "Part of me never wants to return to our place so I don't have to face the memories. But another part can't let go."

Matt knew he should say something, anything to reassure her that it was okay. But her sad face proved the opposite. She wanted to move on, she really did. She simply wasn't ready.

"I still have her wedding ring," Matt said quietly. He glanced down at his own naked fingers and bit the inside of his lip. "Locked away in a drawer where I'll never look at it. But I still know it's there."

He watched Lola's gaze move to her own ring. She turned it upside down, wiggled it back and forth, and then covered it with her other hand. Taking a large, noisy breath, she brought both hands to her forehead. An apologetic smile spread on her lips.

"You must think I'm such a mess," she laughed quietly. She peeked at him, shaking her head when she saw him smiling.

"You are a mess," he teased softly. "But only because of your flip-flops and your need to fix everything on your own." He leaned back on the couch, listening to the crickets and the breeze outside. "Otherwise, I think you're pretty normal."

"Well, thanks, I guess."

Goliath lifted his head and sighed as if exhausted by their conversation. His tongue curled out and unfolded with a big yawn, a tiny squeak erupting from him at the effort. He stood, still wobbly from sleep, and padded over Lola before tumbling to the floor. His skin and fur flopped as he shook himself from side to side.

"Little guy still needs to grow into his body," Matt said as he eyed the pup. "He's going to be a big dog." He bent over to rub Goliath between the eyes, getting an appreciative groan in return. "If he grows into those paws, I bet he'll be close to a hundred pounds."

Lola's eyebrows lifted in worry. "A *hundred* pounds? What am I going to do with you?" she asked Goliath, and he wiggled in delight at the thought. Then he scurried into the kitchen.

"I'll take him out before I go," Matt said, standing quickly. He followed Goliath before Lola could uncurl herself from the couch.

OUTSIDE, THE NIGHT WAS cool, the creek burbling peacefully. Matt watched Goliath in the moonlight, sniffing for just the right place to relieve himself, and gulped in a huge breath of air.

A hell of a mess he'd gotten himself in, he decided. He couldn't deny his feelings for Lola, or his soft spot for Sam. But he didn't have to act on them either. Perhaps the best thing for everyone was to spend less time together, to step back and visit only during baseball games so that by the end of summer it would be easier to say goodbye. He'd return to the routine of teaching in the fall, with barely the time to think about them anyway. It was for the best.

Goliath bumped into Matt's shins with clumsy vigor. He scooped the puppy into his arms and let him nuzzle his cheek, his wet nose leaving damp prints on his skin.

"Don't get too attached, little guy," Matt whispered, rubbing his fingertips over the velvety fuzz of Goliath's neck. "Not much longer and you'll be returning home."

As GOLIATH WORE CIRCLES on his bed in the kitchen, Matt cleared a cup of milk from the table, pouring the waste down the sink. He gave the shiny new faucet a sturdy tug to check that it still worked properly, then walked to the family room to say goodnight.

Lola was sound asleep on the couch. Her eyelids were soft and heavy, her skin like a silk rose. One hand lay on her heart, the other limp over her belly. Her chest rose and fell in peaceful, deep breaths.

It was the second time Matt had found her like this, and she was just as beautiful tonight as she had been that warm day on the grass. Her hair was a waterfall over her shoulder, splaying softly in the hollow of her neck. The creamy skin of her chest revealed a smattering of flirty freckles. Her lace-edged blouse had slipped to the side, exposing one smooth shoulder, and her legs were long and gorgeous, stretched to reveal every muscle and graceful curve.

Matt cursed himself for standing there, for watching her sleep. He simply couldn't pull his eyes away. He could barely keep from pulling her into his arms and carrying her to bed. But no, it would be too tempting to crawl in beside her. And if she woke, which she probably would, she would know he'd crossed the fine line that she had drawn between them.

With a fitful sigh, Matt pulled a blanket from the back of a nearby chair. He laid it gently on Lola's legs and settled it over her shoulders.

One last kiss, he promised himself as he bent to touch his lips to her forehead. He lingered on her warm skin, rubbed a soft finger over her cheek. And then turned and walked away without looking back.

Chapter Fourteen

❧

"Do you miss me yet?"

Lola held the cell phone to her ear and gulped a bottle of water as she listened to her ex-coworker's giddy voice. She imagined Jill would faint if she saw Lola covered in sweat and mowing the lawn.

"I bet you're bored out of your mind by now, aren't you?" Jill teased.

"Actually, I haven't had time to get bored yet," Lola answered, wiping the moustache of sweat from her lip. "My aunt's place is a lot of work, and Sam's been keeping me busy with baseball practice and play dates." Exhaustion suddenly swamped her body, so she leaned against the corner of the house for support. As her arm brushed the siding, thin strips of paint fluttered to the grass.

"So, what are you actually doing there? Like, dusting and housework and stuff?"

Lola rolled her eyes. She thumbed the siding and watched the paint flake into her hand. "No, like, mowing the lawn and fixing broken faucets," she answered with a grin. *Breaking* the faucets was more like it, she admitted with an inward giggle. And finding a delectable handyman to help clean up her mess.

"You know how to mow the lawn? Lola Sommers, I can't even

imagine it!" Jill howled on the other end of the phone and then her voice muffled into the background. "Listen," she said, returning to Lola. "I'm at work right now, so I can't talk long. But I wanted to let you know there's an opening here that would be perfect for you. Great hours and decent salary."

Lola wasn't sure if the flip of her heart was a movement of excitement or of panic. "What kind of job?" she asked. She watched Sam chase a fluttering monarch across the lawn with a bamboo butterfly net.

"It's a coordinator position. They're looking for someone with a little marketing experience."

"At a photography company?" Lola felt a sudden burst of hope. But it was quickly dashed away.

"No, Lola. Have you not read my emails? I was hired by Rowder Merchandising a month after we were laid off. The position is in their marketing department. You'd be perfect for it. Just put in a year or two of the grunt work and then you could move into a manager job when Sam's a little older."

Jill continued with further description, but her words faded into background noise. *Another boring office job*, Lola sighed. She wanted to stomp her feet and have a tantrum, to shout at Jill that she was made for more. Didn't she know that? They had worked together for an entire year, shared their hopes and secrets day after day.

"So, what do you think?" Jill asked, interrupting Lola's silent tirade. "I can just about guarantee the job for you. Paul has the final word, but he trusts that I'd only recommend the best."

Lola frowned, inspecting her nails. They weren't long or beautifully manicured any more, but somehow she was proud of that. "Jill, I can't leave here until the end of summer. I promised my aunt. And Sam, he can't miss the end of baseball season. I'm actually not even sure what exact date we'll be home, I haven't had a chance..." Her voice trailed off as she realized how weak the list of excuses were.

"Lola," Jill said after a pause. "What's going on? I thought you were desperate to find a new job and get back to work here?"

Heat rose to Lola's cheeks. She was thankful there were two thousand miles between them.

"Are you... Lola, did you *meet* someone?" Jill's voice was joyfully incredulous. "You did, didn't you? Oh, tell me what he's like!"

Panic made Lola lift her weary body from the house and pace in the grass. She tried to concentrate on peeling the paint flakes from her clammy hands as she moved. "No, it's nothing like that," she insisted. "I just... I don't know, Jill. I don't know..." But she did know. And it was time that she admitted it to herself.

Lola turned to see Sam hopping with excitement. "I caught one!" he hollered, tugging the net closed with one hand while trying to wave with the other. "Mom! I caught a butterfly!"

"Jill, I have to go, Sam needs me," Lola said. She smiled thankfully at her little boy as she moved toward him. "I'll think about it, okay? I'll call you in a few days and let you know."

Jill's voice turned suddenly softer, confusion and frustration edging in. "Oh, okay. But Lola, they're going to start interviewing next week, so make up your mind fast, all right? I can't hold the job forever."

"Okay. Thanks, Jill." She turned off the phone, popped it into the front pocket of her overalls, and gave Sam's head a quick peck when she reached him. He certainly did have a butterfly trapped in his net, and Lola watched its wings open and close in patience.

"What kind is it, Mom?" Sam whispered.

"It's a monarch. Isn't it beautiful?"

They inspected the delicate wings, the perfect design of orange loops, the fragile antennae and dainty legs.

"What are you going to do now?" Lola asked, bending beside Sam. He stared at the monarch, mesmerized by its beauty, and considered his response. Then he lifted his chin with certainty and let the top of the net open. When it crawled to his finger he lifted it to the sky, smiling wide at his decision. But the butterfly held tight to Sam's skin, letting the light breeze bend its wings.

"Why isn't she flying away?" Sam asked, shaking his finger gently. The monarch lifted off, sailing to a lilac tree beside the house. It landed on the tip of a purple flower, seeming perfectly happy with its first stop.

"I guess she wants to stick around for a while," Lola answered quietly. She smiled, understanding exactly how the little butterfly felt.

AFTER LOLA TUCKED THE old lawn mower back in the shed, she returned to the front yard to find Sam sitting in the grass. He pulled at the freshly cut blades and kept one eye on the lilac tree where his monarch continued to rest.

Lola's eyes moved beyond the tree, to the white paint that peeled from this side of the house as well. In some places near the ground, huge strips were completely missing from the siding. It made the house look decades older.

"I wonder how many gallons of paint it would take to cover the entire house," Lola mused aloud.

Sam studied it with one eye closed against the bright sun. "I think five would cover it," he finally answered.

Lola glanced at Sam and laughed. "Do you think so? It's a really big house, you know. And it has four sides."

Sam plucked a blade of grass and stuck it between his teeth while he studied the house another minute. He lifted his fingers up and down, painting the siding in his mind.

"Okay, maybe twenty-two," he decided, giving a single nod of confidence.

Lola lifted an eyebrow. "I'd say that's a better estimate. Are you as good at painting as you are at guessing?"

They figured it would take a good week, maybe two, to paint the entire house by themselves. They would start with ten gallons of paint - white, of course - and begin at the front of the house and work their way around. It would be a gift to Aunt Louise, a way to say thank you for letting them vacation at her place all summer. And if it took more than two weeks to paint it, that was just fine too. They weren't going back to California for another month at least, and Lola wasn't fooling anyone with the job search.

Best of all, Lola decided, it would be an excellent distraction.

They made a list, and that afternoon Lola and Sam took another trip to the hardware store.

"AFTERNOON, CHARLIE," MATT CALLED, waving to his old friend. Charlie shelved power tools in the back corner and grunted his familiar greeting.

"Whatchya up to today?" Charlie rumbled. He huffed a breath of air when he stood, holding the shelf for support.

"Fixing up Christine Satter's deck. The stairs are falling apart."

Charlie winked. "She sure has a lot go wrong with that house of hers. Makes you wonder if she's out there at midnight breakin' it herself." A little snort escaped him as he walked the length of the aisle.

Matt shook his head and grinned. He was used to the wise cracks of the guys around town. They thought it was hilarious that many of the women in Hope River - single and otherwise - found an abundance of repairs needed on their homes when Matt was off for the summer.

"Gives the town something to talk about, I guess," Matt said. He walked down an aisle of nails and screws, losing sight of Charlie. But he could still hear his low, rolling voice.

"Seems to me the town's already got enough to talk about concerning you," Charlie said.

Matt lifted a handful of boxes from the shelf and studied their labels. "Oh yeah? Why's that?"

"Plenty of rumors going around about you and Miss Lola. I'd say they were all full of beans if I hadn't seen you two at the kids' baseball game the other night."

Matt dropped the boxes in a clatter on the floor. "What kind of rumors are those?" he asked, bending to scoop the screws that had scattered. He could hear Charlie's low, long laugh rumble from the middle of the store.

"Oh, you name it, they've whispered it. I say who gives a damn. You two might be just right for each other."

Staring at the mess he'd made, Matt tried to form a response.

But his mind couldn't work out a single thing to tell his lips to say. Small towns were known for gossip that spread like wildfire, and he was used to that. But Lola wasn't, and he sure as hell didn't want her or Sam to have to endure a bunch of bored townspeople's wagging tongues.

"You helping Lola with her house today?" Charlie asked, oblivious to the panic building in Matt's gut. "She's got a pretty big job ahead of her. Don't know if she realizes how much work that's gonna be."

Shoving the fallen boxes of screws back together, Matt quickly piled them on top of each other and stood. He marched to the end of the aisle and glared in Charlie's direction. "What do you mean, big job?" he asked, his voice tense. "What's she up to now?"

Charlie's face paled. A little cough escaped his chest and he cleared his throat. "She's painting the house. Didn't she tell you?" Guilt dripped from his voice.

"Painting *what* in the house, exactly?"

"Well," Charlie swept his hand absently over the countertop, trying to act casual. "I don't reckon she'll be working on the *inside*. Seems she's intent on repainting the outside of the house...the whole damn thing."

"Jesus, Charlie, why didn't you tell me?" Matt tucked the screws into the crook of his arm and moved toward the front door. Turning back, he scrubbed his free hand over his face and closed his eyes. "When is she starting this?" he hissed. A headache began to slice at his temples.

This time Charlie didn't try to hide his laughter. He could hardly get the words out between the guffaws. "She bought the paint yesterday. Ten gallons of white and a bunch of rollers and brushes. Said she and Sam were going to start this morning. I thought you knew."

"This isn't funny, Charlie," Matt said, shaking his head at the old man. "You don't realize what kind of damage she's capable of doing." What was she thinking? For God's sake, painting an entire house by herself?

Balancing the boxes in one hand, Matt yanked the door open and nearly sent the jingling door bells into the street.

"You gonna pay me for those later?" Charlie called between fits of laughter.

A stream of curses rolled from Matt's lips as he realized he'd almost walked out the door with unpaid merchandise. He set the boxes on a nearby shelf with a loud thud and glowered at Charlie, who was nearly buckled over his countertop. "This isn't funny, old man," Matt warned, though he couldn't control his own pitiful laugh that bubbled as he bolted out the door.

ONE DAMN DAY. MATT scrubbed his chin at the thought. It had only been one day since he'd vowed to leave Lola alone, to avoid her as much as he could. And here he was, racing to her house to check on her.

That's all he'd do, he promised himself. Quickly check on her and Sam, make sure nothing bad had happened, that no one had fallen off a ladder or accidentally swallowed paint.

What the hell was she thinking? Hadn't she promised him just days ago that she'd ask for help when she wanted to work on that rickety old house? And now she wanted to paint the whole damn thing.

Tension gnarled in Matt's stomach as he crossed the small bridge to Lola's. But his panic eased when he saw the house, still old and worn-looking, without a lick of new paint on it. Sam and Lola were nowhere to be seen.

Matt parked his truck beside the Chevy and killed the engine, studying the big home before he slid from his seat. They must be around, he decided, but he was certainly glad to see that Lola wasn't yet painting. There was still a chance he could change her mind or convince her to get some help. And it was a safe bet that she hadn't yet hurt herself or damaged her aunt's place. It would only be a matter of time before the combination of Lola and home improvement would end in more disaster.

As Matt stepped from his truck, Goliath charged from behind the house, howling a warning before recognizing Matt. He rolled over on his back, legs in the air and kicking with excitement as Matt approached. The tummy rub was so delicious that his tongue tumbled from his mouth and flopped in the dry grass.

"Where is everyone, boy?" Matt asked, rolling him over and pulling him into his arms. Goliath licked his chin, warm doggy breath damp on his skin.

It wasn't until he rounded the back corner of the house that Matt's heart jerked in his chest. His original fear was that he'd find Lola and Sam covered in paint from head to toe, cans tipped over and chaos ensuing.

This was a thousand times worse.

Lola teetered on the top rung of a ladder, nearly two stories high. The metal ladder leaned against the house, not at all anchored or sturdy, and while she kept one foot on the rung, the other was balanced out beside her like an acrobat's as she reached to scrape old paint from the siding. And even though Lola was clad only in short, faded, cut-off jeans and a blue tank top that didn't quite cover her curving waist, for once, Matt's heart pounded for an entirely different reason.

"Lola!" he shouted, setting Goliath on the ground. The puppy flopped over in the sun and exposed his tummy again. Lola continued to scrape, her back to Matt, her arm moving methodically over the siding and sending small pieces of crusty paint floating to a tarp below. Her hair was pulled back in a long ponytail and iPod buds were stuck in her ears. She even moved a little bit with the music and swayed on the ladder, sending Matt's nerves into dangerous territory.

"Lola!" Matt shouted again, this time waving his hands in the air and moving so that he would be in her peripheral vision. She turned quickly, her balance offset, and grabbed the sides of the ladder with both hands. Once she found her balance, she pulled one bud from her ear and smiled.

"You surprised me," she called in a chipper tone as she readjusted herself on the slim ladder rung.

Matt shoved his hands on his hips and tried to return the smile. He willed his voice and demeanor to remain calm. "Sorry," he called. "*Please* come down."

She frowned and shaded her eyes to get a better look at him. The worry on his face must have surprised her, because she slowly turned and descended the ladder, step by step, watching her feet as she touched each rung. Matt held the ladder in place, his fear subsiding with every inch that she moved closer to him. And though his blood pressure should have leveled out when she'd nearly reached him, it betrayed him and spiked, making him dizzy. Without permission, his eyes feasted on her legs, her tiny, sexy shorts, the tanned glow of her skin and tiny freckles on her calves and thighs. He gripped the ladder and forced himself to breathe.

"What's wrong?" Lola asked when she reached the ground. She turned to face him, only inches from his frozen body. "What happened?" Panic spread across her soft features as she searched his eyes.

Stepping back, Matt shook his head. *Focus, dumbass*, his mind roared. Blood slowly returned to his brain. He glanced at Lola's feet for a moment, then lifted his eyes to her questioning ones. His frustration returned in full force. "You're thirty feet up a ladder, dangling off the side of it, and you're wearing *flip flops.*"

The color drained from Lola's face. Anger flashed in her dark eyes. "You're worried about my shoes?" she asked. The paint scraper waved carelessly in her hand and Matt had to step aside to avoid it.

He'd never seen her look so ticked off. Good, he thought. Maybe he could finally get it through her thick head how stupid she was being. "I'm more worried about you being thirty feet off the ground while doing ballet moves, but the flip flops don't help. Neither do the facts that you're not wearing a helmet or covered in bubble wrap. And you're out here all alone - what if you fell? Where's Sam?" He was on a roll, he thought with a steadying breath. And he knew this was full teacher mode, but Lola needed a lecture more than his careless teenagers did.

Lola's eyes narrowed. She took a step back from Matt and crossed her arms over her chest as she studied him. Finally, her voice came out in a low, quiet growl.

"Matt, I'm a grown woman. If I want to scrape paint off this old house by myself, then I can. If I want to wear *spike heels* on the top of that ladder, then I will." She watched him for a moment longer, her eyes more fierce than the first day he'd met her. "As for Sam, he's over at Rena's playing with Caleb for the afternoon. Is there anything else you'd like to lecture me about, Mr. Dawson?" she snarled, enunciating every syllable of his name.

A small smirk twitched on Matt's mouth as he watched her fume. She was cute when she was mad. Perhaps he'd gone a little overboard, he realized. Been a bit too over-protective. But, damn if he could do anything about it now. He cared about Lola, about Sam. He'd just wanted to protect them from harm, protect himself from pain and grief.

He'd never forgive himself if he let something happen to them too.

At the sudden realization, Matt shifted uncomfortably and gave an apologetic smile. "Sorry," he said quietly. "Charlie told me you were planning to paint the whole house, and I just..." he brushed a hand through his hair as he fumbled for the right words "... with your track record..." He thought it might make her smile, but the words only made her more angry. She turned and stalked away.

"You know, Matt, I'm not a child," she hissed over her shoulder. She turned enough to send one more glare in Matt's direction but kept moving a little faster, a little more angrily in the opposite direction of where he stood. "I'm not one of your students you can just boss around and expect to obey. I'm perfectly capable-"

Matt watched Lola tumble to the ground then, her words lost in a faint scream as her body turned in one direction and her foot, caught in a small hole in the ground, moved in another. She tumbled to the grass, catching herself hard with her hands.

Matt was beside her in an instant, along with Goliath who licked her face and nipped her ears in excitement.

"Are you all right?" Matt asked. He could feel himself smiling a little, mostly because Lola was squirming from Goliath's sloppy kisses and pushing him away without success. Matt pulled Goliath back, holding him against his body as he wriggled. He watched Lola roll to her side and then flop to her back. She covered her face with grass and dirt-stained hands. "Well, that told you, didn't it?" she sighed, her voice resigned beneath her palms.

Slowly leaning over her, Matt peeled Lola's hands from her face, keeping his fingers wrapped gently around her palms. He smiled as he looked her over, enjoying the soft flush in her cheeks and the way her eyes danced. "Are you okay?" he asked again, his voice quiet.

A gasp of embarrassed laughter hissed from Lola's chest and she nodded, her smile revealing tiny dimples. "I think so. Only my pride is a little damaged," she answered, and Matt felt relief swamp his heart. Goliath returned to poke his nose in Lola's sides and lick her fingers, urging her to get up and play. She pushed him gently away so that he rolled over on the grass, his white puppy feet suspended in the air in surrender.

Slowly, Lola propped herself up on her elbows. With steady hands, Matt plucked a few blades of grass from her hair. She was covered in freshly mowed grass clippings, her palms and knees streaked with dirt and her body sprinkled with flecks of old white paint. Her hair fell from its ponytail and she looked disheveled and embarrassed and incredibly vulnerable. He'd never seen her more beautiful.

"Does anything hurt?" Matt asked, carefully watching her for signs of injury. "Other than your pride."

Lola made a face, then frowned as she looked down the length of her body. She winced when she moved her foot. "My ankle is throbbing a little," she said. She glared at the offending ankle and then scowled even harder at the small hole beside her foot. When she tried to sit up she flinched again and caught her right wrist in her other hand. Before she could collapse back to the ground, Matt gently pulled her up by her elbow and took her hand in his.

With a gentle touch he moved his thumbs over Lola's wrist bones. Her face scrunched when he tried to rotate her hand. Already the area had begun to swell, a slight pink color tinting her skin. "You might have torn a ligament," he murmured. "I don't think it's broken, you'd be in more pain." He let his eyes slide down the length of her legs and knew before he even touched her ankle. It was swollen and slightly discolored, a purplish-pink just above her ankle bone. "Your ankle could be broken," he added. He heard Lola whimper in frustration. "Or it may only be a sprain. We'll have to take you in to find-"

"This is all your fault, you know," Lola interrupted. Matt lifted his gaze and watched her face cloud.

"My fault? How's that?" he asked, only a little concerned by the return of her temper. His eyes moved back over her body, assessing. Maybe 115 pounds, probably wouldn't put up much of a fight, he thought. He could easily carry her to his truck and drive to the clinic.

"I was doing just fine up there," she said, jutting a finger at the ladder. "If you hadn't made me get down-"

"-from thirty feet high," Matt calmly reminded her.

Lola scowled but continued. "-and ticked me off with your bossing-"

"Your ladder was wobbling and you were dangling off of it on one foot," he cut in, but Lola was on a roll.

"-then I wouldn't have been running away from you and tripped in this damn hole!"

Matt's own frustration threatened to bubble over. "Maybe you should just stop running away from me," he said through gritted teeth.

Lola's cheeks burned, and they studied each other intensely, their breathing ragged and quick. A fire sizzled in Lola's eyes like it had the first day they'd met and Matt suddenly felt as he had back then. Heat burned deep in his belly and a flash of fury momentarily blinded him. He leaned close, his mouth inches from hers, his eyes locked with her deep brown ones. With one quick movement, he scooped Lola into his arms and pulled her to his chest, causing her to squeak in surprise. She clamped an arm around his shoulders, too stunned to protest, as he stalked around the side of the house.

"I'm burning those flip flops," he muttered as he held Lola's trembling body tight against his chest.

Goliath nipped at Matt's ankles and barked at Lola. She frowned down at her flip flops, then wrapped her fingers around Matt's neck. "God, you're bossy," she whispered, and let her forehead rest against his jaw.

A low, throaty rumble of laughter was Matt's only answer.

Chapter Fifteen

"Is she all right?" Rena asked when Matt walked into her kitchen. Grace was perched on her hip, holding a bottle of milk and grinning from ear to ear. He kissed her soft blond curls and leaned against the counter.

"She's fine," he said. He rubbed a hand over his neck and sighed. "The doc took x-rays at the clinic. She sprained her ankle and twisted her wrist. She's lying down at her place right now. I told her I'd bring Sam over in a few minutes."

Rena set Grace in her high chair and placed a bowl of cut oranges in front of her. She turned to Matt and watched him carefully with her best counselor expression. Matt rolled his eyes.

"Are you going to make me drag it out of you?" Rena scolded.

Matt couldn't help but smile at his old friend. She knew him so well, and if Gabe were home Matt was certain he'd be getting this from both of them.

He was lucky, he knew. They were his family, his foundation, and he'd be lost without them. They'd been there when his marriage was falling apart, steadied him when Ali was sick. And they'd held him up for so long after she'd died. Now, whether he was ready to admit it or not, he needed them as much as ever.

His shoulders were tight and his head ached. He pressed his finger and thumb into his eyes and ran them over the bridge of his nose. "Where's Sam?" he asked quietly. He glanced out the window toward the empty playground and sand box.

"In Caleb's room playing video games."

Matt nodded. He crossed his arms over his chest as he watched Rena settle beside Grace at the table.

"I don't know, Ree," he began with a sigh. "One minute I'm at Charlie's getting some things for Christine Satter's place, the next I'm racing to Lola's, sure there's an emergency. I think I'm losing my mind."

Rena frowned in confusion and then jumped when Matt suddenly swore.

"I forgot to call Christine. I told her I'd be back in ten minutes." He glanced at the clock on the stove and let out a desperate laugh. "That was four hours ago." He squeezed his eyes closed, trying to keep the throbbing in his forehead under control.

"Don't worry about Christine," Rena said with a sniff. "She can wait another day or two to drool over you." Matt barely noticed Rena's words, or the sisterly tone of her voice.

"Lola's trying to fix up her aunt's house and she's in way over her head. I need to park an ambulance there for the inevitable."

A suspicious twinkle glistened in Rena's eyes. "She's not the only one in over her head. Don't you think you're being a bit overprotective?"

Matt frowned. Of course he was being overprotective. The woman was a walking time bomb and he was desperate to keep her safe. But he certainly wasn't going to explain this to Rena.

He couldn't even explain it to himself.

Rena stood and pulled him into a hug. "Matty," she whispered into his shoulder, "what happened to Ali was never your fault. You couldn't have saved her from any of it, even if you'd have known." She pulled back and laid the palms of her hands on Matt's scruffy cheeks, holding his face so he couldn't look anywhere but into her eyes. "I know how you feel about Lola. And it's normal to want to keep her and Sam safe from more pain and suffering. Lord knows you've seen enough people get hurt. But there are just some things you can't control."

Matt took her hands in his, willing himself to keep calm. He swallowed the lump in his throat and smiled weakly. He needed to move, to breathe, to find a release for this knot that twisted in his gut. Letting go of Rena's hands, he paced to the door and back.

"I should get Sam home," he finally decided. Before Rena could try any more counseling, Grace distracted her by dumping the bowl of oranges on the floor and squealing in delight. With a thankful grin in Grace's direction, Matt kissed Rena's cheek and called for Sam.

"Mommy!" Sam shouted, running through the kitchen and into the family room. He dove onto his mother's chest and wrapped her in a big hug, burying his face in her neck. "Are you okay?" he asked, his voice muffled.

Matt leaned in the doorway and watched Sam cling to his mother. It was a scene that made his heart squeeze, and he wanted so much to be a part of it that he ached. He shoved his hands in his pockets and spoke quietly into the room.

"Rena sent dinner over, you just have to heat it up in the microwave. I bet Sam can handle it for you." He winked at the boy as his eyes lit up with the thought of helping his mother.

Lola pulled herself to a sitting position, running her good hand over mussed hair. Her other hand, wrapped tight at the wrist, lay gently in her lap. She looked tired but content as she snuggled with her son.

"Will you join us for dinner?" she asked. Her cheeks were rosy and her eyes sparkled, and it took every ounce of willpower to turn her down.

"I can't," Matt answered. "I have a few things to finish before the sun goes down." Like calling Christine, for one. He was certain her gossip had circled around town at least three times. And Charlie was probably still buckled over his desk in laughter, waiting for Matt to pay for the damn screws. "Do you need anything before I go?"

Lola shook her head, not hiding her disappointment very well.

Matt felt a bitter disappointment too, but he needed some time to think things over. His head ached with confusion and he needed to clear his thoughts, to make sense of why his heart felt like it might break in two.

"We'll be fine. I have a good helper here." Lola squeezed Sam and kissed his cheek. He wiped it off with a smile.

"I'll check on you tomorrow," Matt said, turning toward the kitchen. After two steps, he stopped and glanced back at Lola, his eyebrows raised. He couldn't help himself. "*Please* don't do anything stupid," he begged. He wanted to repeat the doctor's list: stay off your feet, take plenty of ibuprofen, get some rest. And add a list of his own: no painting, no climbing, no trying to fix *anything*. "And call me or Rena if you need any help. Rena said she'd stop by in a few hours to check on you and help put Sam to bed."

Lola grinned sheepishly and nodded. She lifted her good hand for a sassy salute. "Yes, sir," she teased. Her dimples peeked out, flirting with Matt, making him soften.

Before Matt could disappear into the kitchen, Sam jumped from his mother's lap and ran to him, wrapping his arms around his waist. He squeezed with every muscle in his little body and giggled.

"Bye, Matt," he said, his face pressed against him. Sam looked up with worshipful eyes and a grin that melted Matt's heart. Trying to keep that dull ache in his chest from becoming a sharp pain, Matt rubbed the boy's head and quickly pulled away.

"Take care of your mom tonight, okay?" Sam gave a quick nod and ran to the kitchen door to see Matt out. Before Matt could follow him, Lola's soft voice beckoned him one last time. He turned to find her eyes shining, hope and confusion swirling in them.

"Thank you for taking care of me today," she said quietly.

If he'd had any sense, he would have given a quick nod and followed Sam into the kitchen. But sense had disappeared the day he'd laid eyes on Lola. He slowly walked to the couch and leaned over to cup her face in his hand. He rubbed a thumb on her cheek, fighting every urge to pull her into him, and touched his lips softly to her forehead.

"I'd do anything for you," he whispered against her skin. He let his fingers caress her cheek once more, then slid his hand from Lola and walked away.

Lola's ankle healed slowly. Cooking meals was awkward, hobbling around the small kitchen nearly impossible, and she and Sam took to living on sandwiches and cereal made at the kitchen table. Rena and a few of the ladies around town dropped meals off. Even Charlie stopped in to visit and to laugh with Lola over Matt's frustration with her.

To Lola's disappointment, Matt only visited once the entire week, and even then he'd been cautious and in a hurry to leave. Lola told herself it was to be expected. She'd been giving him mixed signals from the start, and he was finally fed up.

By Thursday afternoon, Lola was more than anxious for baseball practice, and Sam was thrilled to be leaving the confines of the house. They rode to the game with Gabe and Rena.

Lola hobbled on one good foot and one clunky boot all the way to the stands.

"Just let me carry you," Gabe insisted more than once. He was anxious to help her, to just pick her up and make it easier on everyone. But Lola was determined to take care of herself.

"I could just toss you over my shoulder and we'd be there in five seconds," Gabe grumbled. Lola grinned at him as Rena swatted his arm.

"Not even that clunky boot can take away from those pretty dresses," Charlie mumbled quietly at the stands, showing appreciation for her sleeveless denim dress and her one good leg. He'd arrived at the same time as she had and offered his hand as she climbed a step. With unsteady legs, Lola slid in beside Rena and Grace. Charlie settled beside them and grinned at the field.

"See that little red head over there?" he asked, pointing toward first base. A girl with fiery pigtails brightened when her eyes met Charlie's. She waved joyously, and Charlie wiggled his fingers at her and chuckled. "That's my granddaughter, Molly. My son works the night shift at the factory and her mother is closing at the diner this evening. Me and Miss Molly are having ourselves a little date tonight."

They watched the practice begin as usual, with warm-ups and jumping jacks and a race around the bases as the kids chased Gabe and Matt. Lola tried to limit the amount of time she spent gazing at Matt. He'd already caught her staring once and had smirked in her direction. She loved that smirk. She'd missed it terribly the past week.

But tonight, surprisingly, there was plenty to distract Lola from the handsome baseball coach. The crowd that filled the stands seemed especially curious about Lola, and as much as she wanted to wither and hide beneath the bleachers to avoid their questions, she made friendly talk and explained her injury to all who asked.

By the end of practice, Lola's ankle throbbed and she was exhausted from the unusual attention. She looked forward to going home to the quiet house, to elevating her ankle and resting her tired body. She waited patiently for Sam, who, along with Caleb, helped clean up scattered balls and equipment. She held Grace while Rena gathered garbage and packed up the cooler. And she tried hard to keep her mind from gnawing on the relentless feelings she'd developed for Matt.

But when he looked at her with those clear blue eyes, as he did now, Lola was defenseless. She watched him walk toward her, studied the way his forearm grew more sinewy with each piece of equipment he tucked into his hand. When he reached her, the smile he offered tied her stomach into a knot.

Matt wiggled a finger into Grace's hand and set a handful of bats against the stands. "How's the ankle?" he asked. He studied Lola's face cautiously while pulling Grace into his arms, letting her yank his ear and squish a kiss into his cheek.

"It's healing. This boot is a pain in the-" Lola glanced at Grace and smiled as she bit her tongue.

"You'll probably only need it another week," Matt answered quietly. He held his free hand out for Lola and helped her gently slide from the bleachers. She wobbled to her feet beside him. She didn't want to let go of his hand, but she did. And she didn't want to say goodnight, to see him walk away from her again, though she knew she had no choice.

Rena reappeared, taking Grace from Matt's arms. She had been unusually quiet all evening, barely talking with Lola in the stands. Was she angry? Had she decided, rightly so, that Lola was causing more chaos in peoples' lives than she was worth?

They walked to the parking lot together and arrived to an empty lot that was still brightly lit by the early evening sun.

"I'll take them home," Matt told Rena and Gabe as everyone neared their vehicles. They nodded and grunted responses, and with unusual silence and speed, climbed into their minivan and drove away.

Matt took his time throwing the bags of equipment into the bed of his truck. Finally he opened the passenger door and let Sam hop in the backseat, then helped Lola. She took his hand and smiled warily. "Thanks," she whispered.

"Gabe and Rena seemed in a hurry," Lola mentioned, feeling the worry gnaw at her gut.

"I think they had to get Grace home to bed." Matt's response was quiet and unconvincing. She felt her heart drop further.

Lola sighed as they pulled onto Main Street. "There were a lot more people at practice tonight." Through the open window, she watched the houses pass by, saw a family playing basketball in their front drive.

Matt nodded. "Guess they all wanted to get a good look for themselves," he murmured. He offered a small smile as Lola turned to him. "You didn't think you could get away with all of this without alerting the town gossips, did you? It took about twenty minutes for the whole place to hear the news on Monday. They've been itching to get a look at you ever since."

Lola smiled weakly and shook her head. "Well, they saw me at my best tonight. I hope they enjoyed the show."

A low chuckle rumbled from Matt as he slowed the truck and turned onto Lola's long driveway. "Underneath all of the gossip and nosing, this town has a big heart. They always want to help, they just need to have a good look at things while they offer it."

Lola barely heard Matt's last words. She was too busy gaping at the cars lining her driveway. They poured past the tiny bridge and spilled out both sides, parked bumper to bumper. It wasn't until Matt pulled up to the house that Lola found her voice. "What's going on?" she whispered.

Sam wiggled out of his seatbelt and popped his head out Lola's window. "Cool!" he shouted, eyeing the tall ladders that leaned against the house.

"Looks like your place is under construction for a few days. I hope you didn't have any plans." Matt's eyes twinkled as he watched Lola. He parked beside the shed and shut off the engine.

"I don't understand," Lola continued, blinking at all the familiar faces. Matt leaned on his steering wheel, peering at people as they crawled up ladders and laid down tarps beside the house.

"They're painting your house, Lola. When they heard you'd bought all the supplies and then couldn't finish the project because of your injuries, they decided to do it for you."

"Did you put them up to this?"

Matt laughed quietly. "No, it was mostly Sarah. She's the one you'll want to blame."

Lola opened the door and slowly slid out, her mouth agape. People waved, called out joyful greetings and grinned from ear to ear, sensing Lola's surprise. A few were already high up on ladders, scraping old paint off the wood siding, while others sorted through cans of paint and supplies on the ground. It was a busy little construction site, and Lola was overwhelmed. She knew every face, had spent time and shared laughter with every single person there. But she hadn't realized how many she'd already grown so close to.

Rena waved cheerfully from the porch stairs, her cheeks flushed with happiness. "Surprise, Lola!" she called with a laugh. Nearby, Gabe was on the tallest ladder, Anne's husband beside him. Anne called to the men from the ground, then turned and winked at Lola. She wore a handkerchief wrapped around her hair and old paint clothes. She looked so pleased that it brought tears to Lola's eyes.

Matt rounded the truck and stood beside Lola. Softly, he elbowed her and lifted an eyebrow. "You know you're not allowed to climb any ladders, right?" he asked. He gave her a crooked smile but the warning was still there. He would be watching her like a hawk.

Lola leaned into Matt, barely able to hold herself up. She wrapped an arm around his waist and felt him slide a strong hand over her shoulder. "This is one of the nicest things I've ever seen," she sniffled. She had to wipe her eyes to keep tears from dropping to her cheeks.

THE FOLLOWING MORNING LOLA was up before dawn, baking cinnamon rolls and boiling eggs, frying and cooking whatever she could find in the kitchen to feed those who would return for another day of painting. They had stayed and worked past sunset the previous night, making sure every inch of the house was scraped and ready for its first coat of paint in the morning. Lola had hugged and thanked every single one of them, especially Sarah, and was told to expect them all bright and early the following day.

As Sam and Goliath slept, the house was silent except for the creaking of the oven door and the soft whoosh of the dishwasher. Lola watched the morning slowly come to life outside, and she smiled every time she thought about the generosity of the little town. She had seen it at the Hansons' farm, after the fire, and been in awe. Now she was feeling it first hand, and was humbled. All because of a stupid fall, a silly little ankle twist, but still her new friends had come to help. Lola had never felt so cared for in her life. And never before had she felt such a sense of community. It was a lovely thing to wrap around her heart.

By late morning, the house was buzzing inside and out. All of the breakfast food that Lola had prepared was long gone. But others had brought a buffet of sandwiches, cheeses, casseroles, and desserts in every color and flavor. Ladies bustled around the small kitchen, sorting food on trays and stirring homemade lemonade. Lola soaked it all in through her camera lens, silently capturing the smiles and camaraderie, proof that there was so much to be thankful for.

Lola stepped outside, camera still in hand, and the late morning sun made her squint. She peered through the lens, trying to capture everyone working on the house. Ladders sprawled against the siding and people painted at different levels, whistling, conversing, calling instructions to one another.

Lola hobbled backward until she could see the entire house in her viewfinder. She watched Sarah and her father beside one another on ladders, rolling paint and laughing. Charlie was on the ground, brush-painting his section with one good hand and a satisfied smile. Mike from the auto shop and his two teenage sons crawled up ladders at the corner of the house, racing to see who would paint their share of the siding first. Lola focused and clicked again and again. Not only would she look back at these pictures fondly, but she was certain that Aunt Louise would love them as well.

With every picture she took, her heart swelled. She watched as Anne and the yoga ladies set up a huge fold-out table of food, their faces bright and cheerful. Rena sat in the shade beside the shed with a gaggle of children, Sam included, playing games in the grass. Grace napped on a blanket, her cheeks pink and eyes soft with sleep. Lola's heart felt so full that she was sure it would burst and spill over.

"She's a beauty, isn't she?" Gabe asked from behind Lola. She turned and smiled. "Both of your girls are, Gabe. You're a lucky man."

Gabe's eyes glowed with pride as he watched his wife. "She's so good with kids. I'd have ten more with her if she wanted to."

The look in his eyes made Lola sigh. Such a burly, serious man with the softest heart. "Well, I think you should have ten more, you two make beautiful babies."

Gabe's smile lifted to his eyes. He gave Lola a friendly nudge. "Sam's a good kid too," he said. Together, they watched Sam and Caleb play. "You've done really well with him all by yourself. I've worked with kids who have gone through a lot less than Sam, and he's doing a whole lot better. It says something about you."

Lola's throat grew thick but she managed to swallow and offer a smile. It had been a worry for her since Travis died, that Sam would be off balance with only one parent to guide his way. She appreciated Gabe's words.

"You should take a break and have some food. The ladies are putting lunch out now," Lola said, motioning to a table beside the house. Gabe only nodded, his eyes still on his wife.

"Sounds like a good idea," he murmured. Then he smirked and

lifted his chin toward Rena. "But first I need to go steal a kiss from that gorgeous girl over there."

Lola's heart squeezed. *Oh, to be loved like that*, she thought. She ached to have someone look at her the way Gabe looked at Rena.

She was so tired of being alone.

"Where's Matt?" Lola called before Gabe stepped too far away. She watched him turn with a peculiar look in his eyes as he answered.

"Last I saw he was at the back of the house, setting up for the afternoon."

Lola nodded, then waited and leveled her camera at Gabe and Rena. She captured their smiles, their kiss, the way Gabe squeezed between Rena and his precious sleeping daughter. He wrapped his arm around his wife and pressed his lips to her hair.

With a pitiful sigh, Lola slowly hobbled to the back of the house.

It was quiet as she finally turned the corner and faced the emptiness in the back yard. Lola spied Matt at the far end, his back to her as he set up a few ladders and laid a tarp beneath them. She watched while he worked, studying his movements. Lifting the camera to her eye, she focused the lens.

He was incredibly handsome, she mused. Even in a stained gray t-shirt and ragged old jeans, the man made Lola's body quiver. His strong hands that secured the ladders, working so hard to keep everyone safe. His broad shoulders, bulging beneath his cotton shirt. And those arms. Lola warmed just looking at his strong arms. She imagined it would feel like heaven to fall asleep with them wrapped around her body.

Lola snapped a few pictures and then silently hobbled toward him, giving a wide berth to the mole hole she'd fallen into. Although, it wasn't much of a hole anymore. Someone had filled it in with dirt.

"Are you injury-proofing my backyard?" Lola called. Matt turned, a familiar smirk lifting his cheek. It startled her that she could have easily slid into his arms and offered a warm kiss. It felt as if she'd known Matt all her life, as if they were a couple with a history together and a future to look forward to.

Lola slung the camera strap over one shoulder and glanced up at the ladders, hoping that Matt couldn't sense the strange new feelings in her heart.

"I call it Lola-proofing," Matt said. He glanced at the ladders, squinting in the sunlight. "It seemed to work in the front. I haven't seen anyone trip into animal holes or fall off of shaky ladders yet."

"I never fell off a ladder," Lola reminded him.

"It was inevitable. The ankle sprain is really a blessing in disguise."

Lola poked Matt in the ribs and watched him flinch and laugh. She shaded her eyes and took in the freshly-stripped siding. "This really is amazing, Matt. I don't know how to thank everyone." She turned and studied him, knowing that he had probably done more for her than anyone. "I don't know how to thank you."

"You don't need to thank me, Lola," he said, quickly glancing away. "I like helping you and Sam."

She knew she should deny it, this wonderful sense of surrender that spoke to her heart. But it felt too sweet to ignore. She hobbled to Matt and clutched a fistful of his shirt, pulling him to her. The movement went against every warning in her head. But today her heart was winning.

Lifting her face to his, she studied his striking eyes and smiled. "I'm thanking you anyway." She pulled him to her until his lips covered hers, soft and warm and even more comforting than she remembered. Her fingers slid up his chest until they reached his shoulders and dug into his skin. She felt herself move into him, felt his hands grasp her waist, slide up her back and whisper over her neck. She was falling, so quickly spiraling into the warmth of his touch that she couldn't breathe, couldn't speak, couldn't think. Her body melted into his, her feet lifted from the ground.

And a tiny voice echoed in the slippery recesses of her mind.

"Mom!" Sam cried faintly from around the far corner of the house. Matt quickly set Lola back on her feet. She pulled away, dizzy and disoriented, and sucked in a quick breath. She watched Sam appear in the backyard and instinctively pulled at her shirt, feeling a flush on her cheeks. She couldn't yet breathe, couldn't clear her head enough to make sense of the rush of heat that buzzed through her body. Her fingers brushed gently over her swollen lips and slowly, steadily she felt the air return to her lungs.

Sam reached her with a huge grin on his face and a paintbrush in his hand. "Mom!" he cried, completely oblivious. He nearly tumbled beside her in his excitement. He was breathless as he waved the paintbrush in front of her nose. "Charlie said I can take over for him while he has lunch! I just painted a whole big square of the house!"

Lola glanced anxiously at Matt, who smiled as he watched her son. How could he stand there looking so calm when she'd nearly swallowed him whole only a moment ago?

"Better you than your mom," he teased. "Don't let her have that brush or she'll end up painting herself." He threw her an easy, careless grin, but Lola could see it. Behind that mask of calm his eyes smoldered. The pulse on his throat hammered to the beat of her heart.

Slowly, the buzzing in her brain subsided. The heat in her body leveled. She aimed her gaze at Matt and smiled sweetly.

Sam bent with giggles and she pretended to laugh at Matt's joke. She made a mocking face and took the brush from Sam's hand.

"I'm very good at painting," Lola announced. With one quick stroke, she wiped the brush over Matt's nose and chin. "See?"

Sam fell to the ground, rolling with delight, and Lola's mouth dropped open in staged surprise. She stepped back from Matt, still holding the paintbrush up in defense.

A grin spread slowly over Matt's painted lips. He wiped his chin, inspected his white fingers before lifting his eyes to Lola's. They were calculating and mischievous. Lola had to bend a little to keep her gasping laughter from crippling her. She tried to step backward, but when Matt charged her she simply threw the brush at him and turned to run. Even with the huge boot on her foot she tried to escape, hopping and hobbling and nearly galloping on the grass with Matt a step behind her and Sam howling after them both.

Matt caught her by the waist and slung her over his shoulder.

"Did you really think you could get away?" he crowed breathlessly, shifting her so that one arm could wrap around her thighs.

Sam jumped beside them, loving every minute of the wrestling match. And when Matt scooped him up in his free arm and held him by the waist, Sam melted in giggles that nearly brought him to tears.

"Let's go find some paint to dunk you two in," Matt teased as he walked briskly around the side of the house.

From her point of view, which was upside down and slightly fuzzy from the pressure of laughing so hard she might cry, Lola could see the front lawn full of friends. She could also see their knowing nods and delighted smiles, the way a few of them clapped joyously as she hung from Matt's shoulder. And she knew, without a doubt, this would provide plenty of good gossip for days.

"ARE YOU GOING TO watch the fireworks tonight?" Sarah asked as she closed the lid on an empty casserole dish and set it on the kitchen table. Lola flinched at the question. She'd been so lost in her own world of injury and self-pity all week that she'd lost track of the days.

"That's tonight?" She lifted a hand to her lips, gasping at the realization. "Everyone gave up their holiday to work on the house..."

Sarah rolled her eyes. "It's not like I had to beg people to come. I mentioned it to Rena and the word spread like grassfire. We all thought this would be the perfect day for it. And besides," she added, touching Lola's arm softly, "we wanted to help you."

Lola shook her head apologetically at Sarah. "After everything your family has been through, I can't believe you took the time to organize this." Lola wrapped Sarah in a quick hug, squeezing her tightly. "How are your parents?" she asked.

"They're just fine. The contractors are starting on their place next week and say that my parents will be back in their home by the fall." Sarah sighed with relief as she stepped back and smiled at Lola.

Beside them, Dolly swept into the kitchen with an empty tray, a whistle sliding from her lips. "Have you seen how gorgeous the house looks?" she asked.

Anne hustled in behind her carrying a small cooler. "They're nearly done in the back now. I think it'll be fast-going tomorrow when the second coat goes on."

Lola set down the dirty dishes she was holding and wrapped an arm around each of the women. She pulled them together with one quick squeeze and tried to keep herself from choking up. "You all are just angels," she whispered. She kissed Anne's forehead and sniffled, and the ladies embraced her with sniffles of their own.

When they pulled apart, wiping their glistening eyes, Dolly sighed. "Well you deserve it, honey. You're a sweetheart yourself. I'll hate to see you go in a few weeks."

Lola turned back to the kitchen sink where she'd been elbow-deep in bubbles. She didn't want to think about it, any of it. She wanted to stay right there in the moment, filled to the brim with love. If she let herself dwell on the inevitable, her heart would surely break. In only a month's time, she'd not only fallen hard for Matthew Dawson, but had become attached to the whole darn town as well. The thought of leaving them, of losing Matt, made her throat swell.

"I was just telling Lola about the fireworks tonight," Sarah mentioned, noticing that Lola's eyes had begun to swim. "They start around ten o'clock, right?" she asked the other ladies.

Dolly nodded, licking brownie frosting from her finger as she closed the lid on the remaining desserts. "Ten o'clock sharp. And the best place to see them is at the fairgrounds. You won't even have to drive, Lola, with that nice little shortcut beside your property."

"Lola, before I forget," Anne interrupted, letting a plate slide into the soapy sink where Lola's hands worked. "Has anyone mentioned the Fireman's Ball to you?"

Lola shook her head. "No. What about it?"

"Oh, that's right," Dolly murmured.

Sarah closed her eyes and grinned. "My favorite event of the summer," she hummed.

"The Ladies Auxiliary has been talking," Anne continued as she leaned against the countertop. She studied Lola's face with her own dancing eyes. "We were thinking of hiring a photographer for the Fireman's Ball this year. Are you interested?"

Lola's eyes popped. "Are you kidding?"

Anne clasped her hands over her chest and laughed. "I take that as a yes! It's in two weeks, on Saturday night. There's not much in the budget for it, but-"

"I'll do it for free," Lola interrupted. She nodded and lifted a soapy hand to quiet the protests. "After what everyone's done for me today, I insist." The look she gave the women and the tone of her voice silenced them. "Use that money for something else this town needs. I'm sure there are plenty of other things you ladies can do with it." Dolly and Anne smiled at each other, plans reeling in their minds.

"Oh, I love dressing up for the Ball," Sarah laughed, turning a slow circle in the kitchen. "I feel like a princess all night, and Clint is my Prince Charming."

Lola nibbled on her lip. "I don't actually have a dress for a Ball." The women all gawked at her in surprise.

"What are you talking about? You have a closet full of beautiful dresses," Sarah insisted. Lola glanced down at her clothing. Today was one of the few days that she sported shorts and a faded t-shirt.

"Sure, I have summer dresses, but nothing appropriate for a fancy evening. What does everyone wear?"

"Let's just say it's the only time we see our men in suits and ties," Dolly said.

"Harold even gets out his old tuxedo for the occasion," Anne laughed. "He calls it his monkey suit." The other ladies giggled with her.

"I wonder who Lola will go with?" Sarah teased, raising an eyebrow. Dolly and Anne hummed in unison.

"Sam will be my perfect date," Lola answered. He'd enjoy it, she thought. Dressing up and dancing with her, playing with the other kids in the back of the hall like she had when she was little.

Dolly wiggled her eyebrows. "I have a feeling you'll have *two* handsome men accompanying you."

The porch door closed hard before Lola could squelch the conversation, and all of the women caught their breath as Matt ducked into the kitchen. They eyed him with smiles and quiet nods, taking in his handsome face and the way he simply filled the room.

"Speak of the devil," Sarah giggled, patting Matt's shoulder.

"Well, girls, I'm heading out," Dolly announced, picking up an armload of Tupperware containers. She pointed at Lola and winked. "I'll see you tomorrow morning, sunshine. Only a few more hours of work left on this place and it'll be good as new."

Lola hobbled to Dolly and wrapped her in another hug, pulling Anne into it as well. She waved as they shuffled from the kitchen.

"I'll see you at the fireworks tonight?" Sarah asked, giving Lola's arm a squeeze. She patted Matt's shoulder on her way out the door, puckering her lips and batting her eyelashes at Lola behind his back.

When the kitchen had emptied, Matt frowned. "Should I be worried?" he asked with an uncertain laugh. He crossed his arms over his chest and studied Lola.

Heat quickly swirled in her stomach, making it hard to breathe. She needed to move, to distract herself. She hobbled to the sink and emptied the dishwater. "We were just talking about the Fireman's Ball. They asked me to do the photography this year."

"Did you accept?"

She nodded and grabbed a towel to dry her hands.

"Good," Matt said. "You seem to be getting quite a few jobs around here now."

Excitement and fear twisted in her chest as she realized the weight of his simple statement. And the old adage "be careful what you wish for..." sang in her mind.

Lola turned around, leaned against the sink. She clutched the countertop with both hands to keep steady. If it wasn't the idea of her dream job suddenly coming true that made her dizzy, then it was the handsome man with the warm touch and delicious eyes in front of her.

She grinned and shook her head. "You still have paint on your nose."

Matt wiped a hand over the tip of his nose, but the paint remained. It had dried hours ago.

"I still owe you," he seemed to remember, moving slowly around the table. Lola watched him walk to her, feeling paralyzed and helpless. Her mind told her to run, to escape before she did something she would regret. But not a muscle in her body would obey. Her heart thundered and she pressed her fingers into the countertop until they ached.

As he stood over her she saw it. A flash of uncertainty in his eyes, a whisper of fear passing over his face. She knew instantly what he felt. It wrapped its tight fingers over her heart as well.

But this man, she decided, was worth the risk. The risk of a broken heart, of a story without its happy ending. She leaned forward, nodding, inviting him to her. She cupped a soft hand around his jaw, brushed her thumb over his lips.

"We didn't get to finish our conversation earlier," Matt whispered, wrapping his big hands around her hips and pulling her against him. He bent and touched his lips to hers, a whisper at first, and then a deeper, longer kiss that made her eyes flutter and close.

And so quickly, so easily, she was lost. Lost in his warmth, his firm hands squeezing her hips and touching her sides, pressing her to him until she'd forgotten how to breathe. She clutched his back as he kissed her, as his lips parted hers and his tongue moved in a slow and gentle dance with her own. Her hands slid beneath his shirt, to the smooth skin of his back where her fingertips feasted on rippling, twitching muscles and a trim, firm waist.

He was delicious, she thought. Absolutely delicious.

Matt pulled back. "I thought you said this was a bad idea," he whispered. Without waiting for an answer, he leaned over and kissed her, harder this time, with so much passion that her knees nearly buckled.

"It is a bad idea," she managed when his mouth lifted from hers. Her head fell back as he kissed her cheek, her jaw, and finally rested his lips on her neck.

"But I don't care anymore," she added, pulling him closer. She felt him nuzzle into her throat, felt his cheeks widen with a smile. And when he brought his face to hers, touched her forehead with his own, she found that she truly didn't care. She would gladly pay any consequences if it meant he would kiss her, touch her, again and again.

The voices outside the porch forced them to pull apart. As the door creaked open Matt moved beside the table, but not before he threw

Lola a quick grin, one that she could easily translate into *we'll finish this later.*

Hell yes, was all she could think.

"Hey," Rena called as she and Sam made their way into the kitchen. She eyed Lola and Matt for a moment, then rubbed a hand over Sam's head. "Gabe and I are taking our kids to the fairgrounds in an hour. You guys want to come?"

"Can we, Mom?" Sam begged. He bounced to Lola and wrapped his arms around her waist. She smiled down at him, running a hand over his forehead.

"Sure. Are you walking over?" She brushed her lips with her fingers, struggled not to look at Matt.

Rena nodded. "We'll come by about 9:45." She grinned again and winked at Matt, then quickly disappeared out the porch door.

"Are you coming too?" Sam asked, moving to Matt and pulling on his fingers with his own little hand.

"Sure. But I'm going to run home and clean up, first," Matt said. Lola nearly invited him to shower there, but pushed the idea away quickly. It would be confusing to Sam, she knew. And too much temptation for her, she was certain. Imagining Matt naked, slipping into her shower...She trembled from the thought.

"You still have some paint on your face," Sam giggled as he pointed to Matt's nose.

"I do? Where?" He knelt beside Sam and let the boy step closer, pointing to the paint. "Here?" Matt asked, touching his cheek.

"No, here," Sam said, poking the tip of Matt's nose. In that same instant Matt grabbed Sam by the middle and tickled him, sending Sam into a flurry of wiggles and screeches of laughter. They wrestled until both were breathless and exhausted. Matt stood and pulled Sam into his arms.

"I can take care of that paint for you," Lola said. She stepped toward Matt and licked her thumb, raising it to his face.

Both Matt and Sam shrieked with disgust, and Matt held Sam out as an offering. He dropped him into Lola's arms, where Sam writhed with giggles.

"Mommy spit only works on little boys," Matt called, backing out of the kitchen. He winked at Lola before he disappeared.

In the sudden quiet, Lola snuggled her face into Sam's, calming him with her touch. They settled together at the kitchen table, their sides aching and their hearts full.

Chapter Sixteen

By the time Lola and Sam set foot in the woods with the rest of the group, the night had grown cool and the moon was only a sliver of gold overhead. "Will it be loud?" Sam asked, tugging on his mother's hand as he jumped over sticks on the path.

Still hobbling a little from her boot, Lola pulled her thin jacket closed with her free hand and shivered. "No louder than the fireworks we saw last year with Grandma," she answered quietly.

Caleb turned to Sam and grinned, a newly-missing front tooth giving him a comical look. "We get to lay down and watch the fireworks explode above our heads!" he cried. The thought garnered a breathy gasp of excitement from Sam.

The crowd was larger than Lola expected. Families and couples, spread out on blankets or relaxing in folding chairs, covered the entire grounds where carnival rides had been only weeks ago. They talked quietly, laughed together, sipped drinks while waiting for the show to begin. A few faces were familiar, most were ones she'd never laid eyes on.

"We're known around here for our fireworks display," Matt said quietly, noticing the surprise on Lola's face. "A lot of people come from nearby towns. Some even visit from Pine City." He shook an old quilt in front of him and let it settle to the ground, laughing as he watched Caleb and Sam pounce on it.

When the boys were settled, Matt touched Lola's shoulder as he passed by. "I'll be right back." She watched him wind through the crowd until he reached a fenced-off area, beyond which a huge old fire truck sat. Matt greeted a few firemen, shook hands and laughed with them. She watched them discuss what seemed to be safety, as they pointed to the area where fireworks were set up, to the area around them where people sat waiting. Matt checked his watch, planted firm hands on his hips, inspected the truck's gear. Lola smiled. As usual, Matt was doing everything he could to keep his town safe.

Settling on a corner of the blanket, Lola pulled one leg to her chest to conserve heat. She touched Sam's cheek, finding only warmth beneath her fingertips. Beside them, Rena and Gabe snuggled together on their own blanket, with Grace sleeping soundly on Gabe's shoulder. Lola envied the little girl's fleece blanket and fuzzy pink hood that covered her blonde curls.

When Matt returned, he stretched out behind Lola and the boys, leaning back in the grass. He wore a black sweatshirt with the Hope River High School emblem splashed across the front, and a pleased grin on his face. He looked satisfied with the night. And he looked so very warm. Lola ached to curl up beside him.

To be fair, Lola silently acknowledged, it wasn't that she thought she couldn't. She knew that she would get no complaints from Matt. But that was her struggle, really. Was she ready to show affection for someone else? Ready to trust him, and herself?

Sam weighed most heavily on her mind. If he saw her with Matt, would he be sad or angry? Was she ready to explain the complexities of a new relationship? Chewing on these worries, she remained where she was, clutching her arms around herself with slight desperation.

By ten fifteen, the crowd had grown impatient. A few clouds passed over them, covering the slice of moon. But with a sudden burst of light and smoke and ear-splitting noise, the first firework sailed into the sky. It was met with whistles and cheers and soft murmurs of excitement.

Slowly and steadily, fireworks sprayed above them in every color and shape imaginable.

Sam and Caleb scooted to the bottom of the quilt, lying on their backs beside each other, hands cupped beneath their heads and huge grins on their faces. "This is *so* cool," Sam whispered and Caleb agreed with delighted wide eyes.

Lola shivered and pulled her jacket tighter over her chest. She wrapped her arms around her knee for warmth.

And felt something small and hard hit the back of her neck.

A tiny pebble rolled beside her. And then another.

"Pssst."

Turning in surprise, Lola found Matt beckoning her with his index finger. A mischievous smile played on his lips.

She frowned and shook her head, glancing anxiously at Sam.

Matt rolled his eyes. He reached out to rub a hand down Lola's arm and tugged her toward him.

Perhaps it was because she was so blasted cold, or because Sam was so completely engrossed and distracted by the show. Maybe it was because Matt's eyes lit with the vivid colors of the sky, and his charming smile warmed her inside and out. Whatever it was, Lola sighed in surrender. She shifted backwards until she was next to Matt, until her arm brushed against his and his hand slid around her shoulder. She let herself lean into him, soaking up the warmth of his body.

And she couldn't deny how wonderful it was to feel something, someone, again.

With a firm arm, Matt pulled her close. He touched his lips to her hair, to the soft skin of her temple. And with a smile, she realized it wasn't all that long ago when she'd first met him, that he'd touched her gently in the very same place.

"I KNOW WHO WILL be sleeping in tomorrow morning," Lola whispered as her fingers brushed her son's cheek. He smiled sleepily at her, his face squished into Matt's shoulder as he was carried through the woods. The scent of smoke and metallic residue lingered in the air, and Lola felt the need for a hot, relaxing bath.

She had enjoyed snuggling with Matt tonight. Leaning into his broad shoulder, soaking in the comforting smell of his soap and aftershave. She had rubbed her cheek against him like a kitten, trying hard not to purr like one too. And in the darkness of the night, with the distraction of fireworks, no one had taken any notice of them.

Lola walked beside Matt, brushing against him on the narrow path. She warmed at the sight of her little boy in Matt's arms and realized that she simply didn't stand a chance against her feelings. She was falling, deeply, quickly, head over heels in love.

"You probably won't have everyone on your doorstep so early tomorrow morning," Matt said, interrupting her thoughts. "But it shouldn't take more than half a day."

"I still can't believe they're coming at all," Lola answered.

Walking around ladders and tarps and cans of paint, they made their way through Lola's front yard. They walked silently to the porch stairs where Lola took Sam from Matt's arms and cradled him over her own shoulder. Sam's eyes fluttered and he let his arms fall to his sides. His legs grew loose and clumsy around her waist. "He's getting heavy," she said with a little laugh.

"He'll be as tall as you before you know it," Matt whispered. He touched Sam's head softly, brushing a hand over his hair and down his back. He leaned in to Lola, kissing her softly on the cheek. "Good night," he whispered.

With rubbery legs, Lola turned and walked Sam to the top stair. Her stomach swirled with confusion.

"Lola," Matt called gently after her. She turned to look at Matt, tilting her head and smiling. He was so darn handsome, standing at the bottom of her stairs, peering up at her with a grin and his hands shoved in his pockets.

"Would you and Sam like to go to the Fireman's Ball with me?"

She couldn't control the smile that slipped so quickly to her lips. "We'd love to," she whispered.

Matt's smirk bloomed into a full, handsome smile. "Maybe we can try another slow dance."

If Sam hadn't been clutched to her chest, Lola was certain she'd have skipped down the stairs and slipped into Matt's arms for a slow dance that very moment.

BY THREE O'CLOCK THE following afternoon, Lola was practically pushing people into their vehicles and sending them home. They had arrived early to finish the painting, full of smiles and energy and once again carrying armloads of food. Most of the same friends had come, with an additional few who wanted to lend a hand. And like the previous day, Lola was overwhelmed by their generosity.

"Really, Sarah, I promise," Lola cried, nearly shoving her into the car. "It won't take much at all to clean up the kitchen. You've already done so much!" She considered buckling her seat belt for her as well. "Go enjoy the rest of your weekend."

Lola closed the car door gently and squeezed Sarah's shoulder through the open window. A line of cars made their way down the driveway, and she clasped her hands over her heart as she watched them leave.

Charlie was the last person that Lola had to wrangle up. She found him in front of the house, gathering paint-speckled tarps and plastic lining into a huge pile.

"Charlie, go *home*!" Lola lectured. "You've already done too much! Who's watching the store for you today?"

Charlie chuckled and stood straight. His silver hair curled at his temples and stuck to his forehead. "My nephew is there today. Gets him a few extra dollars to pay for his fancy car and take the girls out," he said with a little laugh.

"Good, then you can go home and relax." She grabbed a tarp from his hand and tossed it aside. "I'll clean up the rest. You go on and enjoy the rest of the weekend with your family."

"That ladder there's about to fall apart," Charlie warned, scowling at an old wooden ladder that lay on the ground beside the house. "I'll have someone swing by and pick it up for the garbage in a few days. Don't go usin' it or you'll break your other ankle…or your head," he added, trying to keep his smile under wraps. "And then Matt will have *my* head."

Lola nodded obediently. "I won't, I promise." She wrapped her arms around Charlie's big middle for a hug. "Thank you so much, Charlie," she whispered. He accepted Lola's embrace with a huff and a smile.

When they reached his truck, Charlie turned to Lola and smiled kindly. "My wife would have liked you, Miss Lola." He shook his head thoughtfully. "Been five years since she passed away."

Lola squeezed his hand in hers. "I'm sorry I never had a chance to meet her."

Charlie nodded. "I certainly know what you're going through, losing a spouse and all. Though, I wasn't young like you, raising a child all on my own. You're doing a good job, you know." Charlie's eyes twinkled. He squeezed her shoulder before climbing into his truck. When he'd slammed his door closed, he leaned out the window and grinned. "Stay off those ladders, all right?"

Lola stepped back and listened to him bring the old truck to life, then waved as he rumbled off over the bridge. After two days of controlled chaos, the quiet that greeted her was welcoming. She turned to the house, admiring how it glowed with the new coats of paint. How surprised and pleased Aunt Louise would be! She didn't even care that there were piles of cleanup inside and out. She was so full of love and appreciation for everyone in this adorable town that she had the energy of Superwoman to take on the tasks.

THAT ENERGY DWINDLED AS the afternoon wore on and disappeared completely by the time Lola's body fell into the hammock that evening. She sunk into the netting, letting it catch and fold around her, cradling her like a newborn baby. Her hair dripped from a steaming shower, her feet were bare and sore, the boot absent over her now barely-discolored ankle. Her back ached, her ankle throbbed, and even her wrist, which had felt nearly normal again, was sore.

She had spent the afternoon cleaning garbage, emptying paint cans, and collecting paint cloths from around the house. She'd soaked every brush in turpentine and piled supplies back into the little shed. She'd even cleaned the entire kitchen top to bottom.

Sam had been a handful all afternoon as well. Tired from too much excitement and not enough sleep, he'd been cranky and more to manage than usual. Now he slept soundly in his cool, dark room, freshly scrubbed behind the ears and gently cuddled after bath time. He wouldn't be stirring until morning.

Breathing in the serenity of the creek, Lola pulled her legs to her chest and covered them with her soft cotton skirt. She rubbed her hands together. Her skin was dry and her fingers achy from all of the work and chemicals she'd exposed them to in the past days. The cool, smooth wedding band on her finger looked out of place with its shiny gleam against her worn hands. Twisting it off her finger, she sighed.

The ring, like her heart, held many sweet memories. But it also held some painful ones. She let it roll in her hand, studying the dents and nicks and dull spots from every angle. It wasn't perfect, just as her marriage hadn't been. She and Travis had experienced their ups and downs, and it hadn't always been blissful. But they'd had love and trust. And he'd given her their sweet little boy who endlessly filled her heart.

She knew she was lucky.

But now Travis was gone. And Lola knew it was time to let go. Time to forgive him for leaving her and Sam, for not giving enough of himself to them when he was alive. It was time to move on.

A hot tear slipped down her cheek. She let it spill, along with others, over her chin until they dripped down to stain the cotton that covered her heart. She held the ring in her palm and squeezed it tight, sobbing silently as all the pain, disappointment, and fear burned in her chest.

Her cries finally subsided and all that was left were hiccups and deep sighs that still caught in her chest. She heard the crackle of tires on the gravel driveway and quickly wiped the moisture from her face.

She was relieved to see Matt. He and Gabe and two others had left shortly after noon to respond to a call, a large accident on the Interstate. Before he'd left, Matt had squeezed her hand and promised that everything would be just fine.

She'd known better. When it came to accidents, no one could make such a promise.

But here he was, and she sighed with relief. Nearly even cried with it. She watched him walk silently to her, watched his face light up as he neared her.

"Hi beautiful," he whispered. He ran his knuckles over her cheek and smiled. His eyes were heavy with exhaustion. "The place looks great. I wish I could have helped with cleanup."

Lola smiled weakly, trying to hide the emotions that had brewed inside of her for the last hour. "It didn't take much," she lied. Patting the netting beside her, she shifted over to make room for Matt.

He gave her a wary look. "You're going to flip me upside down, aren't you?" Gingerly, he slid in beside Lola. The white netting folded around their shoulders and supported their backs, and their weight made them lean into each other. Matt rocked them gently.

"Is everyone okay?" Lola asked.

Matt nodded and gave a small, satisfied smile. "They'll all be fine. The driver of a truck fell asleep and crossed over the highway, but thankfully the oncoming minivan swerved in time to avoid it. A few cars ended up in the ditch, one of them rolled."

Lola felt her throat tighten and her stomach sink. Her eyes began to mist. A front page newspaper picture of Travis' mangled car, of the eighteen-wheeler that had broadsided him, flashed in her mind. She squeezed her eyes closed, trying to block the vision and the empty, angry feeling in her gut.

Seeing her reaction, Matt wrapped an arm around her shoulder. "I'm sorry," he whispered.

Lola shook her head, but let Matt pull her against him. He felt so good, so safe. She needed to let him protect her against the misery, needed to know that it could go away. "It's okay," she said. "I'm okay. Tell me what you did there." She wanted to keep him talking, to hear his soothing voice.

After a hesitation, he continued. "We administered first aid on the cuts and bumps, sent a few to the hospital with broken bones and one head injury. But otherwise they're all going to be fine. It took a while to clean up the cars and fuel and glass."

With gentle hands, Matt folded damp hair behind Lola's ear. He caressed her cheek, waiting patiently.

Lola tried to muster a smile. Her lips quivered, then fell. She studied Matt's comforting eyes and felt hers quickly fill with tears.

"I'm sorry," he whispered again. He kissed her hair, still holding her tight against him. Lola sniffled and shook her head, trying hard to gulp down the sobs that wanted to return.

"It's not your fault. I was thinking about him before you even arrived." Slowly, she opened her hand and revealed the wedding band tucked away in her palm.

A slow breath escaped from Matt's chest. "Oh." He lifted the ring from her hand, let the evening light dance on the gold. His fingers were so large compared to it, but gentle as he studied it. He set it back in her palm and closed her hand around the ring. Turning, he kissed Lola's forehead and wiped her tears with his thumb.

Matt took a deep breath and rested his cheek against her. "There's something I want to tell you," he said. He laid his hand over her unclenched one and laced his fingers through hers.

"Right after Ali was diagnosed, I started coming home for a quick lunch every day. I wanted to check on her as much as I could, make sure she was comfortable." His voice was nearly a whisper, and the night quieted as if preparing for his story.

"One day at lunch she held my hand for a long time and told me it wasn't my fault. I didn't understand. I thought maybe she meant how she had never been happy in Hope River, but I couldn't stay and talk about it. So I tucked her into bed and said we'd talk when I got home. I went back to school, just like every other day."

"All afternoon my gut told me something was wrong. When classes ended I raced home to check on her again. I opened the garage door and found her car running. It was hard to breathe. The car was empty but it had been running a while, and the door to the house was open.

It led to a small laundry room that was closed off from the rest of the house." He shook his head, and Lola heard a click in his throat when he swallowed. "I should have known, but I just didn't think... I went to the door and the laundry room was foggy like the garage. It was dizzying. I could hardly breathe."

Hot tears welled in Lola's eyes as she listened. She gripped Matt's fingers and watched while he spoke calmly into the night.

"She was sitting on the floor, leaning against the wall. Her eyes were closed, and there was a peaceful smile on her face. When I touched her I knew."

With absent eyes, he looked toward the creek, shaking his head at the nightmare from his past. "She had tried to say goodbye to me, I just didn't realize. I got to her too late. I couldn't save her. Even with all the training I have, I couldn't save her."

Lola wiped tears from her cheeks and laid her head on his shoulder. She wanted to sob, to scream at the unfairness of it all. A man so giving and loving should not have lost as much as he had. A newborn daughter, a wife he loved and cherished as he did...the cruelty of it twisted in her gut.

"The moment the doctors said 'cancer,' she gave up. I was so angry at her for that. So angry that she took her own life. I missed her, but in the beginning, more than anything, I was just mad. She didn't let me say goodbye. She didn't let me try to help her. It took a long time to forgive her. And then it took a long time to not miss her so much, and to move on with life." He brought Lola's hand to his lips and gently kissed her knuckles. "Eventually I figured out how to move on. I never thought in the beginning that I would. But I did. And you will too, I promise."

Matt gently ran his hand over Lola's hair. She laid her head on his chest, let him rock them in the silence of the night. They stayed this way until the moon was high and the night owls began to call. When Lola finally sat up, she opened her palm and stared at the old wedding band.

"You'll know when you're ready, Lola," Matt whispered, looking at the glistening ring with her. "And I'll be here for you, however you want me, when you are." He climbed from the hammock, then turned and offered his hand. He led her through the grass, pulling her into his arms when they reached the porch stairs. His fingers were gentle on her shoulders, his lips soft on her cheek. "Goodnight," he whispered.

Lola watched him turn and walk into the darkness of the night. The passionate, playful kisses they'd shared earlier in the day seemed like a dream, and Lola understood that their relationship had changed. What they shared now was deeper. Two people, making their way from the pain of their pasts, finding the courage to love again.

"Good night," Lola whispered. Her heart ached and swelled all at once as she watched Matt disappear. She walked slowly into the house, climbed the stairs and slipped into her bedroom.

Her bed was soft and comforting. Her head throbbed with exhaustion and her heart felt heavy. She curled up beneath the warm quilt, and with the ring still clutched in her palm, fell into a deep, dreamless sleep.

Chapter Seventeen

❧

" *L*ola, I have a surprise for you!" Anne cheered over the phone early Monday morning. Lola tried to clear the heavy fog of sleep, wondering why her ring had rolled from her hand when she'd awoken.

"What kind of surprise?" she mumbled, rubbing her eyes as she flopped back onto her pillow. She slid the ring onto her finger and stared at it, slipping it over her knuckle and back a few times. Somehow, it didn't look right on her hand any more.

"If you come to the shop this morning, I'll show you," Anne teased.

The previous night's memories slowly oozed into Lola's mind. She'd swung gently on the hammock and laced her fingers with Matt's. She'd held back tears as she listened to his heart-wrenching story. She'd clutched her wedding band in her hand and hated herself for finally wanting to take it off. And in the quiet of the night, Matt had given her hope, offered her permission to move forward with her life.

If she could only find the strength to take the first step.

The ring felt heavy and awkward on her finger. Lola slipped it off and set it on the bedside table, staring at it as her insides quaked. "We'll be there in an hour," she whispered into the phone. Hanging up, she rolled over and buried her face in the pillow.

AFTER FEELING LIKE AN invalid for so long, it amazed Lola that she barely limped any more. The doctor had promised she'd be back to normal in a week, but still, the ease with which she moved without her boot surprised her.

Lola climbed into the old Chevy and wrapped her fingers around the cool, thin steering wheel. "I'm going to miss this truck when we-" She stopped short. *You don't have to go home* a little voice announced. Sam frowned at Lola as if he'd heard it too.

The morning was warm and sticky. Children played in sprinklers on their lawns and ducks bobbed and splashed in the river. Pots of geraniums glistened and dripped from their early morning drink and bees hovered over the sweet breakfast. Mothers dragged their children into stores as they began their daily errands.

As Lola and Sam entered the photo shop, Anne threw her arms out wide. "You're never going to believe this!" She wrapped Sam in a warm hug and quickly led him to a bowl of candy on the countertop. When he'd plucked out a lollipop, Anne moved behind her desk and held up a large manila envelope. "It came first thing this morning," she said, breathless as she thrust it at Lola.

The envelope was hard and the return address peculiar. Lola frowned at Anne. "What is this?" she asked.

"Just open it," Anne hissed. She wrung her hands as she watched Lola pull back the lip of the envelope.

Lola pulled out a photograph of the Chevy at Aunt Louise's house - the very truck that was now parked outside the store reflecting the morning sunlight. It was the picture Lola had taken their first week in Hope River.

"I submitted this to the fair contest," Lola said. She raised her eyebrows at Anne, hoping for an explanation.

"There's a letter in there," Anne urged, flitting her hands at the envelope. "Dear Lord, you're going to give me a stroke. Just read the letter!"

Lola dug it out and began to read aloud. *"Dear Ms. Sommers, We are delighted to inform you that your photograph has been chosen..."* Unaware that her voice had disappeared, her lips continued to move as she read.

"What is it?" Sam asked, leaning in for a peek. Lola lifted her face to Anne's, frozen with shock.

"Check the bottom of the envelope. Go on," Anne said, covering her smile with trembling fingers.

Slowly, Lola slid her hand to the bottom of the envelope and pulled out a small piece of paper. A check for five thousand dollars, written out in Lola's name, nearly fluttered to the ground with her surprise.

"Holy shh..." she gasped. She covered Sam's ears with her palms and gawked at Anne, silently mouthing it again - *holy shit!*

Anne let out a boisterous laugh. "I knew that picture was special," she cried. "My husband and his car buddies went nuts over it, so I sent it to that classic car magazine to see if they had any interest in it. I hope you don't mind." Anne pulled Sam into her arms and squeezed him until he turned purple. She bent and hummed in his ear. "I guess they liked it, huh? Your mom's pictures are something special."

Still confused, Sam stepped to his mother and tugged the check from her fingers. The lollipop nearly tumbled from his lips. "Holy shit!" he bellowed.

"Sam!" Lola cried, grabbing the check and covering her heart with it. She gaped at him in disbelief.

"We have to celebrate!" Anne decided as she flitted toward the back room. "I'm sure I have a few sodas back here. Sam, lend me a hand for a minute." He bolted after her, avoiding his mother's scolding gaze.

It took a minute for Lola to settle her breathing. She peeked at the check once more and let it sink in. *Five thousand dollars.* She'd never seen a check with that many zeroes next to her name.

At the moment, she wasn't desperate for money. Travis' life insurance had left them enough to get by for a little longer. But the thought of making her own money, of supporting herself and Sam by doing something she loved, gave her a sense of freedom that she'd never before experienced. And it gave her hope.

She followed the excited voices echoing from the back room. Leaning against the door, she watched Anne and Sam move boxes and chairs as they searched for a celebratory drink. The room was painted a bright white, the walls empty, the floor clean. Like a freshly-taken Polaroid picture, it invited Lola to dream, to imagine the possibilities. A photography studio was slowly revealed on the film of her mind, and equipment and clients emerged. As if by magic, a flexible schedule appeared, a career she adored, a small town that surrounded and supported her like family.

"Orange soda!" Sam cried, making Lola jump. He held two cans in front of her as he passed through the door.

Anne shoved a plastic cup full of syrupy orange liquid into one of Lola's hands and a piece of paper into the other. It was an old blueprint of the empty room that Lola had just been staring at. She lifted one eyebrow at Anne, who gave a wicked smile in return.

"To possibilities," Anne cheerfully toasted. She clunked her cup against Lola's and Sam's, sloshing soda on their hands. And as Lola took a sip and eyed the empty room behind her, she felt goose bumps burst on her skin.

"I HEAR YOU AND Matthew Dawson are an item now," Dolly announced during yoga the following morning. Lola let out a cough of surprise but continued to hold her pose.

"Someone told you wrong," she answered. Her voice muffled as she pressed her forehead harder into the blue mat. "We've just been spending some time together. Sam really enjoys having him around." She inhaled a quick breath as she moved into the next pose.

"A little birdie told me that she caught you two necking at the park the other day," Rae added, mischief dancing in her eyes. Her gray hair sprung from her head as she tilted upside down.

Lola locked her elbows and knees so she wouldn't collapse to the floor. "This town needs something else to do besides make up stories about my love life," she laughed. "We haven't been necking anywhere." *Except in my kitchen. And behind the house. And in my dreams.* She flopped onto her back and stretched her arms and legs as far as they would go, trying to suck in a deep breath. On exhale she wheezed, "Matt and I are just friends. You all forget that Sam and I are only visiting for the summer. It wouldn't make sense to start anything – even if we wanted to."

"Well, who wouldn't?" Dolly laughed. "He's such a handsome young man."

"And very nice," Anne added. "Kind-hearted just like his parents."

Floating from one pose to the next, Betty smiled knowingly at Lola. "Is it true he's taking you to the Fireman's Ball?"

Lola didn't answer immediately. She finished her stretch first. "Yes," she finally answered on an outward breath. "He's taking me *and* Sam."

"Everyone will be there this year, that's for sure," Betty decided, raising her perfectly plucked eyebrows. "They want to see the Belle of the Ball with her Prince Charming." She giggled at herself, but Lola rolled her eyes.

Grunting, Anne rolled to her side. "Lola's taking pictures this year, that's why everyone's going. A good photographer will spice things up a bit. Now just leave the poor girl alone and let her do whatever she wants with that handsome Dawson boy."

Lola glanced at Anne and frowned, not sure if she was helping.

After their final pose, Dolly glided to a standing position, refreshed and energetic. Betty followed, tucking her dyed blonde hair behind her ears and adjusting perky young breasts that didn't quite match her sixty-eight year old body. Rae and Anne remained on the floor, flat on their backs, laughing at the predicament of trying to heave their sprawling bodies into standing position.

"What are we going to do without you?" Rae laughed as Lola pulled her to her feet. "I'm going to miss this sweet face of yours." She patted Lola's cheek and squeezed her shoulders. Lola moved to Anne next, pulling her up slowly as well. They laughed as they stumbled to get her upright and steady.

"Well, she's not gone yet," Anne said quietly, a twinkle in her eye.

The other women filed inside for their customary tea and croissants. Anne patted Lola's shoulder as she passed through the kitchen door. "And I think you and Matthew make a wonderful couple," she whispered.

"DAMN IT!" MATT BIT back on a string of curses and clenched his fingers around his throbbing thumb. It was the third time in an hour that he'd smacked it with the heavy hammer.

"Can I get you another iced tea, dear?" Mrs. Brisby called from her perch on the deck. She lifted her own glass of the muddy drink and smiled eagerly at Matt.

"No thank you, Mrs. Brisby. I still have some left." He lifted the tall glass to his lips and took a swig, choking it down with a smile. He'd give her one thing - it may have tasted like the dirt he knelt on, but at least it was cold.

Plucking the fallen nail from the ground, Matt tried once again to hammer the boards of the fence he was building and avoid his fingers. His mind just wasn't in the right place today. Earlier he'd measured two boards wrong and only realized it after he'd cut and tried to fit them. At the rate he was going, he'd be visiting Charlie's hardware store for another pallet of lumber before the day's end.

Truth be told, Matt knew he'd been off all week. And whether he wanted to admit it or not, he knew exactly why.

It had everything to do with Lola Sommers.

It had been three days since he'd seen her or talked to her. Three days since he'd found her in the hammock, eyes red and swollen, knees tucked to her chin as she struggled with her misery.

Years ago, he'd been where she was. He knew her pain, her confusion and anger. He wished someone would have told him then that he was going to survive, maybe even flourish and find love again.

So he'd told Lola what he thought she should know about love and loss and moving on with life. He'd promised her that although life would never be the same, she and Sam would be okay. That she wasn't a bad person for wanting to move forward, that it was actually important that she did.

He'd thought he was helping. But now he wondered if he'd just made everything worse.

Pounding the hammer with a satisfying whack, Matt watched the nail bury into wood. He knew when he left Lola on Sunday night that he'd changed things. That he'd told her, in so many words, that he would be here, waiting patiently, if and when she was ready to move on. With life, and with love.

He was trying to give her time and space, but the fact that he still hadn't heard from her was worrisome. He'd known this might happen, hadn't he? He'd known that his words might do nothing more than scare her. That she may not be ready to move on with life, much less give new love a chance.

And if that was the case, then he'd get over it. He'd lick his wounds, do his best to enjoy her and Sam's company at the Fireman's Ball, and say goodbye with a brave smile when they returned to California.

Life would go on, as it always does. Whether he liked it or not.

"Have you seen Matt lately?" Lola asked Rena late Thursday morning.

"Mmm," Rena nodded, savoring her sip of morning brew. She paged through the newspaper on her kitchen table, pausing at the Health section. "He stopped over this morning on his way to Mrs. Brisby's. I think he's building a fence in her backyard."

Lola tapped her fingers on the table and glanced out the window at Sam and Caleb in the sandbox. Steam swirled from her untouched coffee. "Does Mrs. Brisby live in town?"

"She lives in the yellow house across from the high school. Want me to call and tell her you're coming?" A slow smile spread over her face.

Lola frowned. "No, I was only curious. I'm not..." She bit her lip as she seriously considered it.

"I think Matt would be happy to see you, Lola." Rena eyed her friend over the rim of her coffee mug. "We've been putting up with him all week. He's a sorry case, wandering around like a lost puppy, sulking and grumping about who-knows-what." Taking another slow sip, she watched Lola carefully, a knowing twinkle in her eye.

"I don't want to hurt him," Lola blurted. She shook her head and laughed at the silliness of the comment. How could she explain it when she didn't even understand it herself?

Rena set her coffee mug on the table and sighed. "Lola, I've been Matt's friend for a long time. Believe me when I tell you, he's a big boy. He can handle whatever happens, or doesn't happen, between you two. The question is, can you?"

Lola looked out the window once more and studied her little boy. His hair was streaked with white highlights from the sun and his skin was a golden tan. He was smiling and laughing. It wasn't a question of how Lola would deal with a new relationship. It was a matter of how Sam would.

"He's getting to be a big boy too," Rena said, following the path of Lola's gaze. "Have you talked to Sam? Asked him what he thinks of having Matt around, of sharing you with someone new?"

The question made Lola's throat close. She shook her head. "I've barely come to terms with it myself."

Rena put a warm hand over Lola's and squeezed. "Go find Matt. Talk to him about all of this and tell him how you feel. He deserves to know. And then you two can figure this out together."

In a rush of emotion, Lola stood, nearly knocking her coffee over. "Sam-"

"Go," Rena scolded before Lola could utter the words. She pulled her into a quick hug and then pushed her toward the door. "I'll watch Sam today. Go find Matt."

"WELL, LOLA SOMMERS, WHAT a pleasant surprise!" Mrs. Brisby crooned from her front porch. She held the door open with her squat body, her pink cotton housedress nearly blocking the entry. A broad and welcoming smile made her face wrinkle like a raisin. "I was just on the phone with Dorothy Treble - Lord, that woman can talk - and insisted I had to go because Lola Sommers was walking up my sidewalk."

Lola had seen her perched in the front window when she'd arrived, watching the street like a hawk. "Hi Mrs. Brisby. I'm sorry to bother you."

"Oh, heavens, it's no bother at all!" She grabbed Lola's elbow and pulled her inside. "I've been meaning to invite you over for a glass of my famous iced tea all summer. And where's your little boy, Sam is it?"

"He's playing at a friend's house. Thank you," Lola said as she stepped reluctantly into the bright front room. She tried to remain close to the front door but Mrs. Brisby had other ideas. She set a strong hand on Lola's back and ushered her to an old tapestry couch.

"I'll only bother you for a minute," Lola insisted as she fell into the firm cushions. "I'm actually looking for Matthew Dawson. Is he here?"

Mrs. Brisby's eyebrows shot up to her fine white hair. "Well, dear, he was here all morning building a fence out back. I'm hoping it will keep those pesky little rabbits from eating up my flowers." She disappeared into the kitchen but her booming voice continued to carry to Lola. "I'm certain he'll be working on it for a few more days. He's scheduled to build a small deck for Tina Christianson after that, and next I believe are some bookshelves for Joanie Plum."

Mrs. Brisby returned with a sugar bowl and two large glasses of mud-brown liquid on a plastic serving tray. Ice clinked against the glass as she handed one to Lola. "I suspect someone told you you'd find him here?"

Lola offered a polite smile and nodded. "Rena Wesson. She and Matt and Gabe are all very close."

"Well, of course they are. I've lived in Hope River all my life. And I've known Matthew since he was a baby." She squeezed her body into a rocking chair and looked down her narrow nose at Lola. "He's a very good man. An excellent teacher I hear, and he's always been wonderful at building and maintenance. Though I suspect half the women around this town hire him on so they have an excuse to ogle him."

She gave a quick tsk of disapproval before bringing the tea to her lips. After a long drink she patted her mouth with a napkin. "Quite a shame, what happened a few years back with his wife. He's such a handsome man, I can't believe no one's scooped him up since then. You know, I've been meaning to set him up with my niece Lucy." She leaned over the end table and proudly plucked from it a framed photo of a gorgeous young blonde. "She modeled in New York for years. She's going to graduate school in Pine City now, to be a lawyer, I think." With a satisfied smile she showed Lola the picture and then set it back on the table. "Smart as a whip, that girl is. Quite a catch, isn't she?"

Lola narrowed her eyes at Mrs. Brisby. A fire slowly built in her gut. The hell if she'd let this crazy old woman set Matt up with a supermodel.

Mrs. Brisby gave Lola a shrewd smile. She raised her eyebrows and looked expectantly at Lola's untouched glass of tea.

"I think Matt is already seeing someone," Lola announced. She watched Mrs. Brisby's eyes widen in blatant curiosity.

Lola's fingers trembled as she lifted the tea to her lips. The liquid was grainy and ice-cold in her mouth. She held the drink in her cheeks as she considered Mrs. Brisby and her irritating plans. She needed to find Matt and… and…

The tea began to burn her tongue and threatened to either go down or come out. Lola chose the polite route. She swallowed it down with one giant gulp. A bitter, dirt-like flavor filled her throat and she coughed and sputtered violently. Through tears, she saw Mrs. Brisby's face turn white.

"Must have…swallowed wrong," Lola gasped, coughing once more and clearing her throat. She lifted the glass and peered at the foggy liquid. "It's… amazing. Did you make it yourself?" Tears stung the back of her eyes.

"Of course! It's my secret recipe. I've been making it for forty years. My husband Ralph, God bless his soul, used to take a gallon to the factory with him every morning and share it with the men. He said it was so unique, he swore it was made straight from the earth." She lifted her chin with pride.

One more small cough burst from Lola's chest. "It is *quite* unique, Mrs. Brisby. I've never tasted anything like it. May I?" She gestured quickly toward the sugar bowl and added two heaping spoonfuls to her glass.

Mrs. Brisby straightened in her chair and smoothed the housedress over her legs. "Well, you're looking for Matthew? I expect you're doing some more maintenance on your aunt's home." Her eyes glowed with what Lola assumed was desire for juicy gossip. "I heard there's been some plumbing work and painting done. That house of Louise's was in desperate need of it, I'll tell you that."

Lola sipped her tea more slowly and only half-choked it down this time. She set the glass on a crocheted coaster and slid to the edge of her seat. "I think I'm finished with the home projects for now. I actually need to see him about something else."

Mrs. Brisby studied Lola, waiting for more explanation. "A... personal matter," Lola added. "Do you know where I can find him?"

Mrs. Brisby's eyes twinkled. "I'm afraid he's gone to the hardware store and then to lunch, dear. But he'll be back in a few hours. Why don't you join me for some sandwiches and more tea?"

It took Lola a full five minutes to convince Mrs. Brisby that she couldn't stay. She had to promise to bring Sam the following week for some sugar cookies and, God help them, more of her famous iced tea.

As Lola climbed into her Chevy, she saw Mrs. Brisby in the window, perched once more in the seat with a view. The phone was glued to her ear.

No doubt that news of Lola's search for Matt would spread faster than she could travel to the other end of town.

If Lola wasn't mistaken, Charlie actually looked a little panicked when she charged through the door of his hardware store.

"Hi, Charlie," she called, desperately trying to sound cheerful. It was a stark contrast to the panicked, irritating desperation that swirled in her stomach. The town was as small as an ant farm, yet finding one man was turning into an ordeal more difficult than finding the needle in the haystack.

Charlie's forehead wrinkled with worry. "You know I can't sell you anything or Matt will have my head," he warned. A guilty smile tickled one corner of his mouth.

"Don't worry Charlie, I'm not here to buy anything. I'm looking for Matt."

Charlie's shoulders fell with relief. He huffed with laughter and rubbed his hand over his belly. "Well, he was just here about thirty minutes ago. Needed another box of nails for that fence of Mrs. Brisby's. Said he'd bent up half the other box already." His brows furrowed at the thought. "He's never had a problem with nails before. Either he had a bad box or I reckon his aim is off today." He scrubbed his chin with his fingers and then seemed to realize that Lola was waiting anxiously for his help. "I can give him a call and track him down if you like."

She'd considered it herself, even had his number tucked away in her purse. But she couldn't have this conversation over the phone. "No, that's all right." Wringing her hands, she paced between the paint aisle and light fixture displays that hung from the ceiling.

"I guess some things are better said in person," Charlie said softly, setting a hand on her shoulder. He smiled kindly, nodding as if he were in on the secret. "He told me he was going home to grab some lunch, but I wouldn't be surprised if you'd find him at the fire station now. He goes there to do paperwork when he's got a lot on his mind. Seems to me today would be one of those days."

Lola reached up on tip toe and planted a soft kiss on the stubble of his cheek. "Thank you," she whispered. And with new determination, she quickly slipped out the door.

HE HEARD THE DOOR of the fire hall creak open, saw the sunlight dance across the floor. County paperwork sprawled on the countertop and his ham sandwich sat untouched in the plastic bag beside him. It was hot, he was tired, and today was one of those days he would rather just be alone. Matt considered ignoring the intrusion, hoping the visitor wouldn't notice him. But something in his chest, a sudden squeezing of his heart, made him glance up.

Lola stood in front of the door, hands in fists by her sides, shadows dancing over her face. She was beautiful. And just a little bit scary. If he didn't know better, he'd swear she was glaring at him.

Matt frowned and turned his body on the wooden stool to face her. "Hey," he said, his voice lifting in surprise. God, it was good to see her. It felt like weeks since he'd held her in his arms. Since he'd buried his face in her soft hair and felt such comfort just being with her.

Lola only stared, narrowing her eyes as if ready to charge across the room and slap him. She clenched and unclenched her hands, then wiped her palms over her hips and down her thighs. She took a tentative step, and then another, and then she moved quickly, practically darting across the room. Matt slid off the stool to his feet, bracing for whatever had put that angry glint in her eyes.

When she approached him, Lola didn't slow her pace. She lifted a hand to his cheek, slid her fingers to his neck, and let her body crash against his. Her lips were on his, soft and warm and urgent, her hand cupping his neck and fingers lacing through his hair. He didn't question it, didn't even let his mind consider it. He simply let her fall against him, let her body meld with his. Her lips tasted like sugar, her hair smelled of flowers.

Matt circled Lola's waist with his arms and pulled her against him. Slowly, she opened her eyes. He watched them crinkle with her smile.

"I thought you were going to punch me," he whispered.

She laughed and pressed her forehead against his. "You have no idea what I've been through all morning looking for you. I didn't even know what I would do when I found you."

Stepping back, Matt took her hands in his. With a sudden leap of his heart, he realized there was no longer a ring on her finger. He rubbed his thumb over the bare skin, studying it carefully, then lifted his eyes to hers.

Matt framed Lola's cheeks with his hands. She looked so vulnerable. His heart ached at the way her eyes glistened with tears.

"Matt, I don't want anyone to get hurt. You, or me, or Sam." She shook her head and bit her trembling lip. "I don't know what's next for us, and I can't make you any promises."

He lifted her chin and studied her dark eyes. Amidst the pain and fear that swirled in them, he could see the hope. "I don't need any promises, Lola. I just need to be with you. We have time to work out the rest."

A tear slid down her cheek, but Matt quickly wiped it away. He kissed her cheekbone where it had been.

"I'm falling in love with you, Matthew Dawson, whether I want to or not."

Pulling her closer, he brought his lips to Lola's and kissed her tenderly. "I think I've been in love with you for twenty years, Lola Sommers," he whispered. A smile spread over her lips and lightened her eyes.

They both jumped as the door gave a thud.

"Hey Chief, Will said I'd find you here-" Clint's words stopped short as he spied Lola and Matt embraced in the shadows. His throat moved with an audible swallow. "Oh, I'll... ah... Sorry." He grinned and then pointed awkwardly to another door that led to the garage. "I'll just go... be in there..." He slipped through the door, laughing as he went.

Lola dropped her head against Matt's chest and sighed. He bent into her, pressing his laughter into her hair.

"That'll get the rumor mills going again," he teased softly.

When Lola lifted her face to Matt's, her eyes were clear, her cheeks rosy and soft. A playful smile filled her face.

"I went to see Mrs. Brisby and Charlie before I found you," she said, kissing Matt's cheek, his chin, his lips. "I'm pretty sure the whole town knows by now." She wrapped her arms around his shoulders and kissed Matt so hard that he thought he saw stars. Then, leaning back to gaze into his eyes, she smiled. "We might as well give them something worth talking about."

Chapter Eighteen

LOLA STOOD IN FRONT of the full length mirror, paying little attention to the scooped neckline of her wine-colored satin dress or the way the curls of her hair were piled precariously on top of her head. The delicate hairstyle was perhaps a poor choice for such a busy evening.

But it wasn't her biggest concern.

It was the shoes that had her worried. Three inch satin heels that she'd found tucked in the back of Aunt Louise's closet. They were half a size too small and made Lola's ankles wobble when she stood in one place.

But the shoes matched the dress. The entire ensemble made Lola feel like a princess. And she certainly couldn't show up to the Fireman's Ball in flip flops, could she?

Using her bedroom walls for support, she wobbled to Sam's door and peeked in. He sat on his bed, dressed in cute slacks and a proper shirt, his clip-on tie dangling crookedly at his throat. A wide, adorable grin splayed over his lips.

"Sam," Lola gushed, pressing her hands to her heart. "You are the most handsome date I've ever had." She bit her lip to keep from whimpering. When had he grown into such a young man?

Sam giggled as he jumped off the bed. "I like your dress, Mom. You look like a princess."

Before Lola could pull him into a hug, a knock on the porch door sent Sam brushing past her to the hallway. "It's Matt!" he cried. He sailed down the stairs and landed with a thud in the kitchen.

"I'll be down in one minute," Lola called after him. She moved slowly to the bathroom and checked her hair and makeup one last time, listening to Matt's low voice mix with Sam's high-pitched eager one.

It had been a long time since she'd felt so giddy. Butterflies tickled her stomach and she couldn't help but laugh at her reflection. Her skin glowed. She looked and felt healthier than she had in years.

Downstairs, Sam and Matt laughed together, their voices quiet and silly. Lola took one last look at herself in the mirror, flicked off the bathroom light, and jittered her way to the stairs.

Lola's heels touched the kitchen floor, her knuckles white on the railing. She clung to it, steadying herself from a sudden rush of emotion as she gazed at Matt and Sam.

Matt grinned at Lola and whistled quietly. "You look... stunning," he decided, his voice soft. His hand slid from Sam's neck where he'd been adjusting the boy's tie. He straightened, tall and handsome in his dark suit, and faced Lola.

Grinning from ear to ear, Sam slipped his hand into Matt's and gave it a little tug. "Told ya," he said, glancing up at him. "Just like Cinderella."

"Thank you," Lola giggled. Using the table for support, she reached Sam and bent to kiss the top of his head. Slowly, she straightened and touched Matt's tie. "Look at you two. I'm going to be the most envied girl at the Ball."

They stared at one another for a moment, Lola's fingers wrapped around Matt's tie while his lips curved into a playful smirk. He lifted a finger to her dangling earring and gave it a gentle flick.

Sam glanced back and forth between the two, waiting patiently for someone to speak. He tugged on Matt's hand, sighed, and when there was still no response, he reached over and poked his mother in the leg.

"What are you guys staring at?" he asked. A rip of laughter burst from Matt and he squeezed Sam's hand. Lola glanced away, trying to hide the flush that warmed her cheeks.

"We should probably get to the fire hall so I can set up," she said. She had to clear her throat to get the words out. Sam rushed out the porch door, but Lola was much slower. Walking unsteadily to her equipment, she gathered her bags over her shoulders. But before she could walk with them, Matt was beside her, pulling the bags from her shoulder and sliding them over his. He glanced down at her satin shoes, and with a sigh, lifted his eyes to hers.

"You're killing me," he muttered. A familiar disapproving scowl etched into his forehead, but a small smile still managed to tease his lips. He silently slipped his fingers under her arm and escorted her to the door.

THE SOUNDS OF LAUGHTER and conversation mingled with dinner music in the busy fire hall. Matt stood behind a wall of waist-high counters, his eyes scanning the room as he manned a huge pot of steaming noodles. He and four other fire men, Gabe included, were clad in spaghetti-stained aprons as they served a crowd of beautifully dressed, and very hungry people.

Scooping a plateful of noodles, Matt greeted Mr. and Mrs. Thompson as he served them the traditional Fireman's Ball dinner. As he waited for the next person in line, his eyes drifted and fell on Sam. He sat in a corner with Caleb and another little boy, playing cards and laughing hysterically at one another.

It was amazing how much Sam had changed over the summer, Matt mused. He'd arrived at Hope River timid and quiet, with barely an ounce of meat on his bones and a dull ache in his eyes. Now he giggled and hollered louder than the other children and his frame had filled out from a summer of endless play and home-cooked food. He looked healthy. And so incredibly happy.

With a quick burst of surprise, Matt realized the feeling in his chest. It was a paternal, instinctual throb that was terrifying and comforting all at once. When had he fallen so hard for the boy?

Stirring the spaghetti sauce and ladling a mound on Mrs. Patterson's plate, Matt wondered how he'd found himself in such a state. Falling for a little boy and his mother had been the last thing he'd expected. But somehow, though he hadn't realized what was missing, they'd made his life feel full again.

A bellow of laughter rang through the fire hall. Heads turned and eyes darted to the middle of the room. The noise had come from Charlie, sitting at a table beside his family and smiling up at Lola. He held his belly as he laughed. Beside him Lola laughed too. She clutched a camera in one hand, her other on Charlie's shoulder. She was beaming, and she was beautiful.

Matt watched her, as did so many others in the crowd. Her dress was stunning. It draped from her shoulders and poured over her curves, exposing just enough cleavage to make a man's heart patter. The glossy wine fabric tucked at her knees and draped to her heels like a curtain. One leg peeked out, long and creamy and slim at the ankle, and her feet were soft and bare.

Seeing Lola's toes, Matt laughed and then coughed to cover the noise.

"What are you grunting about?" Gabe asked, setting a pan of hot garlic bread on the counter beside him. He followed Matt's gaze and his eyes landed squarely on Lola. He poked an elbow in Matt's ribs to snap him from the daze.

Flinching, Matt shot his friend a warning glance. But he couldn't help the smile that remained on his lips. He was glad she'd ditched her neck-breaking heels. Doctor's permission or not, it was one less thing for Matt to worry about.

"Better watch yourself, buddy," Gabe teased. "Girl like her can pull you under."

Matt glanced at his best friend and frowned. "I thought you liked her."

"I do. But I'm still keeping my eye on you. Someone has to." Gabe slapped Matt on the shoulder and leaned in close. "Just want to make sure you know what you're getting into, that's all."

Before Matt could answer, Mrs. Brisby was in front of him, holding her plate out expectantly. She nudged the woman beside her and grinned.

"Aren't these firemen so handsome in their suits and aprons?" she giggled.

The old woman beside her snorted. "I say any man who cooks is a handsome man." She laughed with Mrs. Brisby and then held her plate out to Matt as well.

The women moved ahead to pile more food on their already heaping plates. Matt rubbed a hand over his tired neck and considered Gabe's comment. What exactly *was* he getting himself into?

He glanced over the crowd once more and let his eyes settle on Lola. He studied her smile, her dark eyes, the curves of her slight body. He had certainly fallen for her. Hard. But he'd also told Lola that he didn't need any promises, and he intended to keep his word. He wouldn't ask her for any more than she could give. He would take what she offered and be content with that. It seemed simple enough.

As if she could feel his eyes on her, Lola turned and caught Matt watching her. He knew it was too late to look away or to cover his dopey grin. And he was far beyond trying to hide his feelings from her. He held her gaze, his eyes surely revealing how much he longed to hold her. She lifted her camera and caught a quick picture of him, then winked over the lens.

WHEN THE TABLES WERE cleaned and stowed away and the firemen were busy tidying up in the kitchen, the hall lights dimmed. The band kicked it up a notch, causing children and couples young and old to begin a sort of boogie on the dance floor. Elegant gowns swirled and shimmied and men unbuttoned their waist coats. The atmosphere of the room was electric and fun as Matt neared Lola. He loosened his tie, feeling warm and constricted after so many hours of working in the kitchen. But Lola stopped him with a soft hand over his.

"Just a little longer," she pleaded, standing on tip toe to tighten it again and smooth his shoulders. "I want a picture of the three of us."

Matt frowned, but moved closer to her, tapping a finger beneath her chin. "Only if I can take it off after that," he said. She smiled and gave a little nod. Leaning into him, she settled her body so close that her lilac scent made shivers dance through his chest. He circled her waist with his hands and breathed deep.

"Can you find Sam for me?" Lola murmured. Her liquid eyes danced with his while she ran fingers down his chest. He was paralyzed by her beauty, by her touch. He nodded, swallowing hard. And as he moved away in search of Sam, he promised himself that he would get a dance with the most beautiful woman at the Ball before night's end.

"LET'S FIX YOU UP a bit," Matt suggested, tugging Sam's shirt and tie back into place. The boy looked like he'd been wrestling beneath the tables, with spaghetti smeared on one sleeve and dust rubbed into his pant legs. His hair was disheveled and sticking to his forehead.

"What did you get into?" Matt scolded, but his smile made Sam giggle.

"Riley showed us a new game where we jump off the chairs and-"

Holding up a hand, Matt shook his head and closed his eyes. "Never mind, I don't want to know. If you tell me I'll just have to explain it to your mother." He ruffled Sam's hair and pulled him into a quick hug. "She wants a picture with us, so you have to stay out of trouble for a few minutes."

They walked hand-in-hand through the crowd, stopping every few feet for a quick conversation or to suffer through a pat on Sam's head and a squeeze of his pink cheeks. Reaching the corner of the hall where Lola was set up for portraits, they watched Mr. and Mrs. Jensen pose and smile.

"Say spaghetti!" Lola called, enticing genuine smiles and laughter from them. The camera flashed and they thanked her, Mrs. Jensen giving Lola a quick hug before moving back to the crowd.

"Sam!" Lola cried when she spied him. "What on earth?" She

grabbed him by the shoulders and looked him up and down. Sam peeked at Matt, his eyes begging for backup.

Matt sighed. "Just the usual boy stuff," he said, quickly grabbing Lola's hand and pulling her to the backdrop. "If you think he's bad, you should see how filthy the other kids are." He winked at Sam and then waved to Anne and her husband as they approached.

"Don't you all look beautiful together!" Anne cried. She covered her heart with her hands and sighed.

Her husband shifted beside her and rolled his eyes. "You look as comfortable in your suit as I feel in mine," he teased Matt. Both men grumbled and fiddled with their ties.

"Anne, could you take a picture of us?" Lola asked, pushing Matt's hands off his tie and fixing it for him once more. She slipped on her shoes, making her calves curve like a seasoned dancer's.

Those legs, Matt sighed internally. Dear God, how he wanted those sexy legs wrapped around him.

"Awww, Mom," Sam whined, holding back from the portrait area. Lola posed in front of the camera, both hands on her hips and a scowl etched into her forehead.

"Please, Sam. Just one," she pleaded

Picking him up by the shoulders, Matt dropped Sam beside his mother. "If I have to do this, Champ, you do too." He tugged on Sam's little ear and wrapped a hand around the curve of Lola's waist. Nearby couples on the dance floor turned to gape and point and smile, and before a word was said the flash blinded them and Anne let out a hoot of approval.

"Perfect!" she cried. Which was all it took for Sam to sprint from his mother's grip and back to his mischievous adventures with friends.

"Sam, wait!" Lola called after him, but Matt had pulled her tighter against him, his lips an inch from her ear.

"I need to dance with you," he whispered.

Another flash blinded them and they turned to see Anne smiling from behind the camera. "Oops, my mistake!" she giggled. Stepping back, she winked at Lola and took her husband's hand, following him to the dance floor.

Matt's grip tightened on Lola's waist as she tried to pull away. "But Sam-" she mumbled, still blinking from the flash.

"He's fine," Matt assured. His lips touched her ear lobe, making the dangly gold earring shiver.

"I have to make sure everyone's had their picture taken," she insisted, though she no longer pulled back from Matt. Instead her hands wrapped around his waist, her fingers smoothing his crisp shirt.

"Dance with me," Matt whispered again, this time his lips soft on her temple. "I need to hold you."

A whispery sigh tumbled from Lola and she let him guide her to the floor where music beat softly and the crowd swayed as one. Matt pulled her into his arms, his hands caressing the silky skin of her neck and shoulders, moving down her arms until they settled at her waist. He held her hand against his chest and moved slowly with the music. He felt her relax, and smiled down into her eyes.

Like an endless night sky, Lola's eyes were twinkling and soulful. He could see so much in those eyes. A mixture of fears, of hopes and dreams. How far she'd already come and how far she still needed to go. She had so much to give, and, whether she was ready to admit it or not, there was so much that she wanted to receive.

If she would let him, Matt would give her everything she ever hoped for. He knew she couldn't offer him any promises, and he understood why. But he could. And when she was ready, he would offer them. He would tell her that he wouldn't give up on them, that he wouldn't let the threat of time or distance break them apart.

Pulling Lola against his chest and resting his cheek on her tumble of curls, Matt decided that he had one promise for himself as well.

This time, he wouldn't give up on love.

IT WAS NEARLY MIDNIGHT when Lola slid from the truck and watched Matt tuck her son in his sturdy arms. The cool night air kissed their warm cheeks and moonlight lit a path to the house. Sam's head bobbed until Matt cupped it with his palm and laid it gently on his shoulder.

The way that Sam held him, half asleep yet still clutching Matt like a boy clutches his daddy, made Lola's heart ache.

After whispered instructions Matt crept slowly up the stairs, still cupping Sam's sleepy head, and deposited the little boy in bed. Lola watched from the doorway, arms crossed over her chest and a shiver dancing through her body. The man was an endless giver, his heart so big that it filled the room. It was no wonder he'd become such an important part of her life so quickly.

Absently, she shook her head when Matt pointed to the shoes still on Sam's feet. She would peel his clothes and shoes off after Matt left. At the moment, she only wanted to look at the gorgeous man in front of her. To find a way to thank him and tell him how alive and wonderful he made her feel.

Matt rubbed a gentle hand over Sam's thick hair, then inched to the doorway. He moved quietly into the hallway with Lola and closed the door behind them. Standing inches apart, they listened to the silence of the night, suddenly unsure without the music and atmosphere of the Ball to cushion them.

"I had a really nice time-"

"Thanks for-"

Together they laughed and glanced at the floor, fidgeting and shifting in place. Silence overwhelmed them again.

Matt sighed. "Was it as awkward as you remember?" he asked. Lola raised her eyebrows curiously. "Dancing with me," he clarified.

Relaxing her shoulders, Lola studied Matt's pale blue eyes. She felt herself blush, and before she could talk herself out of it, she looped a finger over the waist of his black dress pants and pulled him close. "There was nothing awkward about being in your arms tonight," she whispered.

Matt studied her face for a moment, taking in her eyes and mouth, and a look of desperation passed over his own. He leaned over Lola, slowly, still studying her, until finally his lips touched hers. He kissed her softly, gently at first, as if savoring her flavor. An explosion of heat and desire burst in her chest, and Lola pulled him against her until her back hit the wall. Wrapping a strong hand behind her neck, his thumb caressed her cheekbone and he pressed his hard body against her. She couldn't breathe, couldn't get him close enough to her. Desperately, she pulled at his shirt and tugged it from the waist of his pants.

A sudden, intense lust startled her, making Lola pull back and suck in a breath. They were plastered together, their breath ragged. She watched Matt's face as he waited, pain and desire swirling in his eyes. She grasped a handful of his crisp white shirt in her fist and pulled him to her again, kissing him with all the passion she'd felt since the first day they'd met. Her body screamed to be touched, her skin ached for his hands. She slid along the wall to her bedroom door, pulling Matt with her, his body still hot against hers, his mouth devouring her mouth, her neck, her shoulder. God, how she wanted him in her bed - where was her damn bed? Using her hand for guidance, she blindly felt their way through the door and back until her legs bumped the mattress. His hands slid to her hips and he rocked her against him as she clawed at his back. The heat from his body seeped through her satin dress, warming her straight to the bone. With trembling fingers, he slipped the dress from her shoulders, kissing the newly exposed skin. His hands trailed down her sides and back up over her breasts. He nipped her ear, teased her neck, greedily cupped her in his hands until Lola shuddered with blinding need. She pulled Matt over her and fell onto the bed.

Lola closed her eyes and savored his touch, arching as Matt's lips wet her collar bone and his hands tugged her hips against his. She pulled his shirt up, yanked the buttons open, desperate to feel his warm skin in her hands. Her fingers slid up his back, groping every bulging, rippling muscle. And when Matt's hands found her bare thighs and slid beneath her dress, up to her hips and under the lace of her panties, the darkness of Lola's mind exploded with desperate flashes of light. She ached to taste every inch of him, to feel him make love to her, their bodies so close that they could not find the end of one or the beginning of another.

Matt abruptly froze. He lifted his head, hovering above Lola, and frowned into the darkness of the room. Slightly turning his head, he listened, then looked back at Lola with concern.

Then she heard it too.

"Mo-om," a quiet voice whimpered from across the hall. Lola's head swirled as if she were caught under water. It took one more whimper from Sam before she could sit up, before Matt rolled off of her. She pushed her dress down to cover her legs, adjusted the shoulders and glanced at Matt. It was so painful to leave him, to see the disappointment on his face that reflected her own. With a weak smile, she slid from the bed and moved across the hall.

Sam was half-sitting on his bed, nearly toppling over from exhaustion, trying to pull a shoe from his foot. His eyes were closed, his hair was disheveled, and Lola sighed in relief. He didn't even know he was up and surely hadn't heard a thing from his mother's room.

Lola lay Sam gently back on his pillow, pulled his shoes and pants off, then tucked his legs under his blanket. She wrapped it over his shoulders, let out a huge sigh of relief as she watched his face relax with the peace of sleep, and kissed his forehead. She could feel her hair toppling in chaotic strands down her neck, could feel the moisture of lust on her back. Her knees still trembled.

When Lola closed Sam's door, Matt was sitting on the edge of her bed, leaning over his knees with his chin in his hand. He looked up anxiously.

"Is he okay?" he whispered, worry in his eyes. They'd been so careless, so wrapped up in each other that they'd forgotten. Lola nodded and gave a weak smile.

"He's fine. He wasn't even really awake. He was trying to get his shoes off."

The expression on Matt's face passed from relief to humor. He smirked, then let out a quiet belt of laughter as Lola's face exploded in an embarrassed smile.

"I'm sorry," Lola whispered through her laughter. She stood between his legs and ran her fingers through his hair while he rested his forehead on her stomach. He held her by the waist, his hands no longer urgent on her skin, but soft and careful. He shook his head and stood, slowly wrapping his arms around Lola's shoulders. Her body still tingled under his touch.

With a sigh, Matt pressed his forehead against hers. "I should go home," he whispered.

She didn't want him to go. She didn't want the night to end, to lose the chance of being with the man she had fallen in love with. But she wrinkled her nose and nodded, knowing it was best.

They took turns fixing each other's clothing. Lola slowly buttoned Matt's shirt where she'd forced it open, smoothing the wrinkles they'd made. He adjusted the silky fabric of the dress on her shoulder, his fingers soft over her skin. They trailed her neckline, tender and patient, and stopped to press over her heart.

Leaning into her, Matt bent until his nose touched hers. He brushed his lips against her cheek, whispered a kiss against her mouth. With a desperate sigh, she held his shoulders and fought to keep her control. He felt so good. So perfect.

Matt backed away and hung his head, laughing quietly. "I'm going to go home and take a cold shower," he whispered. He kissed Lola quickly before letting go of her, then took a step back. A flash of regret danced over his face and he pulled her toward him again, cupping her face in his hands, and kissed her with so much passion that her knees gave out. Her heart stopped beating, then nearly burst when his mouth left hers. He brushed a thumb over her lips and stepped into the hallway.

"Goodnight," he whispered, and she nodded and bit her lip, following him to the stairs.

"I had a great time tonight..." she said, a smile playing at her lips. She was going to need a cold shower too, as soon as he stepped out the door.

Matt grinned so wide that lines piled up on his cheeks, making Lola's knees feel like wet noodles for the hundredth time that night. "Me too," he replied, a knowing twinkle in his eye. "Me too."

Chapter Nineteen

❧

"How did it go last night?" Sarah asked. Lola flinched in surprise. Her face instantly flushed thinking of how things really did go the previous night, rolling around on her bed with Matt in a fit of lust. It had been delicious, mind-numbing, and so intense that the cold shower Lola took afterward hadn't done a thing to calm her.

She was still wound up this morning.

Lola set her dessert on Rena and Gabe's picnic table. She'd made a huge pan of zesty lemon bars at five a.m., after a night of fitful sleep and delicious dreams. Though not even baking had eased her thoughts of Matt.

People slowly trickled in, still smiling from the evening before, ready for the traditional picnic of leftovers from the Ball. Lola swallowed hard and braced herself for a quiet conversation with Sarah. She needn't have worried.

"When do we get to see all of the pictures?" Sarah asked.

"Oh." Lola stood straight and clasped her hands in front of her. "The pictures! They'll, um... they'll be on the Ritz Pix website tomorrow. You can call Anne or swing by and order what you'd like."

Sarah's grin was bright. "What a great idea! It'll bring so much new business to Anne's shop." She gave Lola's arm a friendly squeeze. "I can't wait to see our pictures. Wasn't Clint so handsome in his suit last night?" She gave a little giggle and wiggled her fingers at her husband across the yard. "Matthew was quite dashing last night too," she added, raising her eyebrows at Lola.

Lola felt her cheeks flush once again. She swallowed the lump in her throat and smiled weakly. Rena's loud voice interrupted.

"Eat up, everyone!" she called as she hauled a large pan of spaghetti to the line of tables. Gabe followed behind with an even larger pan full of sauce and meatballs, and the crowd began to swarm. Lola backed toward Rena's porch and the protection it offered.

Across the yard on the swing set, Sam waved. "Watch, Mom!" he cried as he and Caleb leapt from the highest point of their swings. They tumbled to the ground and rolled into laughing, squirming heaps. Lola gasped and clutched her chest as the boys stood and brushed themselves off, laughing hysterically and giving high fives.

"Boys, you're going to break your necks doing that!" Rena shouted as she walked to the porch. She shook her head and joined Lola in glaring at their sons.

"Aw, c'mon," Gabe teased, a step behind his wife. "Every kid does it. Did you ever know anyone who broke their necks leaping from the swing?" He brushed past Rena and opened the porch door. "Let them be boys!" One by one, he pulled the women by their arms and stuffed them through the door.

Inside, the kitchen was steamy and warm from heating food all morning. Gabe flipped on the ceiling fan and wrapped a strong hand around the back of Lola's neck. "You look like you could use some cold lemonade," he decided.

Lola nodded, trying to calm her heart rate. "Thanks." She peeked out the window to make sure that Sam was still alive, then turned to watch Gabe pull two gallons of lemonade from the fridge. He poured her a glass, thrust it in her hand, then trudged outside with the gallons clenched in his fists. Rena watched him and rolled her eyes.

"I wonder how long until he remembers the ice?" she muttered. She moved to the counter to sort a tray of cheese and meat.

"How are you today?" Rena asked, glancing at Lola and then back to the tray. "You're awfully quiet this morning."

Lola sipped her lemonade, puckering her lips a little as she considered how much to reveal.

"I'm good, actually. Really good. Really, really good." She nodded and sipped again, still rolling thoughts of Matt around in her head.

"That good, huh?" Rena teased, smirking at her. She leaned against the kitchen counter and raised an eyebrow. "Spill it," she demanded.

Lola swallowed the lemonade with a gulp that made her cough. "Spill what?" she asked when she recovered. Was she really that easy to read?

"Matt took you home last night."

Lola felt her eyes bulge. "Yep. Yes he did." She studied a piece of lemon floating in her glass.

"And you're glowing. I haven't seen you glowing since I met you. What's making you glow?" A wicked grin spread over Rena's lips.

"I'm glowing?" Lola asked. She looked at her hand, her arm, studied her skin. "I'm not glowing."

The porch door slammed closed, making Lola jump. Matt walked into the kitchen, whistling a tune as he moved. "Hi Ree," he called. When he noticed Lola, an instant smirk touched his lips. She smiled in return and could feel her face flush. *Now* she was glowing.

"Hi," Matt said, tilting his head as he smiled at Lola.

Lola nodded, her blush deepening. "Hi," she chirped.

Rena watched the exchange. "I knew it!" she cried, pointing a finger at them both. "The two of you are like giddy teenagers!"

Matt and Lola started at the sudden outburst, and then laughed as Rena hummed and wiggled her eyebrows.

"Rena, it's not like that," Lola insisted, holding a palm up. "We didn't, we aren't..." She shook her head in denial but couldn't finish her thought. Matt only set his hands on his hips and grinned, offering no help at all.

"Well, whatever this is, I get the feeling you two could use some time alone," Rena offered, turning back to her tray. A flash of relief spread through Lola. She *could* use some time alone with Matt. It might take a few minutes to get used to him again, to catch her breath and wrap her mind around what exactly was going on. Last night had changed things, and Lola wasn't sure what to make of it yet.

Rena plucked a small knife from the drawer. She swung it around, slicing salami in time with her words. "Lola, I'm going to take Sam tomorrow night. Caleb's been begging for a sleep-over for weeks. Which leaves you-" she pointed the knife at Lola and grinned mischievously, "-free to do *any*thing you want to." She sliced the last of the salami with gusto and tossed the knife in the sink with a clatter. "For example, you could go on a date with a strapping young fireman."

Rena lifted the tray and swung around, facing Lola and Matt squarely. They were both speechless, eyebrows raised in surprise.

"A date?" Lola murmured. She hadn't been on a date for so long that just the word made her stomach flip.

Rena swept past them. "Just an idea!" she called over her shoulder.

She walked out the porch door, her shoes clapping on each wooden stair. Matt turned to Lola and laughed at the look on her face.

Lola felt herself tremble. A date? Was she ready for that step? Could she explain it to Sam?

Without a word, Matt took Lola's face in both palms and pulled her gently to him, planting a long, delicious kiss on her lips. She leaned into him, her body surrendering before her mind had a chance to decide. With a breathy sigh of relief, she let her hands fall on his waist. She could stay here, in this moment, forever.

"It's about damn time!" Gabe shouted, blowing into the kitchen. He eyed Lola and Matt with a huge grin, his face bright. "I thought you two would never figure it out." Matt and Lola, caught in the act already, didn't bother to pull apart. Instead they held each other, foreheads together, and laughed as Gabe slapped Matt hard on the back. Lola peeked over Matt's shoulder and watched Gabe go to the freezer, yank out a bag of ice and slam the door closed. He turned and winked at Lola, then whizzed past them again.

"Forgot the ice," he called over his shoulder, and was out the door just as quickly as he'd arrived.

Matt kissed Lola's forehead. "What do you think?" he whispered, leaning down for another kiss.

Her eyes fluttered closed and she lost all ability to concentrate. About what? She tried to figure it out, but his lips were soft and breath so warm against her skin. His fingers danced over her neck and shoulders, sending pleasure all the way to her toes. About sneaking into the other room and making out uncontrollably? Going back to her place and finishing what they started last night?

"I'd like to take you out," Matt said, breaking Lola's thoughts. "Anywhere you want." His fingers whispered over her arms and down to her hands. He held them in his own and stepped back to get a good look at Lola's face. Still in a breathless daze, she nodded and grinned.

"I'd like that," she whispered. And she would, Lola decided as her head slowly cleared. She really, really would.

"So, is this like a date?" Sam asked innocently from his perch on Lola's bed. She could see him in the reflection of the mirror, his pointed chin propped in his hands as he lay on his belly, his feet wiggling in the air behind him. She continued to fidget with her earrings, trying to hide the fact that she needed to swallow the baseball-sized lump that had suddenly clogged her throat.

Lola had been avoiding this conversation with Sam for days, but couldn't ignore it any longer. "No, not really a date," she began, studying his reflection. Sam frowned.

"Sam, honey, I miss your father very much, just like you do. I loved him. I always will." She swirled around to face Sam on the bed, her sleeveless berry-colored dress spinning at her knees. "But life moves on and I think it's important that we do too. Even when it's hard, or scary, or strange..." She swallowed hard and instinctively tried to roll the old wedding band on her finger, momentarily forgetting it was no longer there.

"Part of moving on," Lola continued as she stepped toward Sam and watched his serious face, "is meeting new people and getting to know them. And, well…" She shrugged, not sure what to say next. Sam simply waited.

"So, actually, this is kind of… a little bit… like a date." Hearing the words come from her mouth made Lola panic, and she reached for Sam's hand. "But baby, I won't go if it bothers you. I know things haven't been easy these past couple years and I don't want to confuse you or rush into anything…"

"No, it's okay," Sam decided. "I miss Dad too. But I like Coach - I mean, Matt. He's nice to you." He smiled bravely at his mom, and by the look on his face, Lola knew he was being truthful. "You should go. It'll be fun."

Lola took his chin in her hand and kissed his forehead. She sat beside him and pulled Sam into a hug.

"Are you going to kiss him?" Sam asked against her chest. His words were muffled, but the question was clear. Lola flinched at it, but she tried to keep a calm expression. Her cheeks betrayed her as they grew warm and she let out a little giggle.

"I don't know, honey. We're just keeping it simple. But you don't have to worry about anything, okay?"

With an easy nod, Sam wiggled from her arms and moved to the doorway. "Okay. Can I go to Caleb's now?"

Nodding, Lola let out a long breath of air, like a balloon slowly leaking. Relief and despair clashed in her gut as she watched Sam disappear down the stairs. Her palms were sweaty, her head throbbed, and butterflies flopped in her stomach. Her anxiousness over an evening with Matt had been nothing compared to worrying about this little talk with Sam.

She flopped backward onto the bed and covered her head with a pillow.

LOLA WAS GRATEFUL WHEN Matt's truck pulled into the driveway.

And pure relief flooded her body when his arms enveloped her.

"I missed you," Matt whispered, snuggling her to his chest. She wrapped her arms around his neck and let him pick her up, her eyes level with his. The warm kiss that he planted on her lips made Lola's stomach quiver.

"I missed you too," she said, feeling her face bloom with a smile.

Matt set her down and stepped back. "Where's Sam?"

"I already walked him over to Rena's. He was too excited for the sleepover to wait for you."

Did she detect a small pout on the man's face? It soothed her heart to see that he cared for her son as much as Sam adored him.

"Don't worry," she teased as she rubbed her fingers over his smooth cheek. "You're still his favorite." The comment made a smile return to Matt's lips. He gathered her hand in his and set a soft kiss on her skin.

If Lola's heart could beat any louder, she was sure that Matt would hear it. She'd known the man nearly two months, yet she trembled like a child. "I'll just run upstairs and grab my purse," Lola said, letting her hand glide over his chest as she backed away. It would do her good to take a few minutes to gather herself, to catch her breath and calm down. She gave Matt a brilliant smile, then slipped up the stairs.

MATT WASN'T SURE WHAT to do with his hands. He ran them anxiously over the back of his neck, then shoved them in his jeans pockets. He'd decided years ago that dating was for the birds, and now he remembered why.

Glancing around the kitchen, Matt tried to take his mind off the restless desires that burned in his gut. He felt like a high school kid again, hungry for Lola's body and mouth and skin...

He shook his head, closing his eyes and letting a muffled groan escape. *Get a grip, Dawson.* This was supposed to be an easy evening together, a night to enjoy each other's company.

Matt walked to the kitchen counter and leaned against it, glancing out the window to the back yard. Evening was falling upon them, the sun casting a pink glow over the trees. The perfect color for a romantic evening with the woman he'd so quickly fallen in love with.

Turning with another frustrated sigh, Matt spied Lola's black laptop. It sat in a pile with her paperwork, in the same corner of the kitchen it had been all summer. Dust had actually covered the top, making Matt grin. It eased his heart to see that Lola hadn't been busy with a job search or looking for a reason to go back to California in August. Maybe she would stay. He could only hope.

Don't get ahead of yourself, Matt warned his eager mind. Absently, he tried to tuck a bent paper back into a folder beside the laptop. His fingers were too big to gracefully tuck it away, so Matt pulled it out and smoothed the wrinkled paper over his chest. As he reached to the folder to slip it back inside, a picture on the paper caught his attention. He glanced at the stairs, making sure Lola wasn't returning.

It only took a moment to recognize the faded blueprint. The room was large and spacious and part of a building labeled *Ritz Pix.* And in tiny, penciled lettering, almost as if it were trying to whisper a secret, someone had labeled the room *Lola's Studio.* Equipment was drawn in one corner next to a wall marked *backdrop.* At the entry, chairs and end tables were sketched in, and a small section was labeled *play area.*

Matt smiled at the dreams that sang from the paper, at the dreams it inspired in his own mind. Would she risk everything and decide to stay? His hopes soared at the thought, but crashed back to reality as he heard Lola's footsteps on the stairs. Quickly, he shoved the paper beside the folder and turned in time to see Lola stepping into the kitchen.

She was gorgeous. Even more stunning than a minute earlier when he'd watched her walk up those same stairs. She hadn't done anything different; it just seemed that every time he saw her she grew even more beautiful. And now she was one step closer to being a permanent part of his life.

"Ready?" Matt asked. As much as he wanted to ask questions, he wouldn't tell her what he'd seen. She would unveil it in her own time.

Matt held out his hand, eager to start the night. It was a new beginning for them, a chance at something real. He wouldn't push it, he'd stick to his promises. But he also wouldn't deny the possibility that a new chapter of their lives was unfolding before his eyes.

"OF ALL THE PLACES for our first date, you choose to stay in Hope River and go to a bar called *The Outhouse.*" Matt shook his head and lifted a glass of beer to his lips.

"I wanted to try out the local food," Lola insisted.

"You wanted to stay close to Sam."

With a twinkle in her eye, Lola took a sip of her beer and licked the foam from her lip. "This place is cute," she added.

"Cute?" Matt laughed. "I guess I've never heard it called that before. It's been around since before I was born and they probably haven't changed a thing about it in all that time. But they serve good food."

"Beats the atmosphere of half the restaurants in my big city," Lola said. She smiled at the animal heads hanging over the bar and the row of local patrons seated on the stools. "Long lines, stifling waiting areas, crabby servers…and all for some stinky, expensive seafood."

Matt chuckled. "You're not a fan of seafood?"

Lola wrinkled her nose. "Not really. I'm more of a pasta and salad kind of girl."

Lifting a worn single-page menu, Matt glanced over the list of food. "Well, they have a salad bar and I think they serve spaghetti…" He shifted his gaze to Lola's and smirked. "But you have to remember that you're in a town of German heritage. Folks around here like the food to stick to their ribs."

Lola swiped the menu from Matt. She eyed it for a moment, feeling Matt's gaze on her, then looked up with certainty. "Ok, then I'll have pork chops and dumplings."

Matt's eyebrows raised with approval. "Good choice." He plucked the menu from her hands and laid it on the table. "Steak and potato for me."

"Goin' a little crazy, aren't you?" Lola teased. Matt found her foot with his, nudging her softly beneath the table.

The meal turned out to be delicious, but in Lola's mind the company was even better. She hadn't had an uninterrupted dinner conversation with another adult in years.

"Tell me about your family," Lola said as she used a knife to spear the juicy pork chop. The aroma of their meals had her mouth watering. She tried to eat slowly to savor the food.

"I have one sister. She's a music teacher and lives in Massachusetts. My parents lived in Hope River all their lives but moved to Idaho a few years ago. They've always wanted to live in the mountains."

Lola chewed the squishy dumpling, soaked with butter and gravy, and nodded as she listened. "And you've been friends with Gabe all your life?"

"Since we were four. He took a swing at me for stealing his Tonka truck in the playground sandbox. We've been like brothers ever since," Matt laughed. "I grew up with half the guys around here. We've all been through a lot together."

"You're lucky to have friendships like that," Lola sighed. "I don't keep in touch with many of the people I went to school with. Our classes were huge, over a thousand in my graduating year. You'd think with all those students you'd have a better chance of bonding with someone, but really, it just felt lonely. Too big, too overwhelming."

Matt studied Lola before taking a sip of his beer. "What about your family? You've spent all your life in California?"

She nodded, pushing the food around her plate. Her stomach had filled quickly with the heavy meal. "I was born in L.A. and we moved to San Francisco when I was eight. It was just me and my parents. When I was eighteen my parents divorced. Dad moved to Florida, my mom went to Sacramento, and I buried myself in college life. That's where I met Travis." She took a small bite of pork chop, chewed thoughtfully, then added, "Travis' family was all we had when Sam was born. They went through so much with us. I know they miss Sam a lot, and they're heartbroken over Travis."

The waitress appeared at the table then, a tray balanced in one hand and the other hand on her hip. "Can I get you two another beer?" she asked, eyeing Lola carefully. No doubt, Lola decided, the waitress was gathering as much gossip as she could. Tomorrow the whole town would know more about Lola and Matt than they probably knew themselves.

Lola sighed. She wanted to explain to Matt that she felt like she was breaking her in-laws' hearts. That she had taken their only grandchild away from them so quickly after their son's death. If she didn't return, didn't bring Sam back to them or find the proper closure for everyone, the guilt might just swallow her whole. Their return was necessary. It would be as much for her in-laws as it would be for herself.

But the words wouldn't form on her lips.

"Are you saving room for dessert?" Matt teased. Lost in her worries, Lola had stopped eating, though her plate was still half full. She leaned back and rubbed her stomach. "I feel like I swallowed a bowling ball."

Matt grinned. "That dumpling is probably five pounds of potato and flour alone." He leaned forward to inspect her plate. "But you did pretty well for an amateur."

"Want some?" Lola asked, pushing her plate toward him.

He lifted a hand in protest. "No, thanks. You might have to carry me out as it is." Leaning back, he gestured politely to the waitress for their bill. He smiled when his gaze returned to Lola.

"What would you like to do now?" he asked. He reached for Lola's hand and held it softly in his.

"What is there to do around here?" Lola asked.

Matt sat back and crossed his arms in thought. "Well, there's cow-tipping," he began with a smile. "Or we could go throw beer bottles off the water tower. Or, we could go hang out at the railroad tracks and play chicken with the train. That's always entertaining."

Lola laughed. "Is that what you used to do? Were you a *troublemaker?*" She couldn't imagine that the upstanding citizen across from her had once been a mischievous menace.

Matt's face filled with a guilty smile. "Small towns don't offer a lot of options. That's why we're so big on sports."

Lola tried to imagine Matt as a teenage boy. She would have had a huge crush on him, she decided. "I've always wanted to climb a water tower," she said, lacing her fingers through his.

The quick glint in Matt's eyes was both frightening and exciting. She'd never realized he was a bad-boy gone good.

It made her feel like a fluttery teenager all over again.

"WE'RE GOING TO GET arrested," Lola whispered through her giggles. She crouched behind Matt, holding his hand as they made their way around the fencing of the water tower.

"Don't worry, I know the sheriff," Matt whispered back. "I'm sure he'll only throw us in jail for one night."

Lola stopped in her tracks, tugging Matt backwards. They'd tip-toed in hysterics past the sign that warned *No Trespassing*, but suddenly it wasn't so funny. What if she did get thrown in jail? How would she explain it to Sam? She'd always been a good girl, never breaking the rules. Why start now?

Matt rolled his eyes and laughed. He pulled a key from his pocket and set it in her hand. "I'm the fire chief," he reminded her. He pulled on her hand to get her moving again. "I have access to the tower for emergencies."

Lola allowed herself to be pulled to the locked gate. "But this isn't an emergency," she murmured.

Matt glanced at Lola's feet and sighed. "There might be one with those damn flip flops." When he lifted his eyes to hers, they were wary and scolding. It was a look she was getting used to. "Can you climb up here without breaking your neck?"

The question made Lola lift her chin a fraction and scowl. "Of course I can. It's just a bunch of silly stairs."

After studying her for a moment, Matt finally unlocked the chain. The metal gate squeaked open, echoing into the night. Lola glanced behind her and stepped anxiously through, a smile building on her cheeks again.

There were sixty-one stairs in all. Lola counted carefully, her eyes on her flip flops as she took each step, her hand gripped tightly in Matt's. When they reached the top, he guided her along a narrow walkway, their backs against the curving bubble of the tower where bright, bold letters spelled the town's name.

The sky was inky black without a star or the moon to break its length. The only light came from Main Street, where street lamps shone and occasional car beams danced over the road. The tower was set back from the street in a small empty field, hidden from view. Matt tucked Lola against him protectively, then leaned against the railing. Although the tower wasn't huge, the distance down still gave Lola the shivers.

"What do you think?" Matt asked quietly. He gave her shoulders a little squeeze and kissed her temple. "Wish you had picked cow-tipping instead?"

"This is the best date ever," Lola laughed. She meant it too. She couldn't remember ever having so much fun on a first date.

"You're a strange woman, Lola Sommers," Matt teased. He rubbed a thumb over her cheek. "Small town life suits you somehow. I never would have imagined saying that when we first met."

Lola pressed a playful fist into Matt's chest, but knew he spoke the truth. She wouldn't have believed that small-town life suited her either, if she hadn't just delighted in an entire summer of it.

A light breeze made strands of hair whisper over Lola's neck. "It's beautiful up here," she decided. She gazed over the glowing streets and shops below and squinted beyond the city limits. "I bet you can see for miles during the day."

Matt pulled her tight against his chest. Leaning down to press his cheek against hers, he pointed into the dark night. "Greenhills Park is over there. You can see the forest and part of the lake when it's light out." Shifting, he pointed in another direction. "Glen City and Amberton are about eight miles that way. You can see their water tower lights blinking."

Matt took a few steps left, holding Lola close as he moved. He leaned against the tower and wrapped both arms around her shoulders. "See that faint glow over there?" he asked, gesturing in front of them. She snuggled against his chest and felt dizzy from the scent of him. Burying her cheek into his neck, she nodded.

"That's the Jensen farm. My land is about a quarter mile west of it."

Lola frowned and lifted her face to Matt's. "Your land?"

"I own eight acres out there. Part of it is forest, part is field, and there's a creek running along the edge. It's a pretty piece of land."

He'd never spoken of it before, and Lola sensed there was a story behind it. She waited patiently, knowing he would continue when he was ready. His face was stone-still, his eyes lost to a faraway place full of memories.

Matt's voice was quiet when he continued. "I bought the land with Ali when we were first married. We had plans to build a big house on it when we'd saved enough money. It seemed perfect. All that space, lots of room for a growing family. But even when we had the money, we never went ahead with it. Ali just wasn't happy here. And then when the baby..." Matt shook his head and stared into the dark night.

Lola felt his body tense, watched his jaw tighten. She brushed a hand over his arm and turned to face him. "After everything you went through, you still held onto it," she whispered. She wrapped her arms around him and hugged him close, fighting against the chill of the cool night's breeze, against the ripples of anxiety that danced up her spine. He hooked his fingers behind her back and rested his cheek against her hair.

"I guess I've always hoped I could still make a home there. Have a big family and a dog, a huge yard to mow and children to chase." His eyes twinkled as he laughed at himself.

Lola thought of what her dreams of home and family had once been. A fancy house in the Bay with her husband and children, a sea of faces and an endless list of shops and restaurants at her fingertips.

So much had changed.

Now, it was a simple life that she pined for. A quiet existence in a town where faces came with names. Where summers were filled with baseball games and picnics by the creek, slow walks through the park and enough peace that she could hear herself think.

And a place where dreams could be planted, tended, and grown to fruition.

"Sounds perfect," she decided with a little hum. She rested her head on Matt's heart and let herself dream with him.

Lola tensed as voices floated up from below. She pulled herself from Matt's arms and leaned over the railing.

"Do you think someone knows we're up here?" she whispered. Disturbing thoughts of trespassing and jail time returned. Her flip flops dangled over the edge as she squinted at the ground, searching for movement. Matt slipped his hands around her waist and pulled her back. "No one knows we're here." He pressed his lips, warm and soft, against Lola's jaw and nibbled down her neck. "Stop worrying. You won't be thrown in jail tonight," he added before playfully nipping her shoulder.

A shiver built at the base of her neck and rippled all the way to her fingertips. She was helpless in his arms. She sank into him until her body molded against his. His hands surrounded her, glided over her skin and caused every nerve to hum. She turned and pressed her lips against his, feeling her blood bubble with heat. Soft and warm and slightly desperate, his mouth offered promises that made her tremble.

Lacing her fingers through his, Lola surrendered with relief. "Let's go to your place," she whispered into the darkness.

NEITHER OF THEM SPOKE on the short ride through town. The sexual tension was too thick for conversation. It was almost too thick for Lola to notice that Matt pulled his phone from his pocket and thumbed a button. He read a text message while pausing at the stop sign.

A slow breath of air escaped Matt's lips. Lola watched his chin fall to his chest.

"What is it?" she asked. Her thoughts quickly tumbled to a terrible car accident on the highway or a four-alarm fire. Her palms went clammy, her breathing quick. Was it at Gabe's? Was Sam hurt? "What's wrong?" she insisted.

Matt stuffed his phone in his pocket and took Lola's hand in his. "Everything's fine. That was Rena. She said Sam is still awake and he doesn't want to stay overnight."

Relief swept over Lola, followed by disappointment. She frowned at Matt as she rubbed a hand over her forehead. In a matter of moments, their hot, lusty evening had iced over.

"I guess I'm not surprised. He's never had a sleepover before." She squeezed Matt's hand and nodded in resignation. "I better go get him."

Chapter Twenty

"And then we painted and then we made s'mores and then we pretended we were sleeping in a tent." Sam's words spilled from him as they walked through the dark woods between the houses.

"If you were having so much fun, why didn't you stay?" Lola asked. She glanced over Sam's head and scowled at Matt in frustration. He smiled gently in return.

"Because I couldn't go to sleep. Their house smells different than ours and the floor creaks different, too." He looked up at his mother forlornly, squeezing her hand in his and pulling it softly to his face. "And I didn't want to be so far away from you." His eyes were big as a puppy dog's and he rubbed Lola's hand over his cheek so softly that she could only smile. Sam's steps slowed as a huge yawn consumed his little body.

"I'm tired," he whispered.

Sam stumbled up the porch stairs in exhaustion. Lola turned when Matt remained at the bottom of the stairs.

"Aren't you coming in?" she asked, desperation clawing in her chest. He couldn't leave. A cold shower wasn't going to fix her this time.

Matt offered a small smile, his eyes answering for him. "I should go."

A responsible parent would say good night and plan another date, Lola warned herself. But for once she didn't feel like being responsible.

"You don't have to go," she insisted.

With surprising speed, Sam brushed past her and jumped down to Matt. His little arms circled Matt's waist as he smiled.

"G'night, Matt," he whispered. With a shuddering yawn, he clambered back up the stairs and waited for Lola at the porch door. His eyes were expectant, his face weary.

Lola gripped the railing with desperation. "I had a lovely time tonight," she said, studying Matt's face in the shadows. She touched her lips as she thought of the kisses they'd shared, hungry for what it could have led to. Blushing, she glanced out at the dark night and laughed.

"Me too," Matt answered. A knowing smirk lit up his handsome features, making Lola ache.

MATT WATCHED THEIR SHADOWS move through the house, lights glowing in different rooms as Lola and Sam made their way to bed. The night had chilled enough to make Matt shiver, but still he stood in the darkness and watched them.

He felt such a strong need to protect them. His heart was inside that home. Everything he wanted from life was behind its white walls. It went against every cell in his body to leave them, but he couldn't stay. He couldn't risk the problems it might cause.

Walking slowly to his truck, Matt tried to swallow his disappointment. Lola's face had shown what he was missing tonight. The thought made him ache. Her flowery scent still lingered on his shirt where she'd nuzzled into him. He still felt her soft skin on his fingertips, still tasted the sweet flavor of her lips.

What he wouldn't do for one last kiss.

Climbing into his truck, Matt slid the keys in the ignition and turned the engine over. He shifted to reverse and looked over at the glowing white house once more. As he backed up and turned so his headlights faced the small stone bridge, Matt's gut tightened in protest.

"Go home," he warned himself. Staying would only complicate things. He'd made her a promise. He wouldn't ask for more than she could give.

But hadn't she told him to stay?

Matt wrapped his fingers tightly over the steering wheel and willed his foot to press the gas pedal.

Just one more minute with her. He wouldn't stay for long. He just needed to see her one more time.

He parked his truck on the far side of the house and turned off the engine.

The gravel driveway crackled beneath his shoes as Matt made his way to the front of the house. He considered knocking on the porch door but thought better of it. Sam might still be awake.

Lola's curtains glowed from the soft bedroom light. Matt smiled as he bent and scooped a handful of tiny stones. *Only for a minute*, he promised himself. He gently tossed a stone against her window and listened to it tap the glass. It slid down the white siding and scuttled to the ground. Slowly, he tossed a few more, making a sound like rain drops echo into the night.

A shadow moved behind the curtains and Matt felt a thrill spread through his body. He'd never called on a woman from outside her window, not even in his mischievous teenage years. Now, at thirty-two years old, he was either a complete fool, or hopelessly in love.

Lola pushed the curtains aside and peeked out. Her forehead crumpled as she bent to open the window. Slowly, the frame slid up and she leaned out cautiously. She pushed the hair from her eyes and laughed when she saw Matt. "What are you doing?"

She'd changed into a satin pink nightgown, one that was making Matt's body light on fire. The gown scooped low and revealed the soft freckled skin of her chest. Her cleavage was gorgeous from this angle.

Matt chuckled as he wiped a hand over his jaw. *One minute.*

"I couldn't leave without a goodnight kiss," he whispered.

Lola's eyes squeezed closed as she smiled. When she opened

them again, she leaned a little farther over the window sill. "I just threw on my pajamas. Give me a minute, I'll meet you-" "No, just stay there," Matt interrupted, holding up a hand. He turned, having spied an old ladder lying on the ground. It was probably left from the weekend of painting, and Matt was grateful to the person who forgot it. He set it against the house and quickly climbed the rungs.

"Matthew!" Lola cried. "You can't use that ladder! Charlie was supposed to throw it away."

Matt slowed his climb, considering for a moment. "What's wrong with it?" he asked, bouncing on the rung to test if anything would break. While Lola hissed with laughter, Matt smiled up at her. It felt pretty sturdy to him. Hell, he was moving too fast to fall anyway.

He was breathless when he reached her. His heart threatened to beat through his chest, and more than anything he simply wanted to pull her into his arms and never let go. But he willed himself to take a breath, to slow down and offer only what he'd come for. Holding the windowsill with one hand, he lifted the other to her face and kissed her with so much passion that his legs went limp.

Lola folded her hands around his neck, leaning over Matt so far that she nearly tipped out the window. They teetered backwards, laughing as they continued to kiss and cling to each other.

"Get in here," Lola giggled. She yanked Matt toward her, pulling at his arms and shoulders. Her eyes were dark and playful and her lips twisted in a sultry smile.

She dragged him in after her, barely giving him time to slide his hips through the window and lever his body inside. He stumbled to his feet, his heart pounding from the adrenaline rush.

Lola didn't wait for Matt to steady himself. She wrapped her arms around his neck, a leg around his thigh, and crushed her body so hard against his that it was all Matt could do not to drop her on the spot and tear her gown off. With one hand he pulled the curtains closed, with the other he lifted Lola by the waist. He walked to her bedroom door with her body wrapped around him, bumping against the bed and dresser as they moved.

"Is Sam asleep?" he whispered. With a quick nod she wrapped both legs around his waist and slipped her hands under his shirt. He fell with her against the door, his hands beneath her nightgown on the soft skin of her hips. With trembling fingers, he fumbled for the door handle and locked it. They laughed in hushed tones and kissed and sighed together, relief swamping them both.

Matt carried Lola to the bed and dropped her on the quilt, his body still attached to hers. He hovered over her, greedily kissing her soft mouth and the fragrant skin of her neck and shoulders. He lifted her night gown above her hips, exposing the long smooth legs that had been wrapped around him, and moaned. How long had he wanted to feel those legs? He ran a hand over them, from the ripple of her calf to the curve of her hip, until his hand glided over her lace panties. He wrapped a finger around them, aching to rip them from her body.

"Don't stop," Lola gasped. She fixed her gaze on Matt, slowing enough to take a deep breath. She ran a finger over his cheekbone, down his jaw, over swollen, desperate lips. "Please don't stop," she whispered, and covered his mouth with her own.

Her hands moved quickly as she pulled his shirt off. She slid it from his body, her fingers gliding over his chest and arms, her mouth warm and wet as it followed. She unbuttoned his jeans and slid hands over his hips, a whimper escaping her lips.

Never had he felt so out of control, so swallowed whole by his desire for a woman. Her beauty, her body, her heart and soul, she completely overwhelmed him. His mind scrambled as he tried to fight her spell, but it was useless. With a shuddering breath and desperate hands, he lifted the silky gown from her hips, up over her breasts and past her silky shoulders, over her stunning lips and eyes…and let it fall to the floor.

With every taste of her skin, every whisper of her body against his, any and all thoughts of complication disappeared. He was breaking no promises.

He took only what Lola offered, only as much as she could give.

And tonight, it was everything he needed.

A STRANGE SENSATION FILLED Lola the next morning. She felt a heady mix of exhaustion and exhilaration, a tingle that rippled from head to toe. Her face was tucked in the crook of Matt's neck and her naked body was warm against his.

Watching Matt in the new morning light, Lola smiled. He lay with both arms spread out beside him, one leg poking from beneath the heavy bedding. His face was soft with sleep, his eyelashes still over his cheeks.

Lola set her hand gently on his chest, feeling the deep rhythm of his breathing and heartbeat. She could lie like this forever, she decided, basking in the warmth and safety that surrounded them.

Her eyelids grew heavy and would have fluttered closed had she not heard car doors slam outside. She peeked at the clock- 5:45 a.m. - and tried to clear her mind. What day was it? Her heart burst with the realization.

Yoga day. The ladies had arrived, and not once during the summer had Lola missed a morning with them. If she didn't join them soon, they would come up looking for her.

Lola carefully shifted her body and slipped from the bed. The cool morning air made her bare skin prickle and she nearly laughed out loud as her feet landed on piles of clothing. They'd been tossed so easily, so carelessly the night before. It made Lola shiver all over again.

As she quickly dressed, she listened to the quiet whispers and stifled laughter of the women entering the porch. Had they noticed Matt's truck? He'd told Lola, as they'd snuggled under the covers in the early morning hours, that for Sam's sake he'd tucked it out of view on the far side of the house. God bless the man for thinking ahead.

Now it was Lola's turn to think ahead. At her door, she turned and studied Matt. He hadn't moved a muscle since she woke. He looked so peaceful, so content that surely he'd sleep for another hour. *In her bed.* She smiled at the thought.

The key was exactly where Lola remembered it, above the door frame lying snug against the wall. One key that could lock any of the second floor bedrooms from the outside. It was there for emergencies, Aunt Louise had once told her.

Today was definitely an emergency.

Silently, she closed the door and turned the skeleton key in the old lock. The little boy across the hall would likely sleep a few more hours, but she wasn't going to chance it. A locked door was a guarantee that he wouldn't find any surprises in her bed this morning.

Downstairs, the warm sun slanted through the windows and mirrored her mood. "Good morning, dear!" Dolly called quietly, arms open wide for a hug. She smiled and squeezed Lola to her ample chest. Pulling back, Dolly lifted her eyebrows. "You're practically glowing. Have you done something different?"

Lola casually shrugged her shoulders. *As a matter of fact, I did. And he's in my bed right now, thank you very much.* She moved to her mat and settled down, hoping the women would follow suit.

"There is something different..." Rae decided, pursing her lips in thought. She studied Lola curiously, tilting her head as if the angle might enlighten her.

Lola offered a tight-lipped smile. "Just slept really well, I guess." *In the two hours of sleep I actually got - thank you very, very much.* Lola lay on her back, facing away from the women's nosey stares. She bit her lip to hold in the huge smile that threatened to take over her face. With a quick check of her watch, she moved into pose. The women reluctantly followed her lead.

If all went as usual, Lola mused, they would be out of her house by seven. In the last few weeks Sam had taken to sleeping later, sometimes even until eight. With any luck he'd stick with the pattern, giving Matt enough time to sneak from the house after yoga was finished. It was a perfect little plan.

And, for a while, everything ran accordingly. Yoga was quiet and peaceful, actually helping Lola forget that she had a time bomb ticking away upstairs. Everything seemed to be on schedule. Moving through the final stretches, Lola basked in the satisfaction of her pleasingly achy muscles. They'd had a delicious workout overnight.

"Good morning, Sam!" Anne cried from her position near the door. Lola lost her balance and tipped to the floor as she watched Anne pulled Sam to her. In his half-awakened state, he stumbled into her arms and pressed a cheek against her shoulder.

A desperate whimper escaped Lola's mouth. "You're up early!" she crowed, her voice a little high. She pulled herself from the floor and tried to keep a pleasant smile on her face as panic spread through her limbs.

Sam pulled from Anne's embrace and frowned at his mother. "Why is your bedroom door locked?" he asked. Four sets of suspicious eyes turned and narrowed on Lola.

"Oh. Well, that door sticks sometimes, baby. Come here." She ignored the women's curious stares and held her arms out to Sam. With wobbly legs he walked to her and slumped in her lap.

How would she get Matt out now? She wiped a hand over Sam's warm cheek and cursed herself.

"Why don't you go back to bed for another hour, Sam?" Lola suggested. "You look exhausted." Sam rubbed his eyes and yawned deeply.

"I'm not tired," he croaked.

The knot in her stomach rose to her throat. "Okay, then go curl up on the couch and watch some cartoons. I'll make you breakfast in a little bit."

Sam perked up with the idea. But his answer wasn't what Lola had hoped for. "I can make a bowl of cereal, Mommy, remember? You showed me how the other day." His face brightened with pride.

Lola felt her posture slump but tried to hold onto her smile. The effort made her cheeks hurt. Across the porch, Rae set hands on her hips and raised an eyebrow.

"Sure! That's fine! Then you can take your breakfast in the family room, okay?" Change of plan. She would move the ladies along and sneak Matt out while Sam was busy watching cartoons. Easy enough.

Sam frowned. "But you said I have to eat my cereal at the table, Mom. I might spill in the family room. Besides, I want to eat with you this morning." He planted a squishy kiss on her cheek and bolted to the kitchen to demonstrate his newfound independence.

"Okay, baby," Lola whimpered. She flopped backward on the mat and covered her eyes. Of all times for him to practice responsibility.

"All right, ladies," Dolly said, clapping her hands to focus everyone's attention.

"Into our final pose. Face down, stretch your arms and legs top to bottom." Her voice became muffled as she demonstrated the belly pose. Everyone rolled to their stomachs, imitating Dolly's movements.

Everyone except Lola.

Still on her back, she was too busy gawking at the man crawling from her bedroom window. She sat up quickly and turned, covering her mouth so the gasp in her throat wouldn't escape. Would they see him?

In various positions, but all remaining face down, the women continued to keep their eyes closed as they stretched and talked quietly amongst themselves. Lola rolled over and squished her cheek against the mat. "This feels so good!" she said a little too loud. "Let's do this one for a long time!"

Anne and Rae amiably agreed, and when Lola lifted her face to spy on the women she was relieved to see they hadn't yet moved. She raised herself from the floor to look out the porch window, clenching her teeth as she waited for Matt to make his way down the ladder. Why was he going so slow? She glared at his progress, then glanced back to the ladies, still lying flat on their stomachs. Betty groaned.

"Oh, one more minute! This is really stretching us out today, huh?" Lola cried. She turned back to the window, silently begging Matt to move faster. A dozen more steps and he'd be home free.

Watching him, Lola realized he looked a little disheveled. His shirt was wrinkled and untucked, his hair stood up on one side, and... were those pillow marks on his cheek? Lola bit her lips to keep from laughing.

And then she nearly screamed.

As Matt's left foot touched an old wooden rung, it split in half and he fell awkwardly, catching himself another two rungs down. He dangled for a moment until he dropped to the ground.

"Oh my God!" Lola cried, and she covered her mouth and ducked back down to the mat.

"Are you all right?" Dolly asked, propping up on her elbows. The women stared at Lola.

Lola nodded violently. "Yep! Fine! Just..." she shook her head, then nodded enthusiastically, confusing herself with which lie she was about to tell. "... felt a little back spasm when I looked up too quickly. Have to do that one slower next time." She rubbed her back and waved a hand. "As you were, don't mind me." With curious frowns, the women slowly resumed positions, face down.

"Hold it for ten more seconds, girls," Dolly instructed. Lola lifted to her knees and peeked out the window. Relief swamped her. Matt had clambered to his feet and was brushing his hands and pants off. There was a grass stain on his knee and one of his shoe laces had come untied, but he was alive and moving.

Run! Lola silently urged, and she watched him glance up at the ladder with hands on his hips before walking toward the front of the porch. *The other way!* Her mind cried, and she waved frantically at him. Behind her, Dolly counted down. "Eight... seven... six..." Giggles twisted in Lola's stomach and burbled up her throat until they rolled around in her mouth. She slapped a hand over her lips and gasped for air as the laughter threatened to overcome her. Outside Matt noticed her and frowned at Lola in confusion. She jabbed a finger at Betty's blue Bonneville in the driveway and felt the hysterics rise to her throat. When Matt flinched and quickly crouched low in burglar pose, she couldn't hold it in any longer.

With one huge burst of laughter, Lola grabbed her chest and swirled around, ready to tell the ladies the truth. But Sam beat her to it. He stood in the porch doorway, a guilty look on his face.

"Mom, I spilled milk on the-" His sorry face twisted in surprise and he lifted on his tiptoes. Over Lola's shoulder he'd spied Matt. "Matt's here!" he screamed. He burst through the porch and threw open the screen door, tumbling down the stairs.

"Hey, Champ!" Matt called. He smoothed his shirt and ran fingers through his hair, then clapped his hands together. Sam jumped into Matt's arms, hugging him with arms and legs.

"Are you going to have breakfast with me?" Sam asked, his voice high with excitement. Lola covered her mouth, trying with everything she had to wipe the surprise and laughter from her face. Betty, Dolly, and Rae all giggled and chattered at once, greeting Matt and pulling him onto the porch.

"Mom, Matt came to have breakfast with me!" Sam called, and Lola nodded and gave a corny thumbs up. She didn't dare open her mouth for fear more peals of laughter would spill out. The bewildered look on Matt's face was priceless.

"What are you all doing here this morning?" Matt asked, surveying the ladies who surrounded him. He quickly glanced at Lola, his eyes daring her to break.

"We're just practicing some yoga," Betty chirped. She rubbed a hand over Matt's muscular forearm and clutched her chest.

"This early, huh?" Matt answered. His eyes slid to Lola's once again and he gave her a wild-eyed look of reprimand. Lola shook her head, desperate to keep the laughter inside. Her eyes watered as she sniffled and bit the inside of her lip.

Matt hoisted Sam in his arms and smiled. "Well, Sam, looks like it's just you and me for breakfast." The ladies clucked and talked at once as they pushed Matt into the kitchen.

"Oh, we just finished up here!" Betty exclaimed, her hand once again on his forearm, guiding him inside.

"Join us for a cup of tea, Matthew," Dolly insisted.

Rae followed Matt, inspecting his snug jeans and nodding her head as she clapped her hands in a silent cheer.

"I'm just going to clean up out here," Lola managed, as air spilled from her lungs. Her face actually ached from holding herself together.

Matt glanced over his shoulder as Betty dragged him into the kitchen. His eyes sparkled as he winked at Lola.

As everyone else made their way into the kitchen, Anne stood in the doorway and grinned. She raised her eyebrow in a knowing fashion and pointed out the porch window.

"Might want to move that ladder," she whispered.

"WHAT DID YOU DO then?" Gabe asked, an amused expression on his face. He took a swig of his beer as he waited for Matt to continue.

"I had breakfast with Sam and the yoga club ladies," Matt answered. "Sam thought I'd just arrived. What else was I supposed to do?" He shrugged and took a healthy swallow of his own beer.

The two men didn't often visit The Outhouse in the late afternoon on a weekday. But today they'd made an exception. Matt's insane morning had warranted it.

A crisp jet of laughter echoed from Gabe and through the near-empty bar on Main Street. It would be a few hours before the locals arrived, and Matt was thankful for the lack of eavesdroppers.

"So you haven't even been home today?" Gabe asked. He grimaced as he looked over Matt's shirt and hair. "You look like hell, by the way."

"Thanks," Matt answered, smoothing his wrinkled, grass-stained shirt. He took another sip of beer. "I haven't been to my place since yesterday afternoon. I had a job at Stephenson's first thing this morning and finished up Vicki's place this afternoon." He wiped a tired hand over his brow and glanced at his watch. "I need to go home and shower pretty quick though. Sam and I are making dinner for Lola tonight."

Gabe's smile slowly disappeared. "You guys playing house now?" he asked.

Matt felt a flash of anger course through his veins. "What's that supposed to mean?" he asked. His fist clenched as he studied his friend's face.

Gabe sighed and set his beer on the bar with a thud. "I don't know, man." He shook his head. "I'm happy for you. Lola's great." He raised his eyes to Matt's and scowled. "But she's leaving in three weeks. A few days ago she told Rena that she'll be on a plane the first of August. She's going back to California, Matt."

Thoughts of a hidden floor plan flashed in Matt's mind. He leaned back as he studied Gabe. "Maybe not."

Gabe rolled his eyes.

"She likes it here. She and Sam have settled in and she's even found some work."

"That doesn't mean she's staying," Gabe murmured.

"I know it doesn't. But before we went on that date, I found a floor plan in Lola's place."

Gabe shifted on his stool to face Matt better. "A floor plan?"

"Yeah, a faded one of Anne's photo shop." Matt ran his fingers over the bottle of beer, wiping droplets of condensation from it. "There's an empty room in the back that she could turn into a studio." He felt the hope rush through him. "She's thinking about settling in Hope River."

Gabe thought about Matt's words for a moment. He took another sip of beer and frowned. "Why hasn't she said anything?" he asked.

"I don't know." Matt sighed, then shrugged as he glanced out the window. He watched Mr. and Mrs. Franklin shuffle down the sidewalk, holding hands and smiling as they had for the last forty years.

"I think she just needs some time," Matt said. He looked at Gabe again, hope still strong in his chest. "I don't want to push her. We're just making sense together and I don't want to lose that."

Gabe nodded and slapped Matt on the shoulder. "I hope you're right, buddy." He finished off his beer, then pulled a twenty from his wallet and tossed it on the bar.

"Well, time to go home and face the crazies," he said, a faux shiver rippling over his body. "You watch out, man. Keep heading in this direction and you'll have a handful of little monkeys waiting at home to jump all over you too." He smiled and lifted his eyebrows in warning.

Matt elbowed Gabe as they walked together out the door. "I can only hope," he laughed.

Chapter Twenty-One

"Darling! How are you?" a voice echoed through the telephone. Lola smiled at her aunt's crackling, distant voice. Even halfway across the world, it was as chipper and energetic as ever.

"Aunt Louise! Where are you?" she asked. Sam and Goliath scuffled through the kitchen, a ball bouncing and dog nails clicking as they ran outside. Lola plugged her ear so she could hear Louise's response.

"I'm still in India, but I've been traveling around a bit with my friend Yogesh for the last few weeks. I'm flying home in ten days. You'll still be in Hope River then, won't you?"

Lola unplugged her ear and leaned against a kitchen chair. Ten days? In ten days it would be August? Aunt Louise would be home and the summer would be over. She swallowed the lump in her throat.

"Lola, are you there? Oh, this damn phone…"

"I'm here!" Lola lifted her chin and inhaled a deep breath of air. "Sam and I will stay here until you get back. We want to see you for a few days before…"

Somehow, she couldn't finish her sentence. She didn't know how it was supposed to end.

"Fabulous!" Louise cried. "I can't wait to see my Samuel! And you,

Lola. Oh, I can't wait to hear all about your summer. There must be so much to tell."

The comment made a small smile return to Lola's face, and she felt her cheeks flush. Yes indeed, she thought. There was a lot to tell. And a lot more that still needed to be figured out.

Lola hung up the phone and wandered to the porch window. Outside, Goliath snored in the sun while Sam played on the driveway. He talked quietly to himself, driving his dump truck through an imaginary construction site.

She could watch him for hours. In fact, she probably had. She'd had the time to sit and relax and watch him play all summer. But when had he changed so much? Their summer in Hope River had made her little boy grow so big. He'd put on a few pounds and grown at least an inch. No longer were his clothes baggy, and among his friends he didn't seem so small anymore. His hair was bleached with blonde streaks, his skin tanner than it ever had been in California. And his demeanor - he was a different child than Lola remembered from three months ago. The sullen, quiet boy was gone, replaced with a boisterous one. He wanted to play and run and laugh and just be... happy.

And so did she. Hope River had changed her as much as it had changed her son. And so had Matthew Dawson.

For the last two weeks, they'd spent nearly every day together. Along with Sam, they'd shared late afternoon picnics and long walks in the park, kickball games and warm evenings of swimming at the beach. They'd even visited Matt's land outside of town, playing in the small creek and chasing each other through the woods.

And late in the evenings, Lola and Matt shared time alone. She cherished their late dinners and conversations, a good movie while they lay together on the couch. They'd even had a few more dates. Most nights Matt left late. But occasionally Lola would convince him to stay and she'd wake up with him beside her, feeling as happy and blissful as she'd ever remembered.

The summer had healed her. She hadn't felt this content, this healthy or happy since before Travis had died.

Life, it seemed, was finally moving on.

The phone rang, startling Lola from her thoughts. She returned to the kitchen and picked up the receiver.

"Do you feel like some fresh berry pie?" Rena asked. Her voice was playful, making Lola laugh.

"That's a silly question," Lola teased.

"I have a blackberry pie in the oven that's just begging to be eaten," Rena added.

"We'll be over in ten minutes." Lola didn't wait for a response. It had become their ritual - one of them baking and inviting the other over, taking long afternoons to laze and gossip and enjoy their friendship while Grace napped and the boys kept themselves busy. Hanging up the phone, she anxiously reached behind the computer for the rumpled sheet of paper that had been gnawing at her thoughts all morning. She folded the paper and placed it gently into a pocket of her cotton dress.

Lola grabbed the sunblock and Sam's baseball cap, then headed for the door. She touched the paper in her pocket as she tapped down the stairs to the warm grass. Today was as good as any to test her ideas on a friend.

"GOD, THAT SMELLS GOOD," Lola sighed as she entered Rena's kitchen. The porch screen creaked behind her, then slammed as the boys darted outside to play.

"Wait until you see how pretty it is," Rena beamed. She shoved thick oven mitts on her hands and scooped the pie from the oven, then held it in all its juicy glory under Lola's nose. Purple bubbles oozed from small slits in the golden crust.

The aroma of tart blackberries tickled Lola's nose. "You're going to tell me that you picked the berries yourself, aren't you?"

"Gabe did. He and Caleb walked the riverbank a few nights ago and found a huge patch." She set the pie on a cooling rack and slipped off the oven mitts, then pulled two large glasses from the cupboard.

Lola closed her eyes and sighed. "Fresh berries from your own backyard," she marveled. "I never knew how much I loved small town

America. And I certainly never imagined I'd enjoy the countryside or mowing grass or baking pies…" She accepted a glass of cold iced tea and grinned at her friend. "But I do. I love it all."

"Which is exactly why you should stay," Rena decided. It was the first time she'd said so out loud, and she grinned wide at Lola's surprise.

"You are considering it, right?" Rena asked. She set her tea on the countertop and folded her arms over her chest as she waited for Lola's response.

Waves of panic danced with hope in Lola's stomach. Her fingers slid to the folded paper in her pocket. "I might be," she answered. She glanced out the kitchen window to avoid Rena's gaze.

"There are plenty of good reasons to stay," Rena said. She leaned against the counter and thrust a finger out as she listed them off. "You and Sam are happy here. I can feel it." She nodded, knowing she was right.

"You both have good friends here. Everyone in town loves you. You have me. You have all of us. You're a part of our family now." She smiled at that. "You'll have your Aunt and can stay with her until you find a place of your own."

Rena had counted off every finger on one hand and moved to the other. "You've found work that you love and you're great at. My sister loved her wedding pictures and there are others who have asked about your photography," she added.

Lola touched the paper in her pocket again. It felt like lead, too heavy to be pulled out but such a burden to keep hidden. She wanted to tell someone, to share her dreams, to make it all real.

"And then there's Matt," Rena added with a sparkle in her eyes.

Lola loosened her grip on the paper and smiled. "And then there's Matt," she repeated. She was so in love with him that it scared her silly.

Where should she start? Lola wondered. There was so much to tell Rena, so much that she'd been holding back about Matt, about the studio, about Sam. She opened her mouth, wondering what would tumble out first.

It turned out that nothing would. An alarm began to shriek in the kitchen. Both women jumped and Lola's hand slid to cover her racing heart.

From a small desk in the corner, a black radio blinked rapidly and crackled to life. "Emergency services requested …" it blared. It continued with a location and details.

Fire. A large house, a few miles from Hope River, possible occupants inside. Lola's heart hammered as she listened, as she watched Rena grab her cell phone and punch a message quickly on the keypad. The voice repeated on the small radio, calm and steady, asking for all units from local towns to respond. When Rena finished her text she walked to the radio and turned the sound low.

"Gabe will want to go to this," she said, worry slowly spreading to her eyes. Her mouth was tight as she walked to the porch door to check on the boys.

"And Matt?" Lola asked, feeling her chest tighten.

Rena slowly nodded. "He's probably already on his way," she answered softly. She squeezed Lola's arm and pulled her to the kitchen table. They settled quietly into wooden chairs and stared at each other while the calm voice on the radio continued. The voice in Lola's head was anything but calm.

After a few minutes, the radio went quiet. The silence of the kitchen was ominous. "How long have they been volunteering?" Lola asked. She folded her hands on top of one another and absently touched her bare ring finger.

"Ten years now. They both joined when Matt moved back." She reached across the table and gently covered Lola's hand with her own. "Don't worry, they're careful. And they look out for each other. They'll both be fine."

Lola nodded bravely. "Do you ever get used to it?" she asked.

Pulling her hand away, Rena leaned back in her chair and heaved a loud sigh. "Not really. I always worry until I hear from him." She jumped when her cell phone beeped. Lola watched her read a text message, holding her breath.

"They're on their way. Gabe, Matt, and Will so far." Setting the phone down, she stared at Lola. "There's nothing we can do now but try to take our minds off of it. Come on, let's have some pie."

A tiny laugh burst from Lola and she smiled gratefully. Rena always knew how to settle the nerves. She watched her friend cut generous pieces of pie and slide them onto white porcelain plates, then glob a heap of whipped cream on top. She turned with a plate in each hand and a wicked smile on her lips. "This should keep us busy for a few minutes," she said.

LATER, THE BOYS BURST into the kitchen with tales of worms attacking sand castles and dragon flies with silver wings landing on Caleb's head. They gulped cold lemonade and gobbled up cookies, and with rosy cheeks and sweaty heads begged to turn on the sprinklers. When they'd received permission, they yanked their t-shirts from their bodies and leapt down the stairs, the screen door slamming after them.

"How did they survive previous summers without each other?" Rena laughed as she set her plate in the sink.

Lola shook her head in amazement. "Sam's never really had a best friend before. Everything about this summer has been a new experience."

"See?" Rena scolded. "You can't leave. We'd *all* miss you too much."

A little cry from upstairs interrupted them. Instinctively, both women glanced toward the stairs and Rena frowned. "She's not napping as long as she used to," she moaned as she headed up to her daughter's rescue. "God help me when she starts skipping naps altogether."

It had been a long time since Sam had napped. Lola peeked outside, watching the boys race through the sprinklers and scream in delight from the cold shock of the water. No longer sporting any baby fat, their bodies were lean and tan, their legs and arms gangly.

Her little boy was changing so quickly. Before long he'd want to know about girls and cars and shaving. He was soon going to grow into a young man, Lola realized with a flush of panic. One who needed a father figure for advice and guidance.

Moving back to the table, Lola listened to Rena singing to Grace.

Her voice was soft and sweet, quietly carrying down to the kitchen. The floor creaked with their movement overhead and Lola could hear Grace squeal as she sang along with her mother.

Lola jumped at the sound of the radio crackling back to life. The voice was quiet but urgent, and Lola quickly turned the volume up. "Ambulance requested..." Lola heard. She twisted her hands at her chest and leaned over the radio, but the thumping and singing from the stairs blocked the sound. Lola turned the volume higher and laid a hand on her stomach. Suddenly the pie wasn't sitting so well.

"First responders are at the scene, an ambulance requested immediately for medical treatment and transport. Repeat, fireman injured, CPR being administered, ambulance requested immediately..." Lola's hand moved to her mouth and she covered it to stop the sudden cry from escaping. Her body flashed with heat and adrenaline as she fought a strong wave of nausea. She turned to see Rena on the bottom step, listening with wide and fearful eyes, and wondered if her own face was as shockingly pale as her friend's.

It took a moment for the information to seep in. They stared at one another, unsure if they should acknowledge their terrified thoughts. Rena was the first to break the trance as she bolted to her cell phone. Grace bounced on her hip, struck silent by her mother's sudden mood change.

"Tell me you're okay," Rena whispered as she pressed the phone to her ear. Lola watched her, dread and fear and anger filling her body, higher and higher until she was sure she'd suffocate. Outside the boys streaked across the lawn, still laughing and playing, oblivious to the choking fear that flooded the kitchen.

"Shit," Rena hissed, pulling the phone from her ear and pressing another button. She looked at Lola and shook her head, her eyes filling with tears. "I'll try Matt..." Lola swallowed hard, the lump in her throat like a piece of hot coal. She lifted a hand to Rena, trying to comfort her friend even as panic unraveled in her own chest. Memories of Travis swirled in her brain. The emptiness, the shock, the hopeless feeling of loss...

"They can't answer when they're fighting the fire," Lola said, her voice so soft she could barely hear herself. "They won't hear the phone in all the chaos." She nodded, trying to convince herself of this, trying to stop the cold fright that squeezed at her throat.

Slowly nodding, Rena lowered the phone. She pressed Grace to her chest and kissed her silky blonde curls. Over the top of her daughter's head, her dark eyes met Lola's and held.

Once again, there was nothing to do but wait.

Chapter Twenty-Two

*W*hen Travis died, there had been no warning. There had been no waiting, no wondering if she would see him again. There had only been the facts, given to her by a kind policeman with solemn green eyes. He had knocked on her door, held her hand, offered support when her knees buckled.

It was raining the day Travis died. Lola remembered the water dripping from the police officer's hat and the dampness of his hand on her arm. She remembered the burning scent of noodles boiling over on the kitchen stove and Sam's hungry whimpers as he tugged on her shirt. She remembered that time had gone still, that everything moved in slow motion, and that it seemed the world had suddenly swallowed her whole.

Please, God, not again. The prayer ran through Lola's mind over and over as she rocked herself gently at the picnic table. The afternoon sun peeked through the thick leaves overhead and she watched Rena wring her hands and twitch her foot in a panicked rhythm. A fireman was injured, how severely they didn't know. Nor did they know if either of their hearts would be broken when the news finally reached them.

Both women jumped as Rena's cell phone vibrated on the table.

She grabbed it and fumbled, nearly dropping it as she tried to thumb a button. She pressed the phone against her ear and covered her eyes.

"Babe?" she asked. Lola watched Rena's entire body relax, her hand drop from her eyes to her stomach. "Oh, thank God, Gabe," she whispered. She listened for a moment, and when her eyes lifted, Lola saw painful news in them.

Lola tried to swallow the thick lump in her throat, but it only rose farther. She watched as Rena shook her head and reached for her. Aching chills spread quickly over Lola's arms and legs, and her vision blurred. *It was Matt,* she told herself. She stood, shaking her head, covering her mouth to stop the sobs that were building. Hot, thick tears fell down her cheeks. Time came to an abrupt stop. The world opened its big angry mouth to swallow her whole.

Rena reached across the table to grab Lola. She shook her head furiously, her eyes narrow, her mouth twisted in protest. Her fingers wrapped around Lola's wrist and her voice sounded as if she were underwater. Lola pulled away and let an angry sob break from her chest.

Through the stormy sound that thrashed in her head, Lola heard Rena's voice. "It was Will," she'd said. "He's going to be okay." The voice was far away, as if in a dream from which Lola knew she should wake. She collapsed to the ground, catching herself with her hands, and leaned over the soft grass. Tears dripped down her nose and she gasped, desperate for air.

"Honey, it was Will. Matt's okay, I just heard his voice." Quickly, Rena was beside her, arms around Lola's shoulders, hands holding her tight against her body. She pulled Lola's face to her own so their eyes met. "Matt's just fine," she said again, and this time her words were stern.

The afternoon swirled around Lola as she let the words register. She closed her eyes and breathed, her chest hitching, her body flashing with mixtures of relief and guilt. Slowly, sounds returned to normal volume and texture. Sam and Caleb were still playing in the sandbox, their laughter floating across the warm afternoon. Grace, a few feet away, babbled to a blanket full of toys.

Matt's alive. Suddenly feeling foolish, Lola leaned back into the cool grass. What had just happened? "I'm sorry," she whispered. She swiped at her wet eyes and pulled her knees to her chest. Rena settled in the grass beside her.

"Honey, I didn't realize..." Rena began, but Lola shook her head and waved a hand to stop her.

"He's really okay?" Lola asked. She wanted to touch Matt's warm skin, to feel the rhythm of his breathing and heartbeat beneath her fingers. She wanted to be sure.

Rena nodded.

"And Will's okay?" Lola added.

With a relieved sigh, Rena nodded again. "He's on his way to the hospital. A wall fell and knocked him out for a few minutes, but the others pulled him from the building right away. They'll take good care of him."

"And Gabe's okay?" Lola asked, feeling like a broken record.

Rena nodded and smiled, her face relaxing. "He's fine." She shook her head and wiped a finger over one lone tear on her cheek.

Lola touched the skin where her wedding band used to sit. "I'm sorry," she whispered. "I don't know what happened. I was so scared I'd lost him too. It was like going through Travis' death all over again." More tears welled in her eyes and threatened to open the dam. She angrily wiped them away.

"It's okay," Rena whispered as she hugged Lola close. "You won't lose Matt too. He's not going anywhere."

IT WAS LATE EVENING when Lola and Sam finally made their way through the woods. They'd stayed with Rena to pass the time and to bask in the knowledge that their men were safe. When Gabe had stepped through the kitchen door, he'd scooped both women into his arms and kissed their cheeks.

"You girls worry too much," he'd teased. But Lola saw the exhaustion in his eyes and knew they'd had reason to worry.

Now, as she held Sam's hand in her own and felt the soft pine needle floor beneath her feet, Lola tried to soothe her heart. While she was desperate to see Matt, to hold him and feel the life pulsing through him, she was also angry with him. Angry because he'd scared her, angry that he'd put himself in harm's way.

More than that, she was mad at herself. She'd let all of this happen. She'd allowed herself to fall in love with Matt, and now she couldn't turn back. She was in too far.

Rubbing a hand over her churning stomach, Lola followed Sam to their property. Her footsteps faltered as she glanced at the house and the man standing in the shadows of her porch.

Matt was striking as he waited at the foot of her stairs. His tall, strong body cast a shadow over the ground. Lines creased his forehead and cheeks, evidence of a difficult day. He looked completely exhausted. His eyes were smoky, his cheeks flushed, his hair in a spiky mess as though he'd toweled off from a shower only seconds before.

Lola covered her mouth with a trembling hand and willed the tears to stay hidden behind her eyes. He was the answer to her weary heart - absolutely beautiful, leaning against the porch stairs, waiting only for her and Sam.

"Matt's here!" Sam cried. He flew through the grass and leapt into open arms. He wrapped himself around Matt's chest and squeezed, holding tight to him for a full minute. Lola watched as Matt closed his eyes and pressed his face into her son's neck.

When his eyes opened again they were focused on Lola. She remained a few feet away, her hands deep in her pockets. The folded paper slid through her fingers, the edges sharp against her skin. She smiled quickly and then glanced away. Already, she knew he'd seen the storm that brewed in her heart.

"Did you have a fun day?" Matt asked Sam, leaning back so he could see the boy's bright face. Sam exploded with exciting details. Stories of sand castles and worm fights and sprinkler fun with Caleb poured from him as he slid from Matt's arms and back to the ground. He jumped to imitate a move over the sprinklers, then looked at Lola and made a face.

"Mom, I'm *hungry*," he moaned. Matt chuckled.

Lola cleared her throat to make sure her voice was steady. "Grab some fruit from the kitchen, and then it's bedtime. I'll be up to tuck you in in a minute." Sam grimaced at the mention of bed but seemed too hungry to argue. He bounced up the stairs and onto the porch, the screen door clapping shut behind him.

When Lola finally lifted her eyes to Matt's, she found his gaze intense. A frown furrowed his brow.

"Are you okay?" he asked softly. He took a tentative step toward Lola, but she lifted her chin and bit her lip in warning. She played with the drawing in her pocket, wanting to crumple it and tear it into a thousand pieces. It was dangerous there at her fingertips, threatening to break her heart. This whole damn town was threatening to break her heart.

"I'm fine," Lola answered, nodding her head desperately. She watched Matt take a step closer, and stepped back herself. *Don't come any closer!* her mind screamed, and she felt her eyes fill with tears. Making a fist in her pocket, she dug her nails into the palm of her hand.

"Lola," Matt began, and before she could stop him he was in front of her, pulling her to him, wrapping his strong arms around her body. He settled his lips against her ear, into her hair, his breath warm and comforting. "Tell me what's wrong," he whispered.

Her throat hitched, and Lola let herself be held. Her hands reached desperately around Matt and clutched him to her. Nuzzling into his broad chest, she buried her face and her tears in his shirt. *Thank you, thank you, thank you,* she repeated. He was there, in her arms, in the flesh.

"Tell me," Matt whispered again, kissing her forehead. He lifted her face gently with his fingers.

"I thought it was you. We heard the radio, that someone was hurt and I thought…" Her voice was soft, childlike to her own ears. She shook her head and laid her cheek in the warmth of his neck. "I don't know if I can do this again," she pleaded, sniffling up tears.

"I'm fine, Lola. And I'm not going anywhere," Matt said, pulling back so he could look into her eyes. He touched a gentle finger to her cheek and gave her a playful smile. "You're not getting rid of me that easily."

The small ripple of laughter felt heavenly on her lips. She sank back into Matt's chest. "Is Will going to be okay?" she asked.

Matt nodded, his chin moving up and down on her forehead. "He's fine. He was released from Fairview a few hours ago. Just a few bumps and bruises and minor smoke inhalation. A good rest and he'll be back to himself in a few days." Matt buried his fingers in Lola's hair and brushed his lips over her temple. His voice grew clouded as he continued. "Most of us have trained for years. We've experienced enough to know the dangers." He rubbed a hand over his jaw, the movement making a sandpaper sound. "But Will is still young. Sometimes he dives in before he thinks, and it's my fault for letting him get in this mess. I should have been watching him more closely. When he's recovered we'll all get in some extra safety training and..."

She couldn't bear to listen any longer. Lola covered his lips with her own and melted into the kiss. She felt his muscles soften, his fingers dig deeper into her sides. When she pulled away, she laid a gentle hand on his cheek.

"Matthew Dawson, you can't fix everything. Just for one night, take a break from saving Hope River. Come inside. Stay with me."

Matt's eyes smiled even before the sentiment reached his lips. It made her heart tremble. He was so precious to her now, something she had never expected.

She laced her fingers through Matt's and pulled him up the porch stairs. "Tonight you get to rest," she said quietly. "I'll take care of you for a change."

Chapter Twenty-Three

❧

"This is going to be totally awesome!" Sam cried as he jumped from his seat at the kitchen table. The morning sun had barely risen above the trees, but Sam was wide awake and bursting with energy. Lola, on the other hand, was dragging.

"Sam, eat the rest of your toast," she scolded before he darted from the room. "You have a big day ahead of you." She rubbed her fingers over a temple and closed her eyes for a moment. The stress of Sam's upcoming adventure had worn her nerves thin.

She hadn't slept for days either, blaming the heat, though inside she knew the truth. The summer was winding down and still Lola hadn't decided what she and Sam would do. She had no job to return to in San Francisco. There was no permanent home or steady job to speak of here. Life was completely up in the air and she was a basket case. A basket case in love.

"Matt's here!" Sam screamed. Lola covered her forehead with a palm to stop the throbbing. She followed Sam out the porch door and witnessed him jumping off the top step and tumbling to the ground in a rolling heap. Before Lola could dash down the stairs and begin CPR, Matt was beside Sam, scooping him up and setting him back on his feet.

"Whoa, Champ," Matt said with a laugh. He wiped dirt from Sam's back and grass from his head. "Take it easy or you'll run out of steam before we even get to the fishing hole." He ruffled Sam's golden hair before glancing up to Lola with a generous smile. As soon as he saw the terrified look on her face, his smile faded.

"Lola," he said softly, walking up the stairs and standing one step below her. He raised an eyebrow in scolding fashion. Setting firm hands on her hips, he pulled her to him and leaned his forehead on hers.

"What?" he whispered.

Usually she found it endearing how easily that gentle smirk slid to his lips. But this morning it only annoyed her. She glanced over Matt's shoulder and watched Sam - her baby, now so tall and strong - bouncing around in excitement.

"He's going to be fine," Matt insisted. "He'll be sitting in a big, safe boat between two grown men. We'll watch him every second. He won't even be able to swat a fly without asking first." He kissed the tip of Lola's nose and squeezed her to him for reassurance. "We *are* trained in first aid, remember?"

Lola's eyes flashed. She felt panic rise in her stomach once more.

"Not that we'll need any first aid," Matt quickly corrected. He shook his head and laughed. "I'll tell you what. I'll put him in a bubble before we leave if that'll make you feel better."

The idea of her son rolling around in a bubble made a tiny smile creep to her lips. "That would help my nerves, actually," she whispered. She closed her eyes and leaned into Matt, letting him smooth her hair. Her heart beat fast, no longer from the worry but from Matt's delicious touch. They'd spent every night together over the past week, bodies wrapped together, making love and whispering into the early morning hours. They'd even managed to avoid the use of ladders outside her bedroom window, having Matt slip out the front door before Sam woke up.

"We'll be careful," Matt said again, and ran a thumb over her chin. He turned down the stairs and met Sam halfway to the truck.

"Wear your lifejackets!" Lola called, wrapping her arms tightly over her chest.

"Okay, Mom," Sam answered with a hint of boredom.

"And no standing in the boat!" she cried.

"Got it!"

"Put another layer of sunscreen on every two hours!" Lola's foot tapped anxiously on the wooden stairs.

"Mo-*omm*!" Sam whined, his shoulders falling in embarrassment. Matt laughed and watched Lola with twinkling blue eyes.

Biting her tongue, Lola studied them as they moved toward the truck. Sam looked adorable in his baggy cargo shorts and small fisherman hat. The hat had been a gift from Matt earlier in the week when he'd asked Sam, with Lola's hesitant permission, if he wanted to go on a fishing trip - guys only. Sam had been ecstatic.

"Sam!" Lola suddenly shouted. She charged down the stairs as Sam turned warily toward her.

"Do I get a kiss goodbye?" she pleaded, trying to lighten her voice. She smiled pitifully and prayed her six year old was not yet too cool to give his mother a kiss. Her heart sank when he studied her, then soared when he charged at her with a devilish grin. He plowed into her legs, nearly bowling her over, and hugged her middle so tight that Lola couldn't breathe. She bent to kiss his hair, to smell his fresh, childish scent, and nearly melted when he lifted on tiptoes to plant a mushy kiss in return. And then, just as quickly as he'd arrived in her arms, he was gone.

SAM BEAMED AT MATT as he slipped into the life vest. Tiny freckles spattered his nose and cheeks, and a toothy grin filled his face.

"Are you excited?" Matt asked. He smiled at the little boy that he loved like his own and clipped the vest securely around his body.

"Yeah, I never been fishin' before," Sam answered. He adjusted his hat and tried not to wiggle while Matt tugged and tightened the straps.

Matt grinned and squeezed Sam's arms. "There, you're all set. Except for the plastic bubble, I think we've got you as safe and prepared as possible."

Sam giggled. "Yeah, my mom worries about me a lot," he said thoughtfully. "But I know it's just 'cause she loves me so much."

"She sure does, Champ." Matt tapped Sam playfully on the nose before rising. With a protective hand on his back, he steered Sam toward the river. "Now let's see if we can get you into that boat without falling into the drink."

When everyone was settled and the boys were wide-eyed beside one another in the middle seat, Gabe pushed them gently from the landing and started the engine with a roar. Matt gazed up at his uncle's small cabin and smiled. Many a childhood memory had come from the place, and he was happy to see the two little boys making memories of their own.

"Where to?" Gabe called beside the noisy motor. They glided over the rippling waves of the river, scattering water bugs in their wake. The sun was warm and blinding as it reflected off the water.

Shielding his eyes, Matt looked down river. "Head over to the north bend," he called, pointing beyond a patch of forest. "I had good luck there a few weeks ago." The boys giggled as the boat lifted with the higher speed.

As they neared the fishing hole, Sam and Caleb saw a great blue heron at the shoreline. It lifted its wings in preparation for takeoff, then quickly launched into the air. With mouths wide open in wonder, they watched it fly gracefully overhead.

The motor slowed, then cut, making the sudden peace deafening. Waves rushed against the shore and the songs of red-winged blackbirds trilled from the trees. A few feet from the boat, a fish smacked at the water's surface.

"Sounds like the fish are hungry this morning," Matt said, nudging the boys with a finger. They perked up, scrambling for their small fishing poles, falling over each other to find the worms.

"Sam, have you ever been fishing before?" Gabe asked, pushing the tip of Caleb's pole away from his face. He leaned over and took the pole from his son, handing him the worms instead.

Sam shook his head. "My dad never took me," he said. His face twisted in concentration as he tried to work his fishing reel. "I don't think we have rivers in San Francisco anyway, just the bay. And it's full of sharks."

Matt rubbed a hand over his lips and tried hard not to laugh. He winked at his best friend and leaned toward Sam. "Want me to show you how to put a worm on your hook?" he asked. Sam nodded, his eyes round and intense.

With experienced fingers, Matt pulled a fat earthworm from the container and laid it gently in his palm. It writhed and wriggled, creating letters of the alphabet with its body. Sam wrinkled his nose as it left a trail of slime on Matt's skin.

"Fish like to eat those?" Sam asked. This time Matt couldn't keep his laugh inside. It burst out quickly, and Sam joined in.

"You take the hook like this," Matt began, pulling the line from Sam's pole and placing the hook between his finger and thumb. "Then you poke it here." Sam squirmed and lifted his eyes to Matt, trying to hide his disgust.

"That's the hard part," Gabe called, watching Sam's face with enjoyment as he helped Caleb cast his line into the water. "The easy part is catching the big one."

Matt showed Sam how to hold his fishing pole, then practiced casting with him. They waited a minute, Sam twitching with anticipation as he watched the fishing line laze on the surface of the river. His bobber quickly disappeared to the rocks below. With a quick howl and a delayed jerk of his arms, Sam yanked the fishing pole up and fumbled with the reel. "I got one!" he shouted, pulling the fish toward him. "I got the big one!"

It fought playfully, a small bass trying to swallow the fat worm whole. Sam nearly fell over the side of the boat as he simultaneously pumped the reel and peered into the water.

"Whoa," Matt laughed, grabbing the back of Sam's life jacket. Caleb and Gabe cheered as Sam dragged the fish in. Its body thumped heavily against the aluminum boat as it was dragged over the side and onto Matt's feet.

"I caught a fish!" Sam howled, and the pure joy in his eyes filled Matt's heart to the brim.

Later, when the boys were settled on their respective sides of the boat and sharing exaggerated tales of Sam's first catch, Gabe glanced at Matt and smirked.

"What are you laughing at?" Matt murmured. He watched Gabe lift his pole at a possible bite, then patiently lower it again.

Gabe shook his head and let the smirk grow into a broad smile. He glanced at the boys and then back to the depths of the water. "You know, buddy," he began, lifting his chin to make the coming words sound as macho as possible. "I've been looking forward to this day for a long time."

Matt listened to the sound of water lapping against the boat and the occasional burp of a bullfrog.

"I always imagined we'd take the kids fishing together. Remember going out with our dads? All crammed in that rickety canoe of yours?" Gabe laughed at the thought. "Now it's our turn."

A part of Matt's heart soared. He'd often imagined doing this as a father and friend too. Yet, still unsure of how this would end, he couldn't fully celebrate. Would Lola stay? Would she let Matt be a father to Sam, let them be a family together?

With a snort, Gabe leaned back on the motor and puffed his chest. "I think I'm allergic to this sentimental stuff," he mumbled, and he scratched a bite on his forearm. A grin still played on his lips, but machismo returned and he lifted his chin to the water as if casting a spell on the fish.

"Time to catch some trophies!" he cried, and was answered by whoops of excitement from both boys.

THE HUM OF MATT'S truck engine was the sweetest sound Lola had heard all day. She sprang from her position on the kitchen floor, clad in a dirty apron and wet rubber gloves, and tossed the tooth brush into the bucket of soapy water. The grout she'd slaved over all afternoon was probably cleaner now than it had been the day it was installed.

Racing to the porch door, Lola pushed it open and let the cool evening air wash over her. Relief washed over her too, at the sight of her two favorite guys walking toward her, both rosy and weary from a full day of fishing.

"Did you catch dinner?" Lola called. Sam giggled and ran to her, wrapping Lola in a grimy, fishy-smelling hug.

"We ate at Dairy Queen," he mumbled into her apron. He rubbed his nose against her, too tired to scratch it himself, and closed his eyes.

Pulling her hand from the yellow glove, Lola ran her fingers through Sam's thick hair. A sigh that had been trapped in her chest the entire day slid gratefully from her body.

"He caught enough bass for dinner tomorrow night," Matt announced. "I'll even cook." He wrapped a warm hand around Lola's arm and kissed her gently on the cheek. He smelled of fish too, but Lola didn't care. She was so glad to have them home.

"I'm ti-red," Sam moaned. He pulled back from his mother and grinned at Matt, who ruffled his unruly hair.

"Run upstairs and we'll give you a quick bath before bed," Lola said as she gave Sam a little push toward the porch stairs.

"'Night, Champ," Matt called after him. Sam beamed and waved weakly before staggering into the house.

Lola pulled the other glove from her hand. "He looks like he had a great time," she said quietly.

"It was really fun, tangled lines and all. We never even needed our first aid kit," Matt teased. "He's filthy though. We moored at a beach for lunch and the boys played with frogs and clams on the shore. They had a blast."

Lola flapped the gloves against her leg, back and forth as she listened to stories of their day. She was happy they'd enjoyed themselves. But there was also something in her gut, something she couldn't yet put a finger on that whispered warnings to her heart.

Matt seemed to sense this. "Have you been worrying all day?"

"No." She quickly shook her head in denial, then sighed. "A little."

"Lola, you know I'd never let Sam get hurt. He's like a son to me."

A sudden dizziness threatened to send Lola to her knees. She'd known he felt this way about Sam all along, but the words still shocked her. Anger and confusion warred inside. Shouldn't this kind of statement from Matt satisfy her? Make her feel more safe and secure, make her happy for her son? She gripped the railing for support, and forced a smile. "I know," Lola answered softly.

With a sigh, Matt touched Lola's face and pulled her in for a lingering kiss. His touch was tender, his lips comforting. Lola hid her face in his chest and begged for composure.

"You should get up to Sam. He's so exhausted he'll fall asleep in the tub if you don't hurry."

Silently, Lola pulled from Matt's embrace and stepped to the porch door.

"Fish fry tomorrow night?" he asked as he watched her.

"Of course," Lola answered. And before she could change her mind, she slipped inside.

UPSTAIRS, WHILE THE WARM bathwater ran, Sam slowly peeled the filthy clothes from his body, too tired to even toss them in the hamper. He yawned hugely and looked up at his mother with bleary eyes.

"So you had fun?" Lola asked, settling on her knees beside him and helping him pull off his socks. They were caked with dirt and smelled like a swamp.

"It was *awesome*," Sam answered, perking up a little. "I caught the first fish. It was huge. It was green and yellow and had really pointy fins on its back and big sharp teeth. Matt showed me how to put worms on the hooks the first time and then I did 'em myself after that. And he let me and Caleb row the boat while him and Gabe fished too." His smile was a mile wide until another yawn overtook him. Lola helped him climb into the warm tub where he sank into bubbles as he continued.

"And at the beach me and Caleb found some frogs and caught three of them and played with them in the water. And then Caleb got a leech stuck on his toe and he cried, and I got bit by a horsefly." He lifted his elbow to show off a dime-sized welt, red and angry, puffing from his skin. "And when I smacked it we threw it in the water and it wiggled around until a fish ate it!" His eyes popped at the memory and made

Lola laugh. "Matt said it was probably a sunfish that ate the fly, and that next time we can put a fly on a hook and catch a huge fish with it."

Sam closed his eyes tight while Lola poured water over his head. As she rubbed shampoo into his hair, Sam sucked in a big breath and continued. "Matt said the biggest fish he ever caught was a muskie." He put his hands out in front of him, spacing them about two feet apart to show the fish's size. "He said he got it in the wintertime when a lake was covered with ice. Did you know you can go fishing on the ice?" Sam looked up at his mother with utter surprise. "You have to drill holes and pull the fish from them!" Fascinated, he finally quieted and let Lola scrub around his ears and neck. He kept silent, lost in his thoughts, as he fingered the rainbows that glistened on the soapy bubbles.

"You like Matt a lot, don't you?" Lola asked quietly.

Sam's eyes darted to hers and a guilty expression spread over his cheeks. He nodded slowly. "You do too," he answered shyly. "He kisses you like Daddy used to."

Lola felt her cheeks warm but tried to act as though the words hadn't surprised her. She should have known. Children always knew more than adults realized. Her chest tightened anxiously.

"Well, yes," Lola acknowledged, pouring water over Sam's shoulders and chest. "But it's different than it was with Daddy." She tipped his head up by his chin and rinsed the soap from his hair.

Poking a finger in his ear to clear it from water and bubbles, Sam frowned at his mother. "Why is it different?" he asked.

Lola considered for a moment. Why was it different?

Lola loved Matt in ways she had never felt with Travis. The realization made it hard for her to breathe.

"Well, your daddy and I were married, for starters," she answered slowly. Her mind raced to argue. *It was necessary to get married when you learned you were pregnant. Would you have married Travis otherwise?* Her fingers trembled at the thought.

Lola tried to keep her hands busy by washing Sam's back and arms. Sam suddenly turned to her, his cheeks bright and gray eyes sparking with intensity.

"Maybe we can ask Matt to marry us," Sam decided. "Can he be my new dad?" His eyes were hopeful and smile turned shy as he watched Lola's face. She swallowed her surprise and tried to laugh, but knew from her little boy's expression that this was no laughing matter. He was completely serious.

"Sam, honey," she began, gently rubbing his back. "That's... that's not really how it works."

His expression quickly fell. He nodded and focused on the bathwater that was murky with faded bubbles and grime.

"You don't think he wants to be my dad," he mumbled.

Lola felt her heart nearly crack in half. "No, Sam, it's not that. Matt *loves* you. He thinks you're the best kid in the world. It's just that...it's complicated."

With a noisy sigh, Sam frowned at his mother. "If he didn't want to marry you and be my dad, then he wouldn't play with us all the time. And he wouldn't have sleepovers." *Sleepovers?* Lola felt her cheeks flush. She thought they'd been so careful.

"And today Gabe even called me Matt's kid!" Sam cried in exasperation. His eyes welled with tears and lip quivered. His teeth chattered with cold.

Panic rushed through Lola's body and pulsed inside her head. She grabbed a towel and tried desperately to stay calm. "I know, Sam, it's all very confusing. Even for me it's confusing. Let's just get you out of the bath, and we'll figure things out okay?"

Sam stared at Lola for a moment, water dripping from his hair as he shuddered. Slowly he seemed to realize that he'd upset her. He stood and wrapped his wet arms around her neck and nuzzled into her cheek. She wiped her tears before he could see them.

Guilt poured into Lola's chest. Hadn't she come to Hope River to help Sam recover from the suffering and loss they'd experienced, to heal his fragile heart? But all she seemed to have done was threaten to break it further. She'd pulled Sam away from his grandparents, from the safety and security he knew in San Francisco. And now she'd allowed him to latch onto a man that could leave them just as quickly and tragically as Travis had.

They had to get away from Hope River before it was too late. Returning to San Francisco was their only option. Lola could protect Sam there. It was a safer place for both of them, where there was nothing more to lose.

Chapter Twenty-Four

*M*att arrived the following afternoon with flowers in one hand and a small cooler of fish in the other. "For you," he said with a smile as he handed Lola the bouquet of lilies. He got a high-five from Sam before handing him the cooler and watched him heave it proudly up the porch stairs.

Matt had been desperate to see them since the evening before. It had been a long and sleepless night worrying about Lola. Seeing her now made his heart feel better, though he still could sense her unease.

Leaning into her, Matt offered a kiss. She turned her face awkwardly so that his lips landed on her cheek. After glancing anxiously at Sam she turned back to Matt with a tight smile.

"Come inside," she said, nodding toward the house. Matt watched as she stuck her nose in the lilies and avoided his gaze. With a twist in his gut, he followed her inside.

It was as though someone had flipped a switch, Matt decided. He pretended to be busy with the fish fry, finding pans and preparing a bowl of cornmeal and egg. But it was hard to ignore the difference in Lola.

There were differences in her kitchen too. Ones that made that twist in Matt's gut feel more like a knife wound. The laptop had been dusted off and moved to the table, the folders arranged in a neat pile beside it. Fresh handwritten notes filled a new notepad and all evidence of a floor plan, of a dream of what could be, were gone.

Lola was quiet as she worked on the salad. If Sam hadn't been in the kitchen, setting the table and chattering endlessly about their fishing adventures, the room would have been consumed by silence. Matt made conversation with Sam, but Lola only nodded, lost in her thoughts.

He'd never seen her this way before. Was she angry? No, he'd seen her angry. Angry wasn't this calm - and it was her calmness that worried him. She quietly distanced herself, her eye contact minimal, and by the time dinner was over Matt was prepared for the worst.

"Can I go to Caleb's now?" Sam asked, shoving the last bite of fish in his mouth. Lola glanced at Matt, then studied Sam. She cut into her filet, slowly twirling the fish around on her plate as she considered. She seemed reluctant as she nodded, but Sam jumped from his chair, oblivious.

"Only for an hour," Lola insisted. "Be back by six-thirty. Do you have your watch on?" Sam nodded and thrust his wrist out to show her before darting from the kitchen. At the door, he stopped quickly and grinned at Matt. "Wanna play catch when I get back?" he asked.

"Sure, Champ." With a quick wink, Matt felt his heart warm as he watched Sam run off.

When Matt turned back to Lola he found her sitting stone-still, studying her plate. Her face was pale and eyes slightly swollen. Panic swelled in Matt's heart.

The slam of the screen door made them both jump. With Sam gone, the silence that lingered in the kitchen was deafening.

Matt laid a hand gently on Lola's. *I can fix this*, he promised himself. Whatever it was, he could make her feel better and put a smile on her beautiful face again. He would show her all the reasons to stay, to be with him - if she'd only give him the chance.

Lola set her fork down and slipped her fingers from Matt's. She folded her hands together in her lap, watching them intently. Chewing on her bottom lip, she seemed to agonize over what she wanted to say.

The emptiness on her face was ominous. Had he offended her? Done something stupid while fishing with Sam? He had taken every precaution to keep the boy safe, had protected him as if he were his own.

Studying her somber face and aching eyes, Matt slowly recognized what was hidden deep inside of Lola. It wasn't anger that she was harboring. It was fear.

"How was your day?" he asked quietly. It was a stupid question, he knew. But he was desperate to avoid what was coming. He sensed it, with every tensed muscle in his body. Things were caving in.

Lola lifted her face and tried to smile. "It was fine. I did a little cleaning." Her throat clicked when she swallowed. "And I packed."

Matt went still. "You're leaving," he said softly.

Lola's eyes glistened with tears, but before Matt could acknowledge them she sucked in a shaky breath and stood. Like a trapped animal, she swung around behind her chair, hands tight over the backrest. She swiped tears from her eyes and stared at the ceiling.

"Travis' parents are expecting us. And we have a house... Sam and I have a life back there that we can't just abandon." She met Matt's gaze as he studied her.

"Are you coming back?" Matt asked quietly.

Lola bit her trembling lip and turned away. "I don't know." She gulped in a breath of air and looked back at Matt. "We knew this summer was going to end, Matt. I told you... I *told* you that I couldn't make any promises."

"I'm still not asking for promises, Lola. I just want to know if you're coming back here. If you'll consider it."

Lola's face began to crumple, but she pulled herself together and shook her head. "I got a job offer today from an advertising firm in San Francisco. My friend knows the director and said the job is mine if I can be there in a week."

Air wheezed from Matt as if he'd been punched in the gut. An angry heat flashed through his body, but he held a steady face. *Calm,* he warned himself. *You need to stay calm.* He folded his arms tightly over his chest.

"What about Hope River?" he asked. *What about me?* he wanted to shout.

Lola shook her head and continued to avoid Matt's gaze.

The anger rose to Matt's throat and threatened to overflow like boiling water. He stood and tossed his dishes in the sink harder than he'd meant to. His plate cracked into three pieces.

"What about your photography studio?" he asked, his voice raw. "I know you had plans for it."

Lola's dark eyes widened. "How...?"

The answer didn't matter. Matt watched her, letting Lola simmer as he tried to rein in his desperation.

Outside, the sun had disappeared and a gusty wind rattled the house. Lola rubbed trembling fingers over her forehead and paced to the window. "That was just a stupid idea. I never imagined..." She shook her head, refusing to continue. When she turned back to Matt, her face was stormy. "That was none of your business."

"None of my business," Matt repeated. He stared at Lola hard, his blood at boiling point. "And I suppose you're none of my business either? Or Sam?"

"What do you expect me to do?" Lola shot back. Her voice strengthened to match Matt's and her hand gripped the table until her knuckles turned white.

"I expect you to do what's best for you and Sam!"

"I don't know what that is!" Lola cried in desperation.

He couldn't play this game any longer. He had to know the truth, had to find a way to fix whatever she saw as the problem.

"Why, Lola?" Matt demanded. "Why won't you stay? Sam loves it here. *You* love it here, I know you do. You haven't spoken of the city once, haven't missed a day of it. You're falling for this little town, this simple life." He'd moved close as he spoke and was only inches from her. "So what is it, Lola? What are you really afraid of?"

Tears spilled over Lola's cheeks and she covered her mouth with a shaky hand. She leaned against a chair and shook her head desperately.

"I know what you've been through, Lola. I know how scared you feel." He reached out, desperate to make her understand. "It tips your world upside down and makes you lose trust in life. But running away is not going to solve anything."

"I'm not running away," Lola insisted. "I'm protecting Sam. I've watched my son lose one father already and I'm not about to let him lose another. He *adores* you, Matt. He worships you. He wants you to be his..." She lifted her hands in the air with exasperation. "How am I supposed to tell him that it's not that simple? That you're dangerous for us? You run off to save lives and fight fires and risk your life - that's admirable, Matt. It really is. But the other day, I thought we'd lost you." She shook her head and let a sob tumble from her lips. "He wouldn't survive it again, Matt. And neither would I."

Her startling words gave Matt a sudden hope. Beneath all of this fear, she wanted to be a family. She wanted to be with Matt but was too afraid she'd lose him.

"Marry me."

Lola's eyes widened in disbelief. "What?" she cried.

"I want you to marry me, Lola. I love you. I want you to be my wife. I want Sam to be my son. I won't hurt you and I won't leave you. I'll protect you." He heard the desperation in his voice but didn't care. He wanted nothing more than to wake up to her and Sam every single day for the rest of his life. Didn't she want that too?

One lone tear slid down Lola's cheek. She took a step back and shook her head over and over. Matt reached out to touch her, but she pushed his hand away. "We don't need you, Matt. We don't need your protection. We're fine just the two of us." She turned away, her entire body trembling, and then swirled back. "You can't just do that!" she cried, her voice quivering with anger. "You can't just ask me that and expect everything to be okay!"

It felt as if the walls were caving in. He'd known this would happen, hadn't he? He'd known it all along. There was nothing he could do. This sudden understanding nearly buckled his knees. Just as Ali had, Lola was pushing him away.

"I love you, Lola. I need you in my life. I need Sam." He stepped toward her once more, but she flinched away.

"Sam's already lost one father. I won't let him go through that again."

Matt wanted to grab her shoulders and shake some sense into her. "He's not going to lose me, Lola. I'm not going anywhere. You're the one who's leaving and taking him away!"

A fire burned in Lola's eyes. "It was a mistake to let him get so close to you."

"Were you and I a mistake too?" Matt shouted. He nearly shook with his anger. Lola was lying through her teeth, and she knew it. They'd been good for each other, he and Lola and Sam, they were happy together. He watched Lola, his heart pounding, fists clenched as he waited for her to answer.

"Sam and I are going back to California," she whispered, anger still dark in her eyes. They softened as more tears threatened to overflow.

His hand already in a fist, Matt contemplated putting it through a wall. Instead he pounded it on the kitchen counter, making dishes rattle in the cupboards. Lola turned away from him, hiding her face. He could see her wiping tears, covering her mouth with a trembling hand.

Frustration clouded the shame he should have felt for losing his temper. How could she throw this away so easily? He needed some time to think, to figure out a way to put things right. To convince Lola that she could trust life again, trust *love*.

He charged to the kitchen door, stopping as his hand wrapped around the handle. He stood for a moment, collecting himself.

"Lola, just give us a chance..." he said quietly. He turned toward her, hoping he might still get through.

Lola shook her head, her back still to him. She wouldn't turn, wouldn't face him to see how she was breaking his heart.

"No, Matt." Her voice was quiet but steady. "This is one thing you can't fix."

Memories from seven years ago flashed through his mind. It was Ali all over again, only this time Lola wasn't taking her own life. She was taking his hopes and dreams and a belief in second chances.

Something inside of Matt begged him to reach out, to hold Lola one more time and tell her that he would be there for her, forever. To convince her that he wouldn't leave the way Travis had.

But it was a promise he knew he couldn't make. No one could. In silent surrender, he walked out the door.

IT WAS EXACTLY SIX-THIRTY when Lola heard the porch door slam. Sam skipped into the kitchen, his hair tousled and a wide smile on his lips. Through the windows behind him, Lola could see that the sunny day had given way to towering, dense clouds. They were as ominous as the ache in her chest.

"Mom, where's Matt? I have to get my mitt from my room-" Sam froze in the doorway, all color draining from his face as he surveyed the boxes and bags on the table. "What are you doing?" he asked in a small voice. The look on his face told Lola he already knew the answer.

"Baby, we're heading back to California soon," Lola began. She tried to act casual and keep a steady hand as she placed books and a few folded blankets into the largest box.

"But I don't want to go back," he said quietly. Lola heard him swallow hard before his voice returned a little louder. "Mom, I don't want to go back. I like it here."

She watched his face grow darker. "School begins in a few weeks, Sam. Aren't you excited to see your teachers again? Your friends? Mam and Pap?" He only frowned at her words.

"I want to stay *here*," he insisted. His fists clenched against his legs and he scowled harder. "Where's Matt?" he insisted. "I want to play catch with him." His eyes quickly filled and Lola had to bite her lip to stop hers from doing the same.

"He went home."

Shaking his head frantically, Sam stepped closer to his mother. "I'm sorry I upset you yesterday," he cried. "I won't ask him to be my dad, I promise. I won't say it anymore."

Her hand flew to her mouth and she shook her head desperately.

"When's he going to take me fishing again?" Sam asked. One tear slipped down his ruddy cheek. Kneeling before him, Lola took his clenched fists in her hands. She wiped his tear and held Sam's cheek in her palm.

"Maybe next summer. Maybe we'll come visit Aunt Louise next summer for a few weeks and you can see him then."

More tears, and his lip trembled. He shook his head, the anger building, and glared at his mother. "I don't want to come back next summer. I want to stay here now!" He pulled back, shoving her hands away. "I want to stay *now!*" he screamed. The shrillness of his voice made Lola jump.

"Honey, calm down." She put a shaky hand over his chest, trying to soothe him. "It's just that… it's my job, as your mother, to protect your heart. It's complicated, and…"

Sam didn't let her finish. Pushing away, he sent her a look of pure hatred. "My heart's *fine*, Mom!" he screamed. "*Yours* is the one that's broken!" Tears spilled down his face, pouring from his pained gray eyes and staining his dusty cheeks. He yanked himself from Lola's grasp and darted through the porch door, letting it slam behind him. The windows rattled as he pounded down the stairs.

Still on her knees in the kitchen, Lola watched in horror as her little boy disappeared.

Chapter Twenty-Five

She knew she should run after Sam, but Lola was too weak to move. Her legs felt like lead as she knelt on the floor.

Goliath rose from his warm bed, his plump body wiggling with uncertainty, and nudged her arm with a wet nose. *Go after him*, he seemed to say as he bumped her again with his head. Planting a hand on his soft back, Lola used him as support to lift herself up. With Goliath at her heels, she ran through the porch and down the stairs.

Outside, there was no sign of Sam. Only the howl of the wind and Goliath's eager whine filled the air.

"Sam!" Lola cried. Goliath touched his nose to the ground, sniffing at the grass. In the distance, the sky rumbled and moaned, sending chills through Lola's body.

"Sam!" she shouted again, this time with such force that Goliath flinched.

Still, there was no response. She gasped for air, finding it hard to breathe, to think. Where would he go? He'd never been so angry before. She scanned the stream, the shed, the woods as an emptiness echoed through her chest.

"Gabe! Is Sam here?" Lola cried as she crashed through the brush at the edge of his lawn. She nearly fell over him before she could slow herself. He'd been sitting on the ground beside his lawn mower, examining the exposed engine with a handful of tools. He jumped to his feet when he saw the look on Lola's face.

"He left at 6:30. Didn't he go home?" Panic rose in his wide eyes.

Nodding helplessly, Lola covered her face with both hands. A helpless sob bubbled from inside and she bent and gripped her knees.

"We… we had a fight. He got upset and ran out," she cried. "He's never done this before."

From the corner of her eye, Lola saw Rena dart from the porch, the door clapping behind her. She was at Lola's side in an instant. "What's wrong?"

"Sam's run away," Gabe answered, and Lola nodded desperately.

"He couldn't have gone far," Lola insisted, glancing around the yard. "He only ran off a few minutes ago."

"Caleb!" Rena hollered as she turned to the house. *Please,* Lola prayed, *let Sam be hiding inside. I'll never forgive myself if…*

"We haven't seen him since he walked home." The look of panic on Rena's face made Lola's fear twist tighter. "Why did he run?" Rena asked.

Gabe scowled at Lola, waiting for her to answer.

She stared at them, hesitating. God, she was a fool. "He wants to stay here," Lola answered quietly. She fought against the rush of tears and guilt. "He wants to stay in Hope River and be with Matt."

Gabe and Rena studied one another. "Matt," they whispered together.

"I'll call him," Rena shouted as she ran back to the house. "Sam might go to him."

Lola's heart galloped with hope. It didn't matter that she'd had a horrible argument with Matt only hours ago. If Sam had gone to him then he would be safe. Matt would protect her little boy.

"I'll drive around and look for Sam," Gabe called, pulling keys from his pocket.

Lola was through the woods and back at her place in seconds. Goliath met her with eager yips. He followed her as she searched every hiding place she could think of - behind bushes, under the porch, by the stream. They ran around the house, into the shed, even back inside to check every room. The search left her empty-handed and more convinced of where he'd be.

Sam had to be with Matt. Where else would he go?

She was climbing into the old Chevy when she saw the dust flying on her driveway. Matt's truck barreled toward her. She'd never been so relieved to see him. She was at his truck window before he even parked, desperate to see her little boy sitting beside him.

But he wasn't there. "He's not with you?" she cried, leaning into the cab to search the seats. The sky rumbled overhead and a swirling wind made Lola's hair slap across her cheeks.

Matt slipped from his truck and steadied Lola by the shoulders.

"Where would he have gone?" she whimpered, then covered her mouth once more to stop the terrified sobs. She'd wanted so desperately to protect his little heart and only ended up breaking it herself. What an idiot fool she'd been. Her body trembled and threatened to crumble.

Matt pulled Lola to his chest and held her against him. He stroked the hair from her cheek before taking her by the arms. "We'll find him," he promised.

They drove slowly on Main Street, squinting through the darkening evening at every sidewalk and home.

"What happened?" Matt asked as he leaned forward to peer down a side street. Thunder rumbled overhead, making Lola shiver.

"He saw me packing when he came home," Lola began. She felt her teeth chatter as she relived Sam's disappointment. "He was angry. He wants to stay but I told him…" She swallowed hard and tried to finish, but couldn't. Her throat tightened and chin crumpled. She just couldn't do anything right, could she? Stay or go, it would be a poor decision.

Matt took Lola's hand in his own, squeezing it softly. "It's okay," he said quietly. "We'll find him."

His hand was so warm over hers, his fingers so gentle on her skin. Comfort and love swamped her heart and she nearly cried out in her frustration.

Who was she kidding? She did need Matt. And so did Sam. Yes, they could survive without him. They'd done it for two years and could go on that way for plenty more. But why would Lola choose that for them?

She gazed at Matt as he searched the town, looking for signs of her son, signs of a little boy who she knew Matt loved like his own. *Why am I doing this to him?* She heard her heart whisper. *Why am I doing this to myself and to Sam?* As if a veil was lifted from her eyes, she could suddenly see it so clearly.

She loved him. She wanted a life with him. And though no love in the world held any guarantee, she trusted Matt's promise. He wouldn't leave them. She laced her fingers through his, holding tight as she continued to search the streets.

Beyond the windows, the dark and roiling sky flickered with lightning.

"He's out there alone," Lola whispered as she watched the sky. The pain of this nearly choked her.

They searched the schoolyard and playground, battling the angry wind as they looked for signs. Sam was nowhere to be found.

Huge raindrops splattered on the windshield as they raced next to the ball field. Lola was out of the truck and running to the stands, calling over the wind and storm before Matt even stopped. The raindrops struck the dusty earth of the outfield as Lola searched the bleachers and covered dugout. Nothing. Everywhere they looked, nothing.

Her panic grew so fierce that Lola became angry with the rain, with herself. She ran hard, aimless and desperate until she could no longer breathe. She stopped, gasping in the field, and looked beyond to downtown, the bridge, the river...

The river.

She sprinted recklessly to it, sloshing through puddles and over fallen branches. She could barely see past her own hands. Thunder crashed overhead. Lola wiped rain from her eyes as she looked up and down the river. She needed a clearer view. Turning, she struggled up the muddy bank toward the bridge.

In the distance, Matt called to her, shouting her name again and again. Through the rain she saw him pointing over her head at something across the road. His voice was muffled and distant, and she couldn't make out his words. She turned to look where he pointed, and saw.

It was Sam. Across the road, against the fire station, hiding safely beneath the front door's awning. He held his little arms around his body in tight desperation. He was crying, his face crumpled in fear, and Lola's heart simultaneously broke and burst with utter relief. She charged over the bridge, onto the edge of the road, her feet carrying her with speed she had never known before. "Sam!" she cried. He saw her, relief flooding his face, and stepped out from the awning. She saw the apology in his eyes as he ran to her.

"*Stop!*" Matt's voice cried from behind Lola. It echoed in her ears, so close and desperate. The wind changed direction and the rain pelted her back. A headlight flashed dimly over the street. Sam jumped from the curb into the street. She couldn't stop him.

Time collapsed. Rain fell from the sky in slow motion. Even the thunder sounded distant and part of another world. Yet it all happened so fast.

It came from nowhere, a huge white delivery truck with windshield wipers swishing frantically. One headlight was out, the other seemed dim, but so close to Lola. So very close. Across the road she watched the shock slip over Sam's face. He jumped back to the sidewalk, to safety, but held a hand out to his mother and screamed.

Before she could cry out in the pain that she knew would come, before she could brace herself for the impact of that white truck striking her side, she felt her body lurch and tumble toward Sam across the road. Strong hands were on her shoulders, pushing her, tossing her like a rag doll away from danger. Tires wailed and the truck slid one way and then the next as it battled with the road. Lola's body crumpled to the ground, into a deep puddle against the curb. Her forehead hit the sidewalk. Pain flashed through her temple and warmth trickled down her face.

Behind her the truck slid sideways and thumped to a stop. A heavy silence spread thick over Lola.

Moments later, as if she'd been pulled from the depths of the water, every sound flooded her senses and rang in her ears. Rain pattered the road, thunder rumbled low and ornery. An engine hummed and ticked, and feet splashed through puddles as they ran. Time expanded and Lola was thrown back into reality.

Sam's frozen hands were on her, his voice desperate in her ear. "No!" he sobbed.

I'm okay, Lola wanted to whisper, but the words wouldn't come out. She lifted her face to reassure him, but his eyes weren't on her. Instead, he stared helplessly at a man's body lying lifeless in the road.

She knew his face, those large hands. The wide shoulders and strong legs. And she knew she would never forgive herself for the pain she had caused him on this day. Matthew Dawson, the man she had grown to love more than she'd known possible, lay limp in front of the truck.

A burst of adrenaline had Lola on her feet in an instant. As she moved on steady legs, the driver of the truck kneeled beside Matt. Lola pulled Sam to the curb and kissed him hard on the forehead. "Stay here," she warned. "Don't move!" Sam watched her with terrified eyes and nodded.

"Call 911!" She shouted as she shoved the driver away. Confused and scared, he looked at her with glassy eyes. "Now!" she screamed, and he snapped from his trance and ran to the truck. Lola dropped to her knees.

"Don't you dare do this to me Matthew Dawson," she warned, touching his cheeks gently. She watched his chest for movement, then leaned an ear against his mouth. Short, slow breaths, so shallow she could barely feel them, slipped from his mouth. She laid her cheek on his chest and fought the fear and panic.

His chest hitched once, then continued with shallow breaths. Lola leaned close and pressed her lips gently against his.

"Stay with me," Lola whispered to him. She leaned over and waited for him to move. "Just breathe," she said, swallowing a cry. "Let's just breathe…" With a hand on his chest, she willed it to rise and fall in even rhythm with hers. Her eyes flooded with tears and burned her cheeks.

"I lied," Lola said, bringing her face close to Matt's ear. "I lied when I told you we were a mistake." She sniffled and wiped a tear from her nose. "We were never a mistake. I love you, and I want to be with you forever. I want this little town to be our home, and I want you to be Sam's father." She sucked in an unsteady breath and laughed a little, watching the faint pulse on his neck. "I want to have more children with you, Matthew Dawson. We have so much to look forward to. You can't give up." She let herself cry a little then, the tears falling down her cheeks and dripping onto him. Leaning over him she kissed the bruises on his jaw, the cut below his eye.

"I love you," Lola whispered again, her lips warm against his skin. "When I said Sam and I can make it on our own, I wasn't lying. But I wasn't telling you the truth, either. Because the truth is, we don't want to make it on our own. We want to be with you." She pressed a gentle hand over his heart and closed her eyes.

"Please," she whispered. "Don't leave me."

Epilogue

The day was unusually warm. It had been warm all summer, though Lola was used to it now. She'd lived in this little town for nearly three years, watching the seasons come and go, enjoying the frigid winters and hot steamy days of the summer.

She loved the crazy weather here. And the crazy people. She loved this little town.

Glancing down the street, Lola surveyed the cute benches where families sat and watched the traffic crawl by. The flower pots beside them exploded with petunias and pansies of all colors. Shop doors opened wide as people of Hope River went in to pay their daily visits. It was these people who had become Lola's family.

They'd all pulled together after the accident on that awful stormy night years ago. They'd found solace in one another and had been a comfort to Lola and Sam. They'd supported her, let her cry on their shoulders, given her hope that life would move forward, one day at a time.

She was stronger now. Stronger than she'd ever known she could be. She had a business she was proud of, a sturdy and cozy home that she'd helped build herself. And she'd found happiness in the simple act of living one day at a time.

"Afternoon, Lola!" Charlie called from across the street. He waved a hand in the air and chuckled as she lifted the screwdriver in her hand and waved it at him.

The tool felt familiar to her now. She used it, and so many others in the handy little tool box at her feet, almost on a daily basis.

Today she was adjusting a shiny new plate on the wall beside the door. She'd ordered the plate at Anne's suggestion and now, next to *Ritz Pix,* a fancy little plate announced the addition of Lola's studio. *Sommers Photography* had officially been in business for nearly eighteen months. And already, wonderfully, she was overwhelmed with clients.

"Mom, look what I got!" Sam cried as he ran to her. His feet slapped the sidewalk and he nearly crashed into her with his triple-scoop ice cream cone. Lola didn't dare bend to kiss him like she used to. Sam had passed through the phase of enjoying his mother's attention in public. But he beamed at her as he always had, with eager gray eyes and a smile that lit up his face. He stood beside her, his head nearly reaching her shoulder.

"You're going to get a stomach ache if you eat that whole thing," Lola warned, ruffling his hair. She laughed as he tried to fit the entire top scoop into his mouth.

Turning to place the screwdriver back in her tool box, she surveyed the neat placement of tools and then closed it with a snap. With her back to Sam, she gathered the box in her hands. "Where is everyone else?" she asked, glancing once more at her shiny new plate. Sam answered unintelligibly around a mouthful of ice cream. He stepped inside the shop and let the door slide closed behind him.

"You're getting good with those tools," a deep voice teased.

Lola turned and let out a quick laugh as she saw them. The little girl in his arms grinned wildly and held a dripping ice cream cone in her pudgy fingers. Her straight brown hair shone in the sun and her eyes were as bright as blueberries. Lola kissed her daughter's soft cheek and then studied the man in front of her. His eyes twinkled playfully and one corner of his mouth lifted in a familiar smirk.

She loved that little smirk. Through two years of surgery, recovery, and therapy that little smirk had kept everyone going, kept them believing that the town hero would make it through and return as the man they'd all once known. Lola studied the light scar that streaked beneath his eye - the one that reminded her to just breathe, to treasure each and every precious day that she had with him.

"Do you need any help, Mrs. Dawson?" Matt asked, pulling her into his strong arms.

Lola leaned against his chest and planted a soft kiss on his lips. "No thank you, Mr. Dawson," she said, smiling wide. "I fixed it all by myself."

Turn the page for a sneak peek at
Bonnie J. James' next book, coming in 2013.

Chapter One

"Well for heaven's sake, young lady, when am I going to see a ring on that finger of yours?" Mrs. Oaks asked. Her wrinkly face scrunched in disapproval. "If I were you I'd tell that man to either piss or get off the pot."

Kate Kettering gripped her rotary cutter and sliced a yard of fabric in half. She was used to the sassy opinions of the old ladies who frequented her shop, but Mrs. Oaks surely won the prize for most obnoxious.

"We haven't discussed marriage yet, Mrs. Oaks," Kate said, smiling politely at the prunish old woman. "But I'm sure you'll be one of the first to know if we do." She folded the vintage flower fabric into a perfect square and handed it to Mrs. Oaks, then glanced anxiously at the clock.

Mrs. Oaks raised an eyebrow and clucked her tongue. She poked a bony finger into the woman standing beside her. "I was married with three children by the time I was her age," she said, gesturing at Kate.

"Well, Sis, at her age you didn't own a quilt store or have any ambitions other than to be a mother," the woman answered. She rolled her eyes at her sister and shooed her from the counter.

"Hi, Norma," Kate said thankfully, taking the bolt of fabric from her. She unrolled it quickly, letting it flop with a thud against the countertop.

"Don't mind Annie," Norma whispered from behind her fingers. "She's always got an opinion about something. I say you take as much time as you need before getting a ring on your finger. Your Anthony is a handsome one, but if he has any sense he'll hang around as long as you need him to."

The smile Kate plastered across her lips was nearly painful, it was so fake. If these women only knew that just days ago she'd had a three carat diamond engagement ring on her finger for all of two minutes, they'd be squawking like wild birds.

"Two yards, please," Norma said, patting the blue cotton fabric. "I'm making a blanket for my grandson. He wants rockets this time, but Lord help me if I can find a pattern for that."

"I think we have one in the children's section," Kate answered. She glanced at the clock again and sliced two yards from the bolt with such efficiency that it made Norma flinch.

As she folded the fabric, Kate called across the room to her shop manager. "Pearl, can you show Norma the space rocket pattern in the children's-" Before she could finish, Pearl waved a hand and hurried away. *God love that woman,* Kate told herself for the thousandth time.

Katie May's Quilt Shoppe would tumble to pieces if it weren't for sixty-two year old Pearl Groves. She'd been with Kate since the very idea of a quilt shop popped into her head, and now Kate couldn't imagine a day without her. Surely she was an angel sent from heaven. The thought made tears prick behind Kate's eyes, but a cool rush of air swept through the shop doors and steadied her.

Two robust women entered the store and caused a noise akin to hens joining a henhouse. Voices lifted and clucked with laughter and conversation. The entire scene made Kate sigh with satisfaction. She loved the sound of her busy quilt shop on a cool autumn evening.

Outside, the cold September sky was gray and dreary. A light rain began to pelt the line of windows that faced the historic Baker Street, but there was a warmth inside the shop that made everyone's cheeks glow. It was the beginning of quilting season, after all. As many of the local men of St. Claire, Minnesota, geared up for hunting and fishing, their wives were preparing for a sewing marathon that would last them through the spring.

"Kate, what do you think for the color of this binding?" Peg, a long-time customer, held out a nearly-finished quilt and made a face. "Lime green or berry red?"

Kate gave a pleasant gasp of approval. "Oh, definitely the red, Peg. That's gorgeous. Will you bring it to the guild meeting on Monday night? You have to show it to the other ladies."

A pleased blush spread over Peg's cheeks. "I guess I'll buy a few yards real quick so I can finish it by then," Peg said.

As Kate measured and cut fabric, she saw the old street lamps blink to life outside. Seven forty-five. She wouldn't make it on time at this rate. Kate rushed to finish Peg's order and ring it up.

"I'll take care of that. You go on," Pearl insisted. She nearly knocked Kate over with the swing of her ample hips as she squeezed next to Kate behind the register.

"Thanks, Pearl," Kate whispered. She patted her old friend's arm and slipped from behind the counter.

Kate's heels clicked desperately on the wooden floor as she streaked past rows of fabrics and tables of sewing projects. She kept her head down and made a beeline for the back of the shop.

The phone was ringing as she entered her bright white office, but Kate didn't dare answer it. She grabbed her raincoat from the coat rack and the quilted tote bag she'd made a few months ago and darted to the door. Her head pounded from the day that had started over fifteen hours ago, and the arches of her feet ached miserably. But nothing on her body hurt nearly as much as her exhausted heart.

How ironic, Kate realized as she hurried through the dark, damp air to her car. The man she loved more than life itself was breaking her heart in two. Yet, without fail, she rushed every night to be by his side.

Two years. What the hell happened? It had only been two years.

Guilt and anger rushed through Mitchell Fyn's veins as he gripped the steering wheel of the old Lincoln Town Car. He watched the rain pelt the windshield and listened to the splashing of tires in the Care Center's parking lot.

Two goddamn years. When Mitch had last seen him, his grandfather had been frail and slightly confused. But this? This just wasn't fair. Aunt Carol had warned him, but still the sight had been shocking. His Gramps, at age seventy-two, a white ghost of a man in a cold and lonely room. All skin and bones, sunken cheeks, and eyes that stared at nothing.

Damned Alzheimer's. Damned everything.

They should be out fishing right now, Mitch decided as he cuffed the steering wheel with his palm. They should be laughing about old times, sharing stories of Mitch's childhood, talking about government and world politics, about Gramps' construction company and the latest bridge Mitch had built in Iraq.

They had so much to catch up on. If only he'd come back sooner.

Turning the key, Mitch started his grandfather's old car and listened to the engine purr. The last time he'd been home, Gramps had handed Mitch the keys and told him to use the Lincoln whenever he came to town. He probably hadn't expected it to take two years for Mitch to return.

Damnit, he should have come back sooner. He should have taken leave when it was offered, gotten out of that hellfire desert he was in and come back to visit while Gramps was still... *here.*

Because Gramps was long gone now.

The rain fell harder, pelting the car with huge wet drops that bordered on slush. Mitch forced the car into reverse and blindly searched for the windshield wipers as he backed out. His fingers fumbled on both sides of the steering column, setting off the blinkers before he finally turned on the wipers. They squeaked across the windshield, clearing the icy rain, giving Mitch a clear view of the three-story building where his grandfather lay in a cold hard bed.

He'd come back tomorrow, Mitch thought. Maybe in the morning there'd be a chance that Gramps would wake up for a few minutes, open those mischievous blue eyes and recognize the boy he'd practically raised as his own son.

Mitch's head jerked backward and slammed into the headrest. He heard a loud *crunch* from the back of the car. He stomped on the brakes and squinted into the rear view mirror.

"*Shit*." Throwing the car into drive, Mitch inched forward until he was back in the parking spot. He put the car in park and rubbed a weary hand over his face, then opened the car door. "Shit," he murmured again.

The rain had slowed to a steady drip but still felt icy on his face. He might have found it refreshing if he wasn't so preoccupied with the woman who stood behind his car.

"Look at what you did!" she cried, throwing her arms in the air. She turned to Mitch and narrowed her eyes at him. They glinted for a moment as the lights from another car passed by. "You're supposed to look before you back out!" she scolded. She bent to survey the damage on her car. The fender was crumpled above the front tire.

"I don't have time for this," she growled.

"Look, I'm sorry," Mitch began. Excuses ran through his mind - distraction caused by an ailing grandfather, an unfamiliar car and bad weather, sleep deprivation from traveling halfway across the world that very morning... He sighed and lifted his hands in surrender.

The woman only glared in return. If Mitch wasn't mistaken, there may have even been steam rising from her head. "I can't do this now," she spat, glancing at her watch. Turning back to her car, she jerked the door open and grabbed a bag. With quick movements, she unzipped a pocket and rifled through it, then yanked at another zipper.

It gave Mitch a moment to study her.

She had to be five foot ten, even without the three inch heels. Her legs were stunning, with muscled calves that only runners could boast of. Her skirt fell to mid-thigh and was partially covered by a raincoat that wrapped around her torso, tight enough to show a few curves.

"Do you have insurance?" the woman barked, still tearing through her bag.

Mitch cleared his throat and nodded. "Yes, I-" For a moment his heart thumped. Surely Aunt Carol had kept up the insurance on this old thing. "I'll grab it for you." He slipped back into the Lincoln and dug through the glove box, relieved when he found an updated insurance card. When he stepped back out to the rain, the woman was coming at him with a hand extended, a card in her fingers. Her heels click-clacked hard on the pavement and her long dark hair, now curving with dampness, stuck to her cheeks. Her teeth chattered as she thrust the card in his hand. He handed his over as well.

"Are you okay?" Mitch asked. Such an idiot. He hadn't thought to make that his first question minutes ago.

"Just cold," she said, sticking his card in her purse and turning away. Mitch grabbed her arm and turned her gently back.

"I mean are you hurt?"

She studied his eyes for a moment, her own hazel ones softening. Mitch caught a glimpse of something in them. Grief? Pain?

"I'm fine," she answered. She pulled her arm from Mitch's grasp and walked briskly back to her running car, her shoes clicking on the pavement in even rhythm. "But your insurance better pay for this," she warned before slipping back into her seat. She threw her bag on the passenger side, gave Mitch one last warning glance, then slammed the door.

Mitch watched as her car's red tail lights dimmed in the parking lot and disappeared around a corner. "Shit," he whispered once more. It was the only word he had energy for.

With the woman's thin insurance card between his fingers, Mitch stared into the darkness and let the rain fall around him. The icy water dripped down his cheeks and seeped into his shirt and he wondered, not for the first time that night, what in the hell had just happened.

The Golden River Care Center hallway echoed with the sharp sound of Kate's shoes snapping against the hard floor. She shook the rain from her coat as she passed the open lounge, where the television quietly droned an eight o'clock update on the evening weather. She tried to dry her damp hands on her skirt, but it was no use. Every inch of her body was shivering with cold and wet.

"Visiting hours are over, honey," a plump nurse called from behind the desk that guarded the rooms beyond. Kate glanced at the wall clock and held back the urge to roll her eyes. Three minutes past. Surely she wouldn't be carried out by security if she popped into her father's room for one minute. She put on her most pleasant smile and waved at the nurse. "Hi Shanice. I'll only be a minute, I promise." Kate didn't slow her stride, just continued walking briskly past the desk. She ignored Shanice's raised eyebrows and hum of disapproval.

"Hi Daddy," Kate said as she quietly slipped into the room. She crossed over to the bed and planted a quick kiss on her father's forehead, then dumped her purse and coat into a nearby chair. With efficient speed, she grabbed the straw cup of water on his bedside and filled it at the sink, snapping the lid in place before setting it beside him again. She scooped up a few wrappers on the table, straightened the pile of books-on-tape beside the CD player, and plucked a few dying flowers from the vase she'd filled a few days ago.

"What's got you all worked up?" George asked in a slow and quiet voice. He kept his eyes closed as he lay in the bed, but a slow smirk played at his lips.

Kate tossed the dead flowers and wrappers in the garbage and moved to the window. She opened and closed the blinds. Twice.

"Some jerk just hit my car in the parking lot," she hissed.

"You okay?" George asked.

"Yeah, I'm fine." Kate adjusted the blinds once more before running a hand through her tangled, wet hair. Her pulse was slowly calming and the adrenaline that had shot through her minutes ago now made her limbs ache.

George weakly shifted to one side of the bed. "It's just a car," he said as he patted the blanket beside him. "Come here."

As Kate turned to face her father, she wasn't sure if she should smile or cry. The old worn man in the bed resembled the father she'd grown up with, but looked so frail and tired that she sometimes didn't recognize him. Tonight though, a little twinkle in his eye and a lift at the corner of his mouth reminded her of who he would always be. She slipped off her shoes and climbed on the bed beside him.

Since she was a little girl, this had been Kate's favorite place in the world. Tucked against her father's strong body, her chin on his chest and cheek nuzzled against his neck. The world was always safe when she was there.

George patted her leg with a trembling hand. "It's your birthday tomorrow," he whispered.

"Don't remind me."

"I might not remember tomorrow. Happy birthday early."

Tears stung Kate's eyes. She swallowed the lump in her throat and vowed that she wouldn't cry. It only made him feel worse.

"I'm sorry I was such a pain in the ass growing up," she said against his shoulder. She laughed a little at the thought of all she'd put her poor father through. He'd had to raise her on his own since she was ten.

George grunted and his eyes slowly crinkled with a muted laugh. "You weren't that bad," he said. His hands weren't strong enough to squeeze her, but she felt the pressure of him trying. "Just had a bit of wild child in you. Turned out good though."

"You had your hands full with me, Daddy. I bet you wondered if we'd make it through." Kate smiled at George. "Skipping school, rowdy friends, breaking curfew. Remember when I jumped off the railroad bridge?" George grunted at the memory as Kate continued. "God, I'm lucky I didn't break my neck."

"You're lucky that cop didn't haul you to jail," George muttered. "You didn't think twice when it came to taking risks. Got that from your mother."

Kate stiffened. She didn't want to think about her mother tonight. Only the fact that she had the luxury of a sweet conversation with her father. It came less and less these days.

"Speaking of taking risks," Kate said as she shifted in the bed. She took a moment to clear her throat. "Anthony proposed."

Thinking back to the incident three nights ago nearly made her break out in a cold sweat. She glanced at her father's face to gauge his reaction. His eyes were closed but he nodded knowingly.

"You knew?" she asked.

A smile lifted one corner of George's mouth. "He came in last week. Asked for my permission."

"What did you say?"

George opened one eye to peek at her. "Said it wasn't up to me."

A small laugh bubbled from Kate's chest.

Slowly, George moved his hand until it found Kate's. He blindly felt her fingers and tried to squeeze them in his. "No ring," he whispered. "You said no?"

Kate sighed and laced her fingers through her father's. "I said... I didn't know. He's working overseas for a few weeks, so I have time to think about it."

The small smile that caused George's cheeks to widen made Kate frown. "You think this is funny?" she asked.

"Nope. Just want my girl to be happy."

Kate studied her father for a moment, watching him close his eyes once more. His breathing was labored and his face was gaunt with exhaustion.

From the corner of her eye, Kate saw the door crack open. Rubber-soled shoes squeaked on the floor and Shanice stepped into the room with a hand on her hip.

"Visiting hours are over, Miss Kate," she warned. Kate nodded as she continued to watch her father. Her eyes filled with tears.

Shanice stood in the doorway watching Kate and her father and finally sighed. She turned off the florescent overhead light so that only the bedside lamp glowed. "You need some rest too, young lady," Shanice said. Her voice had softened and her dark round eyes showed worry. "Take another minute and then I'll lock up behind you." She slipped from the room, closing the door behind her.

Kate snuggled back into the warmth of her father's neck. She felt him shift his head slightly until his cheek rested against her forehead. The tears that Kate had held at bay for so long silently slipped down her cheeks.

"THANKS FOR LETTING ME crash here, Bryce," Mitch said as he poured himself a cup of coffee. He glanced at his cousin and offered a thankful nod. "I appreciate you and Shelby taking me in."

Bryce lowered the newspaper he'd been scanning and shot Mitch a quick grin. "I'd be pissed if you didn't stay with us while you're home. Though, you may regret it after nine days in this nuthouse." He lifted his coffee to his lips, the steam swirling in front of his laughing eyes. "What are your plans while you're here?"

Mitch considered as he leaned against the kitchen counter. Bryce would be at work all week, and from what Aunt Carol had reported, he'd be putting in long hours at the office. Shelby was home with the kids all day but Mitch certainly didn't want to get in her way.

"I'll visit Gramps. Maybe get my bike out if the weather is warm enough."

"Some of the old crew is still around, you know. Birch said you should give him a call when you're settled. We'll have to go out one night and relive the old days." Bryce smoothed his fancy tie and crisp shirt and offered a mischievous smile.

The old days. Thoughts of his teenage years with Bryce and Todd Birch made Mitch chuckle. The three of them, only months apart in age, had worked together every summer for Gramps' construction company. They'd also gotten into a helluva lot of trouble when they weren't on the clock.

Shelby breezed into the kitchen, clad in a long blue robe and fuzzy slippers. "I expect you to have dinner with us, too," she announced. Her short blonde hair stood in curly tufts and Mitch found her just as cute this morning as the day Bryce had introduced them eight years ago.

Mitch shifted away from the coffee machine so that Shelby could pour herself a mug. "Shelbs, you don't have to cook for me. I'll take care of myself while I'm here."

Shelby made a face and wrapped a hand around Mitch's jaw. She made him look her in the eye. "Of course I'll cook for you. I want to, and if you don't let me I'll be mad at you."

"Better listen to her, Mitch. She's mean when she's mad." Bryce ducked as Shelby swatted at him. She turned quickly, but he grabbed her by the waist and whisked her into his lap.

Mitch watched them laugh, saw Shelby's face light up as Bryce nestled his face in her neck. A dull ache of envy washed through Mitch's body, and he turned away. He nearly fell over the little girl standing at his side.

"Who are *you?*" she interrogated. She clutched a stuffed monkey to the front of her princess pajama dress and stared up at Mitch. Her eyes were the color of pennies and as round as them too. But they narrowed as Mitch leaned away.

"Mia, this is Daddy's cousin Mitchell. You were only two the last time he was here, so you probably don't remember him." Shelby came to her daughter's side and ran her fingers through the girl's tangled dark hair.

"Wow, she grew up fast," was all Mitch could manage. The girl was making him nervous. "She looks just like you, Bry." He breathed a little easier when Bryce scooped her up in his arms and set her on his knee.

"Four years old now," Bryce said, giving her a little bounce. "Wait until you see Rex. We call him 'mini-me'."

A strange noise carried from another room. "You can meet him now," Shelby said. "I think I hear him stirring." She set her coffee on the table and slipped from the kitchen.

Mia continued to stare at Mitch from the perch of her father's knee. Her scowl had eased but still she assessed him with suspicious eyes.

"I have to get to work, Princess," Bryce announced. He wrapped his arms around his daughter and planted a kiss in her hair, then slid her off his knee. She stood beside the table and continued to eye Mitch.

"I'll see you tonight," Bryce said. He slapped Mitch on the shoulder and pointed a finger at him. "Make sure you're around for dinner so we can catch up. And one night we'll have a few beers and hit the pool table. Just like old times." His mouth lifted in the crooked smile that Mitch remembered from childhood.

Bryce disappeared from the kitchen, leaving Mitch and the little girl alone. She hadn't moved since her dad had slid her from his knee. Was she even awake? Mitch waved a hand in front of her eyes.

"Do you have a gun?" she asked.

Mitch flinched and glanced anxiously at the door. Where was Shelby? He wished she'd return to the kitchen and protect him from this scary little girl. Though Shelby probably wouldn't be impressed to find them discussing guns.

"Uh, not on me," he answered.

"My dad says you shoot bad guys."

Mitch studied Mia and scowled. How old did they say she was? Four or fourteen?

"Mostly I just build bridges." He swallowed, waiting for her to say something. She only stared. "In countries far away," he added, hoping it would appease her.

The kitchen clock ticked away as they continued to stare at each other.

Finally, Mia tilted her head and frowned. "Do you get scared when you're far away from home? Sometimes I get scared when I have a sleepover at Grandma's."

The girl's eyes were shining up at Mitch as she waited for his answer. She was an intense little thing, but she was actually starting to grow on him.

"Sometimes," he admitted. The truth was, he didn't really know where home was anymore. He never actually had. But that didn't seem to matter, because the childhood feeling of being lost and scared followed him wherever he went.

Mia nodded and pursed her lips as if she completely understood. She held her stuffed monkey out to Mitch and smiled when he accepted the toy.

"You can have him while you're here. He'll make you feel better." At that, she spun on her heel and walked away. Mitch felt the soft worn fabric of the animal in his fingers and wondered what he was supposed to do next.

"What's his name?" he called after her. Mia slowed and glanced over her shoulder, a tolerant look on her face.

"Monkey," she answered.

Of course. "Monkey," Mitch repeated. He lifted the toy so they were eye to eye.

As Mia left the kitchen, a chubby little boy toddled in. A pacifier dangled from his lips and he sucked it so hard that his cheeks dimpled. Mitch studied the mini replica of Bryce.

"Errr," the boy growled.

Mitch laughed. "Hi there. You must be Rex."

"Errr," Rex answered. He pointed at Mitch and nodded, then turned and ran away.

Standing alone in the silence of the kitchen, Mitch laughed at himself. Only forty-eight hours ago he'd been in a completely different world. Though somehow, life in this house seemed far more foreign.

About the Author

Bonnie J. James has traveled and lived abroad, but many of her fondest memories are from the small Wisconsin town where she grew up. She loves to weave her hometown setting and rural upbringing into the lives of her characters. Bonnie lives with her husband and two young sons in Minneapolis, Minnesota. She is currently writing her next novel and loves to hear from readers! Visit her website at bonniejjames.com.